SEASON OF STORMS

Volume Two of
The Summerlands

ELLEN FOXXE

DAW BOOKS, INC.

DONALD A. WOLLHEIM, FOUNDER

375 Hudson Street. New York, NY 10014

ELIZABETH R. WOLLHEIM
SHEILA E. GILBERT
PUBLISHERS

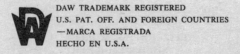

DAW TRADEMARK REGISTERED
U.S. PAT. OFF. AND FOREIGN COUNTRIES
—MARCA REGISTRADA
HECHO EN U.S.A.

PRINTED IN THE U.S.A.

"THE SHIP IS SINKING!"

As the shifting of the deck confirmed her first mate's words, Captain Vendeley threw open the door of the nearby cabin and was met by the scent of burning. With a curse, she leaped at the gray-garbed man who was burning sheets of parchment over a candle flame. Sparks and charred bits of paper flew everywhere as she tore the smoldering sheaf from his hand, and they struggled for possession of the fragments.

Rolande threw him against a table, knocking the breath from him, but when she tried to examine the documents, she found that only scraps remained. "You'll tell me about the new weapon, then!" she shouted at the man, pulling him to his feet.

He swayed unsteadily, gasping, "God's curse on you—pirate bitch—I'll die first!"

**Ellen Foxxe's
brilliant fantasy saga**

THE SUMMERLANDS:

SEASON OF SHADOWS (Volume One)

SEASON OF STORMS (Volume Two)

ACKNOWLEDGMENT

The author would like to thank Mark Freedman for giving her the benefit of his technical expertise.

Chapter 1

The shot from the Acquitanian sloop smashed into one of the smaller guns on Rolande's vessel, driving it aft where it splintered the taffrail and barely missed crushing a man standing near the tiller pole.

"Turn her, you witless toadspawn!" Rolande yelled at the pilot, who clapped the helm hard about. The battle had been raging since midmorning, but now the crewmen on the other vessel seemed more concerned with taking cover than with fighting back, and Rolande sensed victory within her grasp. All about her, rugged men and women swarmed across the decks, swiveling the guns as their ship came abreast of its target again. "Now!" Rolande shouted, and the guns discharged a broadside at the other vessel. The roar of the cannon was deafening, and the reek of black powder hid the smell of sea salt. When the smoke cleared, the enemy ship struck its flag, and Rolande's crew let forth a spirited cheer.

"Bring us close enough to board her," Rolande ordered the pilot, keeping a weather eye on the other vessel lest the captain change his mind and try some treachery. But the decks had been all but cleared by the fleeing crew of the merchantman, and there were only sporadic reports of gunfire as the ships were lashed close and Rolande's people gained the deck. They encountered little resistance as they surrounded and disarmed those who had not yet retreated belowdecks.

While the rest of the crew was occupied securing the captured ship, one lookout remained high in the rigging of Rolande's own vessel, alert for any further sign of danger. He was a young Yerren, with the dull brown feathers of the clan from the swamps to the east of the colony of South Oriana, on the junction of the Wherrisovir River and the sea.

In the years since the first Albinites had been banished to the shores of the Summerlands, the stream of emigrants had increased to a raging torrent, and with them the settlers had brought a variety of evils, including diseases previously unknown to the feathered denizens of the New World. These plagues had taken a worse toll upon the winged ones than their most deadly interclan wars, reducing their population to a fraction of its former magnitude.

But the invasion had not been without its advantages—at least as far as the younger generation of surviving Yerren were concerned. By nature prone to flying as far as their wings would take them, the young Yerren had been fascinated from the first by the ships of the travelers from across the sea. A few, such as Rolande's crewman Hrivas, had been quick to realize that by serving on such vessels they could travel to far places—in a way that had never been possible for them before.

Many were the Yerren myths of heroes who set off across the sea and passed the point where they could hope to return before the strength of their wings failed them. Some were said to have found magical countries far across the waves, populated by all manner of monstrous and marvelous beings—creatures of living stone, water-dwelling folk with scales instead of feathers, Yerren with feathers of silver and gold, who lived forever, whose powers of flight were such that they could soar to the stars. . . . Hrivas had loved these tales all his life and longed to venture beyond wings' reach. But nothing in the old stories was as strange, he thought, as the *Ysnathi*—the featherless clan who had truly come from beyond the horizon, riding the waves in their floating cities.

Many mariners considered the Yerren bad luck, and refused to have them aboard, but Rolande was of those who saw at once the Yerren's value as lookouts, perched high in the rigging, on yards that wouldn't bear the weight of a human sailor, or soaring higher yet, and flying out over the sea. Scouting on the wing for signs of ships, her Yerren crewman could search farther than the best spyglass. Where Hrivas was concerned, Rolande stood for no superstition from her crew, and took on no sailor who objected to serving alongside a featherling.

The Yerren were not fond of enclosed places, and Hrivas rarely ventured belowdecks. Remaining high on the mainmast on watch, while the others herded the merchantman's crew below, he saw someone creep across the waist of the captured ship to the fife rail. Hrivas watched with a hunter's eye, ready to fly across to the rigging of the merchantman and fell his prey with an arrow or a pistol shot, if he suspected any threat to Rolande's people. But the skulking figure only tossed something over the rail, then turned and scurried back toward the forward ladder. Hrivas wasted no time but launched himself into the air and swooped down to snatch the oilcloth-wrapped packet still drifting on the surface of the sea. Captain Vendeley might want a look at the thing, he thought, whatever it was.

* * *

When the rest of the sailors had surrendered themselves into the hands of Rolande's crew and been taken below, there remained a single figure standing on the forecastle deck, one hand on the rigging dangling from a broken mast. Rolande approached cautiously, pistol drawn. The man was unarmed, she noted, marking as well that he was tall and well-formed, with thick black curly hair—but these latter observations she set aside for future consideration. "Are you the captain of this worm-eaten hulk?" she demanded.

The man shook his head regretfully. "Would that I were—then maybe those fools would have done my bidding and held their places, instead of fleeing like gulls in a gale."

"Then who are you if you're not in command here?"

"Edward Blythe, merely the surgeon on this unlucky ship."

"A surgeon . . ." Rolande said thoughtfully. Ships' doctors were notorious for being ill-trained and poorly equipped, but at least he seemed sober. "There's work enough for you, then. We've wounded aboard the *Azora*."

"No doubt you have. We did you a fair turn, and if those bastards hadn't given up, we might have held you off."

Angered at his cocksure air, Rolande snapped, "Enough talk. You'll go and treat my crew—and if they die, you'll regret it." She nodded to two of the foremastmen standing behind him, and they placed themselves on either side of the surgeon, pistols drawn.

Blythe spread his hands resignedly. "Very well. But as to saving them all—I'm not a wizard. I can't promise they'll all heal."

"We'll come to terms later," Rolande said, touching

the point of her knife to his chest. "But first, tell me where the captain's hidden himself."

Resentment flared in his eyes, and for a moment he was tempted to refuse. But glancing at the guards who flanked him, Blythe decided he wasn't about to die for the likes of the captain. They would find him soon enough in any case, when they searched the ship. He shrugged. "He's scurried down to the hold where the bales of cloth are stored. A fine example to his men—no wonder they behave like cowards."

Rolande sent some of her people to search the hold for the captain. "Bring him to me when you find him," she ordered, then turned to her prisoner with a tilted smile. "So you would have handled things differently, would you?"

"I'd not have surrendered so easily."

"Then perhaps it's as well you're a surgeon and not a captain, for you'd only have cost the lives of your crew to no purpose."

"Oh, aye, and you don't mean to scuttle this vessel with all hands aboard, I suppose?"

In fact, Rolande had very precise reasons for choosing to board the Acquitanian ship, but she wasn't about to discuss them with this stranger. "Why should I do that, now?"

"I know the ways of pirates like you," the surgeon snarled.

"Oh, you do?" Rolande asked, her interest quickening. "Well then, you should know that we're a privateer vessel. And how is it that you know so much, Surgeon?"

"My last ship was overtaken by a crew led by Captain Brodery, and they slaughtered every man aboard, save me and the cook, because we could be of use to them."

Rolande snorted. "As I thought, you know nothing of the pirate's trade. Our interest lies in capturing a ship with as small an amount of damage as possible. It's the goods aboard we seek, and we'd expose ourselves to no more harm than is necessary to obtain them, nor engage in needless killing. Brodery's a madman who gives no quarter—anyone could tell you that. How did you get away from him, then?"

"The ship made a stop off the southern coast of Acquitania and sent men ashore by boat to trade some of the goods they'd taken, in return for provisions and water. It didn't occur to them that I could swim, so they didn't keep close watch on me. I slipped overboard and swam ashore, then hid until the ship left."

"Well, I have a cook, but now you're here, you can be of use to me. I'll keep in mind that you can swim." She gestured at the crewmen. "Take him aboard."

And if *that* story were true, Rolande thought, then goats could fly—but the man's past was no concern of hers. Everyone at sea was running from something, and most of her crew would be unwelcome on their native shores. As the surgeon and his escort left the deck, Rolande's sailors led the captain before her, having searched the hold and hauled him out from behind the bales of silk. He was a stout and florid-faced man, who gazed wildly around, searching for a means of escape. "Spare my life for the sake of your soul," he entreated Rolande.

Rolande looked past him, slapping her pistol impatiently against her thigh. "You have a passenger aboard this ship . . .?"

"Aye, a number." The captain nodded vigorously, anxious to placate his captor. "Is there one in particular you want? Take the lot—only let me live."

The surgeon hadn't been lying about his captain, at

any rate. Fighting down the desire to shoot him on the spot, she said, "Hold your noise, you whining mongrel. The one that interests me is a Dep courier, a tall fellow, calls himself Hodge. Is he aboard, or no?"

The captain pursed his lips uneasily. "Ah, Master Hodge, now . . . most unfortunate, you see—in the heat of the battle—" He gestured toward the body of a man in Deprivant gray, sprawled lifeless on the deck.

Rolande quickly searched through Hodge's clothes, but found none of the documents she expected. That was strange. He'd not be likely to leave such things in his cabin, supposing he even had a cabin. She took a closer look at the wound that had killed him. A ball from a small, single-shot pocket pistol had made it, a shot straight to the heart, at close range. But her people carried large belt pistols, and there had been little fighting on deck once Rolande's people had seized the ship. Spurred by a sudden hunch, she returned to the captain and asked, "What of a passenger bearing trade charters or contracts from investors in Acquitania to merchants in South Oriana? Have you such a one on your list?"

With an attempt at dignity, the captain replied, "Oh, yes. A fine one, that. Claims to be a banker's clerk sent to arrange imports from the New World. Says—"

"Enough," Rolande snapped. "Where can I find this clerk?"

"Well, I'm not certain of that now. The purser's cabin—for the passage was paid in good silver. But for all I know it may be empty now. A wise'un would have hidden away against your invasion."

Rolande doubted that the one she sought would have done anything so foolish. "Lead the way," she ordered.

* * *

She found her quarry in the cabin the captain pointed out, and, turning to the seamen behind her, she gestured for them to take the captain away. "Tie him to the foremast. I'll deal with him later. I wish to speak to this one alone."

When the captain had been dragged off, protesting at this barbaric treatment, Rolande was left facing a young woman seated at a small table bolted to the plank floor. She was calmly writing in a ledger, as if nothing were amiss, and for a time she continued her calculations without acknowledging Rolande's presence by so much as a turn of her head. She was attired in breeches of the finest wool, and a wide-sleeved linen shirt with a blue velvet vest. She appeared to be unarmed, but Rolande would have been willing to wager that she wasn't.

Finally, she closed her account book, sighed in an irritated manner, and said, "Vendeley. I thought I was rid of you."

"Presumptuous as always, Lady Alicen."

The woman's slightness and cropped hair gave her the look of a lad, but Rolande had seen through Alicen Kendry's various disguises before now. She sat down on the narrow bunk, but kept her pistol trained on the woman opposite her.

Alicen laid aside her quill. "You are come too late for your rendezvous with Hodge, however."

"Yes, so I discovered. You saved me the trouble of killing him myself. You did take his papers, I trust?"

"I fear in the melee they were lost overboard. You may search for them, if you doubt my word."

"Certainly not. Whether you pitched them overboard or whether you have them—not that I would make bold to doubt your word—they'll not reach the Chamber's agent in the Colonies either way. It's all one to me."

"You surprise me," said Alicen. "I had assumed, from sheer force of habit, that you yourself were that agent." She favored Rolande with a long look, lingering on her shirt and leather breeches, smeared with soot from the cannon fire and spattered with seawater. "Though there were reports, to be sure, that you hadn't prospered in the Chamber's employ."

Rolande stiffened, forcing herself to resist the impulse to brush at her clothing. *The trouble is, the bitch sees through me, too.* "How behind the times you are," she purred. "I parted ways with the Chamber of Statesmen four years ago. I'm my own master now."

"Are you? Do you mean that you serve whichever side pays you better? Or are you simply freebooter now—preying on any defenseless vessel?"

Rolande laughed. "Much as it galls me to admit it, we're working on the same side, you and I. It's the Chamber's ships I harry. I'm a privateer, empowered by colonial law to attack enemy vessels."

"I see. And I, a banker's clerk, authorized by a group of merchants in the Lowlands to invest funds in trade with the Colonies."

"What—you, doing honest work for wages, like a commoner? How demeaning for you, My Lady," Rolande sneered. She tapped the pistol restlessly against her leg. "Do not toy with me, Alicen. You didn't even fool that ass of a captain. You were ever the Duke of Wyston's loyal lapdog. You're working for his interests, now the royal family's gone. As king's cousin, is he next in line to the throne?"

Alicen shrugged daintily. "Some say Wyston should be King," she admitted, for such was common knowledge. "And others maintain that the Duke of Halkin has a better claim."

"And you?"

"As they are equal in relation to the House of Obelen, I'll support whichever of them can muster the means to restore the power of the monarchy to Albin. Had I my choice, Wyston should rule, of course. But you know all this," she added impatiently.

Rolande rolled the barrel of the pistol thoughtfully between her fingers. She knew much more than that, but she had no intention of sharing her information with Alicen. There were very few who knew that the Princess Oriana, the true heir to the throne of Albin, was yet alive—and no one, not even the Princess herself, was aware that Rolande possessed the secret. "Your mission is to raise support for the Duke of Wyston among the dispossessed nobles of New Albin?" she asked Alicen, but it was not really a question.

"I am a clerk on investors' interests. And if I were something other, I'd not tell the likes of you about it. Please don't suppose that I *believe* you're supporting the royalist cause now."

Rolande bristled at the scorn in Alicen's tone. "You've reason enough to fear me," she agreed. "I've thwarted your plans more than once in the past, but—"

"You are nothing but a gallowsbird that's grown into a vulture," Alicen said haughtily. "I can believe that you prey on whoever's weakest at the moment, but that's hardly reason to trust you—"

"Alicen," Rolande said, sounding bored, "I am *aware* that you consider me mere rabble—it's quite unnecessary for Your Ladyship to remind me of it every time we meet. Especially," she added softly, "as I hold your life in my hands at present. Is it wise, do you think, to take that tone to me?"

Alicen was silent, but she stared at Rolande defiantly, unflinching.

"But then," Rolande went on, "your daring was ever the one thing I liked in you."

"I can't think of a single thing I like in you, Vendeley—or whatever your real name may be. But how could an upstart brat like you understand loyalty and honor? There are dozens more like me in the Lowlands and Acquitania, and even in Albin itself. You cannot stop us all."

"Oh, maybe I could," Rolande said cockily, "if it were to my advantage to do so—but it isn't, as it happens. Not now." Indeed at this time, it suited her purposes to have as much discord as possible sown in the Chamber's fields. As long as the Chamber of Statesmen held sway, she could not hope to attain any position in Albin, but if she supported a winning faction, then she might yet gain power. "Loyalty and honor are for those who can afford them," she added. "But how could an aristocratic brat like you understand that? When I was the Chamber's agent, I served them well— none better—but now their downfall would serve me. So I've no desire to stop you, you see. Indeed, I'd not come within a spar's length of you, if I had my way, but as fate has seen fit to throw us together again, I may as well make the best of it. I need reliable information, and you generally know where matters stand, I'll say that for you. The rumors change with every passing ship. Are folk as disillusioned with the Chamber's rule as I've heard tell?"

Alicen smiled. To disseminate such information could only help her cause, and she would take particular satisfaction in apprising Rolande of the situation. If Rolande reported her words to the Chamber, she would be telling them nothing they didn't know already, and if she spread the word to others, it could encourage them to desert the Deprivants and join the growing resistance to their rule. "The tide is turning, and a new leader will ascend from the House of Obelen," Alicen said triumphantly. "Conditions worsen daily, and the peasants and the artisans and shopkeepers will not believe the pretty lies of the Chamber anymore. This time only the remains of the army and the Deps themselves will stand against us."

"And the other factions who vie for power with their own claimants to the throne," Rolande suggested. "I hear that Halkin has the support of the Acquitanian court."

Alicen hesitated, but saw no reason to deny the fact. "If he thinks he'll be more than a puppet king, with the Acquitanian army at his back, he's a bigger fool than he used to be."

Rolande rose and stuck her pistol in her sash, then bowed mockingly. "Well, it has been a pleasure, as always, my dear, but I've work to do."

"I know that smile of yours," Alicen said suspiciously. "The last time you had that look, you locked me in a wardrobe."

"If you'd not been hiding in my wardrobe, I couldn't have locked you in it," Rolande reminded her. "You should be grateful that I didn't do worse. I could have killed you—unpleasantly. And you'd have deserved it, too, for the time you lured me into the catacombs under the palace and left me there to rot!"

"Do your worst, then," Alicen challenged her, almost keeping the quaver out of her voice.

So you do have some fear in you after all, Rolande thought, savoring the knowledge for a moment. "Oh, but how can I, and you such a helpless little thing?" she said sweetly. "It would be like treading on a henchick. That's the worst of having you underfoot—one can't deal with you as you deserve, without feeling like a coward who bullies babes."

Alicen blanched with fury. "If you mean to shoot me, Vendeley, do it—but spare me your scurrilous, ill-bred remarks!"

Ill-bred . . . Rolande turned to the door, refusing to be baited further by Alicen's contempt. "Believe what you like," she said indifferently. "But if I were still in the employ of the Chamber, why would I let you go? I'll leave you to puzzle over that. My work's done here."

Alicen frowned. She *was* puzzled by Rolande's behavior, but she could not bring herself to admit it. "No doubt your people have looted everything worth taking from this unfortunate ship."

"I certainly hope so," Rolande said cheerfully. "I needn't pay them so much that way."

Having ordered the transfer of goods, Rolande returned to her own vessel to inspect the damage. The original ordnance brig she'd taken over during the Chamber's first attempted invasion of the Colonies had proved too small to attack any but the most poorly armed vessels. Rolande had audaciously captured a sloop some three weeks out of Saxony with a cargo of debtors and petty criminals bound to be sold as slaves. By making her vessel appear a target for the slavers, who were not averse to a little piracy on the side, she'd lured them into a rocky cove, then turned her own guns upon them from the sea while her people amid the rocks fired from all sides. She'd taken the sloop, freeing the captives and turning the brig over to them, after adding its guns to her new ship. The slavers she left to fend for themselves on the rocks.

When that sloop had become too worm-eaten to be

seaworthy much longer, she'd taken a Castilian brigantine, outfitting it with the guns she'd captured, so it held full forty cannon. It was a formidable privateer vessel, but still hardly as well-fitted as any of the men-of-war the Chamber could muster. Rolande had been successful at harrying their trading ships so far, but it was clear that she needed to capture a still larger and more powerful vessel.

But this was her ship for now. She was proud of it, and of her crew—a mixed lot of bandits, navy deserters, transported criminals, freed slaves, and impressed sailors who'd gladly traded servitude on the ships Rolande attacked for service on the *Azora*. Rolande had made them into a disciplined and unified whole, from the lowliest cabin boy to the feathered lookout in the highest reaches of the rigging. She did not believe there was an abler crew on the water.

"How do they fare?" she demanded of Blythe as she descended from the deck into the hold.

He looked up wearily from the planking where he was setting the broken leg of the last crewman. "I'd say most will mend. There are two who I fear are beyond my ministrations." Seeing Rolande's dark look, he said defiantly, "Perhaps if you didn't want them wounded, you shouldn't have put them in the way of cannon."

"If you hadn't forced the battle, you wouldn't have this to contend with now. It's fitting I say that you should clean up the mess you made."

"I made?" Blythe demanded. "You attacked the bloody ship, when we were peaceably going about our business! We are a simple merchant vessel, not a man-of-war. Just because you'd like an easy life, living off other people's property, you think you've the right to set upon anything on the sea!"

Rolande laughed outright. "Who wouldn't like an easy life? But this isn't it, I can assure you! You've never served on a privateer—or a pirate ship—or you'd know that. But you've seen service, right enough, to judge from the way you fight."

Blythe looked uneasy. It hadn't occurred to him that he might be dealing with a person of some intelligence, and he could not afford such miscalculations.

"Your vessel is not so innocent as she seems," Rolande continued, "but that is no longer your concern, for she's cut loose and on her way. And you are here."

"I see. And what do you plan to do with me, now you have me here, Captain?"

Rolande grinned lecherously. *I'd like to find out if the rest of you is as attractive as what I can see,* she thought, but she said, "You've done a neat, workmanlike job on the wounded. I could use such a one as you." *For any number of things.*

"No doubt your crew has need of a surgeon's services quite often," he agreed.

Rolande observed that he had not said that he would object to such an idea out of hand. And this struck her as interesting. So he'd been outside the law before now. A surgeon of his ability wouldn't sign on a ship unless he had reasons of his own to be away from land. "I have a proposition for you," she said, smiling.

"Do you now?" Her interest in him was plain to see, and he leaned back against the hold wall, studying the damp shirt that clung to her sleek form. "What might that be?"

"If you'd join us, I could promise you pay equal to what you've been getting, plus a share in any treasure that we take."

Blythe moved a step closer. "That is a tempting offer. And, as no doubt you mean to force me to go with you, I suppose I've little choice," he said.

* * *

"My Lord, something must be done about that blasted pirate Vendeley!" The merchant Herrel Richter would have liked to use stronger language, but he hesitated to do so before the Governor. He was torn between respect for Sir Andrew's rank, and impatience at the Governor's apparent inability or unwillingness to make the coast safe for mercantile ventures. He had dressed in finery suitable for the audience—in soft doeskin trousers, silk shirt, and brocade vest—and he made a deep bow before he spoke, but he could not altogether control the anger in his face and tone.

Behind him stood two more of the town's most prosperous merchants, also dressed in their best. Mistress Cardif, a skinny, knobby woman in a cerise silk gown, was clutching a petition, which she now laid before Sir Andrew, declaring, "We must insist that you act, for the good of the colony."

Glancing at it, he saw that it was, as he expected, the most recent of a series of complaints about the ravages being wrought on ships delivering goods from Albin—and now, it appeared, on those from Acquitania as well.

In truth, Sir Andrew had little use for those who maintained lucrative trading partnerships with their brethren in Albin. The civil war that had left him and the rest of the aristocracy dispossessed by the fall of the King had brought ruin to large numbers of people in their homeland as well as exile to those like himself. Putting money into the pockets of the Chamber of

Statesmen's minions was not an enterprise likely to win sympathy from Sir Andrew.

But as Governor, he was duty bound to protect the interests of the townspeople, whether he personally approved of them or not, and if Vendeley was, in fact, preying on merchant ships engaged in lawful commerce, then he would have to take steps. Still, he found the work of listening to the endless repeated complaints, day after day, far more wearing than any battle he'd undertaken on the field of war, as King's Marshal in Albin. *I'm not made for this,* he told himself. *This needs someone with a finer patience for fools than I possess.* Not for the first time, he longed to be back in command of an army. He often felt that if one more person presented him with one more petition, he'd draw his sword—now a ceremonial weapon only—and cleave both petition and petitioner in half.

The icy gaze he turned upon the merchants showed that he was unintimidated by the wealth they represented. His strong face was etched with lines of weariness, and his dark hair had started to turn gray at the temples, but he bore himself with all the resolution that had carried him through years on the battlefield. When he spoke, it was in stern, measured tones that commanded their respect. "It is for the good of the colony that I have empowered Vendeley as a privateer to intercept the Chamber's vessels. For if they build up a strong navy, none of us in New Albin will be safe."

"But she is taking neutral trading ships, as well as those within the bounds of her charter!" Mistress Cardif persisted plaintively. "If an end is not put to this vile freebooter's depredations, no merchant vessel will be secure upon this coast."

"We are entitled to receive the goods we pay for," Richter seconded.

Sir Andrew could feel a pounding headache starting. As the third merchant opened his mouth to add his tale of woe, he stood, to indicate that the audience was at an end, and came around the carved mahogany desk that graced the reception room of the Governor's Mansion. "I grant that you are entitled to everything you say. I shall look into this matter personally," he assured the petitioners. Resplendent in russet breeches and coat embroidered with gold thread, and a creamy white shirt with a lace cravat, he towered over them, one hand resting on his sword, as he rang for a servant to show the group out.

"It is said of this Vendeley that she is the devil's mistress, that she can raise winds to spirit ships away," Mistress Cardif said uneasily as the merchants moved toward the door.

Goodman Trudet turned back. "They say she sails with a crew of demons who sacrifice all those they catch to the Evil One—and that she possesses the power to change her form at will."

"Enough!" Sir Andrew barked. "I expect this sort of superstitious nonsense from the gypsies in the marketplace, not from those of your standing in the community. If you do not set an example for unlearned folk, who is to do so? We'll have a panic to deal with before we know where we are. I tell you, I know this Vendeley of old. She is a plague, but she is flesh and blood, as you or I, and I shall see that she is contained." *Although the Good God knows how.*

With this they had to be satisfied, although they took their leave reluctantly, murmuring among themselves. No sooner had the door closed behind them, than Sir Andrew bolted it and pushed his way through the heavy velvet curtain that separated the reception room from the side chamber. He did not seem particularly surprised to find the much vaunted pirate waiting for him there, passing the time in a game of cards with his wife.

Rolande looked up from the green baize table. "Oh, it's too grand!" she exclaimed with a grin. "To think that I have such powers! I'd not have missed that spectacle for all the world." She laughed delightedly, like a child presented with a toy.

Sir Andrew dropped into a turned spindle chair and glared at her. "I've warned you before, Vendeley, you're paid to find out what you can about the state of Albin, not to—"

"And to see her ships come to grief, lest the Chamber take the notion to invade again."

Sir Andrew nodded, rubbing at his aching temples. "I give my sanction to that—as long as they are men-of-war or ships bound on state business. You've no authority for the wanton capture of merchant vessels for your own gain! Especially not merchant vessels flying the flag of a nation other than Albin."

Rolande assumed an air of offended virtue. "I did not take that ship for *my* gain, but for yours."

Sir Andrew sighed wearily. "I've heard your prevarications many times in the past, and I'll have no more of them. How is it to my gain, pray, to have a pack of irate tradesmen set upon me?"

"Well, for one thing, the *Lorisonde* was carrying some very fine Lowland silk, and I've brought you a bolt." She turned to Lady Celia. "Emerald green, 'twill match your eyes to a rarity—"

"If you stay within the bounds I've set you," Sir Andrew interrupted, his tone grim, "I may be able to protect you. If you continue to commit felonies at will, I shall be forced to hang you. Is that understood?"

Lady Celia went to his side, concerned about how

careworn he appeared. The Governorship had taken a heavy toll on him, but his sense of duty would not allow him to abandon it to lesser hands. "She's only baiting you, Andrew. You should know the vixen's ways by now." She gave Rolande a reproachful look and said sternly, "Out with it, now. Why did you seize the *Lorisonde?*"

"I was coming to that," Rolande protested indignantly. "There was a Dep spy aboard the ship you object to my stopping. The Chamber has plans afoot regarding the Colonies. They seek our subjugation still."

Sir Andrew looked up sharply. "Explain yourself!"

For answer, Rolande brought forth the oilskin-wrapped packet that Hrivas had plucked from the sea. "This was carried by a Dep courier on that Acquitanian vessel whose safety so concerns you."

Sir Andrew was on his feet in a moment. He snatched the packet from Rolande and undid it, to find several sheets of folded parchment, which he spread across the card table. As he and Lady Celia perused them, Rolande paced idly about the chamber, thinking, *That silver inkwell must be worth a pretty penny. I could steal it this moment, and they'd be none the wiser. But where's the sport in that? If I asked for the thing, I daresay Celia would give it to me.*

The documents contained a list of instructions clearly intended for the Chamber's agents in New Albin, directing them to sow dissension throughout the Colonies in aid of a new plan the Chamber of Statesmen was preparing to undertake. Further instructions were to be imparted by the Chamber's agent "Serpent."

"Have you no thought as to who this Serpent is?" Sir Andrew demanded of Rolande.

"Not I."

"You did not question the Chamber's agent, in God's name?"

"Ah, that would have been unavailing, I fear, as he was already dead when I boarded the *Lorisonde*. You see, there was another spy aboard—one whom I had a passing acquaintance with, as it happens."

"One of your old comrades?" Lady Celia asked.

"More likely one of yours, milady. Lady Alicen Kendry."

Lady Celia looked thoughtful. "We met at court betimes. A charming girl, but I'd not say we were friends. You say she's a spy?"

"Aye, and a sly weasel, more dangerous than she looks."

"I can believe much of Alicen Kendry," Lady Celia mused, "but not that she'd work for the Chamber. They executed her father."

"No, she killed the Chamber's agent, to prevent him from meeting with me, for she assumed that I was Serpent. She's of the party who would restore the monarchy, with the Duke of Wyston as King. She seeks the support of those who've prospered in the Colonies and wish to return to their homeland. You'll see her here before long, I promise you."

Sir Andrew leaned back again. "I see. Yes, the winds have grown strong lately in that direction. The return of the monarchy . . ." He said the words as if savoring them. "But support for the Duke of Halkin is gaining ground. Even if one claimant were to succeed in overthrowing the Chamber, it might mean no more than the start of a second civil war."

All three were thinking the same—if Princess Oriana returned to Albin to reclaim her birthright, both of the royalist factions might well turn to her, forming a unified opposition to the Chamber. Rolande knew that Sir Andrew had brought the Princess to New Albin, disguised as a member of his household, but she could only guess at their plans for the future. Lady Celia tried to imagine what it would be like returning to Albin with Sir Andrew and their children. There would be little left of their estates by now, long since destroyed by the ravages of time and the hands of the Deprivants. Still, she thought, if they could restore the House of Obelen, return the rightful heir to the throne ... *and return Andrew to his rightful position*—not an official hounded by every petty municipal concern, but Lord Marshal for the Crown, Queen's Marshal. . . .

"Your news interests me," Sir Andrew admitted to Rolande, "but if Lady Alicen killed the Chamber's agent, how is it that you have these documents, not she?"

Rolande grinned. "She threw them overboard when the ship came under attack, but my Yerren lookout saw her and fished them out again."

"Then you ought to have returned them to her," Lady Celia pointed out.

"Do you know, I might have, but the *Lorisonde* was two days gone before Hrivas brought the packet to me. It hadn't occurred to him the thing might be important—you know the Yerren have no understanding of subterfuge. When he saw that it wasn't any sort of treasure or goods, he thought it was just trash. He was using it to polish the rails when my crewman Corey asked where he found it, and bade him show it to me."

"A pity that you and Alicen were working at cross-purposes," Lady Celia said, studying the document, "but that can't be mended now. What are we to make of this?"

Everyone looked again at the one line, on the topmost page, that had drawn their attention irresistibly: "This time our triumph is assured, for our Good God wills it so, by the timely development of a new weapon that will increase our power a hundredfold. . . ."

Chapter 2

"Rub this on your feet, twice in the day, and it should make the swelling go down," Katin said, handing a pot of mallow in sheep's grease to an old woman dressed in a coarse linen farmer's smock. "Once when you rise and once at sundown, say."

The woman nodded solemnly. "Your horehound syrup did wonders for my husband's cough," she said. "We haven't much, but we'll send you a bit of bacon when the slaughterin's done."

As Governor's Ward, Katin had no need to exact a fee for her services, but she knew better than to offend the pride of the poor by refusing what little they could afford to pay. She was well trained in such matters. For a moment, she watched the woman limp away, then sighed and began to straighten up her worktable, returning jars of simples and unguents to the shelves lining the walls of the shed that served her for a makeshift apothecary.

She had escaped from Albin in the guise of a 'prentice herbalist, but what had begun as pretense had soon become a passion, then grown to an occupation, as word of her way with remedies had spread from the estate through the community. Most of her time was now spent in study of medical texts and herbals, in compounding healing mixtures and ministering to the ills of her fellow colonists. In Thornfeld, the first settlement Sir Andrew had brought her to, folk had wondered who she was and what place she held in his household. She behaved, it was said, with too much freedom for one in such a menial position. But her reputation for effective cures had since eclipsed the suspicion and speculation. In Oriana she was accepted for what she claimed to be—a student of pharmacognosy, living under Sir Andrew's patronage and protection. He, in turn, had let it be known that she came of good family, that her people had perished in the Uprising, and that he had sworn to her father that he would look after her interests. All of which was true enough—as Lord Marshal, he had sworn oaths aplenty to defend the royal family.

Evening was drawing on, and Katin expected no further calls on her services that day, so she was surprised to hear someone else approaching the shed. Setting down her jars, she looked out to see Sir Andrew crossing her extensive herb garden, and she went at once to meet him. "Is anything amiss, sir?" she asked, concerned. If the matter were not pressing—or secret—he would have sent for her to attend upon him at the house, so as to keep up appearances.

He smiled, but his eyes were grave. "I have a few matters to discuss with you. Perhaps we might take a turn in the orchard," he suggested, by which Katin knew that he wished to be certain they were not overheard.

"By all means," she said. "We'll not have much more of this fine weather." She gave no sign of reluctance but was, in fact, dreading the conversation they were about to have. She knew what to expect. She had been anticipating it for some time. From travelers she'd heard rumors that the Chamber's hold on the people of Albin was weakening.

When she'd been younger, she'd been able to make herself believe that the power of the Deprivant Church was unchallengeable, that the freedom she enjoyed in the New World would be hers forever. But of late, the reports had been impossible to ignore, and she'd known that the time for a decision was approaching. She was the true heir of the House of Obelen and the throne of Albin. She would have to choose whether to reclaim the crown or abdicate power forever.

"It appears that the time is ripe to strike," Sir Andrew said simply.

For all that she had been expecting something of the sort, Katin nevertheless felt stricken and unready, when the words were actually said. "Then it's true?" she asked softly. "You believe that the people will turn on the Chamber as they turned on their King?"

"All the reports I've received suggest as much. Discontent has been on the rise for some time, as you know. The poor feel themselves betrayed by the Deps' promises."

"With reason!" Katin exclaimed. "And if the Chamber can't depend upon the peasantry, their army will be much weakened. . . ."

The Deprivant Church had succeeded in subverting the peasants who had been trained, all too well, to feed the never-ending demand for soldiers to beat back the incursions of the Acquitanian Army. Incited by the Chamber's promises of land, of a better life in this world and salvation in the next, the common folk—and certain powerful converts from among the nobility—had risen up and defeated King Thorin's army in a long and bloody civil war. The House of Obelen had been overthrown, and those loyal to the Crown driven into exile.

Above all, Sir Andrew longed to see his country restored to the rightful heir, and to take his place at the head of her army again. But in this he knew he was not free to follow his own desires. His actions must be governed by the will of his sovereign, who walked at his side now, barely reaching to his shoulder, hardly able to keep pace with his long stride. With her brown skin, her work-hardened hands and carelessly cropped hair, she looked like a common farm girl, but Sir Andrew knew her to be a queen. He could hear the royal deliberation in her tone as she asked, "And you believe that an attempt to take the country back could be successful now?"

Sir Andrew thought of the message Vendeley had brought him—a secret weapon that could spell defeat for any such attempt. It was imperative that he find out more about that device, before they committed themselves to any irrevocable course of action. "There are dangers we are not yet able to judge. I am seeking to discover what I can about the true strength of the Chamber. For now, however, the critical decision rests with you. A challenge will be made to the Chamber, but who will make it, you or another? The two chief pretenders to the throne will not wait for long. The time has come for you to decide whether you wish to reclaim the rule of Albin in your own name, or abdicate by default. I must have your authorization to act on your behalf."

Katin breathed deeply of the wild, sweet scent of the ripening fruit. It almost brought tears to her eyes. "What action would you have me authorize, then?" she asked quietly.

"With your leave, I shall send word to my old comrade Sir Warren Landervorne, who was in charge of military security before the Uprising. He continues to work covertly for royalist interests, from Acquitania. I will inform him that you live yet, and charge him to seek out those nobles who are most trustworthy and who might be of use to us. We must, of course, proceed with the greatest caution. For the present, more than ever, no suspicion should arise that you are anything other than you seem."

As she hesitated to answer, Sir Andrew went on, "They think you dead, you could go on letting them believe it so. But if you were to lead the challenge, most would probably rally to you." He stopped walking and turned to face her. He felt brutal, laying such a burden upon her, but he had his duty, and she hers. "And if you do not," he said bluntly, "then the Duke of Wyston and the Duke of Halkin will most likely kindle another civil war and tear the country apart between them."

Both knew that by putting the situation in such terms, he had left her no choice. She had been witness to the violence and chaos wrought by the peasant army. The rabble had dragged her family from the ship by which they had sought to flee and turned them over to the Chamber for execution. She herself had only escaped through her own resourcefulness, managing to leap overboard and disguise herself as one of the urchins scavenging the shore. How much unnecessary terror and butchery would there be if she didn't return?

"Further, the Duke of Halkin has the assistance of Acquitania," Sir Andrew reminded her. "Should he prevail, Albin will be little more than a subject kingdom."

At this, anger drove all other considerations from Katin's thoughts. For generations, her ancestors, from

the Warrior Queen Albarosa onward, had fought to resist the annexation of Albin by its powerful neighbor.
She could not shame the House of Obelen and betray
her people by putting any whim of her own before the
safety and sovereignty of her country. "I shall claim
the throne, My Lord," she said.

Sir Andrew smiled. "I never doubted that you
would, Your Highness."

After Sir Andrew's departure, Katin returned to the
familiar and comforting chore of clearing away her
supplies in the shed, lost in thoughts of the changes
that were to come. But once again she was interrupted
in her task, this time by her friend Jerl Smit, a youth
who had served under Sir Andrew in the militia of
Thornfeld and worked on his estate as well. Many of
the militiamen had chosen to follow their commander
when he led the party southwest to found the new colony of Oriana. Jerl had been quick to join them—for
following Sir Andrew meant following Katin as well.

Sir Andrew had warned him to take no liberties
where Katin was concerned, and she herself had con-
fided to him that she was connected to the highest nobility of Albin, but still he cherished hopes of winning
her one day. He'd carved out a farmstead for himself
beside woods at the fringes of the marshland near the
settlement, choosing the spot deliberately, despite its
inconvenience, to allow him to expand his holdings.
He dreamed of a great plantation with a manor house
worthy of any lady, where Katin might consent to join
him someday—and what hard work could achieve, Jerl
would have.

"You've come late for a lesson," said Katin, "and
you don't look in need of healing herbs." She'd been

teaching him to read, when they could find the time, encouraging his desire to better himself.

"No, I came to deliver a load of timber, and I thought I'd find you here. You—" Jerl hesitated, uncertain. During the resistance to the Albinate Invasion, he had proven his courage under fire, but he had never been bold with words. It took all his daring to continue, "you seem to be avoiding my company of late."

Katin had been avoiding Jerl, though much against her own inclinations. *If I had my way, I'd be in your arms now,* she thought, turning away to hide her face, busying herself with some bottles on a shelf behind her. Jerl's tall, strong frame seemed to fill the small shed, and she could smell the sharp scent of wood shavings and resin he brought with him. "Oh, but I've been so busy for some weeks now," she said, without looking at him. "With the turning of the season, folk always fall ill, you know. There have been many in need of my services."

Jerl accepted this, or seemed to. "This town does boast a capable physician—you're not responsible for the welfare of the whole community. You'll wear yourself to a shadow. You look peaked."

If she looked wan and shaken, Katin thought, it was her conversation with Sir Andrew, not overwork, that had left her so. But to Jerl she said only, "You're a fine one to talk of working too hard. *Another* load of timber already! The Governor's Mansion will be finished before we know where we are."

"It's all but finished now. Another few months at most, I'd say. But the way the town's growing, I'll have a ready market for my wood all the same."

"You mean to clear more trees yet?" Katin asked. She began to pour sand on the small brazier in the corner, to douse the flames.

"A good many more. The profit's all to be put back into stock, and the more land cleared the better." Above all, he wished to impress her with his prospects. The money he'd saved from his pay as a militiaman had long ago been spent on the supplies he'd needed to start the farmstead. "I'll own the largest farm in these parts one day," he said seriously.

Katin smiled. "I've no doubt of that." *And if I were free, I could do worse than help you to build it. But how can I? My destiny was set by my birth, my duty stands between us like a castle moat.*

But the temptation was undeniable. As Jerl approached her, in the close shed, she snatched a broom from the corner and began energetically sweeping up the dried leaves and dust from the plank floor, forcing Jerl to retreat out the door to make room. But when she rejoined him, closing the shed behind her, she found matters no easier out of doors. In the glow of sunset, Jerl looked all the more appealing, his tan skin edged with gold, his brown hair shot through with fair highlights. Katin wanted to bask in the warmth of him, and forget for a time who and what she was—as she'd done once before, at their last lesson in reading.

It would have seemed absurd to be distant and proper with Jerl, after the easy camaraderie which had marked their forays through the forest and along the coasts of Thornfeld, during the attempted invasion by the Chamber. Their experiences had brought them so close that it felt altogether natural—indeed inevitable—when Jerl one day turned from the poem he was struggling with and drew Katin into his arms. For a long, sweet moment, she had allowed herself to be what she seemed, a commoner who could be courted by a hardworking youth with land of his own. Katin had not wanted him to stop kissing her. It was the Princess who pulled away at last, making light of the matter with regal tact. "No more poetry for you, my lad!" she'd said with a laugh. "In future we'll read Ansenrath's *History of Saxony!*"

After that, she had turned to Lady Celia for advice, but Her Ladyship's words had been little comfort. "From what I've seen of the young man," she warned Katin, "he does not seem the sort to entertain a light dalliance. And is he not too proud be your paramour, to share your favors with your Prince Consort? If you are not prepared to marry him, and lead the life of a farmwife, I should think it rather . . . unkind . . . to encourage him further."

And at times Katin *had* felt prepared to choose Jerl—though she prudently accepted Lady Celia's offer to chaperone all further reading lessons. But now, after her discussion with Sir Andrew, Katin could no longer deceive herself. She was not a simple country girl who could bed or wed without any thought but for her own welfare. But how was she to explain herself to Jerl? He still stood waiting for her, shading his eyes against the sun, expecting to escort her to the house, perhaps, or walk with her in the orchard, in the heady, apple-scented dusk.

Jerl had lost much of his awkwardness and diffidence over the past four years. He had always believed in his own worth, but before he'd left Albin for the New World, he had not expected others to believe in it. Baseborn as he was, he felt that here in New Albin, he was any man's equal. He worked his own land now— yes, and, by the Good God, he had others working for him. A few years before, he had thought Katin out of his reach, but his experiences in Thornfeld and his success in Oriana had given him the confidence to pursue even that dream.

He took Katin's arm and turned her to face him, forcing himself to speak, before she could question or admonish him. "Katin, you have been avoiding me, ever since we—well, you know, if you want me to stay away, I will. But if it's what Sir Andrew wants—I know he thinks I'm not good enough for you, but what do *you* think? It's for you to say—this isn't Albin!"

Wherever I am is Albin, Katin thought helplessly, unable to meet Jerl's eyes. *I should tell him the truth. That would cure him of his partiality for me.* Jerl, she knew, was no royalist, though he no more held with the Chamber than with the monarchy it had overthrown. Would he despise her if he knew who she was? It would be hard to forfeit his regard, but it would be fairer to Jerl. If he knew she was the Princess, he would understand that he must give up all idea of courting her, and he would understand why. He deserved better than to be turned down without a reason.

But even without Sir Andrew's warning, Katin knew better than to reveal her secret to anyone without direst need, even to someone who would not willingly betray her.

"In this land, we've only ourselves to answer to," Jerl was saying. "No matter what Sir Andrew—"

"It's not that!" Katin blurted out. "It's nothing to do with Sir Andrew. It's I myself who . . ." Her words died at his wounded look.

Jerl released her and stepped back. "I see," he said. "I'll not trouble you again."

For a moment, Katin watched him walk away. She knew she should let him go, and she knew that she couldn't do it. She couldn't allow him to go on believing that she found him unworthy, that she was indifferent to his feelings for her. "Jerl, wait, you don't understand," she cried. "I've no choice in the matter. I *can't* accept you because I'm—I'm—"

Jerl looked back at her, puzzled. "You're what?"

"Betrothed!" Katin said.

She was almost as surprised as Jerl, but she began to elaborate upon her lie at once. "Since childhood—it was a marriage alliance between two great Houses, sealed by oath and bond. Unless the compact is formally abrogated, any other marriage I made would be illegitimate."

"But what can such an agreement mean now?" Jerl protested. "The noble houses were overthrown—they no longer exist!"

"As long as one heir of the line lives, even in exile or in poverty, a House exists," said Katin, who firmly believed this. "For me to repudiate the betrothal, just because I couldn't be called to account for it, would be to dishonor myself and my name."

Having known all his life the problems of the peasantry, Jerl had little sympathy for the problems of the aristocracy. "Look here, do you *want* to marry this lord you're promised to?" he demanded in exasperation.

"No . . . but then I'm not free to do as I want."

"Well, how can the compact be formally abrogated, then?"

"By consent of both Houses—but his consent and mine would do, I suppose, under the circumstances."

Jerl frowned. "Would he hold you to the betrothal if you ask to be released from it?"

"But that's just my difficulty, Jerl—I *can't* ask him," Katin said, inspired. "I don't know where he is, or even whether he's still alive. He fought in the Uprising, of course, but after Breicenshire he disappeared, like so many others. He may have been killed in battle, or executed by the Chamber, or he may have gone into hiding, as I have." Warming to her tale, she went on, "He could be here in the Colonies somewhere, or in Acquitania. Sir Andrew is trying to find out what's become of him, and if he lives, no doubt he's searching for me as well, but we can't let ourselves be found too easily. The Chamber's agents are hunting us, too, you see."

Jerl could understand that well enough. The families of the highest nobility were those related to the royal line. The Chamber would stop at nothing to see the monarchy exterminated, down to its last collateral connections.

"Jerl . . . I'd not tell this much to anyone but you. I know I can trust you," Katin said earnestly, and that much, at least, was the truth.

Jerl nodded glumly. He did not ask Katin what her real name and title were, for she was clearly reluctant to say more. And in truth, if she were of ducal rank, Jerl didn't much want to know about it. "Tell me this—is there anything in this *compact* of yours that forbids you to come to the fair with me?" he asked gruffly. He pulled a handbill from his pocket and thrust it toward her.

Katin took the crudely printed sheet, emblazoned with a sheaf of wheat, a bulbous moon peeking out from behind it, proclaiming a Harvest Fair to be held on the Town Common with games, masques, and dancing. She could think of no reasonable way to refuse. And the prospect of dancing with Jerl was far from disagreeable. "Well . . . perhaps I *have* been working too hard lately," she said, smiling.

* * *

It was an unseasonably chilly afternoon. As yet no rain had fallen, but massive black clouds blanketed the sky, smothering the waning light of the fall dusk, and the air hung thick and stagnant. There was little doubt that the storm would soon come.

Oliver Ruthven's mood matched the tenor of the weather as he strode down the main street, looking in vain for lodgings. He had just disembarked from the *Amaryllis,* a sloop newly arrived from Albin by way of Saxony, and his first sight of the New World did not impress him favorably. The streets in the vicinity of the wharf were lined with one- and two-story dwellings and trade establishments, some built of clapboard, and others merely constructed of wattle and daub. Except for the main street, which was laid with cobblestones, the roadways all appeared to be unpaved. All in all, it appeared a ramshackle place when compared to the capitals of the civilized world, with their old brick and stone edifices and broad thoroughfares.

Ruthven was to have taken up accommodation with Sir Evan Delart, one of the exiled nobles seeking to regain his fortunes by accumulating as much land as possible in the New World. The ship on which Ruthven had sailed had been delayed, however, by the storms which so often plagued crossings from Albin. The delay had cost him more dearly than he had anticipated, for an equerry from the estate had met him at the dock, with word that His Lordship had not a week past been thrown from a horse and broken his neck. It would be best, he was advised, not to impose upon Her Ladyship at this time, for she was yet too mazed with grief to receive visitors.

And, Ruthven thought, *Her Ladyship's loyalties have yet to be sounded.* Better to take up his post where there was no danger of treachery. Sir Evan's death might truly have been an accident, of course, but

Ruthven had survived the Chamber's attempts on his own life, these half-dozen years past, often enough to teach him caution. If there was the chance that a Dep agent lurked in the halls of Sir Evan's manor, then Ruthven would look for lodgings elsewhere. He looked forward with no great enthusiasm to a louse-ridden bed in some rural hostel, but anything would be preferable to another night aboard the *Amaryllis*.

His scowl deepened as he turned from the cobble-stoned street onto Livery Row, which proved to be no more than a dirt path between the rough-hewn buildings. He'd been told that there was a hostel down this way, but he saw no sign of one, and the neighborhood hardly looked the best place to draw custom. He had just passed the butcher's shop with its great wooden ham hanging above the doorway, swinging in the wind, when a grubby urchin girl of some ten or eleven years ran from the shadows into his path and held out a handful of tawdry trinkets. "Buy a charm, sir? 'Twill bring you luck!"

Ruthven threw her a copper and said, "Keep your rubbish. Just tell me where to find an inn in this god-forsaken wilderness. Is it down this way?"

"Aye, just past the livery stable," she said eagerly. "I'll show you!" She started to run toward him, stumbled on the uneven surface of the path and fell against him, grabbing at his jacket to steady herself.

Before she could regain her balance and scamper past him, Ruthven grabbed her roughly with both hands and lifted her clear off the ground.

"I'm sorry, sir," she whined. "I didn't mean to dirty your coat, sir . . . please . . ."

"Do you take me for some country clod?" Ruthven snarled. He set her back upon the muddy ground, and keeping a firm grip on her arm, plunged his hand beneath her gaudy sash and retrieved the leather pouch she'd filched from his jacket.

"Please, sir, don't turn me in to the Watch," she pleaded, grasping at the sleeve of his coat. Ruthven hesitated, then glancing down at his cuff he saw that the silver button had been neatly sliced off. "Cursed gypsy cutpurse!" He swiftly brought his hand up in a sharp blow across her face. "I'll teach you a lesson myself."

As he raised his arm to strike her again, a voice behind him said, "Strike that child and I'll see you taught one, sir."

Ruthven turned, looking over his shoulder to see a slender young woman in buckskin breeches and linen shirt emerging from one of the narrow houses. She carried an empty basket, and he took her for a servant girl on an errand. "Be off about your business, unless you want a beating too," he warned her.

Her scornful look took in his black velvet jacket and knee breeches, silver brocade vest and silver-buckled boots, but neither his obvious prosperity nor his threat turned her from her purpose. Her basket had hidden the small flintlock pistol she wore in her belt, but now she drew the weapon and pointed it at Ruthven's heart with the steadiness of one who knew how to use it. "Let her go. We do not hold with cowards who beat beggar-children here."

"Do you hold with thieves?" Ruthven snapped. "The creature's nothing but a pickpocket."

"We've magistrates to deal with such matters. But as you've already administered justice, of a coarse sort, and you've lost nothing, I'd say you're quits with her. Why not let her go?" She shrugged and returned the pistol to her belt, then looked up and suddenly gave a piercing whistle.

She was answered by a shrill barking from *overhead,* and to Ruthven's astonishment, a middling-sized dog appeared on the edge of the roof of a nearby house and began to clamber down the face of the building like a squirrel.

Taking advantage of his distraction, the child twisted sharply in his grasp and broke free, darting off before he could even snatch at her. He didn't bother to give chase. He had no desire to appear before the local authorities, and the satisfaction of bruising the brat wasn't worth the trouble of catching her. Besides, this handsome, arrogant maid and her extraordinary pet were far more interesting.

The animal, halfway down the wall, suddenly launched itself into the air and glided down the rest of the way on the furred webbing that stretched between its forelegs and hind paws. It landed steadily on the dirt roadway not far from Ruthven, and regarded him with suspicion. Perhaps sensing its mistress' hostility to the stranger, it growled a warning at him, its dark-gold fur bristling, and bared surprisingly menacing fangs.

"What in the devil's name is that thing?" Ruthven demanded.

The young woman laughed, looking even more comely than before. "Well may you ask in the devil's name, for I call him Lucifer. He's a soarhound. They live in the forests to the northeast." She called the dog to her, and it left off standing guard over Ruthven and scampered to her side, wagging its tail. "Good dog," she said, with a sidelong glance at Ruthven.

"And who are you, girl?" he asked, in a more cordial tone. He favored her with a smile that rarely failed to charm.

"I am an apothecary from the estate of Lord

Edenbyrne, the Governor of this colony," Katin said. "And who may you be, sir?"

"I am but a visitor to your shores—in search of lodgings for the night. Your little friend told me there was a hostel nearby, before she tried to lift my purse. Or was she liar as well as thief?"

"It's straight down the lane," she said, with a dismissive wave of her hand in the general direction.

Ruthven made her a mocking bow. "Perhaps we shall meet again, Mistress Apothecary. But if it would suit you, I shall continue on my business now."

"May your business be accomplished swiftly," Katin said with the same false courtesy. "I daresay you'll not want to stay in Oriana any longer than you must."

Thunder rumbled in the distance as they went their different ways.

The front room of the Brazen Horn hostel was full of patrons, travelers taking their evening meals, and a few townsfolk who lived nearby, drinking dark ale and mulled rum. Lorin, whose pawnbrokery stood at the end of the street, lounged at one of the rough oak tables, his long limbs occupying more than his share of space. Over his tankard of ale, he watched a dark gypsy woman move from table to table, her prognostications lost in the babbling of voices. As she passed, he caught her round the waist and pulled her down onto the bench beside him.

She gave a tug at his shaggy hair, which was drawn back and bound with a leather thong. "Want your fortune told, do you, handsome?"

Lorin grinned. "Have you something promising to tell me?" He laid a silver coin upon the table, for his business had been prosperous of late.

The woman glanced at the coin then ran her finger

softly down the center of his palm. "For a man such as you, the future promises great pleasure."

"Does it now?" Lorin leaned closer for a better view of his buxom companion, failing to notice when Rolande walked through the door with Edward Blythe. But few others missed Rolande's entrance. She paused for a moment just inside the doorway, elegant in her long green coat with its gold damask trim. One hand rested on her hip, near the pistol tucked in the belt of her satin breeches.

The fortune-teller snatched Lorin's coin from the table and said hastily, "Indeed, I can promise you a welcome visit from a friend," then slipped away into the crowd. Lorin stared after her, puzzled, then turned and caught sight of Rolande, who was looking in his direction now. He sat back, laughing, but his smile faded when he saw her say something to the good-looking fellow behind her, and motion to him to follow her.

Rolande shouldered her way through the crowd, stopping before Lorin's table. "I'll tell your fortune for free," she offered, taking a swig of his ale. "Murdered by a jealous lover, no doubt."

"Maybe if you weren't at sea more than not, I'd be spared such a fate," Lorin suggested, trying not to show how glad he was to see her. "It's time enough you came back. Brought something with you?" he asked, with a meaningful glance at Blythe. "Who's your friend, then?"

Rolande smiled silkily. "Why, this is Ned Blythe, he's my ship's surgeon—a man most skilled with his hands."

"No doubt. Sawbones, is he? Doesn't look it." Lorin looked him up and down suspiciously. "Lorin's my name," he told Blythe. "Vendeley and I have business ventures in common. And we've matters to discuss."

Blythe raised an eyebrow archly. "I see. I'll leave you to your *affairs,* then. It's no concern of mine. I'll see about those supplies I need—after I find a drink." He turned away unhurriedly and made for the far end of the room.

"Where did you find curly-locks?" Lorin demanded.

Rolande shoved him over to make room for herself on the bench beside him. "Took him off an Acquitanian trader—along with a cargo of fine cloth, in case you're interested."

"Is he really a surgeon?"

"Aye, a damned fine one," Roland said impatiently. "Why not?"

"I don't like the look of him, that's all."

Rolande grinned. "I do."

"Huh—you like the look of anything that might make fair sport."

"And you don't, I suppose?" said Rolande, gesturing at the fortuneteller, who was now reading the palm of a prosperous-looking merchant at a nearby table. "If you're so jealous, you're welcome to rejoin my crew, whenever you like—as my first mate."

"And you're welcome to come work for me, as my clerk."

Rolande took another swig of ale. "Ah, you're right, you know—we're better as we are. There can't be two captains on one ship."

"True. And the only time I have any peace is when you're at sea."

"I thought you missed me."

"So I do, but you're no sooner back than I forget why," Lorin lied.

Under the table, Rolande let her hand slide down his thigh. "I'll remind you of why, a little later, but first to matters of business. I've enough silk and satin—of the best quality—to clothe half the town."

"Good. Half the town'll be wanting new clothes, with the Fair coming up." He reclaimed his ale from Rolande and took a long pull at it. "The merchants will be tearing their hair out for fabric. And they'll be roaring mad that they have to buy it from me because another supply ship was sacked. There'll be trouble over this business, you mark me."

"What—the dread bandit chief afraid of a few whining shopkeepers?" Rolande teased.

"I'm a respectable tradesman now," Lorin reminded her.

"If you are, it's because I made you one! You were living in the wild like an animal when I found you."

"And it was that animal *you* came to for help, when you had all of Thornfeld and half the Chamber's army hunting you—and now you've set the most powerful merchant interests in Oriana against you! I've heard about the *Lorisonde*. It's not me I'm worried about—I can deal with their complaining. It's you they're after, woman. They want your head this time."

"I know all about that," Rolande assured him. "I had my reasons for taking the *Lorisonde,* but never mind. Someone always wants my head, but no one's got it yet." She put her arm around Lorin's neck and pulled him closer, to ask in a low, throaty tone, "What I want to know is, what part of me do *you* want, eh?"

Night had fallen, and the raw air sliced through the thin silk of Alicen's blouse and burgundy satin jacket. She was attired suitably for calling upon the local aristocracy, and had come recently from the house of Sir Evan's widow. As a member of the nobility herself, she had been able to gain access to Lady Ideline, but even so, she had accomplished little beyond tendering her formal condolences. It was evident that Her Ladyship planned to wait until a clear leader came to the fore before she committed her funds to the restoration of the monarchy. *Parsimonious as ever,* Alicen thought.

It had been the last visit of a long and wearying day, and Alicen looked forward to a glass of brandy and a rest. When she had made her way back to the hostel, she told the stablehand to have her horse ready early in the morning, and hurried in out of the cold. But as she climbed the stairs overlooking the taproom, she noticed Rolande deep in conversation at a table by the hearth.

What sort of place was New Albin, if a pirate like Vendeley could confer with her cronies in a public place with impunity? And what was she up to here? Too weary for another encounter, Alicen hastened up to her room before Rolande could see her, but the mere sight of her old enemy was enough to strengthen Alicen's resolve. She was determined not only to succeed, but to see to it that a certain misbegotten freebooter knew of her triumph.

The next morning Alicen set out for the Governor's Mansion. It was inevitable that she would pay a call there before she had spent many days in the colony, but her orders had been to contact certain of the known loyalists immediately upon her arrival—those with whom the Duke of Wyston had been corresponding since the early stages of his campaign. She was to apprise them of the Duke's plans at once, and learn what they could tell her of the disposition of others in the colony, before she approached any whose loyalties were unknown. But as soon as she learned that the

Governor was none other than Viscount Edenbyrne, the Lord Marshal himself, she had changed her plans.

Katin was delivering a tonic of alfalfa seed to the cook for her rheumatism when Alicen rode into the yard. The servant who admitted her lost no time in reporting to the kitchen about the nature of the visitor, describing with relish her fine ruffled linen shirt and pale green vest trimmed with silver lace, beneath a damask jacket. Only minutes later, Katin had secreted herself in the small side room from which she could overhear Alicen's conversation with Sir Andrew.

It was as well that Vendeley had forewarned him of Lady Alicen's plans, Sir Andrew reflected. Otherwise, when the woman had come to him demanding the restoration of the monarchy, he might have assumed that she knew he was harboring the Princess and given the game away.

Instead, he asked her, "And how do you expect me to accomplish that?"

"It's well known that you drove the Chamber's army out of New Albin," Alicen said warmly. "And with you at the head of our forces, we can drive the Chamber from the seat of power, as we are sworn to do!"

The woman's dangerous, Sir Andrew warned himself. It was dangerous to listen to anyone who told one exactly what one wished to hear. It was too difficult to doubt the sincerity of such a passionate advocate, and the temptation to fall in with her proposal, to confide in her, was extraordinary.

"It's true that we were successful, against great odds, in defending the colony of Thornfeld against an invading force," he said cautiously. "But bringing an attack against a standing army is another matter, Lady Alicen. Even supposing that my militia are willing to abandon their homes here to make the attempt, even supposing that your fellows can raise some hundreds of soldiers at each of the other colonies, we should still have half the numbers the Chamber can raise. Do you plan to bring foreign troops into Albin to fight your battle?"

"That is the Duke of Halkin's plan, not the Duke of Wyston's," Alicen said fiercely. "Halkin would sell Albin to Acquitania, to be called King, but why should we throw off one yoke only to bear another?"

"You would not follow the Duke of Halkin, then, though he could restore the House of Obelen to the throne?" Sir Andrew probed.

Alicen hesitated, then said slowly, "Given a choice between the Duke of Halkin and the Chamber, I would follow him. With an Obelen on the throne, we might after all unite the country again, and overthrow the Acquitanian overlords. But that is not the choice we are given. The choice is between Halkin and Wyston, and one is as much an Obelen as the other."

Neither is that the choice, Sir Andrew thought, but he only asked, "Where will the Duke of Wyston find his soldiers, then?"

"We will find them among the people of Albin, who now suffer more harshly under the rule of the Deprivants than ever they did at the hands of the aristocracy!"

"The peasantry? The commonality?"

"Peasants, townsmen, craftsmen. Already there have been uprisings against the Church in Barstowe, Fairfield, Lynehaven—"

"Put down by the Chamber's troops, according to the reports I have received."

"But for each subdued, two more break out—our agents see to that. The Chamber's tax collectors were hanged in Turnstone, and by the time the army forces arrived, there was nothing to be done about it, and they were needed at Bristleton, a hundred leagues south, to deal with an outbreak there. Averwell was under siege at last report, and—"

"Averwell?" said Sir Andrew, startled. It was a major port, but news of the uprising there had not yet reached him.

Alicen nodded in satisfaction. "Further, the Chamber's army shows signs of dissension in the ranks, My Lord. Desertion is rife, and various factions who supported the Deprivants, in the interests of their own local concerns, have fallen away like so many leaves from a dying tree. The people are weary of the burden that the Church's levies place upon them. They are ready to throw off the Chamber as they did the monarchy and the aristocracy—"

"And you think they wish to return to their old masters?"

"No. But there is sentiment among them that the country needs a King—a *strong* King who will keep the power of the nobility and the Church in check. They will follow a true Obelen, and the Duke of Wyston promises a new order, one that will give them a voice in their own fate. He has said that they shall have an assembly, and from it send a minister from among their own number, who will always have the King's ear." Seeing Sir Andrew's frown, she said, "Come, you cannot deny that we were defeated by the abuses of our own class. If it had not been so, the Deps could not have drawn the people into revolt against us."

Sir Andrew sighed. "You can have no idea," he said, "how badly Thornfeld was governed by a council of just such *citizens*. It was *despite* them, at every step, that my militia prevailed."

Lady Alicen, of course, shared his doubts. She, too, had been raised to believe that it was the duty of the aristocracy to rule and to protect the common people, and that the lower orders, in turn, were meant by the Good God to serve their betters. The order of her existence, like his, had been utterly overthrown by the Deprivant Uprising, and she welcomed a new order no more than he. But, unlike some of her class, she did not choose to blind herself to the lessons of the revolution. "The fact is," she said, "that we cannot hope to succeed without them. If we are not to abandon our country to the Deps or the lords of Acquitania, if we are to see the Obelen line restored, then we have no choice. We must *act*, and I tell you, now is the time to strike!"

There they were in accord, though Sir Andrew gave no sign of his agreement. He remained silent for a time, as if weighing her words, allowing her to believe that his reservations about the Duke of Wyston's plans for an assembly of commoners were stronger than they were. It was true that he had little patience for the notions of governance exhibited by his fellow colonists, but he had also seen, at the defense of Thornfeld, what could be accomplished by an army of free folk who felt that the land they were fighting for was their own. If the Duke of Wyston's agents could inspire that kind of resolve in the people of Albin, the Chamber's army of conscripts and hirelings would not stand a chance.

Lady Alicen, he concluded, was potentially a valuable ally. No Kendry had been among the turncoats who tried to wring favors from the Chamber when it was clear the Deps would triumph. Kendrys had fallen at Breicenshire, he knew, and the Baronet, Alicen's father, had been publicly executed by the Chamber, as a warning to those who continued to defy them. There seemed no reason to doubt her loyalty to the House of Obelen, and Sir Andrew could well believe that she would support the Princess, the true heir, above all other factions, if she knew of her existence.

But he could not afford to disregard what Vendeley had told him about Lady Alicen's career as a clandestine agent. Until he had received verification that she was trustworthy, it would be foolhardy to take her into his confidence. He would query Sir Warren as to this point in his next communication, but that would take time. . . .

At last he said, "You are at liberty to say that I am in sympathy with your cause, but I can give you no definite answer without consulting with others, and receiving more information."

"Information about me?"

Sir Andrew waved this aside, as a matter too obvious to require discussion. "Of course. But I am presently awaiting information about the intentions of the Chamber. If, as I suspect, they plan a second attempt to subdue the Colonies, I must take that into account before I can commit myself—or my people—to any course of action."

"As must we," said Alicen, intent on his words. "If they were to send thousands of soldiers here, as they did before, Albin's defenses would be all the more vulnerable to attack. If we knew when they mean to invade—if they do—we'd know when best to strike. But thus far, our agents have heard only threats and promises to seize control of New Albin one day, to bring about the redemption of her heretic sons and daughters, of course, to bring her lost lambs—and their revenues—back to the fold. We've taken it for bluff, no more. It's all they can do to keep order in Albin nowadays. Do you really think they're mad enough to make the attempt now, when they need all their forces to maintain themselves in power?"

Sir Andrew rose and began to pace the room restlessly. "There are those among them mad enough for anything, who believe that they cannot fail because they are about God's business. If they were to accept the defeat we handed them before, it would appear to their followers that they had offended the Good God by their actions. Moreover, if they should succeed, it would go far to regain the support of the people, and to weaken the pretenders' hold. They have no choice but to make another attempt."

"I see. Have you, then, any information as to the time and magnitude of this attempt?"

"Not as yet, but I expect to know more, in time. When I have received the reports of my informants, I shall be able to give your proposal the consideration it deserves. For now, rest assured that your trust is not misplaced in me. We shall speak again, in due course, and I wish you luck in your mission, for the present." Choosing his words with care, he added, "I think it likely that we have the same end in view, and that we shall work together to achieve it." He raised his wineglass in a toast. "To the day when the rightful heir of the House of Obelen will ascend the throne of Albin."

Alicen was far from satisfied, but she could hardly refuse to honor such a pledge.

From her listening post behind the curtain, Katin smiled at Sir Andrew's equivocation. So he was not sure of Alicen Kendry. He had not told her of the message intercepted by Hrivas, much less of the fact that neither the Duke of Wyston nor the Duke of Halkin was the true heir to the throne. Katin had known Alicen at court since childhood, and could not imagine her sinking to the ignominious position of Chamber's spy. Still, Sir Andrew was right to be cautious. If Vendeley, who had long been the Chamber's trusted agent, could join forces with the royalists she claimed to despise, then perhaps a Kendry could betray her class and serve the Chamber. . . .

Like Sir Andrew, Katin had not cared for the tenor of Alicen's remarks about the old order, though she could not deny that there was truth to them. Her years in the New World had taught her more about her people than she could ever have learned at court. She remembered an argument she'd had with Jerl, when he'd first asked her if she thought he could learn to read. Without thinking, she had exclaimed warmly, "Of course! It's a fine idea! You ought to educate yourself all you can. Ignorance is the mother of want and vice. You saw for yourself what disaster was wrought in Albin when the ignorant masses seized power—and in Thornfeld, those unfit to govern would have left the land undefended, had not Sir Andrew brought them to heel—"

For once, Jerl had interrupted her. "Then when all are educated, they will have no need of an aristocracy to govern them?"

Katin had tried not to show how profoundly such treasonous sentiments shocked her. "Why, were such a thing possible, that might be so," she said as gently as she could. "But not all the commonality could be taught, nor would most be equal to the responsibilities that rule entails."

"What I can learn, others can," Jerl said, with uncharacteristic stubbornness.

Katin disagreed, for she thought of Jerl as exceptional. But she could not well explain to him about blood and breeding. Anything she could say would sound like an insult.

"You know some other colonies have founded schools for all the children of the community," Jerl was saying. "We should have one such here in Oriana."

Katin's years of training told her that the rudimentary knowledge of letters and figures imparted by such schooling would not suffice to make statesmen of the children of common tradesmen and laborers. But she could at least agree that a degree of education, however crude, might make folk better subjects—or citizens. "Lady Celia thinks so, too," she assured Jerl. "She's told Sir Andrew that the colony should engage the services of a competent schoolmaster, and establish a school for all children old enough to profit from instruction. She thought perhaps Carl—but he's far too taken up with his own studies. Do you know, he's found a rare species of white bat in the swamps to the east?" And she had thus been able to turn the talk to the less contentious subject of the discoveries made by the naturalist Carl Schellring.

But now, as she considered Lady Alicen's words, she could not help remembering Jerl's. Was it possible that here in the New World education would take the place of aristocracy, and that even in Albin the people were to take part in the governance of the country? If the Duke of Wyston's followers should transfer their allegiance to her, as Sir Andrew intended, must they be given in return a voice in the affairs of state—matters they knew nothing about? If so, the sooner all were educated, the better. . . .

Alicen knew better than to press Sir Andrew further at present, and she took her leave after paying her respects to Lady Celia. So the rumors about the Baroness Lindley and the Lord Marshal had been more than ill-natured court gossip after all. Perhaps Celia would be of use in influencing her husband to champion the Duke of Wyston's cause. She had greeted Alicen warmly, and made clear that she suspected her reason for visiting the Colonies. Though she had given no definite assurance of her support for Alicen's mission, she had nevertheless been most encouraging.

Waiting in the yard for a groom to fetch her horse, Alicen went over and over her unsatisfactory discussion with Sir Andrew. *He's holding something back,* she thought in frustration. She had seen Oliver Ruthven in the Brazen Horn—was it possible that the Duke of Halkin's agents had won over Lord Edenbyrne? Would the Lord Marshal serve the man who would bring the Acquitanian Army past the borders he'd fought so many years to protect? It seemed inconceivable, yet every man could be bought if the reward were great enough. She shook her head. Such an answer didn't fit with everything she knew of Viscount Edenbyrne. She would not give up hope.

If the Lord Marshal were in her camp, others of the nobles, still hesitating, could be won to her cause, she was certain. Many shared the Duke of Wyston's reluctance to rely on Acquitanian aid and allow an enemy power a sure foothold in the affairs of Albin, but they questioned whether the monarchy could be restored without resorting to this drastic measure. If Sir Andrew were willing to undertake the campaign, however, they might well take a different view of the matter. After the rout at Breicenshire, the Chamber had not regarded him as a threat, but his crushing defeat of their invading troops at Thornfeld had put heart into their opponents, and shown that he was still to be feared. *I must succeed in this. He must join us,* Alicen vowed. But she could not neglect the rest of her mission. For now, there were others she must see.

The air had regained its sultry warmth and not a breeze stirred. *What a wretched climate,* she thought, *either too cold or too hot. You'd think he'd be glad enough to leave it.* When her horse was brought around, she took the silver canteen that hung from her saddle and had a long draught of watered wine, wishing for something stronger.

She'd barely had time to replace the cork when she felt a strange tingling numbness creeping over her limbs, and she knew at once what it meant. *Someone poisoned it when the horse was in the yard here or at the hostel.* She opened her mouth to shout for help, but her throat seemed to be too tight to force words through. A coldness seeped through her chest, her vision blurred. She stumbled toward the house, but managed only a step or two before she collapsed to the ground, where she lay as still as stone while the mud soaked her fine lace and linen.

Chapter 3

*S*he's been poisoned—*no doubt of that,* Katin thought, holding the cup into which she'd poured the contents of the flask. She smelled it, then held it up to the light of the oil lamp on the kitchen worktable and used a spoon to fish out a piece of leaf that floated to the surface. She cast an anxious glance to where Alicen lay by the hearth, surrounded by servants waiting for Katin to tell them what to do.

The groom who had brought Alicen's horse, seeing her stricken, had fetched help without delay, and the servants had carried her into the kitchen, calling for Katin. She had sent at once for Carl, but he was somewhere off in the swamps again, and now, listening to Alicen's rasping breath, Katin knew she didn't have time to wait for his return. She'd have to treat Alicen herself. To let her die was unthinkable, despite the risk that she might wake and recognize Katin as the Princess Oriana.

"Keep her head up," she ordered. "That will help her to breathe more easily. Heat water!" Without waiting to see her orders obeyed, she raced out the kitchen door and hurried to her workshed, with Lucifer at her heels. She was gone for only minutes, but by the time she returned, clutching jars of milkweed and foxglove, Alicen was already ashen white, and her lips had a strange bluish tint. Grabbing the bowl of hot water from the trembling fingers of a scullery maid, Katin crushed a handful of the herbs into it, then slipped her hand behind Alicen's head and poured the decoction into her mouth, little by little. Alicen coughed and sputtered, but Katin managed to make her swallow most of the liquid.

It was all she could do, and it seemed so little when she looked at the gray, still form of Alicen, who was somehow all the more pathetic in her soiled finery. But a quarter of an hour later, Alicen was still alive, and Katin was relieved to see that her breathing was stronger, and the deathlike pallor seemed to have lessened slightly. As Katin leaned close to feel her heartbeat, Alicen groaned and opened her eyes, staring straight up into Katin's face. Her vision was still unclear, and the features above her shifted and blurred into a familiar, well-remembered visage. She squeezed her eyes shut, then opened them again. *Could it be? No, the Princess was dead. Then who . . . ?* She tried to focus more clearly. Now the face seemed to change—it didn't look quite the way she'd thought it had, not quite the same, too old, and yet— *It's the poison,* she told herself. *I must be delirious.* Everything seemed to spin dizzily. "Oriana . . . ?" she murmured.

"Aye that's where you are," Katin said quickly, turning away. "Take her to a bed, and keep her warm," she ordered on her way to the door. "And send Master Schellring to her when he arrives. I must let Sir Andrew know how she fares."

"'Twas wolfsbane, or something akin to it," Katin said, coming into the back parlor of the Governor's dwelling, followed as usual by Lucifer. "But I've given her an alterant, and it seemed to answer. I believe she'll mend, with rest."

Lady Celia laid aside her embroidery, and Sir Andrew turned from the correspondence and documents piled on the trestle table beside his armchair. "Wolfsbane?" he said. "Then this was a deliberate—"

But he broke off as a little girl of three years ran into the room, clutching a piece of kindling. She was followed at a run by a harried young nursemaid, a lass of sixteen who looked much at a loss. Sir Andrew once more gave his attention to his work, and Lady Celia rose and crossed to the cradle beside the fireplace. The baby had been wakened by the commotion and begun to fret.

Katin, too, bent over the cradle, beckoning to the little girl. "Look how big your brother's growing. Perhaps he'll be a general like your Papa, eh?" The baby stopped fussing and made a grab for the silver clasp in Katin's hair.

But the child had caught sight of Lucifer and dashed after him, waving her piece of wood with a menacing air. Delighted, the dog seized the near end in his teeth and tugged fiercely at it, nearly pulling her off her feet.

The nursemaid caught her and looked helplessly at Katin, who picked up Lucifer and took the stick away from the combatants.

"Mine!" the little girl objected.

"If you want to throw sticks for doggy to fetch, you must do it out of doors," the nursemaid scolded.

"Not stick—s'ord," the child told her indignantly.

"Oh, I see," said Katin, enlightened. "You're a soldier, too."

The child looked at her in disgust. "No no no— *pi*rate!" She squirmed away from the nursemaid and threw herself at Katin and Lucifer, yelling, "S'ord anna *pis*tol, too!"

"Oho, a pirate, is it? Well, if that's so, I *arrest* you, then, for brigandry upon the high seas! And I'll claim the reward for capturing you and delivering you to the proper authorities." Katin dropped Lucifer, tossed the stick on the fire, and grabbed the little girl, tickling her mercilessly before handing her over to the nursemaid again.

Overcome with naughtiness, the child pummeled the hapless girl, shrieking, "Can't capter *me!*"

"Clara," Lady Celia said quietly.

"Pirate, Mama!"

"That will do," Lady Celia said firmly. "Come give me a kiss." Suddenly meek and tractable, Clara marched up to kiss her mother, the very picture of obedience. Lady Celia's calm authority had subdued, betimes, natures more formidable than her daughter's. "Now kiss Papa, Miss Wickedness, then go take your nap like a civilized person, or I shall be ashamed of you."

Sir Andrew gave up all pretense at working, and regarded his piratical offspring in bemusement, as if she were one of the unknown New World creatures that Carl brought back from the wild. He lifted her onto his lap and said, "I thought you'd decided to be a cavalry officer and ride a white horse."

"Sail onna *ship*," Clara explained earnestly.

"Ah. Well, others besides pirates sail on ships, dear. Your Mama and I traveled across the ocean to come to this land, years ago, but neither of us indulged ourselves in piracy on the way."

Clara received this information in astonishment. It seemed impossible that either of her parents had ever done anything so interesting. "Clara go, too?" she demanded.

"Perhaps someday," said Sir Andrew. "Perhaps soon. If you promise not to run anyone through with a sword."

Clara accepted this proposition, and having further stipulated that Katin would come sing to her later, she went off for her nap without further mayhem.

Sir Andrew shook his head. "You've been letting Vendeley tell her stories," he reproached his wife. "If you must cultivate the acquaintance of a lawless freebooter, you might at least prevent her from corrupting your children."

Lady Celia laughed. "The whole town's agog with talk of pirates, my dear. Children will hear servants' gossip. I can assure you that Rolande takes no interest in the nursery whatsoever." There were very few people who referred to Rolande by her given name, and fewer still who addressed her thus, but Lady Celia had done so almost from the first.

Now that the nursemaid and her charge were out of hearing, the others were free to confer about the disturbing matter of Lady Alicen Kendry. If she'd been poisoned, who was responsible? Had she recognized the Princess, and if so, would she remember what she'd seen when she recovered? Would she accept the story that Katin was an illegitimate connection of the royal family, to account for the resemblance—and could she be trusted with a story even that close to the truth?

All felt that events were already moving beyond their control, but there was little enough they could resolve concerning Lady Alicen until they could question her. Sir Andrew soon turned to another matter he had to discuss with the Princess.

"I have sent word to Sir Warren," he told her, "and asked for his counsel in the event that you lived yet and were determined to regain the throne. He will undoubtedly read the truth behind my question."

Katin nodded. So, they were set upon their course now, past returning. It was chilling to contemplate, but she said only, "How much can he accomplish, do you think, from Acquitania?"

"He is dispossessed of formal power, of course, but he retains much of the web of informants he maintained as commander of military security. We should have word from him within the month, as to the state of affairs in Albin and Acquitania."

So soon, Katin thought.

To protect the colony from another unexpected attack from Albin, Sir Andrew had instituted a relay system that allowed him to receive word of what occurred in Albin more rapidly than the Chamber could obtain information from the New World. He had recruited Yerren messengers who sailed to stations on coastal islands, then flew in relay from island to island, covering three-quarters of the span of the ocean between the colony and the continent beyond the eastern sea. For the last leg of the journey, messages were turned over to human sailors and delivered to the continent by ship, and return information followed the same route in reverse. It would have been impossible, not long ago, to receive news in much under a season, but now it seemed that there was no time for reflection, for regret, for doubt.

"Very good, sir," Katin said firmly.

* * *

Though Ruthven and Alicen agreed on little else, they were of one mind concerning the climate of the New World. Ruthven huddled in his cloak and cursed the wind as he rode along the path that led from Lady Ideline's estate to the main road to town. His belated interview with Sir Evan's widow had been even less promising than Alicen's. Over wine made from apples grown in the estate's orchards, Her Ladyship had told him, with an air of coy regret, that she was afraid her husband, the late Lord, would not have wished her to support the cause of the Duke of Halkin, so long as he maintained his plan to bring the Acquitanian army into Albin.

Ruthven had met with this argument from many of the colonial nobles, and it had been all he could do, on this occasion, to keep himself from flinging his wine into Her Ladyship's complacent, superior face. It was merely an excuse to do nothing, to refuse to make sacrifices for the homeland they claimed to honor! How easy to take a lofty view of the matter from the security and comfort of their estates here, and leave it to the dispossessed to restore Albin to the Crown!

Ruthven had argued, cajoled, and even pleaded, explaining to Lady Ideline that to take such a position was to abandon Albin to the Chamber of Statesmen, to the rule of the rabble in velvet who now lorded it over their betters—but despite his persuasive words and his potent charm, the widow only gazed at him and murmured sympathetic platitudes, without actually promising anything. His one consolation was that she seemed no more disposed to lend her support to the Duke of Wyston's folly than to the Duke of Halkin's plan. She was not, then, completely beyond the reach of reason.

The Duke of Wyston's vision of a populace united against the Deps was the delusion of a madman, Ruthven had declared to Lady Ideline. There was one way to oust the Chamber from power—with the might of Acquitania. And there was one way to unite the people of Albin—*against* the might of Acquitania, once an Obelen was on the throne again. The foreign forces might think themselves an occupying power, but they'd soon be shown that they were no more than mercenaries whose usefulness was at an end.

He might as well have spared his eloquence, for all he received from Her Ladyship was assurances that she would give the matter her most careful consideration, and he knew that she would do nothing of the sort. No doubt the old she-weasel had given the same assurances to Alicen Kendry, who was surely engaged in a mission similar to his own. Kendry's title gave her an advantage over him, damn her, but still her message was one that many of her fellow nobles were not best pleased to hear. He knew that some considered her a traitor to her class, and he should be able to turn that fact to his own advantage. . . .

But suddenly all thoughts of political maneuvers were driven from his mind as his horse's hoof hit an unseen obstacle in the road, and a charge exploded with a thunderous clap, spewing loam and pebbles high into the air. He clutched the reins, hanging on with desperate strength and trying to quiet the panicked horse. Despite his efforts, Ruthven found himself slipping from the saddle as his mount reared wildly, and he grasped the reins close to the mare's head and threw himself across her neck. Unable to throw back her head, the horse was forced to cease leaping, but she took off at a terrified gallop that left Ruthven clinging for his very life.

The horse covered nearly a mile before Ruthven brought her under control. When he did, he immediately turned her back in the direction of Lady Ideline's estate, determined to find out what had caused the explosion. The horse refused to turn onto the side trail from which it had just fled, and he could hardly blame the beast. Tethering her to a nearby tree, he proceeded down the leaf-strewn track on foot, but his own progress slowed as he crept forward to the hole left by the charge. With small concern for the state of his satin trousers, he knelt and swept aside the scattered debris, examining it carefully. In it, he found a half-burnt wick, a scattering of black powder, and bits of metal from the container that had held it. So, someone had known of his plans to visit the Widow Delart today—or followed him, then lain in wait until he was seen or heard trotting in the direction of the trap. The coward had then lit the fuse that would cause the explosion in the path and scare his mount—and then what? Hope that he was injured or killed? Hardly an exact way to kill a man. Or perhaps his enemy's plan had misfired and the charge had been intended to explode later and do greater damage, or kill him outright.

Ruthven had been the target of attacks before, from many sources, but what enemy could he have here, at the far end of creation? His thoughts returned to Alicen Kendry. There was no doubt in his mind that she was aware of his presence, as he of hers—yet he had not raised his hand against her! Very well, if that was how she wished to play the game. . . .

* * *

As Rolande and her crew continued to harry enemy ships, she kept on with her search for some clue to the nature of the Chamber's military plans. When they stopped at whatever ports were momentarily safe, to repair their vessel and resupply food, water, and lost crew members, Rolande assiduously questioned her fellow seafarers regarding the secret weapon the enemy was creating. There were rumors aplenty that the Chamber did not plan to let the rich resources of the New World go unexploited, while their own cupboards were nearly bare, but she heard nothing of the device mentioned in the letter jettisoned from the *Lorisonde*. Yet if the Chamber planned an invasion, there must be those in New Albin prepared to provide whatever support would be required—and Rolande was not one to give up easily.

* * *

"There's one took a room here, a few days ago, who might have the knowledge you seek," a one-eyed manservant told her, at a dockside inn in Dunraven, where she had stopped to repair her ship's mizenmast, damaged in an overly ambitious attempt on an Albinate man-of-war. He set down Rolande's drink before her and waited expectantly till she motioned him to sit.

"Aye? Tell me more," she invited, shoving the drink toward him. She laid a single, heavy silver coin upon the table between them.

Downing the drink hastily, he whispered, "His name be Passmore, and he is of the Deprivants—a cleric." The man spat disdainfully upon the floor. "A liar and a thief like all of them. But he carries papers stamped with the Chamber's seal in red. . . ." He gave Rolande a significant look.

As one who had carried secret documents for the Chamber herself, Rolande knew that the red wax signified a military matter for the eyes of the Lord General only. But how would her informant know what an agent of the Chamber had on his person? "And I suppose he showed them to you?" she asked wryly.

The servingman smirked. "Our young churchman had a bit too much ale one night, and I had to help him up to his room—and not a penny did the cur offer me for my trouble! But when I'd tucked him up and he was snoring away, at peace with his God and all, I helped myself to a just payment for my services, and I spied the packet when I went through his possessions. I paid it little heed at the time, as it was of no value to me, but I recognized the seal from my days in the Chamber's navy—before I lost my eye." He gestured at his scarred face and eye patch. "Served on a ship engaged off the harbor of Thornfeld. When we were hit, we ran aground and a gun exploded, burned my face bad. Being of no good use to them, they left me behind like an old dog to starve."

Rolande nodded thoughtfully. That, at least, was likely enough to be true. "But how did a Dep Minister come to drink more than was good for him?" she asked, with a sidelong glance at the man. "From all I know of the grayfolk, they disapprove of overindulgence in spirits."

"Ah. Well, I may have misspoken—perhaps he was taken ill. It might have been that he had only one drink, but that one proved too strong for a man not used to the like."

Rolande took his meaning. He'd drugged the Dep's drink, then pilfered as much as he dared from him. "A solitary traveler ought to be more careful," she said. "Where can I find this fellow now?" Sir Andrew would pay well for such documents.

Having drunk Rolande's ale and pocketed her money, the servingman slowly stood and stepped back, shaking his head. "I never said you could *find* him,

mistress, now did I? He had his chests sent aboard the
Corina, and she set sail yesterday, bound for Albin."

From the dockmaster, Rolande found out that the
Corina was not bound for Albin directly, but would
stop first at Baradon to acquire spices, then go on to
Castilia to sell them at a profit before finally making
port in Albin. This must have been unwelcome news to
the Chamber's courier, but it satisfied Rolande, for if
she were to set out at once for White Hern Island,
where ships making the trade run between Baradon and
Albin were wont to stop for supplies, she might yet intercept the *Corina.*

White Hern Island was the last of the channel islands where a merchant vessel might take on needed
supplies in safety before sailing across the eastern sea.
There were pirate havens in the eastern sea, as in other
waters, where enterprising freebooters had set up way
stations for their own kind. A pirate ship could obtain
repairs and supplies there, for a price, and the crew
could rest unmolested, but to stray too near such a
place in a merchant ship would be lunacy. As a law-
abiding vessel, the *Corina* would have to take on food
and fresh water at White Hern Island, and if Rolande
could arrive there first, before the *Corina*'s business
was completed in Baradon, she would only have to
wait for her quarry to come to her. But the other ship
had a day's start already.

She harried the shipwrights mercilessly to complete
the repairs on her mast, and set about recalling her
crew to their duties at once. Above all, she wanted to
catch the *Corina* before the messenger could reach
Albin—then let His Lordship claim she didn't do him
good service! Nor was she indifferent to the fact that
the spices would fetch a pretty price at any market—

legitimate booty if she could capture the *Corina* in the line of duty.

As the *Azora* approached White Hern Island, she stopped several times to exchange news with the other vessels that crossed her path, seeking any that might have passed the *Corina,* if the merchant ship were ahead of her. Rolande learned nothing, however, nor had the *Corina* yet been seen at White Hern Island, when the *Azora* made port there. But when Rolande's ship had lain at rest off the coast of the island for the better part of a week, there was still no sign of the vessel she sought. Rolande knew that the *Corina* could not make the final long crossing to Albin without taking on additional supplies, but as more days passed, she began to fear that her informant had been mistaken about the ship's plans, or that her quarry had made an unforeseen detour.

Finally, she sent her Yerren lookout to survey the coast of the small island and report all sail, for she would have to take some action soon. Her crew was growing restless, having allowed a few good prospects to pass unchallenged, in order to pursue this whim of hers, and she could not well explain her mission to them. The less known about her dealings with Sir Andrew, the better—for him. And Rolande had no intention of jeopardizing his position, for her own fortunes might depend upon his.

Thus, she was ready to make sail and seek any prey when Hrivas returned, but his report changed her mind again. He knocked, or rather scratched, at her cabin door, during the evening watch, when she was none too pleased to be disturbed, then stood awkwardly on the threshold as if poised to flee when she flung open the door with a curse and glared at him. Hrivas' command of his shipmates' tongue was reasonably good, but his discomfort at being enclosed belowdecks, coupled with Rolande's impatience, very nearly left him speechless.

His message, though, when he managed to give it, improved Rolande's mood considerably. Hrivas explained that he had sighted a ship a half-day's sail from the island, coming from the south. It was a light, swift vessel of the type commonly sailed by the *Ysnathi* coastal traders, but with one of his own brethren among the crew. He had stopped to rest on deck, and learned that the ship had passed the *Corina* the day before and that she was indeed but a day behind them. "And *now* she's flying the Chamber's flag," he added.

Rolande laughed. "So, we were too early for the rendezvous, not too late! Good work, *criiylash*." She used the Yerren word for "sharp-eyed," one of many that had spread from Yerren sailors to their human crewmates. Equipped with this news, Rolande resolved to sail some little way out of the harbor where they might wait for the approach of the *Corina*.

She dismissed Hrivas and turned back to Blythe, who lay on her bed with his arms stretched behind his head. "We'll take her!" she told him. "She's declared herself an enemy to the Colonies, and that makes her lawful prey for us. But if we've not met with her before three days are past, we'll give her up and go a-hunting."

Blythe grinned. "So you're a champion of the law, are you? It seems to me you take the law or leave it, pretty much as you please."

"And if I do?" said Rolande. "That doesn't suit you?"

"Oh, it suits me well enough. I don't mind saying that this inactivity is beginning to grow tedious."

"I can't have that—nothing's so dangerous as a dissatisfied crew," Rolande said, stretching out beside him on the berth. "Now how can I best keep you occupied in the meantime?"

The *Corina* hove into view a day later, her flag sporting the emblem of the Chamber, a torch on a gold field. On Rolande's order, Hrivas left his place high in the rigging above the main-topgallant sail and swept in a graceful arc over the sea toward the enemy vessel. As he neared the ship, he glided low enough to confirm that it was indeed an Albinate galley, and to count the guns it carried as protection, but he took care to stay out of their range.

The sailors repairing tackle on the quarterdeck stopped and stared uneasily at the foreign monster that hovered over the ship and then disappeared again into the clouds. One man who bore a crude tattoo of the torch and the sword—a symbol adopted by peasants loyal to the Deprivant cause during the Uprising—shouted, "Begone, demon, in the name of Sovereign God!" and made the Deprivant sign of Repudiation.

When Hrivas reported to Rolande how well-armed the *Corina* was, she spat and said, "If that's a trading ship, I'm Albarosa the Great!" No doubt the master of that vessel did carry on commerce, but he did so to disguise his true business—the ferrying of information to and from the Chamber.

At first, as the *Azora* moved smoothly toward the *Corina*, flying a neutral flag, the Albinate captain took no alarm. But when they drew close enough for him to see that the *Azora* carried a large number of guns, he hailed her, demanding the identity of the vessel and her captain. No sooner had Rolande responded than he called for increased speed, with the intent to draw away. Over the past few years, a number of Albinate vessels had fallen prey to a ship commanded by a proud woman captain—a ship with heavy weaponry and a feathered fellow as lookout.

Rolande commanded her own helmsman to make after the other ship, and the distance between them soon began to narrow, for the *Azora* was lighter, faster, and less heavily laden. The captain of the *Corina,* seeing that flight was unavailing, brought his vessel about and discharged his guns. In turn, Rolande ordered a broadside fired on the up roll, hoping to disable the *Corina* without sinking her. As the smoke from the guns billowed forth, the *Azora,* with her superior maneuverability was able to sail closer, at an angle to the *Corina*'s bow.

By eliminating their only chance of escape, Rolande had hoped to intimidate the captain of the *Corina* into striking his colors and allowing them to board, but he refused to give way. Instead the *Corina* raked the deck of the *Azora* with a load of grapeshot in an attempt to inflict such heavy injury to the crew that she would be forced to draw off. But Rolande ordered the *Azora* drawn back only far enough to bring her again parallel to the Albinate ship, then had her gunners deliver round after round of cannonfire, this time on the down roll, aiming to disable the *Corina*'s guns.

Despite the relentless pounding from Rolande's cannon, the captain of the galley refused to strike his colors. The battle raged for three hours, and the sea around the two embattled vessels became filled with debris, pieces of yards and rigging torn from the two ships. The smoke was now so thick that it was nearly impossible for the crews of the vessels to see each other, but as fewer and fewer balls struck the *Azora,* Rolande had little doubt that they had been successful in striking at the *Corina*'s armaments. Still, the *Corina*'s captain refused to surrender.

Peering past the ruins of the mizzenlift, through the thick clouds of soot that separated the two ships, Rolande caught a glimpse of his flag still flying and was infuriated by the Dep's stubbornness. Sooner or later a lucky shot from the enemy would bring down one of the *Azora*'s masts or damage her steering gear, crippling her. She had meant at first to avoid sinking the enemy vessel, so as to let the crew take her safely to land, but now she resolved that she must damage it severely enough to leave the captain no choice but to surrender. And to save her own crew, she must accomplish this as swiftly as possible. Accordingly, she commanded all guns to bear on the enemy square amidships.

"Run up beside them," she ordered her helmsman, knowing full well that she had the chance of only one good volley. If the *Corina* survived to retaliate, at that distance, her own vessel was doomed. The helmsman, stony-faced, steered the *Azora* close to its quarry. On Rolande's word, her gunners fired a broadside, pouring cannonballs into the hull of the facing ship. The *Corina* listed sharply to starboard, and Rolande feared it would sink straightway, yet shortly it righted itself enough for her to consider boarding. "Lash her to us," she shouted, "but stand ready to sever the ropes if she starts to careen—we don't want to go down with her! You, bring me her flag!" she ordered Hrivas.

Now that the guns were still, Rolande crossed the boarding planks and stood on the deck of the *Corina*. The captain, first mate, and two lieutenants all lay dead upon the deck, and all around were wounded men and shattered yards and crosstrees. Rolande ordered her crew to transfer to the *Azora* all who might survive,

that Blythe might attend to them when he had finished
with her own people.

She questioned the remaining officers of the vessel,
and soon learned where to, find the young Deprivant
Minister. As she moved through the press of captives
and wounded sailors along the quarterdeck, her first
mate pushed his way up to her and reported, "The
hull's taken a great hole from our cannonballs, and
she'll sink ere long. We've no time to tarry."

This was no more than Rolande had expected, and it
would mean one ship the fewer for her enemies, but
she preferred that it not founder till she'd found what
she sought. "Carry on, then," she said grimly, as the
shifting of the ship confirmed that time was short.

She threw open the door of a cabin on the starboard
side of the main deck, and was met by a scent of burning, different from the odor of gunpowder that still
hung in the air around the ship. With a curse, she
leaped at the gray-garbed man who was burning sheets
of parchment over a candle flame. Sparks and charred
bits of paper flew everywhere as she tore the smoldering sheaf from his hand, and they struggled for possession of the fragments. Rolande threw him against a
table bolted to the starboard wall, knocking the breath
from him, but when she tried to examine the documents, she found that only scraps remained. "You'll
tell me about the new weapon, then!" she shouted at
the man, pulling him to his feet.

He swayed unsteadily, gasping, "God's curse on
you—pirate bitch—I'll die first!" Rolande had just
time enough to note that he didn't deny that he knew
of such a weapon, but in a moment both of them were
scrabbling for their footing as the ship gave a dangerous lurch.

"She's going down!" Rolande yelled. "We'll both be

drowned—come on!" She raced for the ladder, dragging the unresisting Dep spy after her.

As they burst onto the deck, the first mate cried, "We've sent the crew aboard our vessel, Cap'n, but we've got to cut her loose *now*, or she'll pull us down along of 'er!"

"Get on board yourself, then."

But before she could follow, the Chamber's agent had twisted from her grasp, raced back down below to the lower decks, and disappeared.

For only a few seconds, Rolande stared after him in disbelief, as her crew shouted frantically for her, and the deck listed wildly underfoot. Then she leaped aboard the *Azora* and ordered the mooring lines cut at once. There was no time to chase that Deprivant lunatic through the wings between the decks, with the sea pouring in over both of them. The sailors standing ready chopped through the heavy ropes with hand axes, and Rolande could only watch as the *Corina* was swallowed by the waves, along with its secrets.

Chapter 4

Rolande listened with increasing concern to the report of her ship's carpenter. In the taking of the *Corina*, the *Azora* had suffered severe damage herself. Her foremast was sprung, and she had lost her bowsprit and part of the upper works, so that the vessel could hardly be considered seaworthy. They had to land as soon as possible to make repairs, and with the crewmen of the *Corina* aboard, they didn't dare make for a law-abiding port in the eastern sea, lest they be arrested for piracy. Their warrant to capture ships that threatened the colonies of New Albin would mean nothing here.

"There's no help for it," Rolande decided. "Set a course for Needle Isle." It was a notorious pirate haven. "You know the heading?" she asked her pilot.

"I've been there," he admitted. "The approach is treacherous, with jagged outlying rocks all around, but I can steer us there if she holds together."

"Is it true that Tyrrel rules there?"

"Aye, he was the scourge of these waters in his day, till he got so old. Now he keeps the isle as a place to rest his bones. A merchant ship off his shores will be picked clean in a trice, but a pirate crew can get wood, water, and stores there—for a price. And we'll have to hand over a share of all goods on board, as tribute."

"We'll be provided protection in return, while we make our repairs?"

"Aye, the isle's well defended with cannon and armed ships. But they'll make you swear to engage in no deeds of piracy without Tyrrel's consent, for so long as we're harbored there."

Rolande did not press the man as to how he had become familiar with Captain Tyrrel's refuge, for like many who now sailed with her, he had no doubt served on pirate ships in the past. And while she was, to be precise, not a pirate, since she acted under legal commission, this was not the time to put too fine a point on the matter.

"Well, we're in no shape to mount an attack as it is, consent or no. And our gold and goods will be lost at sea along with our bones if we don't seek sanctuary at Needle Isle, so let us jury-rig the crossjack braces and the topmast crosstrees and pray they hold out long enough," she ordered.

Alone in her quarters, Rolande lit an oil lamp and laid the pieces of paper she'd rescued from the Deprivant messenger on the table. The remains of the pages were charred, and water had smeared the ink in places. After much study, she'd only succeeded in making out a few phrases. "... to accommodate the firing of all guns ... isolated from shipping routes ... off the southern coast of New Lindness, 100 leagues east of the northernmost point of Dunraven ..." *But what exactly is to happen, and when?* Rolande asked herself, furious at her own carelessness in letting the Chamber's agent escape her. Though she herself had never been ardently devoted to the Dep cause, she should have guessed that he might be fanatic enough to drown himself rather than betray his masters.

She turned back to her task in frustration, but could

make no sense of the maddening bits of information. If the Chamber was planning to stage an attack, why were they looking for a place away from the Colonies? But they seemed to want a location in the vicinity of the settlements, and that alone boded ill ... perhaps they meant to secure their secret weapon there for future use? The idea increased her unease—and her determination—but there was nothing further to be learned from the scraps of paper, whose burnt edges flaked off in her hand and drifted away.

For four days they made their way limping, before sighting the isle they sought. The wounded ship was listing badly by the time they gained the narrow strait that led to the final approach to the shore. They managed to navigate between the craggy cliffs, but were unable to adjust the damaged rudder well enough to avoid the sharp rocks protruding from the water. One ripped a greater gap in her side below the orlop beam, and with a ragged groan the ship leaned heavily to port.

Rolande ordered her sailors and the survivors of the *Corina*'s crew into the longboats, then watched in anguish as the *Azora* careened and sank beneath the waves. She had been a worthy vessel, trim before the wind, and spirited in fight. And now Rolande was left without a command, stranded. *Kairas,* she thought bitterly, a Yerren word that meant "with wings clipped."

She was only thankful they were close enough now to row the last league to the isle and gain the safety of the shore. As the oarsmen maneuvered the crafts between the rocky outcroppings, Rolande turned resolutely from the drowned wreck of her ship to study the lay of the land they were approaching. The island was roughly horseshoe-shaped with two narrow curving

necks of land that jutted out into the sea, creating a
narrow strait through which all ships attempting to
close with its shore must pass. Captain Tyrrel had chosen his fastness well, Rolande acknowledged.

Once through the strait they found themselves in a
cove that formed a natural harbor, where a great variety of ships hailing from many nations, and in all
stages of repair, stood at anchor. The island was surrounded by cliffs along its other sides, but here a series
of forested slopes rose gently from the coarse sand of
the beach. At the far edge of the northernmost hill
Rolande could see a solidly built, windowless, square
wooden structure, which gave no sign of its purpose.

But of more immediate concern was the crude
wooden stockade that had been erected upon a rise not
far from the water's edge, bearing batteries of guns
taken from injured vessels that had come to that shore
over the years. Defended by gunners of ruthless and
desperate courage, the isle was rarely bothered by naval ships, and the few that had ever come against them
had been easily sunk. Rolande saw that the isle could
be taken by a large armada, but the cost would be
great. There was not much to fear on that score, she
thought—the navies of the civilized world were so
heavily occupied with fighting each other that none
could spare a large enough force to eradicate the outlaw colony here. And even if a war fleet did succeed in
driving Captain Tyrrel and his followers from his isle,
they would simply reestablish themselves in another
port before long, for such freebooters were as numerous at sea as thieves on land.

Rolande's longboat was in the lead, and as they
pulled closer to shore, she could see that a makeshift
town had been raised beyond the fortifications. Here,
log shacks and scattered tents housed the crews of the

grounded ships that took temporary refuge on Needle
Isle. Nearby, corrals held pigs and cows, and supplies
were stored in shanties. Everything the sailors required
was available from Captain Tyrrel's henchmen, for the
right price. On one of the slopes overlooking the harbor stood a more elaborate house constructed of finished wood planks—no doubt Tyrrel's own dwelling.

When the boat came to rest on the sand, a stocky,
shaggy-haired fellow strode forward from the nearest
guardpost to greet them, looking them over with a decidedly predatory air. "Whence be you from?" he demanded, one hand resting on a pistol among the
weapons that bristled from his belt.

"The freehold of the deep," Rolande answered
promptly.

The watcher nodded, acknowledging the universal
formula with which pirates greeted each other.

"Then you're welcome to—" he began, but suddenly
broke off and pulled out his pistol, aiming it overhead,
where Hrivas was swooping lower over the harbor.

"Leave off that!" yelled Corey, one of the *Azora*'s
boatswain's mates, and the shot went wild as he ran up
and knocked the sentry's arm aside. Hrivas prudently
soared up out of range.

"What ails ye, fool? It's one of those cursed
wing'uns—"

"I know what he is," Corey said hotly. "He's our
shipmate, and you fire on 'im at your peril, scurvy bastard!" There were mutterings of agreement from some
of Rolande's crew, silence from others.

The sentry turned on Rolande. "That thing belongs
to you?"

On her own ship, Rolande had been undisputed master, but here and now she was a shipwrecked outlaw
with no authority, as she knew only too well. Yet she

answered, as if unaware of her own standing, "He's a member of my crew, aye, and a better lookout a ship couldn't have. He's brought us no ill luck—"

"No?" The man's raucous laughter echoed from the surrounding cliffs. Other pirates had been drawn from the stockade by the sound of gunfire, and he told them, "There's their ship scuttled, and the lot of 'em washed ashore like so much driftweed, and they say they've had no ill luck from sailing with a wing'un!"

Rolande joined in the laughter, as if she thought this sally the height of wit. Her people were surrounded. "Why, do you call this ill luck?" she cried. "Here we are hale and whole, on dry ground, among friends— I've had misfortune that makes this look like a frolic. But 'tis no fault of my featherling that we're here—"

"Not one foot or feather does that thing set on this ground, so I warn ye!" the sentry interrupted, seconded by the others. "If you're so partial to its company, you can go join it, and stay there till you rot!" He gestured with his pistol to the reef where Hrivas had taken refuge, at a safe distance, waiting for some sign from Rolande.

She held up both hands in a placating gesture. "Very well, very well, I'll send him away—no need to get into a lather. But belay your fire, for pity's sake. The poor creature's done you no harm, nor means any." Remembering Sir Andrew's relay system for carrying information, Rolande realized that Hrivas would be able to reach the Coral and Goatshead Islands from here, and Blue Mountain Island from there. At Blue Mountain he could find a ship willing to take him over the long stretch of sea—too far for him to fly—to the southern colonies. She would send him with a message for Sir Andrew, she decided.

The pirates who'd come from the stockade made

them surrender their weapons before allowing any of them to move from the shore. Rolande reluctantly handed over her pistol and sword. She could see the sense in preventing disparate crews of buccaneers from going about the island armed to kill, but she muttered to her pilot, "Do you know where they're kept?"

"Everybody knows." He nodded toward the hut at the top of the cliff that rose on the northern side of the isle, abutting the fortifications. "But they're guarded night and day."

Rolande started to ask another question, but fell silent as the pirate sentry stalked up to her again, frowning. "Now get rid of your demon pet!" he ordered. "Then we'll see what's to be done with the rest of ye."

Rolande yawned and stretched in a long shrug, then turned her back on him and beckoned Corey to her. "Take one of the boats—you and you, help him row it—and bring this out to Hrivas." From under her greatcoat, she took a small bundle tied with twine, the remaining scraps of the Chamber's document, wrapped in the flag of the *Corina*. "He's to take this to Sir Andrew and tell him all that's taken place. Give him as many of our waterskins as he can carry." Hrivas would have no trouble feeding himself, Rolande knew, on fish snatched from the waves in his talons, and seabirds caught on the wing. And he preferred them raw. "Have him wait for us there. We'll make for Oriana as soon as we've a ship to carry us."

Now maybe these bastards will let me get some sleep, she thought, as she stepped wearily away from the longboat, but then a deep, harsh voice called out, "Vendeley!"

She looked around to see a man well over six feet tall, striding across the beach toward her from one of the nearby shanties, which rang with shouts and laughter. As the sentry who'd fetched him returned to his post, Rolande stared at the newcomer, taking his measure, but she held her ground and made no move toward him. Let *him* come to *me,* she thought, drawing herself up to her full height, and instinctively taking on a challenging stance.

Every inch of him glittered, from his embroidered damask wide-sleeved coat and breeches to the heavy gold-braided chain around his neck. His hair was long, mostly gray where it had once been black, and tied back with a gold satin ribbon. His eyes were cold and hard as obsidian.

"Captain Tyrrel?" said Rolande.

The man grinned. "And you are Rolande Vendeley, no? It is my business to know who sails these seas. You've come to seek our hospitality, have you?"

"Aye," Rolande said cautiously. "By the courtesy of the sea, for we're without a ship."

The pirate chieftain seemed displeased at this. "And how did you lose the *Azora?*"

"We took the *Corina* for her cargo of spices, but we hit her too hard, and sent her and her nutmegs to the bottom, to flavor the waves!" She shook her head ruefully. "She was better gunned than she'd any right to be, and perhaps I shouldn't have tried her, but overweening ambition has always been my besetting sin. She gave us a few bad knocks ere we sank her—still, we might have mended the *Azora* if we'd made it to land, but your blasted rocky reef here put paid to that. So you see, you've only yourself to blame that we're on your hands." She sounded as if she found the situation inconvenient, but nonetheless amusing.

"Why, you find yourself in difficulties, then," Captain Tyrrel said, with mock regret. He removed a dagger from his belt and began to clean his nails with it. "We've little means here to offer charity. We expect visitors to pay their way—in gold or goods from captured vessels."

"Of course you do," Rolande said smoothly, "and very prudent of you, too. But suppose, now, some unfortunate castaways hadn't anything of the kind to their name?"

Captain Tyrrel smiled unpleasantly, and looked Rolande up and down with evident interest. "That could be most unfortunate—for them. But for you, Vendeley, some special terms might be made. . . ."

Rolande bowed. "Oh, that won't be necessary for *us*, I assure you. The crew of the *Azora* ask favors of no one. Alden!" she called, "fetch the chest in the boat." The first mate climbed into one of the longboats and rooted among the remains of the stores there.

"There's an easy way and a hard way to do things," Captain Tyrrel observed, eyeing Rolande speculatively.

Rolande reminded herself that she was on Tyrrel's ground. She wasn't prone to taking threats from anyone, but she hadn't missed the glint of light on metal in the nearby fortification. His people there were watching, and they wouldn't miss her at this range. "Some things are best not done at all, easy or hard," she said. Bristling as she was at the constraints placed upon her, she kept her temper in check until Alden returned with a small leather-covered chest. Taking it from him, Rolande said, "We couldn't carry much from the wreck but a few stores to see us here. But I wasn't about to abandon this." Opening the box, she showed him the gold and silver coins collected from the *Corina*.

"There should be well on two thousand royals' worth there," she said, enjoying the look of astonishment on the captain's face, "in old royals and new em-

bers." The coins minted by the Chamber, with their
torch insignia, had come to be known as embers. They
were not so heavy as royals, but they were worth their
weight. "Will that buy us your hospitality, Captain?"

Corey left the others in the longboat and climbed up
alone to where Hrivas was waiting. Rolande had sent
him deliberately, knowing that Hrivas trusted him as
much as any Yerren trusted any human being.

"Why do you skinned bears always try to kill us?"
Hrivas demanded, after Corey had delivered Rolande's
message.

"Don't you know why? It's because you demon-
spawn can do what we only dream about—fly free as
the wind and leave us in the dirt. Fair makes us sick,
that does."

Hrivas could sense the goodwill behind his friend's
words. There was between them an echo of the wordless communion shared by all Yerren of the same clan.
It was so with some of the Ysnathi, he had found, but
very few. Indeed, it was said that they had no such rap-
port among themselves, but this Hrivas took for a
spiteful lie, spread by those who hated all Ysnathi and
considered them soulless monsters. "It's not our fault
if you great clumsy featherless fools can't get yourselves off the ground," he said.

"Well, we can shoot you lot out of the sky, anyway,
so watch your wings. Good luck, featherpate. Eh—you
can get to Blue Mountain Island all right, I suppose?"

"Look to your own luck, furface. You'll need it
more than I will, on that island of vipers.

* * *

Peeking from her post behind the curtained doorway, Katin noted that the handsome young man who sat in the wainscot chair opposite Sir Andrew had long, sand-colored hair and strongly-chiseled features. He was dressed in the outfit of a gentleman of means, the lace of his shirtfront spilling from his deep blue waistcoat. His jacket and breeches, like his waistcoat, were edged with gold trim, giving him a foppish look, but from his martial bearing, even when seated, it would have been difficult for Katin to mistake him for anything but an officer.

Captain Charles Fenton had been sent by Sir Warren Landervorne, in response to Sir Andrew's communication regarding the Princess. Once satisfied that the message had indeed come from Sir Andrew, the captain was to pose as the Governor's aide, assist him in establishing the legitimacy of the Princess' claim, and serve as liaison between the colonial loyalists and those of the Albinate nobility still in the Old World.

Sir Warren had agents scattered throughout the colonies, gathering military and political information for the Chamber's adversaries. Captain Fenton had been living in the colony of Hammersfeld far to the north, in the guise of the younger son of a noble family, seeking his fortune in the lucrative fur trade. Though some of Sir Warren's people had been posted nearer to Oriana, for a matter of this import he had naturally selected his most trusted agent, the son of an old friend who had spent his life in the King's service. Young Fenton was not yet thirty, but he had already proved his worth during the Uprising and the dangerous years since.

Now he was saying to Sir Andrew, "As you recommended, My Lord, we approached a small number of those whose loyalty to His late Majesty was beyond question, and acquainted them with the fact that Her Highness is yet alive. All are willing to send emissaries, but they require proof of her identity." He spread his hands apologetically. "As you know, there are already too many pretenders to the throne. If the royalists can be convinced, however, that she is indeed the Princess Oriana, then there is no question but that they will rally to her, to the fullest extent of their resources."

Sir Andrew nodded. "Subject, of course, to Her Highness' approval, we shall receive all such emissaries here, in the strictest confidence. They will be satisfied, never fear."

Katin felt that it was time she joined this conference. Intercepting the servant who was bringing a tray of wine, she took it herself, carried it into the reception room, and set it on the maple table before Sir Andrew. "Will there be anything else, My Lord?" she asked. If Sir Andrew were unsure of Fenton, he would dismiss her, and she in turn would withdraw without a word.

Captain Fenton had ceased speaking upon her entrance, but he had given her no more than a glance, taking her for a serving girl of the household. He was startled when Sir Andrew rose and drew out a chair for her, but he stood at once, and had already mastered his astonishment when Sir Andrew said, "Your Highness, permit me to present to you Captain the Honorable Charles Fenton, of the Third Darhan Cavalry, second son of Lord Copeland."

"Your Highness' most devoted servant," said the captain, making Katin an accomplished bow. As he declared his delight at learning that she had survived the Uprising, and his sense of the honor she did him by such an audience, nothing in his words or manner betrayed his dismay at finding that the monarch whose sovereignty he was charged to confirm had all the appearance of a thoroughly common and coarse-grained peasant girl. How was he to persuade Albin's nobility to accept this unkempt, sunburned savage as their rightful queen? He had always held the Lord Marshal in the highest esteem, but at that moment he could have run him through and dismembered him with the greatest pleasure.

"Pray be seated, sirs," said Katin. Both she and Sir Andrew had an accurate enough idea of what was going through the captain's mind, and she dutifully set about the task of reassuring him. With a smile remarkable for its gracious condescension, she explained, "You will find that here in New Albin, we have neither the leisure nor the inclination to observe court formalities, sir. One must adapt oneself to circumstances, as a soldier will readily understand. You would oblige me by falling in with our unceremonious ways in future, for the sake of expediency, though I trust you will not think me ungrateful for your very proper expressions of devotion to myself and my House, nor insensible to the courage and courtesy which prompted them." *That should satisfy the fellow,* she thought, with the barest hint of a wink at Sir Andrew.

Captain Fenton began to feel distinctly more optimistic about his mission.

Sir Andrew, thinking that he must make Katin repeat her speech later for Celia's benefit, recalled himself to the business at hand and said, "Her Highness' safety was, of course, the reason for this masquerade in the first place. She is known as Katin Ander among us, an apothecary of my household. By carefully maintaining this fiction at all times, in both appearance and demeanor, she has thus far escaped detection for six years—and become an accomplished herbalist," he added, with a smile. "In all that time, no one but my wife has been told the secret, and it has been necessary for us both to accustom ourselves to behaving toward Her Highness as toward a valued retainer—one whose familiarity and license are indulged. If you mean to be of use here, you also must learn to behave accordingly, so as never to betray unawares that the girl is anything other than what she seems."

"May I give you some wine, sir?" Katin asked demurely.

To hear Her Highness referred to as "the girl" was shocking enough to the well-bred captain, and only his considerable self-discipline enabled him to sit by and watch her serve wine to her own subjects. But to follow Sir Andrew's lead, and accept his glass with no more than a polite nod, required a truly heroic effort on his part. He passed a kerchief across his brow, and raised his drink with a hand that was barely steady. "I see what you mean, My Lord, exactly," he said, and took a long, grateful swallow of the wine.

* * *

Alicen waited by the candleberry bush in the hostel's rear yard until she saw Ruthven come out, mount his horse, and ride off. For a silver piece, the stable-girl admitted that the "gentleman" had asked the way to Brynwick Manor, which meant that he would be gone for some hours, Alicen reasoned. He and Sir Francis Silkworth, the master of the estate, would have much to discuss. Sir Francis had given Alicen short shrift indeed, when he'd heard of the Duke of Wyston's proposal for the commoners' assembly. He'd made clear that he wanted revenge on the Chamber, for sending him into what he considered a barbarous exile, but unfortunately he'd also insisted that he would rather see the Acquitanian Army quartered in Avenford than trust the peasants who had turned against him in the past. Ruthven should find him a willing listener.

Now that Ruthven was safely out of the way, Alicen sneaked round to the front of the hostel and entered, making for the stairs as if on the way to her own room. She had continued to pay for the room, and to use it occasionally, so as to disguise the fact that she had moved everything of importance to a small loft in Hannah Franesh's log house near the forest on the edge of the marsh. Hannah, who made her living hunting the giant tortoises and other animals of the marsh, was gone much of the time, and Alicen was provided with a secure and private place from which to conduct her business—a place that Ruthven didn't know about. She had no doubt that he'd already made a search of her room at the hostel, as she now intended to search his.

She passed no one but a girl scrubbing the stairs, and Alicen took care to look back and see that the lass hadn't come into view before she unlocked Ruthven's door and slipped inside. As she'd expected, her key fit his door as well as her own, for all the rooms had simple warded locks that would open to any single-shafted key. Ruthven, too, would have noted the fact—one reason Alicen had rented quarters from Hannah—and it was unlikely that he'd have left anything for Alicen to find, but if he thought he'd succeeded in poisoning her, he might be more careless than usual. There was a chance that he hadn't learned of her recovery, and she'd stayed out of his sight since she'd left the Governor's Mansion. There was nothing to lose by looking, she told herself.

But she had barely begun her search when the door was thrown open and Ruthven advanced on her, pistol in hand, shouting, "Kendry! Just as I thought!" He relieved Alicen of her weapons, then kicked shut the door with a slam and leaned back against it, glaring at her. "Come to finish what you blundered before?"

Furious at herself for falling into his trap, Alicen snarled, "You never planned to go to Brynwick, then."

"Where I plan to go is none of your affair. You take altogether too much interest in my movements to suit me. I like to get back alive from my destination."

"You're a fine one to talk! If not for the Governor's apothecary, I'd be dead now from your poison, you filthy coward."

Ruthven felt he was losing his bearings on the situation. "The Governor's—? A fair-haired lass?"

"Yes . . ." It occurred to Alicen that she'd had only the one glimpse of the girl. "She gave me an antidote."

"Did she now? An interfering creature, that one, and no mistake. But when am I supposed to have given you poison, pray?"

"You deny it?" Alicen sneered. "Why? I've no proof, I can't bring you to justice for it."

Ruthven shook his head. "I deny it because I know nothing about it. It strikes me as an excellent idea, to be sure, but unfortunately my orders don't include killing you. Yet. When I report that you tried to murder me—"

"I was searching your room, no more! And I didn't even accomplish that," Alicen said in disgust.

"Don't come the innocent with me, My Lady! You failed in your last attempt, and you're here to try again. But I warn you this once, if you try any more of your tricks, I'll not wait till I have orders to kill you. And I don't bother with poison. I'll slit your dainty throat and throw you in the swamp. If you're ever found, they'll blame bandits, or those feathered monstrosities that breed in this godforsaken wilderness! Now get out!" He moved away from the door and gestured contemptuously at it with his pistol, then returned the weapon to his coat.

Now it was Alicen who felt at a loss. Did he mean to let her walk out of here? Why try to poison her, and then let her go? What was his game? *But if he thought I was dead, he'd not have set this trap for me.* Thinking fast, but speaking slowly, she said, "Wait, now, not so hasty. . . . You claim that someone tried to poison you, too . . . ?"

Ruthven watched her narrowly. What was she waiting for? Could she really be unaware of the nature of the attack on him, or was she merely feigning ignorance, to put him off his guard? Yet if someone else had tried to kill her, then it was possible that the same assassin was after him as well. She wasn't fool enough to invent that tale of poison; it would be too easy for him to learn the truth from the Governor's household. "No, it wasn't poison," he said cautiously. "Someone set a charge in my path, the first of last month."

"Not I. I was still at the Governor's Mansion, recovering from being poisoned. I can prove it. Question Lady Celia if you doubt me."

Ruthven shrugged. "Then you paid someone to lay a trap for me."

"Oh, *that* would be clever, wouldn't it? I've been trying to be inconspicuous. If I meant to be rid of you, I'd not risk my position by putting my secrets in the hands of some hired killer. I'd just follow you and shoot you through your rotten heart." Alicen smiled, as if the prospect gave her pleasure. "But, aside from mere *dislike,* I've no reason to kill you, and you know it. Halkin would only send another in your place. It's simply not worth the risk." She crossed to a chair by the hearth and sat down, regarding Ruthven thoughtfully. "We both have a problem, don't we?"

Reluctantly, Ruthven nodded. He'd been surprised from the first that Alicen should have tried to ambush him in that way. It wasn't what he expected of her, but it hadn't occurred to him that he had other enemies in Oriana. Now he said with distaste, "And what do you propose *we* do about it?"

Alicen laughed. "The idea's sickening, I agree, but we'd much better work together to find the bastard."

"And kill him?"

Alicen hesitated, but only for a moment. "Or her," she said. *Vendeley? But she'd have thrown me off the* Lorisonde *if she'd wanted to kill me.* "The swamp, as you suggest, is a likely place to dispose of carrion."

Ruthven considered. "And so we're both to seek him out and share what we learn?"

"Why not? We'd have twice the chance of success that way. Whoever tracks him down first will tell the other. Agreed?"

He supposed she was right. He didn't trust her, or imagine that she trusted him, but for once their interests tallied. The situation was not without its amusing aspects. "Very well. But it's to be understood that we're cooperating in this matter only. In all else, we go our own ways."

"Done."

Ruthven poured two cups of wine from a pitcher on the table. "To the success of our venture," he said, handing one to Alicen.

She only toyed with her cup till Ruthven drank from his own, then she almost raised it to her lips, but changed her mind and gave it back to him. "I think not," she murmured.

Ruthven laughed and offered her the wine he had already tasted. "How is our agreement to go forward, if you dare not even drink with me?" he asked mockingly.

"Our agreement only concerns our common enemy," Alicen reminded him. "It makes no provision for drugged wine." But this time she accepted the drink, and sipped from it as Ruthven downed the one he'd intended for her. He started to tell her of his experience in the forest on the return from Lady Ideline's, but he'd barely begun when he slumped senseless to the floor.

After retrieving her weapons and satisfying herself that Ruthven was sleeping soundly, Alicen hastily rummaged through the chest at the foot of the bed, then searched Ruthven's pockets and purse. It stood to reason that he'd keep anything important on his person. In the binding of a small prayer book, which did not look to have seen much use, she found what she was looking for—a folded square of parchment. Pushing aside the pewter pitcher, she spread the paper upon the table and examined a list of names, all nobles resident in the colony, with comments as to the commitment they had made to the Duke of Halkin, and what they expected to gain in return.

Armed with this information, Alicen thought, she might be able to win at least some of Halkin's supporters away from him, by bettering the offers Ruthven had made them. Assuring herself that he was still peacefully asleep, she set to committing the list to memory, a task for which she had a particular talent. Then she replaced paper and book carefully in Ruthven's coat, and, deciding that he was too heavy for her to drag onto the bed, she laid a pillow under his head and quietly slipped from the room.

* * *

Sir Andrew's chess set was a masterpiece, exquisitely carved of ebony and ivory, each piece an individual sculpture in miniature. Rolande had presented it to him, knowing, apparently, that he would be unable to resist it, though he suspected that she'd stolen it from the captain's cabin of some unfortunate foreign vessel. He could only assume that she'd learned of his passion for the game from Lady Celia, during one of those long intimate conversations the two seemed to indulge in whenever Rolande spent time in port.

His wife's partiality for the pirate mystified Sir Andrew, who had long felt that the Good God—or possibly the Evil One—had created Rolande Vendeley for the sole purpose of driving him to distraction. It was diabolical the way the woman always contrived to be too useful to dispense with, while at the same time giving him more trouble than his avowed enemies were able to do. When he asked Lady Celia what two such different women found to talk about, she only laughed and said, "We are not so different as all that. Rolande likes to paint herself worse than she is—I can only suppose that where she comes from there is some advantage to doing so. And no one could be so flawless as you credit me with being, my dear!" Sir Andrew could see no point of similarity between them, but he wisely forbore to press the question further. It might be as well not to know what his wife imagined she had in common with a notorious bandit and spy.

Regrettably, the chess set saw little use, for those few people known to Sir Andrew who understood the game took little interest in it, and could offer no real challenge to his skill. Lady Celia maintained that a *game* ought, by its very nature, to impart refreshment and relaxation rather than tax the faculties to the utmost, and that it ought, moreover, to be engaged in in a spirit of conviviality, whereas Sir Andrew approached the chessboard like the battlefield, in deadly earnest.

Carl had taught Sir Andrew the game, in the course of his education, as a form of mental discipline, and he still occasionally stood him a match—for the sake of the "cerebral exercise," as he put it. But such exercises, he explained, were to be regarded as a means to an end, not as an end in themselves, and it was therefore inappropriate to devote oneself to them as if to the pursuit of philosophy.

Captain Fenton, however, had no such scruples, and was pleased to oblige his host with a game, whenever their various responsibilities permitted. They had spent some days pondering the reports sent with the captain from Sir Warren, laying provisional plans and discussing possible tactics, but little else could be accomplished until actual negotiations with their potential allies had begun. In his guise as personal aide to the Governor, Captain Fenton had received a few delegations of citizens on Sir Andrew's behalf, leaving them with greater respect for a personage to whom "their concerns would be conveyed in due course" than they'd had for someone who was willing to listen to them in person. But such duties as he was able to undertake, or fabricate, left him time enough to become familiar with the Governor's household and estate, to take stock of the community of Oriana, and to contend with Sir Andrew over the chessboard. He had until now considered himself as good a player as most, but he soon discovered that it required all of his concentration merely to stay in play for a respectable length of time. He would have to excel himself even to play Sir Andrew to a draw.

But his mind was not on the game, on an evening not long after his arrival, when the Princess—*Katin,* he reminded himself sternly—burst into the parlor and announced excitedly, "I finally tracked Lucifer to the nest—three whelps no bigger than your fist—in an old tree near Moth Pond." She was dirty and disheveled, with leaves caught in her hair, and bits of bark sticking to her clothes. She had been gone for most of the afternoon.

Some months ago, Hannah Franesh had brought back a young soarhound bitch, from one of her trapping expeditions to the north, for Katin to breed to Lucifer. The wild soarhound had soon escaped from the kennels, but evidently hadn't gone very far. "I've been feeding the bitch on bits of meat, and she doesn't mind me so long as I don't touch the pups. She must know my scent, from smelling it on her mate. I expect I'll be able to move the lot to the kennels soon."

"Mind, you are *not* to let the creatures in the house," Sir Andrew ordered. "Having your pets underfoot is nuisance enough—having them overhead as well is more than I'm prepared to tolerate."

"Yes, sir," Katin chuckled. She turned to Lady Celia and apologized for having missed dinner, then dashed off to the kitchen to cajole the cook into giving her a meal.

"Checkmate," Sir Andrew said to the captain. "You are off your game."

Lady Celia looked up from her book. "Something disturbs you, Captain?"

"It occurs to me that the—the young lady knows nothing of the message received today." That afternoon, a courier from the nearby colony of Oakridge had brought word that Baron Graydon would arrive within the week to discuss "the matter that Sir Warren had kindly brought to his attention."

"True," said Sir Andrew, gathering up the chess

pieces. "Still, we could not be expected to inform her, when no one had the least idea where she was."

"That is what disturbs me, sir. Now that her existence and her very whereabouts are known to others, however trustworthy, the danger that the enemy will learn the secret is increased a thousandfold. Can it be safe for her to go about unattended in this way?"

"Should her enemies seek her out here, they will hardly expect to find her in a tree," Lady Celia pointed out. "But I suppose the situation *has* changed now."

"As it must," Sir Andrew agreed. "It has never been easy to keep a watch on that one. When I first brought her from Albin, I tried to keep her away from others, lest she be recognized, but she took to the life of a commoner so readily that soon she'd transformed herself nearly beyond recognition. When Celia arrived, she looked directly at the girl and asked me who she was, though she'd known Oriana at court."

"But then, I wasn't looking for her," Lady Celia put in. "And I believed her dead. If I'd been sent to seek her . . ." She shook her head. "Well, if she must be protected, she must, poor child, but that lot will fall to you, Captain, and she'll not thank you for it."

Sir Andrew frowned, but said only, "It's true that I can't keep the girl with me, or escort her about."

"Certainly not. It won't do for the Governor to be seen to pay undue attentions to his apothecary. But if she's seen in the company of a young officer, folk will merely assume that I've arranged a suitable marriage for her, and high time, too. Yes, I'm afraid we must rely upon you, Captain."

Fenton clapped the hilt of his sword. "You may rely upon me for anything. Sir Warren charged me to devote myself to Her Highness' protection, if necessary, above all else. No harm shall come to her while I live."

"I have not the slightest doubt of your fortitude and resolve," said Sir Andrew, "but I can assure you from my own experience that you will have sore need of them, if you hope to keep Her Highness out of trouble." He downed the last of his mulled rum and refilled the captain's mug from the steaming jug on the hearth. "I confess that I don't envy you the task."

Katin, carrying a chunk of cheese in one hand and an apple in the other, nudged open the door with her foot and squeezed through. "What task is that, My Lord?" she asked.

* * *

Ruthven was furious when he awoke. The pillow underneath his head he recognized as deliberate insolent sarcasm on Alicen's part, and he vowed to make her pay for it, when the Duke of Halkin gained power. He would have her hunted down, publicly humiliated, even if he had to have agents travel to the ends of the earth to capture her. But he knew, even as he planned vengeance on Alicen, that he was really angry at himself. She'd made a fool of him, but he had only himself to blame for it.

He thought bitterly of Alicen rolling her glass in her hands, as if debating the danger of drinking from it, and deciding not to risk it. She'd had ample opportunity to tamper with it. But then he remembered that she'd even *warned* him that their agreement did not preclude one of them from drugging the other, and he had to laugh, in spite of himself. She'd played him fair, right enough—the conniving bitch—but that pillow, now . . . *that* was an unwarranted insult that demanded retribution. . . .

He was relieved to find nothing missing from his

possessions, but he knew that there was no telling what
Alicen might have discovered. This would mean extra
work, reinforcing ties already established, as well as
forging new ones—and he had nothing but his own observations as evidence of Alicen's activities.

Yet, was that so? Ruthven frowned to himself, reviewing his bewildering conversation with Alicen, half
at cross-purposes, half twisted by their mutual suspicion and accusations. *If not for the Governor's apothecary, I'd be dead now,* she'd said. So—she'd been
conferring with Viscount Edenbyrne, had she? Then it
was high time he, too, paid a visit to the Governor's
Mansion.

He was not sanguine about the chances of swaying
Sir Andrew to the Duke of Halkin's party, for the Lord
Marshal had been engaged for years, before the Uprising, in keeping the Acquitanians out of Albin. *Still, His
Lordship was ever loyal to the Royal House.* If he were
persuaded that the Duke of Halkin was the true heir of
the Obelen line, might he not feel dutybound to support him . . .?

"You know that the Duke would restore you to your
rightful position, and return all your honors and estates," Ruthven assured Sir Andrew, smiling magnani-
mously, as if these favors were his to bestow. "You do
not strike me as a man satisfied to end his days as a
provincial Governor."

"And you expect the Acquitanian throne and court
to accept my reinstatement? They know me too well
from the field. Even supposing that they allowed me to
lead your forces against the rebels, afterward they
would demand my removal."

Ruthven picked up a quill from a small writing table
near his chair and twisted the feathered end between

his thumb and forefinger. "Because the Duke has made an alliance with Acquitania, it does not follow that the Acquitanians will rule Albin. Alliances are formed when they suit the need at hand. In return for the Acquitanian court's support against the Chamber, the Duke has promised future support for the Acquitanian effort against Castilia, no more. It is a simple military arrangement, and one in which no doubt they expect that you would prove a most useful ally."

Sir Andrew chose his words with care. "If a successful invasion of Albin were to be carried out, it would be all we could do to maintain order at home. We'd have no troops to spare for forays into Zaragosa."

Ruthven snapped the quill in two. "After we have established order in Albin, we will have no more need of allies—and we will have an army of the people to drive them from our shores."

It might be done, Sir Andrew thought uneasily, *if there were no alternative.* "We are to turn from fighting the Chamber's forces to fighting the Acquitanians?" he asked. "At what cost? How is the country to sustain two wars more, when it's barely recovered from the Dep Uprising? The land and people would be devastated."

"The people will be *united*," Ruthven insisted, "once they have an Obelen on the throne. Can you doubt it? Time enough then to show the Acquitanians who is master of Albin."

Sir Andrew parried the familiar argument with ease, offering some of the same assurances—and the selfsame toast—he had made to Lady Alicen. It wouldn't do to cut off communication with either party until he knew exactly where they stood, and whom he might enlist in support of Her Highness. His course was fixed and unalterable, but he couldn't help wondering whether Ruthven's reasoning—or Alicen's—would have persuaded him, if he'd not had the Princess' cause in charge.

For his part, Ruthven was well satisfied with the interview. He'd anticipated a far less favorable reception from the Lord Marshal, and had not expected to achieve such a measure of progress without several more meetings, if at all. His Lordship had made clear that he was indeed interested in reclaiming Albin from the Chamber, and restoring an Obelen to the throne. And Ruthven had learned another, perhaps more valuable, fact—Sir Andrew had not given his support to Alicen Kendry's faction.

* * *

Carl Schellring made his way cautiously through the profusion of thick undergrowth that gnarled the marshland. The heavy, oleander-scented air seemed to cling about him, and his boots grew progressively more sodden with each step, but the old man was scarcely aware of the discomfort. As a naturalist, he accepted his surroundings without approval or disapproval; his one concern was to observe, and to account for his observations as far as the laws of nature would allow.

Sir Andrew's father had long been patron of Carl's researches, and Sir Andrew had inherited his upkeep along with the estate that was taken, shortly thereafter, by the Chamber of Statesmen. When Sir Andrew had mounted his expedition to New Albin, Carl accompanied him, not in a spirit of exile, but of exploration.

And it was with this same spirit that he was now seeking the lair of the giant tortoise, hoping to observe them in their natural habitat and learn the secrets of their breeding, to add to the great work he was compiling about the flora and fauna of the New World. The marshes were filled with devilwood, swamp ash and buckthorn trees, and the fallen branches and thick stalks of low-lying shrubs made the footing precarious. Carl had to pick his way carefully, so as not to disturb those creatures he sought to study. He was dressed in moss green and dull brown, the better to blend in with his surroundings. His caution was that of the stalker and the stalked, for it also served to protect him from the sharp eyes of those Yerren who still lived deep within the swamps. They rarely came so near the edge of the human settlement, but they took what chances they could to avenge themselves on the hated Ysnathi, whom they held responsible for the destruction of the Yerren people and the seduction of the remaining Yerren young who left their villages to work the trading vessels.

As he moved through the clumps of fevertree and mangle, stepping silently on cushions of moss, he noted the booming of bull frogs, the harsh cries of herons, the rustling of leaves and rippling of water, then suddenly the sound of twigs snapping somewhere to his left.

The thick foliage kept him from seeing far in any direction, and at first he listened anxiously for the distinctive trilling calls of the Yerren, but it was some far heavier creature that disturbed the undergrowth. Intrigued, Carl turned in the direction of the noise and crept most silently through the clinging vegetation to a stand of ash trees. Could there, after all, be some truth to the colonists' tales of a murderous, manlike monster who stalked the swamps? But what he saw as he peered cautiously around the bole of a vine-draped tree made him shake his head at his own folly. For he discovered not some great and savage beast but two gypsies hunkering down by a tree stump. Behind them was a small handcart loaded with sacks, no doubt the source of all the noise. The gypsy camp lay on the far side of the swamp from the settlement, where they had been wintering for years before Oriana had been founded. Until then, the Wherrisovir River had marked the westernmost boundary of their travels, which took them on a route from the northern colonies in the summer down the coast to the south and then west to their winter camp.

The elder of the two gypsies stood and dug his hand into the pocket of his baggy trousers, pulling out a brass cylinder, roughly three inches long and etched with twining vines. He studied the object thoughtfully. "We've naught to lose by it," he said. "'Tis not our quarrel, so why should we take sides?"

"Naught to lose? Only our necks, if we're found out. What of that?"

"Not a chance of it, I tell ye. We'll be nowhere near, and who's to spy us out?" The elder rolled the brass cylinder in his hand. "And think on the fee, eh?"

"Aye, I do. Well, 'tis all the same to me, for a' that."

The elder clapped him on the shoulder. "Good lad, then I'll meet ye out behind the livery stable, at dawn on the Fair day. None'll mark us i' the crowd."

"An' if they do, we'll offer to tell a fortune or two."

"Now you're usin' yer wits. Then you've only to make yerself scarce an' leave the rest to me. What th' devil! When ought goes bad, other folk'll always pin th' blame to our kind all the same, e'en if we ain't had nowt to do wi' it, so what do we care—I'll take the money and do the deed." He uncorked an amber bottle and took a swig of the contents, then handed it to the younger man. "Let's be gone then, lad, before the rest wonder why we're late." The youth took the handles of the handcart, and the two started across the swampy ground toward Carl, who retreated quickly and silently into the surrounding foliage.

He'd noted a hollow tree earlier, completely eaten away within, and open to the sky. It offered an expedient hiding place now, and he slipped within the empty trunk and held his breath, remaining motionless, till he heard the gypsies pass. But when the sound of the cartwheels had disappeared in the distance, he caught another sound, directly overhead, a soft tearing and smacking noise. Raising his head with some difficulty in the confines of the rotted tree trunk, Carl was startled by a sight that made him forget completely about the pair of gypsies.

A pair of wide, bright eyes were gazing down at him, out of a large, round, flat face covered with greenish-gray fur. In fact, there, hanging from the overarching branch of a devilwood tree, was a giant spotted three-toed sloth, its tongue flicking in and out as it pulled leaves into its mouth. Carl's heart raced with excitement that the threat of discovery by the gypsies had never induced, for the swamp sloth was so rare a creature—known only from the reports of the Yerren— that he had never been wholly convinced of its existence. Almost nothing was known of its habits. *Of course,* Carl thought, *if I could catch one to study . . .* He groped for the net and canvas sack he'd brought along for specimens.

* * *

The jaunty strains of fiddle music greeted Sir Andrew and Lady Celia as they strolled toward the open swath of green on the Town Common, where the local farmers and amateur musicians had broken out their instruments for the dance.

"I miss hearing you play the harp," Sir Andrew remarked to his wife.

"We could do with some music of an evening," Lady Celia agreed. Indeed, her great gilded harp had been the one thing she found hardest to leave behind when she'd been forced to flee from the Uprising. She'd been able to take little more than her jewels—certainly there had been no question of burdening the carriage with a harp too bulky for one footman to carry. But she added quickly, "Still, if I had my harp, I daresay I could hardly find the time to play it now, you know."

She spoke lightly, but Sir Andrew could hear the unspoken regret behind her words. "I must find the means to procure you one," he said, "though I fear it will not be soon." He would have undergone any deprivation to give her back the luxuries of her life in Albin, but such instruments could only be imported at great expense from Acquitania in these times, and establishing the estate and supporting their family through the past several years had taken most of their remaining fortune.

Lady Celia knew this as well as he. "My dear, don't fret yourself—I doubt I remember how to play, after all this time." They had been walking sedately arm in arm, but now she took his hand, like a girl, and led him across the Common, into the midst of the revelry. The field was crowded with folk pitching pennies and horseshoes, watching the acrobats and jugglers, and stopping to exchange gossip with their neighbors.

A cluster of townspeople sat on the grass before a rough wooden stage behind which rose a gaudy canvas backdrop of a city square, whose elaborately painted buildings all looked slightly askew. The audience laughed as the long-nosed villain, in a much patched black costume, was knocked flat by the wooden sword of the masked hero in red hose and tunic. Not far from the stage was the area of the green that had been marked off for dancing, and here young men and women—Katin and Jerl among them—swirled across the grass to the music of fiddle and pipes.

At one edge of the field where the revelers stopped at the plank tables for refreshments, the gypsies in their embroidered tunics and baggy-legged trousers or flowing skirts, were busily plying their trades. They dangled luck-charms, offered love potions, and performed feats of magic. One young man pulled egg after egg from an empty sack, and after turning it inside out to show it held no more, put his hand in it again and pulled out a hen. The spectators, well pleased, threw small coins, which the gypsy children scampered to snatch up.

The music trailed to a halt, and the musicians demanded their due of ale and cider, while the dancers scattered to seek other amusements or sank to the grass to rest till the next tune started. As Katin and Jerl strolled toward the cider stall, Jerl looked around suspiciously and was not surprised to see Captain Fenton following at a discreet distance. "Katin, is he the one you're promised to?" he demanded, though he dreaded the answer. It cost him much to get the words out at all.

Katin followed the direction of his gaze. "Captain Fenton? Oh, no—" she began, then stopped abruptly, her thoughts racing. In the welter of recent events, she had all but forgotten the lie she'd told Jerl about a secret betrothal, but now it seemed the only possible explanation. How else to account for the captain's almost constant attendance upon her? Other folk might find it understandable, but Jerl could hardly be expected to approve. After a moment's hesitation, she lowered her voice and said, "No, he's not the one, of course not, but Sir Andrew's agents did find my . . . my affianced, and he sent Captain Fenton as his emissary."

"Then you've told him you want no part of the betrothal?" Jerl asked impatiently.

Katin looked around worriedly, as if afraid they'd be overheard in the general commotion of the Fair. Naturally, no one was paying the slightest attention to the two of them. "It's not so simple as that," she protested. "I can't settle such a matter by messenger—it must wait until we meet. But it's not safe for either of us to travel at present. Captain Fenton's been sent to protect me. There are rumors abroad that the Chamber's agents may be in Oriana."

Jerl felt the muscles tense in his arms, and he clenched his fists in frustration. *He* should be the one to defend Katin from her enemies! It was impossible, of course. He knew that he was not well suited to such a task, and that he would not be allowed to undertake it, even if he could afford to neglect his own work for the purpose—but— If he couldn't watch over her himself, he'd have far preferred to see her under Sir Andrew's protection than the captain's. . . .

If only Fenton weren't so damnably *presentable,* with his fine uniform and fancy manners. No doubt he had the title to match his aristocratic ways, as well. Was he really no more than an emissary? Katin had been too hesitant, too evasive, in her answers to suit Jerl. If Fenton really was her intended husband, and determined to hold her to her troth, Katin wouldn't want to admit it. And how could any man be expected to give up his right to wed her? In his place, Jerl knew that he would persist till he won her consent. Why should Fenton do any less? Jerl glared at him. "You've not told me the whole truth about that one," he muttered to Katin.

Katin started. What had he guessed? "I oughtn't to have told you anything at all about these matters!" she said, alarmed. "I *want* to, but I haven't the right—don't you see—much more than my own safety is concerned. You mustn't question me, Jerl, please. You'll only force me to lie."

Jerl's bewildered stare told Katin that she was only snarling them both all the more in the dangerous web of half-lies and speculation. Taking herself firmly in hand, she said with perfect truth, "All the same, you needn't think that I like having him at my heels wherever I go, because I don't," and Jerl was somewhat appeased.

Just then the fiddler broke into a reel, and Katin grabbed his hand. "Let's dance." Soon enough she must forfeit this familiar, simple life for the rigors of war—and when they won, she would be faced with the even harder burden of ruling a fragmented and strife-ridden people. At that moment, Jerl seemed to stand for everything that she must sacrifice to duty, on the morrow. But today ... "I want to dance!" she cried, and pulled him into the swirl of young folk, all in their best, most colorful clothes, decked with bright ribbons, rosettes, and cockades.

Jerl couldn't help glancing back triumphantly toward his rival, but Captain Fenton had turned away and was walking purposefully toward the actors' stage. Jerl grinned and joined wholeheartedly in the swift reel. Katin was his partner in the dance, not Fenton's. He was soon lost in the enjoyment of the moment, with Katin's hand in his, and Fenton was forgotten.

Sir Andrew watched with misgiving as they swung past, laughing like carefree children. Seeing his frown, Lady Celia laughed softly and said, "My dear, they're only dancing."

"It may cause talk," he objected. "You've let it be believed that Fenton is courting her."

"Let it cause talk! Far better for folk to think her a fickle wanton than to wonder why a girl of her years and position accepts no suitors. Malicious gossip can't hurt her, but curiosity might."

Perhaps she was right, Sir Andrew thought. Katin looked charming in her simple, wheat-colored frock, with the wreath of braided straw and golden chrysanthemums circling her unruly hair, like a mockery of the golden crown she would one day wear. Romping this way and that in the great circle of dancers, between Jerl and another lad, she looked gay and fetching and flirtatious—but she did not look like a princess.

"I shall just have a word with her, all the same, after this dance," Lady Celia conceded. "It would look odd if I didn't, I suppose."

She waved her fan in time to the music as she watched the reel, and Sir Andrew thought, *She'd like to be dancing, too,* but neither of them knew the steps of these fast, lively country dances. How had Her Highness learned them? "When the house is finished, we must hold a ball to mark the occasion," he said. "It's far too long since we danced together."

Lady Celia flushed with pleasure. "Andrew, *what* a splendid idea! We shall have to bring musicians from Dunraven, I daresay, but there's time enough to arrange for that. Of course I don't know what dances are in fashion at court nowadays, but neither does anyone else in New Albin, so that doesn't signify. Ah, here they are—" The reel had finished, and Lady Celia beckoned to Katin, who obediently left Jerl's side and came to join her.

Sir Andrew stood aside to leave them to their talk, and looked about the green from one end to the other, satisfying himself that all was in order. He caught sight of Captain Fenton among the audience near the actors' stage, then saw that Jerl Smit was making his way through the crowd toward the captain, apparently intent on a confrontation. No good was likely to come of that. It was all very well to say "Let folk talk—gossip cannot hurt her," but a soldier's instinct told Sir Andrew that any circumstance that called attention to the Princess, however trivial, was potentially dangerous.

He started forward, meaning to send Jerl about his business before there could be trouble, but no sooner had he taken a step toward the stage than a barbed hunting arrow came flying straight at him, and buried itself in his chest.

Chapter 5

Sir Andrew reclined, propped up on pillows, in the walnut four-poster bed. He was still weak from loss of blood, and the slightest motion gave him pain, but he had insisted—over the objections of Katin and Lady Celia—on admitting Captain Fenton, to hear his report and discuss how best to deal with the situation.

"Immediately after the attack, I caught sight of someone fleeing from behind the stage, not far from where I'd positioned myself," Fenton related. "It gave a good view of the area, as the assassin also realized, it seems. The Smit lad was nearby, and I thought best to send him to give chase, as Her Highness had told me he was trustworthy."

"I didn't," Katin interrupted, "tell you he was fast."

"Commander Jamison sent militiamen after him as well," Fenton said stiffly, "but he escaped into the woods. I dared not leave Your Highness unprotected to follow the culprit myself. The attack might have been meant for you."

Sir Andrew shook his head, wincing at the stab of pain the movement cost him. "I think not. I've enemies enough of my own, and the shot came too close to its mark for a careless aim." He gestured carefully at his tightly-bandaged chest. "No, I daresay his aim was true—it was only pure luck that saved me."

"It was more than that, my dear," Lady Celia told him. "Had Katin not been at hand, and prevented others from pulling out the arrow, Doctor Justin says you would surely have died of the wound."

Sir Andrew had not heard of this before. "Then I owe Your Highness my life as well as my fealty."

Katin bowed. "I would never have left Albin alive, sir, without your assistance. Still, you might better thank Carl, in this instance. He gave me that ghastly Tuscan treatise about wounds incurred in battle. The one," she added mischievously, "that Your Lordship thought so unsuitable for a young lady's eyes."

Sir Andrew sighed. "A young lady with a proper sense of what is suitable would not take the opportunity to torment a man on his deathbed," he pointed out, and turned back to Captain Fenton. "What else have you learned? Did Smit get a look at the fellow at least?"

Captain Fenton shook his head. "No, he was too far behind to have a good view. He only caught a glimpse of a mask—some sort of animal, he thought, painted red and varnished to a high gloss. He could see that the man was wearing great baggy trousers and a loose shirt of some brownish material, such garb as is common among the gypsies hereabouts—or it could have been worn by any man who wished to be mistaken for one of them."

"Or by a woman," Lady Celia said thoughtfully. At the captain's startled look, she smiled and said, "A mask, and clothing such as you describe could conceal anything."

It was possible, the captain realized. Here in Oriana there were women serving in the militia, and in New Avenford he'd met with women hunters and trappers who could have pulled such a bow as Sir Andrew's assailant had used. It could be a mistake to forget that this, after all, was the New World.... "There is one thing Smit did find," he continued, and produced a small leather pouch from which he removed a brass cylinder, and handed it to Sir Andrew. "Whoever he was, he lost this as he was running away."

"But what is it?" Sir Andrew asked, turning the object over in his hands. It had a hinged top much like a snuff box, but if it were one, it was most unusual in its design, and when he opened it there was no trace of snuff or anything else inside.

None of them could answer. Captain Fenton said, "Perhaps when we know that, sir, we shall also know whom we are seeking."

Katin thought the object looked familiar, but she could not call to mind where she'd seen such a thing before. "What of the mask, then?" she asked. "Were the players questioned?"

"They acknowledge that there was such a mask, along with other properties in a trunk at the rear of the stage. Anyone choosing to obscure himself there could have picked it up. They claim that none of the troupe is missing."

"It could have been one of the gypsies, I suppose," Lady Celia mused. "It's true that the bow is a more common weapon among them than among our colonists. But, Andrew, why should they wish to murder you? When folk have tried to drive them off, in the past, you've put a stop to it. What enemy could you have among them?"

"One who could be bought, perhaps. But who paid the price? If the gypsies know, they'll die before dishonoring their tribe by telling us. Still, we've no choice but to question them. See to it yourself, Captain. Jamison could miss something of significance, as he knows nothing of our plans." He shifted painfully in the bed and fell back against the pillows, as if the effort of talking had exhausted him.

"Enough," Lady Celia said firmly. "Doctor Justin says that you're not to overtax yourself. You must rest now."

"Carl says the same," Katin put in, "and when the two of them agree on any matter, it must be so."

Captain Fenton bowed to the company, but hesitated to take his leave as yet. "As we cannot be *certain* that Your Highness was not the intended target, my duty demands that I make some provision for your safety in my absence. If the household guard were to be increased here, no one would think it odd, after the attack on Sir Andrew, but would Your Highness consent to—that is—might I have Your Highness' word—" Devil take it, *how* did one place one's sovereign under restriction?

Lady Celia came to his rescue. "Her Highness will not set foot outside the house, Captain, I assure you. No one will think that odd either—folk will assume that she must tend to Andrew." She turned to Katin and said sternly, "That is understood, then, my dear?"

Katin saw her cast a glance toward Sir Andrew as she spoke, and rightly interpreted this to mean *don't let him be worried about you now.* "Yes, My Lady," she said resignedly, but couldn't resist adding, "but all this fuss is quite unnecessary, in my opinion—after all, I have Lucifer to protect me!"

"For mercy's sake, don't make me laugh," begged Sir Andrew.

* * *

On Needle Isle they were able to exchange news with the crews of ships that had come from engagements in all the known quadrants of the sea. The latest rumors from Albin, however, were far from reassuring, and only served to increase Rolande's frustration—and her determination to find a way to escape Tyrrel's domain. From the number of Albinate men-of-war other captains had encountered in the months just past, it was impossible to ignore the fact that the Chamber was increasing the strength of their navy. *What is King Magnus of Acquitania doing, when we need him?* Rolande fumed. Was he so occupied with preparing to put his puppet king on the throne of Albin that he'd left off skirmishing with the Albinites along the coast?

"They say that the Chamber's fleet is preparing for a major assault," she told Blythe as he washed his shirt in a bucket outside the hut they shared.

"Another attack on the Acquitanians," Blythe said indifferently. "What of it?"

"Maybe—but there's too much secrecy surrounding these exercises to suit me." Would Sir Andrew be able to make sense of the enigmatic scraps of paper she'd sent him? The need to pursue the answer to this riddle made it all the harder to tolerate her confinement to the island. "I need to know what's afoot—no good comes of sailing blind."

"Why then, when next I address the Masters of the Chamber, I'll be sure to tell them that Captain Vendeley wants a full accounting of their activities," Blythe sneered. "What difference do the Chamber's plans make to us, when we're caught here like fish in a net? First get us off this bloody rock, then you can worry about the Albinate fleet!"

"That's what I've been trying to do for a fortnight, you jackass!" Rolande shouted. "Do you think I want to put down roots here?" She barely restrained herself from pitching the bucket at his head, and instead stalked off to brood upon the situation by herself.

As usual, she stopped on the deserted stretch of shore below the island's steepest headland, and stood studying the cliff face and the approach from the sea. Blythe was right, of course—her first concern was to get herself and her crew away from Needle Isle. She could not really blame him for his impatience, for other captains had offered to take him on when his skill as a surgeon had become known, and so far he had held to his agreement with Rolande.

Though her manner gave little sign of it, Rolande appreciated his loyalty. She was hoping to keep most of her people together, so that when she contrived to acquire another ship, she would have a trusted and able crew. But although she'd approached a number of captains already, none was willing to hire the lot of them, or take them to some other port where she might obtain a vessel. The captains all had their own crews, and Rolande lacked sufficient funds to purchase passage for hers.

She needed a ship of her own, then. But after considering the possibilities with due care, she was forced to abandon, reluctantly, the idea of stealing one from the fortified harbor. Her crew might succeed in commandeering one of the vessels, even without weapons, for the ships themselves were left largely unguarded in the safe haven of Needle Isle. But once in possession of the ship, they couldn't hope to make good their escape, under the eyes of the sentries in the stockade. Ships were not allowed to enter or leave the harbor without Captain Tyrrel's sanction, and the entire island would turn out to stop them, on his order. Without other crews allied to them, they'd not survive the attempt, and what had she to offer others, to make confederates of them?

The main force that kept order among the brigands encamped on the island was fear of Captain Tyrrel. Yet surely his men were outnumbered by the overall mass of pirates. Could she foment a rebellion among them? True, most found the arrangement with Tyrrel convenient ... still, it was rumored that he had amassed a great store of goods and treasure on the island, and the chance to recover the money they'd been forced to pay him, with more besides, might prove too much temptation to resist. . . .

But would a fabled fortune that might or might not exist be worth the risk to them? It would not, Rolande admitted to herself, *not while they were without weapons.* Again she gazed up at the shanty where Captain Tyrrel maintained his captured arsenal, high on the bluff overlooking the beach. It was more than mere superstition, she realized, that barred the Yerren from the island. With a few of the winged warriors at her command now, she could make short work of taking the weapons cache, but Tyrrel evidently thought that the cliffside gave sufficient protection from human marauders.

Rolande thought otherwise. In her days as a 'prentice smuggler, along the rocky southern coast of Albin, she'd scaled cliffs no less steep, and she could do it still, if need be. Yet supposing that she and some of her crew made the ascent, then succeeded in taking the guards by surprise and arming themselves, they would still be outnumbered by Tyrrel's people—and they would still be unable to pass the battery of cannon in the fortifications overlooking the harbor.

Whichever way she turned, she was hemmed in, trapped and helpless. Rolande paced the shore, storming at fate, cursing her luck, and finally facing the fact that she was to lose her crew as well as her ship. It was only a matter of time until she would be forced to allow them to split up and take passage separately, wherever they could. And she herself would have to serve under another captain, on some pestilent pirate vessel, if she ever meant to get off this cursed island.

She would make her way back to Oriana somehow, and those of her crew who did the same could join on with her again, as soon as she had command of another vessel. Sir Andrew would have to help her find a ship—after all, she'd lost the *Azora* in his service, hadn't she? She had failed to intercept the information carried by the Dep agent, but she had also prevented him from delivering that information to the Chamber, and she had destroyed a heavily-armed enemy merchantman. Rolande almost smiled as she pictured Sir Andrew's outraged indignation at her demand that he provide her with a new command. He would refuse outright, he would deny that such a thing was possible, and finally he would agree to see what could be done, no more. And if anything could be done, he would do it. What was most galling was that she would have to accept any sorry little galley that would float, and arm her as best she could, and take on what crew she could find—if she were lucky. She'd hoped to exchange the *Azora* for a man-of-war, and instead she'd be back where she'd started four years ago, with nothing but scars to show for her efforts!

But she was accomplishing nothing here on Needle Isle, and the sooner she made her move, the sooner she could start to make good her losses. She had to speak to her crew, tell them her plans—and cut them loose. If they reached Oriana and didn't find her there, they could report to Lorin, she decided. He'd know where matters stood with her, and he'd have instructions to pay her people what was owing them. There was nothing more she could do.

Grimly determined, Rolande started back to the harbor, meaning to go straight to the *Azora*'s encampment and inform the crew of her decision. But as she passed the stockade, she was met with the news that the *Mantis* had made port only an hour before, and her captain had brought information that made Rolande change her plans once again.

Word spread quickly that a pay ship was bound from Albin to the New World, with gold for the navy in the northern territories, and the captains of the pirate crews in port had soon gathered in Captain Tyrrel's quarters to hold a council of war. "She's three men-of-war as escort," Captain Varrett of the *Mantis* informed them, "so she must be carrying the devil's own fortune, and ours for the taking. They can't but pass through these waters within a few weeks' time."

The promise of vast wealth, to be won with a single strike, was the chance every pirate waited and longed for. Captain Payne of the *Peregrine* licked his lips at the prospect. "With the number of vessels we can bring against them, if we join forces, they'll have to surrender or sink!"

Rolande, too, was eager to join the fray, though for different reasons from the others. If she could report to Sir Andrew that she'd had a hand in capturing the Chamber's pay fleet, he'd be beholden to her for a crippling blow to the enemy. He'd never question her choice of prey again. But beyond that triumph, there were the four ships to be taken, and three of them trim men-of-war. She'd have one of them to replace the *Azora* if she had to stain the sea red with blood to get it. Surely Tyrrel would give her temporary command of one of his men-of-war, for this engagement, if it were to his advantage to do so.

She turned to him and demanded, "Let me take the *Thorn* for this strike, and I'll account for one of the escort for you! You'll have the *Thorn*'s share of the booty, beside, for all I want is the best of the captured ships left afloat when the smoke has cleared—are we agreed?"

Captain Tyrrel had said nothing thus far, and he remained silent for some moments longer, gazing into the fire and letting the others wait for him to speak. Then he said with quiet deliberation, "There's to be no attack on the pay fleet. 'Tis too great a risk."

"Nay, but a prize like this is worth the risk!" one of the others protested. "We could make our fortunes with this one strike!"

"Risk! Where's the risk, with the force we can bring to bear?" Captain Varrett scoffed. "We'll have the lot of them at our mercy!"

Tyrrel spat into the fire, then turned to look full at Varrett with a hard, cold smile. "Aye, we can take her, I don't say we can't. But I say we won't. Let word reach Albin that a pirate armada took their pay fleet, and the navy will send a war fleet next, to destroy Needle Isle and every crew they can catch. That's the risk I speak of!"

"They'll never do it," Captain Varrett argued. "They're too busy warring with their neighbors to spare a fleet of ships to hunt us down." There was some muttered agreement, but no more, for the others had been longer on Needle Isle than Varrett, and knew how dangerous it could be to spar with Tyrrel.

"So they are," Tyrrel agreed, "and I mean to keep it that way, you blind thickwit fool! Our safety's been in striking singly, without warning, anywhere—and now you'd have us a standing target. Aye, 'twould take a war fleet to rout us all out, and we've not been threat enough to warrant such a measure. But if they think we've started to work together, now—if they think they can't send provisions or pay to their forces without losing their ships to a *pack* of us—then we'll be as great a danger to them as an enemy navy, and they'll have no choice but to mount a campaign to rid the sea lanes of us." Tyrrel glared around at the company, demanding, "Now, is that plain enough for you lot of witless loons? If it's too hard for you to follow, just understand this—no ship leaves Needle till the pay fleet's passed and well away from here. Any who try to embark a crew will be food for fish before you come under the bowsprit."

The others, learning that their ships were confined to port, could do no more than exchange furious looks, clench their fists, and bide their time. They were in no position to object—not while Captain Tyrrel held all their weapons.

Rolande saw her hopes for a ship fade and melt away like mist. *In a world swarming with idiots,* she thought glumly, *why is it my fate always to be cursed with intelligent enemies?* Tyrrel was right, damn him— and he had more to lose than the rest. They might take their share of the booty and scatter to the four winds, leave the sea altogether and set themselves up as landowners or tradesmen, with the riches from such a strike. But Tyrrel was comfortable where he was, and he had no intention of letting the others interfere with his comfort. If the pay fleet was struck, he'd either be left to face the consequences, or he'd have to abandon his island empire and begin anew.

Why couldn't he be blinded by greed for that great

treasury of gold, as any other brigand would be? Why did he—rot his eyes!—have to take a *sensible* view of the situation? It was no use now to tell her crew they must part ways, for they would all be trapped here till the pay fleet was long gone, if Tyrrel had his way. That could mean a month or more of cooling their heels on this godforsaken island.

Little as the prospect of serving under another captain had appealed to Rolande, the prospect of doing *nothing* for weeks was even harder to bear. Inaction did not suit her restive temperament, and patience was a quality she did not possess in abundance. Even as Captain Tyrrel uttered his warning and dismissed the company, she was already deep in a scheme to defy his prohibition. The promise of a boatload of gold could win her the confederates she needed to overthrow Tyrrel, and the chance to seize command of a naval fighting vessel was too tempting to withstand. When Captain Varrett caught her eye soon afterward, and fixed her with a deliberate stare, she nodded very slightly and turned away, satisfied. The rebellion was already under way.

Blythe, too, was afire with impatience to be on their way, but he balked at the audacious plan of escape that Rolande laid out to him. "You're a madwoman, and Varrett is a fool," he declared, "but will the rest agree to violate Tyrrel's order? You're asking them to risk no less than mutiny."

"We approached only those who've openly complained of losing the chance at the pay fleet. I think there may be enough of us to mount the assault, but I'll know more tonight, when we meet together. I'll tell them my proposal then."

"Your proposal's the maddest part of the whole harebrained scheme! Tyrrel must have safeguards against such an attack. You can't be the first to have thought of it."

"I've been watching the place since we arrived, and I've seen but few of guards there. The shanty's only far enough back from the edge so as not to be washed away in a storm. And Tyrrel knows there aren't many who'd dare make the attempt," Rolande boasted.

"Tyrrel knows that all who land here are foolhardy and totally impetuous," Blythe insisted. "He hasn't lived past his prime by being careless. Is there no way, then, that I can dissuade you from a course that will only get you killed, and probably the rest of us with you?"

"This is my chance to keep my crew together, and to win a ship worthy of us!" Rolande said angrily. "And my crew will stand with me. You forget yourself, Blythe. I'm your captain, and it's not your place to question my orders."

"I take it that your answer is no." Blythe shook his head regretfully. "I can't stop you from risking your own neck, *Captain,* but I'm not about to follow you and risk mine."

"Oh, I don't expect *you* to follow," Rolande said with contempt. "I'd not allow you to. If we succeed, we'll need you to patch up our wounds. And if we fail . . ." She shrugged. "Tyrrel's not so wasteful as to kill an able surgeon, so you needn't fear for your precious neck."

In a cave on the wooded slope of the bluff, Rolande sat looking around the fire at the other captains gathered to discuss how to deal with Captain Tyrrel.

"He seeks to deny all of us the wealth he himself

has amassed," Captain Varrett pointed out. "Why should we go poor to protect his isle?"

"As you say," one brown-bearded captain grunted. "But he'll not change his tune, nor brook any challenge to his command. I've seen men die for less on Needle Isle."

"True," Captain Varrett agreed. "But if he won't change his tune, still we need not dance to it."

"Are you calling for mutiny?" Captain Payne demanded bluntly. "Out with it."

"Have we taken service under the man? Are we his crew, that he should decide our course and our actions, forbid this and allow that, as he wills?"

"Fine talk! If it's open revolt you'd have, we might as well hang ourselves now and have done with it," Captain Brand of the *Kestrel* objected. "We'll be slaughtered like oxen."

"Maybe so. And maybe we'll be free to go after the pay fleet. Few in our trade die of old age, man. Do you want to die rich or poor, that's the choice before us."

"I for one would rather live, and live rich," Rolande said, knowing that the success of her own scheme hung upon persuading them to go along with Varrett. "And I tell you we can do it, if we work together. I offered Tyrrel a fair bargain, and he'd have none of it, so I say we cut him out—we'll have the Chamber's gold *and* Tyrrel's to divide among us. Folk with that much wealth live to be a hundred and die in their beds!"

Her bravado had its effect on most of the others. "I'm for that, woman!" one of the younger captains declared, laughing. "I've the heart for it, if some don't." He looked toward Captain Brand as he spoke, his words a challenge.

"Aye, the heart of a bull," Brand sneered, "and the

brains of a gnat! We're to fight with knives against swords and pistols, are we?"

"We'll take the weapons shed first, and then the island," Varrett said sharply. "How else?"

"And d'ye think that's not been tried before?"

"Leave that to me," said Rolande. "There is a weakness in the defenses of his makeshift armory. It is built upon the cliffside, which appears to offer a natural point of defense, but the cliff itself is riddled with outcroppings we might use to our advantage." She turned to look at each of the assembled captains in turn, then went on, "Here is my proposition. I will take some dozen of my crew, scale the headland from the shore, and subdue the guards before they can give the alarm. You hide your people in the woods at the top of the hill, staying far enough from the shed not to be seen. When we give the sign, you come forth to get the weapons—quietly—and then we can make a surprise attack on the stockade. With all our crews, we'll outnumber those posted there, and we'll have control of the harbor."

Captain Varrett considered. "How is it you're so certain that you and your lot can climb that cliff? Tyrrel's just as sure it can't be done, else he'd have it better guarded."

"I've climbed the like before—in the dark, with a sack of smuggled booty on my back. And a number of my crew were mountain bandits of New Albin ere I made sailors of 'em. The first time I laid eyes on them, they snatched a member of my party and carried her up one cliff and down another, before I got her back. We'll get to the top, never you fear."

Even Captain Brand thought the plan had merit. "It might be done," he agreed, "but suppose you reach the top and the guards are too quick for you? If they summon help, we'll be trapped with the cliff at our backs."

"And we'll be dead," Rolande snarled. "You'll have a chance to get away through the woods. It's we who'll be most at risk, if we fail, and in return we're to have the *Thorn* for the engagement, if we succeed, and one of the men-of-war for our own, after. What say you?"

"Done!" said Varrett, and the others agreed readily.

Captain Varrett was the first to depart, advising the others to wait and make their way back to their encampments separately. Rolande kept her place till she saw Captain Brand leave, then she slipped out after him and followed silently, knife in hand. If he went toward Tyrrel's cabin, instead of the *Kestrel*'s encampment, she would see that he never arrived there.

He had not gone far through the woods, however, when he suddenly stopped and stood as if listening to something. Creeping closer, Rolande heard a man's voice call softly, "This way!" and she froze, trying to peer through the darkness at the two figures hidden in the thicket ahead. So, the bastard had already arranged to report their plans to Tyrrel, had he? Now she'd have to kill both Brand and Tyrrel's man, curse the luck! Should she follow and wait for them to part ways, or try to take the pair of them together? Best to keep to close quarters perhaps—Tyrrel's spy was probably armed with a pistol.

As she inched forward, barely breathing, she caught a faint flash of metal and a sharp gasp, cut off by the snapping of twigs and swishing of branches, as a body broke through the bushes to the ground. Abandoning caution, Rolande raced to confront the remaining man, and was not surprised to find Captain Varrett standing over the victim. He only glanced at her and remarked, "It doesn't do to leave any weak links," then removed his neckcloth and wiped the bloody knife on it.

Rolande sheathed her own knife and crouched down

beside the body. "Over the cliff with him, I should think, and let the fish dispose of him. Let's go. I'll take his legs."

* * *

Since her recovery from poisoning, Alicen had been troubled by disturbing dreams about the unknown enemy who'd struck at her and at Oliver Ruthven—and now perhaps at Sir Andrew as well. She had only Ruthven's word, of course, that he'd been attacked, but someone had certainly tried to assassinate Sir Andrew, and she could not persuade herself that Ruthven was responsible for that. He'd have no reason to kill Sir Andrew, unless he knew for certain that the Lord Marshal had allied himself with the Duke of Wyston, and that, unfortunately, was not the case. No, whoever was behind the attempted murders wanted all three of them dead, and that could only mean an agent of the Chamber of Statesmen—one who was well trained in dealing death. Someone like Vendeley.

Rolande's claim to be working with the royalists held no weight with Alicen, but it still made no sense for Rolande to leave her alive, aboard the *Lorisonde,* and then try to poison her. And the *Azora* had not been in port at the time of the attempt on Sir Andrew's life. Alicen had inquired at the wharves at once. But if not Vendeley, who?

Alicen herself knew enough of the art of assassination to realize that she was not dealing with an inexperienced bungler. True, the attack on Ruthven might have been mistimed, but black powder was an unreliable and unpredictable weapon in any hands. The blast might have been meant only to make his horse throw him, so that the killer, hidden nearby, could easily dis-

patch him while he was stunned or injured—shaken, at
the least—from the fall. If Ruthven was to be believed,
his own skill as a horseman had saved him, not the enemy's carelessness. She herself would certainly have
died if she had happened to be anywhere else when
she'd drunk from her poisoned flask. The Chamber's
agent could not be expected to know that she would
feel thirsty when someone schooled in pharmacognosy
was within call.

Sir Andrew, too, by all accounts, had come within a
hair's breadth of death when the arrow felled him, but
again the young apothecary had been at hand, to stanch
the wound. The girl haunted Alicen's dreams as well,
as a presence half-seen through a haze of pain and fever, a dim, distant image trying, it seemed, to tell
Alicen something of grave importance, if only she
could make out the words.

But in this dream she was back in Albin, before the
Chamber's rise to power, and the flight to the New
World. She was riding to hounds with the royal hunting party, as she had done from time to time, on state
occasions. The pace was leisurely as they crossed the
meadows, with the hounds still on their leads, and the
young Princess was singing in her pure, childish voice,
a verse of "The Hunting of Wyldendale."

> *"For where the wounded stag had stood*
> *Wreathed all in clouds of mist,*
> *Now stood a man in a bloody shirt*
> *With the arrow gripped in his fist."*

Then suddenly the hounds were away upon a scent,
and Alicen galloped after, with the Princess riding at
her side, laughing with excitement and urging on her
horse. She looked too small for her mount, but no one

who had ever seen her ride would have feared for her safety. The youngest of the royal family, and the only girl, she was a slight, pale child, who could sometimes seem inconsequential, despite her rank. But Alicen knew her for a spirited youngster, and on horseback she showed herself as bold as her brothers. Ever since she was old enough to hold a bow, she'd proved an able archer as well, and she'd been allowed on the hunt at a far younger age than was common. *She's hardly out of the castle, else,* Alicen thought. *No wonder she's like a wild creature set free now.* As they neared the woods, the Princess raced ahead, outstripping the rest, intent upon the chase and heedless of danger or propriety. Her long, sand-brown hair had already come undone and streamed about her face and shoulders, catching on the flights of the arrows in the quiver at her back.

Then without warning, Alicen's horse reared wildly, throwing her from the saddle, and fled at a gallop, back the way they'd come. Alicen felt unhurt, and started to rise to her feet, cursing furiously, when the Princess, somewhere behind her, cried, "Don't move!" and Alicen saw what it was that had startled her horse.

Coiled not a hand's breadth from her was an immense serpent, as thick around as a man's arm, its head poised to strike. As Alicen stared, mesmerized, motionless, the monster stretched wide its jaws, revealing the venomed fangs and the wide, ribbed gullet beyond, which looked to Alicen as broad as a doorway. At that moment, an arrow struck from above, piercing the gaping mouth, splitting the serpent's skull and pinning it to the ground. Alicen looked up to see the Princess perched high among the branches of an oak tree behind her, with another arrow ready on the string, if needed.

Leaping to her feet, Alicen called, "You've done it,

Your Highness, with a single shot! I've never seen the like!" She reached for the arrow, meaning to take the still-twitching carcass to show the others, as a trophy of Oriana's prowess, but again the Princess cried out a warning.

"Don't touch it—'tis not what it seems! Come away!"

Even as she spoke, the great serpent was dissolving into a thick, coiling mist before Alicen's eyes. She backed away, aghast at the sight, but unable to turn her gaze from the place. The arrow still stood buried in the earth, but crouching above it was a human figure, a dark shadow in the swirling mist. It threw back its head to look up at the Princess, as she clambered down from branch to branch, and when it spoke, its voice was hissing and inhuman, as if the words were indeed a serpent's. "Sso! An interfering lasss, that one, and no missstake!"

Ruthven's words about the Governor's apothecary— but it was not Ruthven who spoke. The forest warlock of the song, the unknown enemy that had menaced her with its venom, could not be Oliver Ruthven. "Who are you?" Alicen demanded in a furious shriek.

"Mistress Kendry!" another voice said, from somewhere to her left, and she turned to see Hannah Franesh stride out of the woods toward her. "Did you call to me?" Hannah asked.

What was Hannah doing here, Alicen wondered, puzzled. For that matter, what was she herself doing here? She woke to see Hannah climb over the edge of the loft, looking down at her with concern. "You must have shouted out in your sleep, my lass. Are you well?"

Hannah had started to say "my lady," and quickly changed her mind. Despite her stolid demeanor and rough appearance, she was not as simple as Alicen assumed. Hannah suspected that her lodger was more than the common traders' clerk she claimed to be, for her manners were too ladylike, although she tried to hide the fact. Still, plenty of the aristocracy were in hiding since the Uprising, and Hannah had no objection to sheltering the Chamber's enemies.

Alicen blinked at her in confusion, trying to collect her thoughts, to make them fit into a meaningful pattern. "Mistress Franesh," she said abruptly, "who gave this colony the name of Oriana?"

Still half asleep, Hannah thought, and answered gently, "Why, I don't rightly remember who suggested it, but most thought it fitting. We came from Thornfeld, and that settlement was known as Thorin's Field when it was founded, you see. This was to be a daughter colony to Thornfeld, so we named it after King Thorin's daughter."

Alicen sat up and stretched wearily. "It wasn't Sir Andrew's doing, then?"

"No . . . indeed, he objected that there was already a colony called Oriana along the northern shore, but folk were set on the name, for we'd just beaten back the Chamber's invasion force, and royalist feeling was high among the party. We settled on South Oriana, at last, but here we don't much bother with that. We call the other one North Oriana instead."

Alicen yawned, mumbling, by way of explanation, that she'd been dreaming of the Uprising and the execution of the Princess. As she and Hannah shared a breakfast of fresh-caught fish, she encouraged Hannah to tell her more about the invasion of Thornfeld and the subsequent founding of Oriana.

Hannah, who often spent weeks in the wilderness without talking to another soul, was ready enough to comply. She had stories aplenty of the perfidy of the Chamber and the valiant defense of Thornfeld against the Dep army. Her own sister, she told Alicen proudly, had tricked a young enemy soldier into sending the signal to Sir Andrew that the occupying forces were on the march. "The fellow was among the deserters who chose to stay on, after their defeat, and Sara met him later and told him what he'd done—she made a hero of the lad." Hannah grinned. "They were married last spring."

Alicen feigned interest in such events, waiting to hear more about Sir Andrew's household, without appearing to raise the subject herself. But she listened with sharp attention to Hannah's somewhat confused account of Rolande's part in the colonists' victory. "Aye, the privateer Vendeley—she who sinks the Chamber's trade ships and ruffles the feathers of our merchants. She seized an arsenal ship from the Deps somehow, and delivered the cargo to Sir Andrew on the battlefield—saved the day for us, some say."

Alicen nearly choked on her fish. "Impossible!" she exclaimed, before she could stop herself. "That is, well, *Vendeley*—if 'tis the same woman I've heard of—she used to be a merchant herself, and folk in my trade say she was in the pay of the Chamber."

Hannah nodded, chewing on a mouthful of bread. "I expect she's the one. She kept a shop in Thornfeld that prospered more than most, so there were stories of all sorts about her. But I know it's true about the powder brig, for I heard it from Katin Ander, the Governor's ward, and she was along of Vendeley at the time and had a hand in the business herself."

This was the chance Alicen had been waiting for. She succeeded, with some difficulty, in restraining her curiosity about Rolande, and asked instead, "Ander, the young herbalist? So she's a sailor-lass, too? They say she saved my life when I was taken ill, near the Governor's Mansion." No doubt the story had spread by now. She might as well have her own version about.

"Hmm, I heard something of that from Mistress Wicken, the cook there. She says young Ander did the same for the Governor at the Harvest Fair. Some well-meaning fools went to pull the arrow from Sir Andrew—a hunting-arrow, mind—it would have torn him to shreds—but she made them wait till the physician could be fetched to clip off the shaft and ease the arrowhead out of him properly. But then, the girl knows something of hunting," Hannah added with approval. "I've been days in the woods with that one, and she can bring down her share of game with bow and arrow."

Alicen realized that this was high praise from someone who earned her living by hunting and trapping. "Is that so?" she said, as if mildly interested. "A remarkable lass altogether. You say she's an orphan, in Sir Andrew's care?"

Hannah shrugged. "He's had her in charge since he came to Thornfeld, that's all I know."

"I see," said Alicen, in a tone intended to convey polite disbelief. "So that's the way of it."

Hannah enjoyed telling a story or passing on news as much as anyone, but she was not given to gossip or rumormongering. What she didn't know to be fact she left alone. "Nothing of the kind," she said sharply. "No one takes her for Sir Andrew's get. He's a forthright sort—anyone will tell you that. If the girl was his, he'd own her."

"But if he did, he'd brand her as illegitimate," Alicen pointed out. "Perhaps he thinks it's in her interest to have another name."

This hadn't occurred to Hannah, but it wasn't a question she intended to discuss. "Well, it's not my affair—or yours—whose she is, but Jerl Smit says His Lordship promised her father he'd protect her, and Smit heard that from Sir Andrew himself. That's good enough for me. I daresay she's no commoner, but you know folk don't boast much of their bloodlines since the Deps took power." She gave Alicen a look that said clearly, *She's not the only one who's secret about her origins, my lady.*

Alicen flushed, remembering Rolande's taunt, *You didn't even fool that ass of a captain!* And Hannah, she realized, was more astute than the captain of the *Lorisonde.* But at least she had found out from Hannah what she wanted to know. The Lord Marshal had brought Katin Ander to the New World, and her parentage was a mystery. Smiling at Hannah as if they shared a secret, she said, "Oh, I mean no ill to the Ander girl. I can't but take an interest in her, after all, if she saved my life. I'm in her debt."

That seemed reasonable to Hannah, and suddenly she gave a laugh and told Alicen, "I don't say it to boast, but I know Lady Celia rather well—and if *she* thought the girl was her husband's, she'd make him acknowledge her, and adopt her herself, into the bargain. That would make her legitimate enough to satisfy anyone. Lady Celia already treats her as a daughter of the house, folk say, and if she really were so, Her Ladyship would be the first to see she had her rights. There's no nonsense about *her.*"

"There's something in that," Alicen agreed. "I knew the Baroness a bit myself, in Albin. Indeed, I'd been to call on her, when I was stricken with that sudden fever. . . . I think, myself, 'twas spider bite. Surely a snake couldn't have bitten me, without my knowing."

She shook her head, licked daintily at the fish grease
on her fingers, and added thoughtfully, "Do you know,
I never did have a chance to thank the girl for her help.
By the time I came 'round, they'd sent for the physician to attend me, and somehow I never laid eyes on
Katin Ander, after." *In fact, when I asked to see her,
they always put me off, said she was gathering herbs in
the marshes or seeing to some other sufferer* .... "I
ought to go see her, oughtn't I? I'd not have her think
me ungrateful."

What she was thinking was madness, Alicen told
herself, but she prepared, nonetheless, for a visit to the
Governor's Mansion. So Sir Andrew had promised the
girl's father to protect her, had he? The words suggested more to Alicen than they had to Jerl or Hannah.
If the Princess lived, the King's Marshal was certainly
sworn to her defense.

That proved nothing, of course. But, damn it all,
wherever she turned, she seemed to see the girl—
hiding, hunting, healing. Even Ruthven, at a mention
of her, had said at once, "A fair-haired lass?" Was she
to believe that he could describe every member of the
Governor's household? And what was she to make of
the ambiguous toast offered by Sir Andrew "to the
rightful heir of the House of Obelen"? She had feared
at the time that he might be referring to the Duke of
Halkin, but surely the Lord Marshal would oppose any
scheme to use Acquitanian troops to reclaim Albin
from the Deps. Ruthven must have approached him,
yes—how else could he have known about the girl?—
but Sir Andrew's name had not appeared on his list of
the Duke of Halkin's adherents.

All in all, Alicen was unable to dismiss her suspicions, and the implications of her dreams, however ab-

surd they seemed in the light of day. It would only be
civil, besides, to pay a call at the Governor's Mansion,
to inquire after Sir Andrew's recovery.

* * *

"Nonetheless, with all due respect, the matter of
proof remains," the Baron insisted, sitting stiffly in the
Governor's reception room. Katin, seated in the panel-
backed arm chair, gazed impassively at the visitor,
thinking that it had been a mistake to bid him be
seated. Either he was uncomfortable with the idea of
sitting in the presence of his sovereign, or he felt that
the real Princess would not have suggested it. *I suppose I should guard against such New World notions,*
she thought, *but, really, keeping people thrice one's
age standing about . . .*

Sir Geoffrey, Baron Graydon, looked far older than
Katin had expected. It surprised her that six years
should have changed him so much from the heavyset,
jovial courtier she remembered to the spare, worn-
looking man she saw before her. His carefully tailored
clothes couldn't disguise the fact that the past six years
had taken their toll on him.

"Proof? I ought by rights to say the same, sir," Katin
replied. "You bear little resemblance to the Baron
Graydon I knew—he who used to carry me about on
his shoulders, when I was six."

The Baron smiled for the first time. Perhaps the
crop-haired, sun-stained stranger before him was the
Princess Oriana, after all. She was, he decided, the correct age and bore some resemblance to the child he'd
known at court, but too many years had passed for him
to be certain of her identity now from her appearance.
Sir Andrew might have told her what to say, of

course—he had been often enough at court in those days. Still, hard as it was to accept that this peasant lass was the heir of the House of Obelen, it was harder still to believe that the Lord Marshal would be party to such a deception. His loyalty had never been in question, and then, if he had indeed been hiding the Princess all this time, it would explain why he'd chosen to make his home in the New World, far from the danger of detection or betrayal.

But such changes had been wrought in the aftermath of the Uprising that he could not afford to take even Sir Andrew at his word. "It seems unlikely that anyone would trouble to impersonate *me,* at present," the Baron said ruefully, "but if you are indeed the Princess, you will understand that too much is at stake to allow for the slightest doubt as to your own identity. I stand to commit, not my life alone, but hundreds of others to the restoration of the throne. I cannot do so, in all conscience, unless I am guided by incontrovertible conviction."

Out of the corner of her eye, Katin could see Sir Andrew frowning, impatient to have these preliminaries—and the Princess herself—out of the way, so as to enter into a discussion of strategy with the Baron. But he and Katin both knew that matters were not so simple. Captain Fenton might have been appalled to discover that the Princess could pass for a servant girl, but it had not occurred to him to doubt that she *was* the Princess. It was not for him to question the word of his superiors. The Baron, however, would have to be convinced, and if convinced, he was in a position to add significant strength to their cause. Sir Warren Landervorne had imparted to Sir Andrew that the Baron had been most active, on the sly, in amassing a considerable force composed of dispossessed guardsmen and horsemen from the exiled noble households. Such men now found themselves unable to earn a livelihood in their customary roles of household protectors of the nobility, nor were they suited by training or nature to labor as common workmen. Some had taken positions in the Chamber's army as a means to feed themselves, but few believed in the Deprivants' cause, which had reduced their stature to that of mercenaries, without providing recompense. It was said that the Baron and his agents had traveled most extensively throughout the realm, at great risk to their lives, moving secretly among the camps of the Chamber's forces and other spots where such men were known to gather, enlisting them, a few at a time, into a secret army. Sir Andrew would certainly have been party to such an effort, had he possessed the means, but his personal fortune had never been equal to the support of a private army, and the protection of the Princess had, of course, been his first duty. The Baron's men were rumored to be in several camps in foreign lands, drilling and awaiting his orders, and Sir Andrew was avid to know how much truth there was to such reports. But before Katin dared broach the subject of the secret army, she had to win the Baron's confidence.

She smoothed her skirts self-consciously and said, "Of course you must be wary, My Lord—and you were never hasty by nature, as I recall. You had the byname of Baron Bear, because you were equable enough if left in peace, but dangerous when provoked."

"Anyone might know that," the Baron pointed out, watching her narrowly.

Lady Celia could barely restrain herself from instructing Katin to stop toying with her pearls and sit still. *It was a mistake, I fear, to put her into that gown. She's more regal when she's at her ease in her home-*

spun and deerskin—but she must become used to fine attire again. I shall have to make her dress for dinner in future, every day.

Presented by Lady Celia with the flowing, fawn-silk gown with its golden bows and lace, Katin had only sighed and submitted to necessity, but it was another matter to resume the demeanor that went with such elegant raiment. The ceaseless activity of her life in New Albin had made her restless, and she had lost the habit of holding herself at all times with the majestic composure and patience that never admits to discomfort or unease. Awkward in her unaccustomed finery, she had the air—particularly unfortunate under the circumstances—of an impostor, a maid dressed in her mistress's silks.

Katin herself had not been reassured by her appearance in the glass. Lady Celia and her maid had done what they could with powder and crimping iron to lighten her complexion and dress her hair, but six years in the sun and wind were not to be undone in a day. Abruptly she stood, stripping off one of her lace gloves to reveal a brown, callused hand with traces still of ingrained earth and leaf-stain about the nails, in spite of repeated scrubbings. The others started to their feet, but Katin waved them back impatiently and held out her hand to the Baron. " 'Tis not the hand of a Princess of the Realm, is it?" she demanded. "But a man of your judgment, sir, should not be misled by appearances. You should know an Obelen when you meet her, in any guise, working the earth with her hands or grinding herbs for salves and unguents. I've carried armaments to the battlefield and medicaments to the lowliest laborers' cottages, and I am far from ashamed of the work of my hands, though it leaves me looking like a commoner in your eyes! Would you have had me idle when I might be useful?"

"It has, of course, been necessary for Her Highness to carry out this masquerade, for safety's sake, as you will readily appreciate," Sir Andrew put in. "It would have been an unthinkable risk to do otherwise."

The Baron continued to regard Katin, his face an unreadable mask. "Whether or not you look like an Obelen, you most certainly sound like one," he admitted, "though that could be due to Lady Celia's influence as much as to royal blood."

"I cannot take credit for Oriana's commendable sentiments," Lady Celia said warmly. "I found her already prepared for any sacrifice in the name of duty. If you doubt her, Geoffrey, you must doubt me as well."

"My dear Celia, it is impossible to suspect you of deceit, but it is possible, nonetheless, that you yourself could be deceived."

"Possible perhaps," said Sir Andrew wryly, "but exceedingly unlikely."

"Would you be assured that I've an education suitable to my station?" Katin persisted. "I've been taught history, geography, diplomacy, philosophy, poetry, music, by the most knowledgeable scholars in Albin. I know the lineages of the Albinate and Acquitanian Houses, the Saxon imperial dynasties, the Castilian principalities. I'm familiar with the languages of the civilized world, and the tongue of the near-barbarian Castilian mountain tribes. Would you hear me converse in High Tuscan, or recite the lays of the Old Acquitanian cleric-bards? But that would not convince you either, would it?"

The Baron shook his head. "It would convince me that you were no commoner, but not that you were Princess of Albin. I myself had a hand in the education of the Princess Oriana, however. Tell me this—what gift did I give Her Highness on the occasion of her first hunt?"

A sudden gleam lit Katin's eyes as she answered, "A small jeweled dagger, of exquisite workmanship. I kept it with me always, even till the end, but when I leaped from the *Golden Dove,* I dared not take anything that might serve to identify me." She spread her hands, laughing. "And so, now I find myself with nothing that might serve to do so! Nothing but memories. You had a reputation, sir, for unrivaled skill with a knife, and I gave you no peace till you agreed to teach me some simple moves with the dagger."

"Did I so?" the Baron asked softly.

"You did, and I, ungrateful brat, soon gave you cause to regret it."

"True," said the Baron. "I have still the scar to show for it." He held up his left hand, where an old, badly-healed wound could be seen across the back of his wrist.

For a moment Katin looked puzzled. "But I—" she began, then stopped and shook her head. "Oh, I see— you wish to test me. If I left you with a scar, 'tis on the back of your right leg, somewhat above the knee."

For the first time, the Baron appeared to relax. "So it is, and the devil's own time I have had to explain it—when occasion demanded. It would hardly have been politic to admit—"

"That the King's youngest child had tried to cripple you," Katin finished.

The Baron laughed. " 'Twas no more than a scratch, in truth."

"You did not think so at the time!"

"At the time, I feared I was in danger of being gelded."

Lady Celia raised a scandalized eyebrow. "My dear Geoffrey, explain yourself at once."

He shook his head. "If the tale must be told, let that one tell it. None but the Princess could know the truth of it, for I never said a word of it. I'd have been the laughingstock of the court."

"And I promise you, I never dared tell anyone," said Katin, "for fear I'd be punished."

"Oh, I believe you. If you'd told a single soul, the story would have been common property by nightfall. It would have come back upon me ere long, but it never did—until now."

"His Lordship set about demonstrating to me the different ways in which an abductor or assassin might try to seize hold of me," Katin explained. "He would then tell me what to do to ward off the attack. But he reckoned without my impatience and pride."

"I reckoned without taking into consideration your ingenuity and your small size."

Katin grinned, remembering the mischief she'd wrought. "You see, by the end of the first day, I was quite frustrated by my inability to successfully break any of the holds His Lordship showed me. He told me that it would require much practice to master the methods of defense, but I, of course, wanted to defeat him at his own game. I lay long awake that night, considering how I might get the better of him, and when he fetched me down to the training field the next morning, I asked him to do the shadow attack for me again."

"The shadow attack . . . ?" Lady Celia interrupted.

"An assault in which the attacker comes from behind, obliquely," the Baron explained, "and attempts to catch the victim about the throat with one arm, leaving the other free to club, stab, or otherwise subdue the one captured."

"He'd spent a large part of the previous morning trying to teach me how to use the hilt of my dagger on the point of the attacker's wrist, so as to render his hand numb and force him to release his grip," Katin continued. "Not with any great success, for I was too small to strike with enough strength to produce a suitable shock. But I had since evolved my own solution to the problem. To come at me from behind, His Lordship had to balance his weight with his legs apart, to bend forward low enough to reach my neck. When he lunged at me, I simply dropped to the ground and rolled between his legs, then drew my dagger and swiped at him, aiming for the highest point I could reach—which luckily wasn't very high."

"Heaven preserve us," Lady Celia exclaimed. "And you say that *our* daughter is uncontrollable, Andrew."

"I didn't really mean to cut him," Katin added hastily, "but I was off-balance, and he kicked his leg out at me just then." Abashed as a six-year-old, she said to the Baron, "You bled so profusely, I was terrified I'd done murder."

" 'Twas not so serious as it looked—save that I came dangerously close to committing high treason, by giving Your Highness a sound thrashing."

"I've nearly done the same, a score of times," Sir Andrew observed sympathetically.

"I'd have richly deserved it," Katin admitted, rather proudly.

It was her childlike air of guilty glee at her deed, as much as the tale itself, that allowed the Baron to see in her the willful, winsome child he remembered. "If there was one member of the royal family I'd have sworn would survive the depredations of the Chamber it would have been you, Your Highness," he said, and swept low in a deep bow.

"You are with us, then?" Katin asked, suddenly serious. In the space of a heartbeat, she had changed from a rebellious child to a monarch far older than her years.

The Baron wondered how he could ever have doubted her. "With all my heart," he said.

"And with all your resources, I trust," said Sir Andrew, turning at once to practical military matters. "It is said that you have mustered a private army of some three thousand soldiers."

"I've heard the rumors—they are greatly exaggerated. I have perhaps half that many, as yet. Not what you're used to having at your command, I'm afraid, but I am adding to their number day by day."

"We've the start of an army, then," Katin said hopefully. "Sir Andrew defeated the Dep invaders with little more, at the end!"

"The invasion force was a fraction of the Chamber's army," Sir Andrew reminded her. "Still, we are better started then I'd thought to be."

Katin soon withdrew, knowing that the Lord Marshal and the Baron would prefer to discuss military tactics without feeling that they must stop to explain matters to her at every turn. Sir Andrew would report their conclusions to her in due course, and at the moment she was chiefly eager to change her elegant gown for more comfortable clothes.

Lady Celia followed her, but at the door she turned back for a moment to warn Sir Andrew that he was not to overtax his strength, and to charge the Baron not to allow it. "Don't forget, my dear, you've only been on your feet for a few days. That wound will have no chance to knit, if you do not take sufficient rest." She appealed to Katin. "Isn't that so?"

Katin seconded her warmly, giving her admonitions the force of a royal command.

The Baron had not yet heard of the attack on Sir Andrew. "Wound?" he said. "And was that your doing, too, Your Highness?"

"No indeed. I can produce witnesses to my innocence! I am a fair hand with a small hunting bow, but someone stronger than I was needed to send an arrow with such force across the green."

The Baron frowned. " 'Twas no accident, then . . . ? I see. So the enemy are already among us."

As she dashed down the curving staircase, dressed in simple breeches and tunic, Katin found Captain Fenton waiting to escort her, as usual. "I'm not leaving the grounds," she protested. "I'm just off to the kennels for a moment, then I must tidy up my workshed for the day. I'll be back directly."

"I'll just see you to the herb garden, then, and wait nearby for you," he offered. It was the best he could do to allow her some privacy, without violating his orders from Sir Warren and Sir Andrew.

Katin understood this, and attempted to accept it with good grace, but she desperately wanted to be alone to think about the changes that were overtaking her, and the greater changes to come. She felt too restless to stay in her own rooms, however, so she made an effort to hide her resentment and told the captain about the outcome of the meeting with Baron Graydon, as they crossed the yard to the barn that held the kennel.

"If you were so formidable at six, 'tis small wonder you don't feel in need of a bodyguard now," he said agreeably, but they both fell silent as they approached the barn, where they could be overheard by the kennel hands. Captain Fenton waited below while she climbed the ladder to the loft where the litter of soarhounds had their nest. She had not seen Lucifer since Lady Celia's maid had dropped him out the window and shuttered it, that morning, while Katin was being dressed in the elaborate silk gown. Lucifer's claws were more like a cat's than a dog's, and he was accustomed to clambering into Katin's arms, or jumping onto her shoulder whenever he liked. He made one pounce at the long, trailing skirt and was unceremoniously defenestrated before he could make another.

One of the pups crept out of the straw and nuzzled her hand with its stubby golden nose, but Lucifer was nowhere in sight. The mother had grown used to Katin, and now allowed her to handle the whelps, so she picked up the fat little downy creature and held it to her cheek, comforted by its thistledown softness. She would have to leave so much behind, but she could at least take her soarhounds home with her. *Home . . . ?* she wondered. Could Albin ever be home to her again?

She satisfied herself that the pups and their mother were all healthy, but she was far too unsettled to stay for long. As she descended from the loft, Captain Fenton attempted to hand her from the ladder, and before she could stop herself, Katin snapped, "I've climbed the tallest trees in the woods to see the view, I've climbed the rigging of a brig to sight the enemy, I've climbed a rope ladder a hundred feet high to reach a Yerren treetop city, and I can climb down from a barn ladder without your help!"

Conscious that they were not alone, the captain kept to his role as suitor and replied earnestly, "Katin, if you've been allowed to run such risks, you have been scandalously ill looked after. You shall certainly do nothing of the kind again, if I can do ought to prevent it."

Already ashamed of her outburst, Katin led the captain from the barn, saying hotly, "You'll find that I shall do pretty well as I like," to carry on the appearance of a lovers' quarrel. But as soon as they were away from listeners, she apologized, "Forgive my vile temper, sir. I've the manners of a savage—"

"And I have still the manners of the Old World, Your Highness. They may be out of place in the New, but they are the only manners I know." Captain Fenton was thoroughly versed in court etiquette, but there were no rules of correct behavior for responding to an apology from one's sovereign. Such a circumstance simply could not arise.

Katin picked a flower off a winterberry bush, thinking how much easier it was to talk to Jerl. She suddenly wanted to saddle her horse and ride off to find him, but she would not be able to confide her present troubles to him, and she certainly couldn't call upon him with the captain in attendance. She tossed away the flower and said, "It's just that I found that meeting rather trying—and it was but the first of many. I must accustom myself to civilized behavior again, I know, but you see it's not so easy as climbing a tree!" She gave an unconvincing laugh and added, "And Lady Celia says I must dress like a lady every day, till I can wear silk without squirming like Clara."

The captain smiled, at a loss for words. It was a New World indeed, if a monarch felt obliged to ask pardon for a show of royal temper, or obeyed the dictates of her own subjects, as a matter of course. She had much to learn about being a queen, he thought, but who was to teach her? He felt quite sorry for his young sovereign, but could think of no way to express such an unsuitable sentiment. Both were relieved when they reached Katin's workshed, at the far end of the herb garden.

"I'll stay here in the garden—" the captain began, but he broke off suddenly, listening, and motioned Katin back. "Someone's in there," he said softly, drawing his sword.

Katin, too, had heard a muffled thump from within, but she laughed at the captain's caution. "I must have shut Lucifer inside again," she explained. "He *will* hide up among the roof beams—" But then she stopped, frowning. "Oh, but I couldn't have, could I? He was in the house this morning, and I've not been out since. Well, but it must have been one of the gardeners . . ." she said uncertainly.

The captain was not convinced. It might be Her Highness' dog within, or it might be the enemy who'd failed to kill the Lord Marshal and meant to attack the Princess at closer quarters. He insisted that Katin hide in the nearby orchard while he made sure that the shed concealed no danger. This, at least, was a situation he felt equal to. What satisfaction it would be to bring the culprit to Sir Andrew—preferably alive. When he threw open the door of the shed, he was prepared to find an indignant soarhound or a desperate murderer, but he was not expecting to see Lady Alicen Kendry seated at Katin's worktable, looking back at him as if he were the intruder.

Chapter 6

Alicen hadn't gone directly to hunt for Katin. There had been one more thing she wanted to know, before she had a look at the girl herself, and it was something Hannah could not tell her. She needed someone who'd been with Sir Andrew since before the Uprising, and after observing those employed about the estate, she approached the oldest of the workers putting the finishing touches on the rear portico of the mansion.

"Aye, and his father before him," the carpenter told her proudly, "and my father before me." He dropped the plane he was using onto a half-finished board and waited for Alicen to come to the point. He did not suppose that she was interested in his history, but she was too well dressed to be told bluntly to state her business or be on her way.

"Then perhaps you can help me—it's Katin Ander, the herbalist, who concerns me," Alicen explained, laying a silver demi-ember on the half-planed board between them. "I think, you see, that there's a chance she might be my niece, or at least family of some sort. My sister married a man named Ander, and they'd a young daughter when the Deps deported them, for heresy, seven years ago. I've only had word from her once, in all this time, that they meant to travel to Oriana, where her husband's kin had settled. But now that my business brings me here, I'm told there's no one in the colony named Ander save the Governor's apothecary—and she an orphan girl. She's of an age to be my sister's child, to be sure, but no one seems to know who her parents were."

The carpenter shook his head regretfully. "She can't well be the one, mistress. She came from Albin with His Lordship's household."

"Oh—then she lived at Stoneridge before the Uprising? If that's so, she's no connection to my sister's husband. His people were all from Darhan." Alicen sounded bitterly disappointed.

"Well, no, I don't say she belonged to Stoneridge. 'Twasn't till we sailed for New Albin that the master took her in."

Aha, thought Alicen, and said aloud, "Is that so? I don't know how they made the passage, for I was in the Lowlands at the time. Are you sure she'd no family with her?"

"None that I know of, mistress. Folk said then she'd been orphaned in the Uprising. P'raps 'twas North Oriana your people meant," he offered helpfully.

Alicen sighed. "Still, I suppose if she's not my niece, she might be some relation to the Anders of Darhan."

"Why not ask the lass herself, then?"

"That's what I didn't like to do, till I'd found out where she came from. I've heard talk that she could be . . ." Alicen paused delicately, and shrugged. "And if that were so, she'd not welcome questions about her parentage. But I think I'd best go see her. I may never be in these parts again." Alicen smiled winningly. "Many thanks for your help, friend. Where would I find the girl now?"

* * *

A search of Katin's workshed had revealed nothing
to suggest that she was anything other than a hardworking herbalist, and Alicen was about to go look for
her elsewhere when she heard someone approaching
the shack. By the time Captain Fenton pulled open the
door, she was seated at the table, leaning her head on
one hand and drumming the table with the fingers of
her other hand in a bored, impatient manner. She
looked surprised and faintly annoyed to see the captain, but said politely enough, "Ah, Captain Fenton, is
it not? Is Mistress Ander with you?"

Fenton knew who Alicen was, and he was aware that
she'd been poisoned practically on Sir Andrew's doorstep. It seemed likely that she'd been a target of the
same killer who'd attacked the Governor, and he did
not therefore consider her a threat to the Princess, at
present. He beckoned to Katin, saying, "She will be
here directly," when an overturned crate in the corner
began to thump and scrape on the floor as if it had a
life of its own.

The captain looked from it to Alicen, frowning.
"What, if I may ask, do you have there?"

Alicen glanced toward the source of the noise, but
before she could answer, Katin approached the door,
and the crate broke into shrill, frantic barking and
yelping. Pushing past the table, Katin demanded,
"What have you done to my dog?"

"That thing is a *dog?*" said Alicen. "When I started
to open the door, the creature came flying at my head
like a drunken bat. So I caught it up in my cloak," she
gestured to the red velvet mantle lying across the other
stool, "and put it under there to keep it out of mischief."

"He was only protecting my property," Katin said
indignantly, bending down to lift the crate. Lucifer

leaped up, clinging to her and wagging his tail. "Good dog—aren't you the brave watchdog, then," she crooned, keeping her back to Alicen.

Captain Fenton withdrew with a bow. "You've hardly room for three in here. I'll be just outside."

Detaching Lucifer, Katin set him on the floor, and he scrambled up to the ceiling, staying as far away from Alicen as possible. Katin wished she could do the same. Without looking at Alicen, she picked up an armful of jars from the table and turned to put them on the shelves along the back wall. "What brings you here, m'lady?" she asked without turning from her task. "I trust you're not still suffering any discomfort from your illness?"

"No, thanks to your skill I am quite well. I came to thank you for saving my life."

" 'Twas but my duty, m'lady."

Alicen gathered a few jars from the table and brought them to Katin, trying to catch a closer look at her face, but away from the single oil lamp guttering on the table, she couldn't see Katin's features clearly enough to be certain of the resemblance. She tried to imagine the slight, young Princess grown into this hardy, humble country lass. Could years and sunshine have stained her fair skin brown and burnished her hair to this pale gold? Would the Princess lower herself to play the part—indeed to live the life—of a commoner? "How is it that you call me *lady*, Mistress Ander?" Alicen asked suddenly. "None but Sir Andrew knows of my rank and title."

Cursing herself for her carelessness, Katin countered, "You are mistaken, m'lady. Lady Celia knows you, and she told me."

"A curious thing to tell one's apothecary, is it not?"

Katin bent over a cold brazier and began to clear the

ashes into a sack. "Lady Celia knows that I am to be trusted," she said stiffly. "As you owed me your life, she saw fit to explain who you were. You need not concern yourself that it will go further."

"Oh, I am sure of that. No one who knows Her Ladyship could doubt her judgment. Perhaps she also told you why I have come to Oriana?"

"That could scarcely concern me, m'lady."

"Did you not wonder why I'd been poisoned?"

"In these days, many have enemies. Sir Andrew was nearly murdered, at the Harvest Fair."

"And folk say you saved him as well."

"They are kind to say so, but I am no surgeon. I could not have removed the arrowhead safely."

"Nonetheless, you seem to have disobliged the Chamber's assassins to a remarkable degree."

"The Chamber . . . ?" Katin asked innocently.

"Assuredly, the Chamber must be the author of these outrages. And you yourself may become a target, girl, if they know that you've foiled their plans twice over. Is that why you've a Captain of the Horse Guard in attendance?"

Ignoring the question, Katin answered only, "I'm sure the Chamber'd not be bothered with the likes of me. I'm not important enough to draw their fire."

"No? Yet folk say that you lost your family to the Dep Uprising." As Katin did not deny the fact, Alicen went on, "I daresay you are no friend to the Chamber. Perhaps you would help me with my mission here. I've come to garner support for the overthrow of Dep rule, and the return of the Obelen line to the throne of Albin."

Katin could sense that Alicen was watching for her reaction, and she was careful to give nothing away, but her thoughts were in a turmoil. *Is she toying with me?*

Is she trying to provoke me? Katin was not afraid of
Alicen. After all, Captain Fenton was within call, as
Alicen knew full well. *No,* Katin decided, *she's not
threatening me.* She seemed rather to be inviting Katin
to confide in her—but what did she know already?
What did she guess?

Katin's voice was steady as she asked, "What could
I do in aid of such a cause, m'lady?"

Rather at random, Alicen began to speak of her efforts on the Duke of Wyston's behalf, paying little
heed to her own words as she studied Katin for a clue
to the truth. She could read nothing but reserve and
reluctance in the girl's manner, but that proved only
that she was discreet, as befitted a member of the Governor's household, not that she was the Princess in disguise. "I seek to enlist Sir Andrew in support of the
Duke of Wyston's claim to the crown—but others are
at work to win him to the Duke of Halkin's party. As
Lady Celia places such faith in you, and Sir Andrew is
no doubt grateful to you, as I am, you might use your
influence for the Duke of Wyston's cause, if I could
persuade you of the probity of doing so."

" 'Twould serve no purpose to persuade me, m'lady.
Sir Andrew would hardly be guided by me in such a
matter."

"Yet people hereabout seem to think you have his
ear."

As she spoke, Alicen brought the oil lamp to the
dark corner where Katin was scraping out the sooty
brazier and held it up as if to light her work, but Katin
wearily rubbed one hand across her face, leaving a
mask of soot behind. "So I have—in all matters per-
taining to my calling," she said, "but you surely do not
suppose that he consults his apothecary on affairs of
state or military questions. I cannot believe that you

are in earnest, Lady Alicen." She spoke lightly, even managing to sound rather amused at the idea. "You are making sport of me."

Alicen retreated to the table, leaving the lamp hanging on a peg near Katin. "No, I assure you, my mission is of too much consequence to admit of levity. The fate of Albin is at stake! I would attempt any means, however unlikely, to convince the Lord Marshal to join with us. I tell you, *only a true Obelen can unite the people of Albin against the enemy.*"

Katin met her gaze, and for a long moment the two only regarded one another in silence, each challenging the other to speak her mind. At last Katin said softly, "I shall tell Sir Andrew what you say, My Lady. You may be sure that he will do what is best for Albin." She looked away and wiped her sooty hands on her breeches. "I don't mean to be discourteous, but I am finished here, and I have other duties to attend to."

Alicen stood. "Of course. No doubt Sir Andrew requires your services. I meant to ask before, how His Lordship fares."

"He is nigh recovered, though in some pain still." Katin shook her head. "He would fare better, I daresay, if he would rest himself more, but he is strong and the wound cleanly knit, so he does very well in spite of himself."

"I am rejoiced to hear it," Alicen said, smiling. "I shall not scruple to pay my respects, then. If His Lordship cannot see me, I shall just have a word with Lady Celia." She held open the door for Katin, letting in the strong late-afternoon sunshine, and leaving Katin no choice but to show herself in the light of day.

* * *

The attempt on the weapons shanty did not start at all well. The wind off the ocean, always treacherous, rose to buffet the conspirators as if it, too, were in the pay of Captain Tyrrel. The sky was overcast, promising a storm, but Rolande had chosen just such a night, when the clouds covered the sky so thickly that not a ray of moonlight penetrated to reveal the thieves' presence to the pirates on guard.

Handholds were abundant, and Rolande and a dozen of her crew had no trouble finding purchase in the limestone, but the climb was long and exhausting, nevertheless, even for those experienced at scaling seaside cliffs and mountain precipices. As she crept up the wall of rock, little by little, Rolande kept an eye on the progress of the others, especially that of the cabin boy, Raphe, who perhaps should not have been there at all. He was not one of Lorin's mountain bandits, and Rolande had intended to send him with the rest of the crew to hide in the woods where the other conspirators were secreted, waiting for her signal. But Raphe had been eager to join the attack party, to prove his mettle before Rolande, and she had allowed it, reasoning that he was strong and agile, and could run the rigging as surefootedly as a soarhound. He and the others seemed to be keeping pace with her well enough, from what little she could see in the unrelieved darkness, but she thought that she'd give the lot of them to have Hrivas at hand again.

Blythe she had left behind, at the compound, not wishing to risk his being injured when he'd be needed to tend to the injuries of others. Indeed, she was not sure he'd have obeyed if she had ordered him to take part in the foray—which he considered an ill-advised and foolhardy undertaking—and she was equally unsure of what she herself would do if he defied her orders.

At the moment, however, the task at hand required all her attention, as well as her strength and stamina. The small hand axes clinked as they gouged handholds in the rough rock, but the sound of their approach was masked by the wailing of the wind. Near her Rolande heard one of the others—Ivy, was it?—swear as she barked her shin on a sharp outcropping. Impatiently, Rolande hissed her to silence. They had come too far to let carelessness stop them now. But the ascent went on without mishap, the climbers struggling up the cliffside like so many spiders until, after what seemed a lifetime, they were at last within a body's length of the top.

"We've done it!" the sailor nearest Rolande whispered, grabbing for the top edge of the cliff to haul himself onto solid ground. "Praise the Good God!"

Even in the darkness, Rolande could see that his face was white with strain, and she warned him, "Not so fast, wait—" but he was already clutching the ledge with desperate fingers. Before Rolande's eyes, the earth crumbled beneath his hands, and the rock he grasped broke away, sending him screaming to his death below. The stone at the raw edge of the clifftop had been cut away then replaced in loose chunks held in place by a short wooden brace. Sod reapplied over the bare ledge had given it the appearance of solidity.

Vicious bastard! Rolande thought. Abandoning secrecy, she shouted to the others. "Don't touch the clifftop, it's a trap! Go back!"

Alerted by the clamor, the pirates guarding the shed fired off muskets to give the alarm and sent runners to muster reinforcements. Some came running toward the precipice and fired their muskets downward, but they had to stop far enough back to avoid the deceptive edge, and the balls whizzed past harmlessly or dislodged chips of stone from the clifftop, sending them skittering into the void below.

Rolande and her sailors swarmed back down the rock face of the hill, grasping at the most precarious of handholds in an attempt to reach the ground before a large force of pirates could arrive. But they were still some way from the beach when the sound of shots and shouting voices could be heard in the distance, from the direction of the harbor. Rolande's every muscle ached cruelly, but she kept reaching for each foothold, moving downward. *Too slow.* Pirates from the harbor stockade would reach the shore below before she could climb down the rest of the way. She stared toward the dark waves lapping the shore below and shouted out "Jump!" as she leaped from her perch into the cold sea. Those who could swim followed her lead.

As soon as the black water closed over her head, Rolande was trying to force her way to the surface. Every second lost could make the difference between escape and capture. But when she finally staggered from the sea onto the coarse sand, and stumbled to her knees, she was grabbed round the waist and someone tried to drag her to her feet. Desperate, she twisted around with her fist raised to strike, though she knew she was too exhausted to do much damage.

Blythe blocked her blow. "Leave off! Save your strength for running."

Leaning against him for support, Rolande gained her feet. "You?" she gasped. "You said—"

"I said this was a bad job, and I was right. Maybe you'll listen to me another time—if we survive *this* time. Come on!" He pulled her toward a pile of boulders at one end of the beach, but as Rolande tried to run after him, she lost her footing in the soft sand and tumbled to her knees again.

"Here, I'll help." Raphe clambered out of the waves and grasped Rolande's arm, and the three of them hurried to the shelter of the boulders, where they were soon joined by Corey and Ivy. Behind them the rest of the crew struggled from the water as a group of pirates spread out across the beach and fired at the stragglers descending from the hillside or trying to escape along the shore.

"We can't stay here," Rolande said, as soon as she'd caught her breath. "They'll search these rocks certain."

"Do we make for the woods, then, Captain?" asked Corey.

"No. We swim."

"Swim! Are you mad? Swim *where?*" Blythe demanded.

"Listen! It's the only way. While the pirates from the stockade are searching for us here, we might swim out far enough to escape notice from the shore, then make our way back around to the dock." She gestured toward the beachhead where the harbor lay. "We'll get aboard the nearest of the ships and take her out to sea before the harbor guards return to their posts."

From some distance down the shore the sound of shouting and gunshots rang out loudly in the otherwise still night. "We've got one here, lads," a harsh voice cried, only to be followed a moment later by a shot.

Rolande raced for the waves, without looking back to see if the remnants of her crew obeyed her. Raphe was at her heels, and Corey and Ivy not far behind. Blythe, seeing no help for it, followed the rest.

* * *

The scene at the fair, at the moment when the arrow had narrowly missed the Princess, was indelibly etched on Captain Fenton's memory. In that brief instant, he'd feared that he had failed utterly and miserably in his appointed task, that he and his name were shamed forever. He could still picture the Common now just as it had been at the moment the arrow was fired—the dancing figures moving like ghosts beneath the lanterns strung from tree to tree on the green—the stage where the actors performed their farce, unaware that behind their canvas town an assassin lurked.

And he recalled with particular clarity the gypsies engaging in feats of magic and fortune-telling, nearby the stage. Why had there been so many of them there? Could they have had anything to do with the attempt on the Princess' life—if such it was? The only description of the culprit suggested a gypsy, though Sir Andrew thought it unlikely. What, after all, had they to gain? But even if one of their number were not responsible for the attack, there remained the possibility that one of them might have seen the attacker, or at least have observed something significant. They had been the closest to the stage, aside from the actors.

He would question them on market day, he decided. The gypsies would then be out in force, seeking to earn money by selling trinkets and telling fortunes—and probably picking pockets, he thought. But petty crime in the colony wasn't his affair. His charge was to protect the Princess, and he didn't feel that he had distinguished himself at that task, thus far. Determined to overlook nothing that might aid in the execution of his duty, he strode toward the center of the green, where makeshift wooden stalls had been set up, not much different from those that had stood there on the day of the

Fair. These, however, held fresh vegetables, wheels of cheese, honeycombs, and live chickens.

Ruthven, too, had been giving much thought to the identity of Sir Andrew's attacker, for he, like Alicen, suspected that it was the same individual who had attempted to murder Alicen and himself—one of the Chamber's agents, no doubt. That something of unusual import was underway at the Governor's, Ruthven didn't doubt, for the sudden arrival of Captain Fenton from the north had piqued his curiosity. The captain spent much time in the company of the Governor and seemed most busy, but just what he was engaged in remained a mystery. Folk said he was courting the arrogant little apothecary, but why would a man of Fenton's station take a penniless herbalist to wife? Certainly he went about with her a good deal, but Ruthven—who had considerable experience in these matters—could discern no warmth between them.

Ruthven had made it his business to keep an eye on the activities at the Governor's Mansion, seeking any opportunity or information that he could use to his own advantage, either in enlisting Sir Andrew's support for the Duke of Halkin or in preventing him from assisting the Duke of Wyston. Thus, riding from the hostel on market day, Ruthven was most interested to see Captain Fenton crossing the Common alone. Abandoning his original plans for the day, he made to follow him. As he saw the Captain stop near the cluster of gypsy tents on the far side of the marketplace, Ruthven tethered his own horse to a tree and moved closer on foot.

Captain Fenton's features were set in menacing firmness as he approached a table of trinkets that lay at the end of the row of stalls, near the gypsy tents. He was well aware that even if the gypsies had seen something useful, there was no guarantee that they would willingly share it with him, and he assumed an air of stern authority in consequence—which was quite the wrong approach to take. He was still several feet away from the table when the woman attending it slipped away, and returned with a large, gray-haired man dressed in a voluminous, bright red shirt. He stood firmly in the captain's path and looked him over with a dubious eye. "What do you want here?"

Fenton matched his tone. "I wish to speak to the leader of these gypsies."

"Then it is me you seek. I am Elek Kedzier. I ask again, what do you want here—Captain?"

"If you know who I am, then you know I'm in the employ of the Governor. I've come on his authority to ask your people about the attack upon him, on the day of the Harvest Fair."

The gypsy's manner became even more distrustful. "And of course you look for a gypsy to blame for the deed! Why not one of the featherfolk, eh? They hide in the trees and hunt with bow and arrow. Here are trees enough—they could flit through these branches all the way to the woods, and no one the wiser." There was no love lost between the marsh Yerren and the gypsies, who had to cross the swampland to reach the town from their encampment. Kedzier spat. "They'll attack anything human they can get at. Why don't you go hunt them down?"

Fenton shook his head. "We've considered that possibility, but the Yerren use arrowheads of stone, not iron. And then, a man in gypsy garb was seen fleeing, at the time of the attack. I would be remiss in my duty if I failed to take such a thing into account."

Kedzier frowned and looked away. "None of my

people would be party to an attack on His Lordship. He's no enemy to us."

Following the direction of the gypsy's glance, Fenton saw a dozen men ranged around a makeshift corral where two young men were trying to break a horse. "That, too," he said, "will be taken into account. I accuse no one. Still, those who were at the Fair may have seen something telling. Have I your leave to question them?"

"You've the Governor's leave, haven't you?" Kedzier said grimly. "We've nothing to do with it, I tell you, but we've nothing to hide. I will see to it that all your questions are answered." Without another word, Kedzier started toward the corral, leaving Captain Fenton to follow.

The men stopped their shouting at Kedzier's approach, and he addressed them in their own language. One of them grunted sullenly, but none voiced any objection to his words. "I have told them who you are and what you want," he said to Fenton. "They will answer your questions."

Captain Fenton looked at the circle of hostile faces, so different from the usual accommodating air the gypsies wore when carrying on their trade throughout the town. "Were any of you near the actors' stage when the Governor was struck with the arrow?" he asked evenly.

"I was," the younger of the two men in the corral with the horse admitted. He wiped his face with the end of the scarf around his neck. "But I was too busy with doing magic at the time to take note of ought else."

Captain Fenton nodded, remembering the boy making eggs appear from the empty sack. "What of the rest of you?" he demanded, but the other men all denied having been anywhere near the stage.

Kedzier's eyes narrowed at this, and he turned to a muscular lad leaning insolently on the corral fence. "What of you, Michat? Were you not doing knife tricks over there?"

Michat shook his head, not meeting Kedzier's eyes, Fenton noted. "I was called away by Kamar. Said he needed help unhitching the horses from the carts."

Kamar, an older man with a black beard, nodded in confirmation of this and said, "That's so."

"Aye, I came to bring him sausage for his lunch, and he was not there," a girl's voice said.

Turning, Captain Fenton saw a gypsy girl walk up to Kedzier and tug on his sleeve. "Magdi said to ask you about the horse," she said to the gypsy leader.

"Later." He turned back to Captain Fenton. "You are answered, then. None of them saw anything. If you mean to question my whole tribe, you must come to our encampment."

"Perhaps I shall do so," said Fenton, though he suspected that those who were before him could tell him enough, if they wished. The gypsies seemed to have a remarkable ability to forget things when it suited them. In a last effort to provoke a response from one of them, he took the brass cylinder out of his pocket and held it up to the circle of men, asking, "Have any of you seen this before?" He handed the object to the gypsy nearest him and watched each man's face intently as he received the cylinder, but none betrayed any sign of recognition that the captain could discern. Frustrated, he returned the thing to his pocket and took his leave.

No sooner had Captain Fenton cleared the last of the tents than Kedzier turned a threatening glower on the man Kamar and said for all to hear, "How is it

you've taken to wearing a beard like a townsman? If I
find that you had anything to do with this stupid attack
on the Governor, I myself will chop you into shreds
and feed you to the dogs!"

As Fenton strode away, Ruthven emerged from behind one of the tents and snatched a passing gypsy
child by the arm, dragging her back behind the tent,
out of sight. She opened her mouth to yell, but abruptly quieted when she saw the silver piece that
Ruthven held out before her face. This was business,
then. Perhaps he hadn't even recognized her. "What
may I do for you, sir?" she asked politely, with a rough
curtsy.

Ruthven smiled. "You were listening to the captain
talk to your brothers and uncles, no?" Without waiting
for an answer, he went on, "You saw the thing he
showed them, just now. Can you get it for me? You've
deft little fingers, as I recall, and he's a gentleman—
not like me. He'll be far easier to thieve from."

The child eyed the money and frowned in indeci-
sion. "That's an ill thing," she said hesitantly. " 'Twill
give bad luck, sir. I could get you a much better
charm—"

"Don't talk your cant to me! Bring me that brass
tube, and you'll have this and another like it. Or would
you rather that I told the magistrates how you lifted my
purse, eh?"

"I'll get it if you want it, sir!" the girl said hastily.
"I saw where he put it. Just you leave it to me!" She
dropped another clumsy curtsy and dashed off across
the green after Captain Fenton.

Ruthven smiled as he watched her frisking along beside Fenton, holding out one of her tawdry charms and
chattering urgently. When he stopped abruptly and

turned toward her, she contrived to collide with him, scattering her luck-pieces and whining apologies as she scrambled after them. Ruthven chuckled and retreated out of sight, confident in his minion's skills. The noble captain, he thought, didn't stand a chance against that one.

Already exasperated by the gypsies, Fenton was in no mood to listen to the girl when she dashed up to him, offering some shiny trinket. "Get you gone!" he said curtly. "I've no use for such a thing."

"Not for you, sir, for your lady!" she insisted, running after him. "For the yellow-haired one, a token to protect her—"

That got Fenton's attention. He stopped short—giving the girl a chance to run into him—and when he'd extricated himself from the child and her luck-charms, he demanded, "What do you mean by that? Protect her from what?"

"From all manner of evil," she said earnestly. "She must wear it so, always, always—" She reached into her loose blouse and pulled out a thong she wore about her neck, to show him a charm identical to the one she had pressed upon him, an eye of some silvery metal with an iris of green stone. "I don't want money for it! It is a gift from Arya, tell her. To keep her safe!"

She made one of her crude curtsys, but Fenton seized her by the arm before she could race away. "Why do you want her to have this, child?"

"She has once stopped a man from beating me," Arya explained. "I wish to give her something, a special charm I make, very powerful. It will keep danger from her."

"But why do you think she's in danger?" Fenton persisted.

"Everyone is," Arya said innocently. "Evil is all around us! You will give it to her, Captain, yes?"

Well, Fenton reasoned, if the girl herself wore one, she probably meant nothing by it. He let her go, and she ran back to Ruthven, with the brass cylinder safe within her blouse.

* * *

With all the pirates gone to answer the alarm, Rolande and the remnants of her crew had managed to clamber undetected on board a longboat, where it was anchored at the northernmost end of the spit, and row out to one of the pirate ships that lay at anchor offshore. Rolande had chosen the *Wasp* as their target because in days past she had observed little activity there to indicate a large number of men left aboard as watch. She had only a handful of crew with which to take the ship—and she hoped fervently that they would be enough.

As their boat slid silently up beside the larger vessel, she said softly, "Now, while the hue and cry is on and they're all distracted, we'll disarm the pirates left on guard here and take this ship out to sea." She spoke with confidence, as a captain must, trusting that none of them—except Blythe—would remember that she had laid out her plan for taking the weapons shed with the selfsame assurance.

Blythe, of course, remembered. "Was this your plan all along—to create a distraction to draw off the harbor guard, then steal a ship?" he asked in a whisper. He sounded merely curious, not censorious.

Rolande's breath seemed to catch in her throat and choke her. How dare he accuse her of such infamy? She was gnawed with guilt and regret over the loss of her crew, who'd be slaughtered by Tyrrel's men because they'd followed her into a trap. She meant to see them avenged one day, but she knew that all she could do now was try to save herself and the few who were with her still. And Blythe actually thought her capable of sacrificing most of her crew in order to make an escape herself! It was all Rolande could do to refrain from seizing an oar and breaking his head, then and there.

But she was not one to give her feelings away. "You're a bloody fool, Blythe," she said calmly. "I've cut men's throats for lesser insults, and if I don't cut yours, it's only because we're likely to need a surgeon before the night's out. You can start by bandaging Ivy's arm, there. Tear up your shirt if you have to. The rest of you wait here, too. I'm going to spy out the disposition of the watch."

She took hold of the chain that dangled from the channel of the ship beside them, and was soon climbing up hand over hand, with numb fingers, and arms still aching from the swim around the shore. She had sneaked aboard a good many ships this way, during her days as a smuggler of stolen goods, but it was not nearly as easy as she remembered it. *I'm getting too old for this sport,* she thought, as she finally dragged herself over the waist-high rail above the quarterdeck bulwark and rolled behind the latticed coaming that surrounded the ladderway to the deck below. *Street-thieving's for children, sneak-thieving's for youngsters, and killing's for those full-grown, that's what we used to say.*

She lay on the deck for a while, waiting to regain her breath and strength, then crept on her hands and knees around a wooden winch and over a hatch grating, stopping behind a chestful of spare sails, and peering across the ship's deck. In all, she spotted only a half-dozen sailors left on watch, which was deemed guard enough for a ship anchored so near the stockade. There was little need for more than someone to give the alarm, but those few who were posted on board were heavily armed with pistols, cutlasses, and the wicked curved daggers commonly used by the Castilians. Rolande and her crew, armed only with knives, would have to rely on surprise to overcome at least one or two of the pirates and capture their weapons, in order to subdue the rest.

Rolande foresaw no great difficulty in accomplishing this. The guards were dispersed throughout the vessel, and could easily be set upon one by one. Hidden from view behind a cannon near the companionway rail at the end of the quarter deck, she watched a pirate below in the ship's waist tightening a shroud, and considered whether it would be possible to climb the rail to pounce upon him. She was so intent on her calculations that she started at the sound of footsteps approaching her hiding place. Looking around the cannon, she saw a sailor come out of the poop deck companionway at the far end of the deck where she hid. She waited silently for him to move on, but instead he sat down by a crate of tackle and began to strop blocks, trapping her behind him. *One of us has to leave, my friend,* she thought, and looked around for some means of distracting him. Creeping through the lower part of the rigging, she used her knife to cut the lashing that secured the horizontal boom at the bottom of the mizzenmast. She yanked on the rope with all her weight, until the boom, secured only by a hinged jaw, collapsed, swinging down to hit him square in the back of the head. As he keeled over, Rolande stopped only long enough to remove the pistol from his sash, then slipped away before he could recover and ran back to the quarterdeck rail.

"There aren't many," she told the others when she had climbed back down into the longboat. "With surprise on our side, we should be able to disarm the lot and take her."

Stealing the ship would make her yet more enemies, but she had little choice if she wanted to get herself and her people away from Needle Isle. Tyrrel would probably spare Blythe, might even keep Raphe for slave labor, or sell him, but she and the others would certainly be killed—unpleasantly—for defying Tyrrel's orders. *Besides,* she thought, *of such deeds as this are reputations made, and at sea, reputation is everything.*

Blythe was tying a makeshift sling, made of strips torn from an old piece of sailcoth he'd found in the bottom of the boat, around Ivy's arm and shoulder. "This one will be climbing no chains tonight," he warned Rolande. "That leaves only four of us."

"Very well, four it is," Rolande said, as if any number would have suited her just as well. "We'll hunt in pairs first—Raphe with me, Blythe with you, Corey. Once we're all armed, we can split up and make a sweep of it. The guards are—"

But before she could embark on further instructions, Corey interrupted with a low cry, "Look there, Cap'n—a longboat, yonder, coming this way. That light's too low in the water to be ought else."

Turning, Rolande could make out a single spot of light, such as might be cast by a lantern hung from the prow of a boat like theirs. "By God, they're too far out to be crew from a ship already in harbor—their vessel must be 'round Saber Point, waiting permission to make port. Quick cut athwart them!" As Raphe and Corey grasped their oars and began to row, she said with satisfaction, "Here's our passage out, without risking our necks again. If we warn them off, why wouldn't they take us aboard? We're not too many, and able sailors all. Pull, lads, pull!"

Raphe and Corey soon brought them within hailing distance of the other boat, and Rolande cried, "Halt there and take warning! You land on Needle Isle at your peril!" As if to bear witness to her words, the sound of musketfire came to them from the shore ahead.

"Who are you?" the seaman in the bow of the other boat called back suspiciously.

"Captain Vendeley of the *Azora,* and friend to you, whoever you are. Stand by for us, and go no nearer to shore, for your good."

The seaman in command of the longboat bade the others ship their oars, and allowed Rolande's boat to draw up alongside his. But the light thrown by the lantern on their bow revealed that he and the sailors who sat between the oarsmen were waiting with pistols drawn.

"You may put up your weapons," Rolande told him with calm authority. "My people are unarmed, as you can see."

After a hasty examination of Rolande's ragtag crew, the seaman ordered his comrades to put aside their weapons. "Why do you warn us off Tyrrel's isle, then? What's afoot there?"

"Captain Tyrrel has forbidden any who land here to leave, on pain of death. There's a pay ship from Albin due to pass near, and he would have none attack her, lest they bring down the wrath of the navy on his paradise. A few crews tried to seize weapons from his storehouse this night and failed—it's slaughter that's afoot here, man. If you make port, you'll be bound to stay till the pay fleet's long past, for Tyrrel can make good his threats."

"But what are you lot at?" the sailor demanded. "You'd not have me believe you're escaping to sea in a longboat."

Curse the luck! Another one that's not an idiot! She was not about to admit that she'd been on the point of stealing a ship from his fellow pirates. "We saw your lights from the headland, of course—do you think we meant to row to White Hern Island?" she snarled. "In the fracas we stole a longboat and came out to meet your ship. Now take us to your captain, you bloody great fool, before others sight you and report your presence to Tyrrel! If we're too late, 'tis you who'll answer for it!"

The seaman hesitated only a moment. "A pay vessel, you say," he muttered. "The captain will want to hear about that, without fail. Aye, you'll come with us, and give your news to our captain yourself. Better you than me to tell him we must turn back. Follow us and look lively!"

He glowered at Rolande and gestured with his pistol, to make clear that he was in charge, but she was only too willing to obey, since his orders fell in with her wishes. "Lead the way, then," she said coolly, as both crews bent to their oars.

By the light of the lanterns on the deck, the captain looked them over as if they were so many rats the ship's cat had fetched him. On hearing Rolande's warning, he'd ordered the ship to be drawn back out of range of Tyrrel's cannon, but he'd given no heed to her demand for passage for herself and her people, in return for the good turn she'd done him. They'd been left on deck, under guard, while he saw to the trimming of the sails, and he seemed in no hurry to deal with them.

Rolande wanted nothing more than to lie down and rest, then and there, but she dared not show weakness to one whose goodwill was so uncertain. Bracing herself against the capstan, she watched white foam dancing on the waves, as the ship came about and moved away from the headland. Her clothes were still damp with brine, and she shivered slightly in the chill breeze off the water. A fine salt spray misted her skin and hair. The bunt line on one of the foremast sails was loose, and she could hear it slapping back and forth, back and forth, while they waited. . . . Why didn't someone secure the damned thing? After what seemed an hour, the captain finally sauntered over to them and sneered, "So you're Rolande Vendeley? You disappoint me, woman. From your reputation, I'd expected something more fearsome than a half-drowned cat with a passel of kittens." He gave a shout of hoarse laughter at his own joke, showing a mouthful of gold teeth.

At last, Rolande thought, *a complete fool.* She felt about to collapse, but she spared no more than a moment to draw in a great breath of the fresh sea air, then boldly took a step forward to face him. In a manner that left no doubt she was a captain in her own right, she said, "Aye, I'm Vendeley." *I'm a cat with nine lives and wicked sharp claws,* said her look. The captain stopped toying with his dagger, and his expression changed to one of sharp appraisal—with a gleam of savagery in his dark eyes.

Rolande waved her hand toward the sailors behind her. "This is Edward Blythe, my ship's surgeon—and a handy one—"

"Aye, we've met," the other captain answered coldly. "I remember that one."

"And these are the remains of my crew—able sailors all. I shipped the rest with other vessels, after the *Azora* broke up on the reefs," Rolande lied, wishing fervently that she had done so. She did not intend to let him know that Tyrrel was hunting her. Desperation was no position to bargain from.

"I can use you, Vendeley, with the pay fleet on its way. If half what's said of you is true, you've taken near as many of the Chamber's ships as I have."

"You've been about it longer than I," Rolande pointed out, with a wolfish grin.

The captain laughed again, but he did not sound amused. He turned his gaze to Blythe. "And you, *surgeon,* I've a use for you as well." His glance at the other crewmen was dismissive. "As for the rest of this scurvy lot—"

"I told you they are my crew," Rolande interrupted. "Only the best sail with me, and only a fool would refuse them passage."

"If you think to give orders on my ship, Vendeley, you are the fool," the captain said grimly.

Rolande took another step toward him, and a pirate moved between them with cutlass drawn, but she continued speaking as if she hadn't noticed the blade pointed at her breast. "If you mean to try for the pay fleet, you'll need every hand you can get, and the others hereabout are bound to Captain Tyrrel's isle. We might prosper together, but I'll make no move without my crew." She shrugged. "You can kill me, but you've naught to gain by it, and much to lose."

The captain scratched his beard thoughtfully for a minute, then seemed to come to a decision. "I would relish capturing this pay ship—but with just myself, it can't be done," he admitted. "Now we're bound for the Tintich Channel. We can get the supplies we need at

Ophir Island as well as at Needle. Then we'll capture another vessel or two, the first that come our way, and place some of my men aboard. Aye, my mate Ramey here will captain one, and you the other. That will give us three ships—it's all we've crew to man, even with your mighty company here. That done, we'll intercept the pay ship. And you'll play your part, Vendeley, or you'll never do aught else."

Rolande knew better than to antagonize the man further. She'd shown him that she'd not be easily daunted, and that was probably as much as he could understand. "Very well, agreed," she said, somehow contriving to sound as if she'd been forced to accept his terms, when in fact he had agreed to hers.

He gave a self-satisfied grin and said loudly, for all to hear, "If what you've heard of the pay fleet holds true, we stand to make our fortunes from this venture! Just remember, those who've crossed me in the past have not died easy."

"I think we understand one another," Rolande said evenly.

The captain gestured to the sailors still standing guard, and ordered, "Take Captain Vendeley and her lot below, and see they have all that they need." Abruptly he turned back to the helm, as if he had lost all interest in the matter.

"A moment," Rolande said, and the captain looked back, frowning. "You know who I am. Would you think it unreasonable of me to ask who *you* are, and what ship this is?"

"This ship's the *Black Swan*." The captain doffed his plumed hat in mock courtesy. "And I am Captain Nicholas Brodery."

Chapter 7

Lady Celia's warning and the Princess' command had their effect. Baron Graydon conferred with Sir Andrew for only an hour before taking his leave, and no protests of Sir Andrew's could dissuade him. He could see for himself that his host was exhausted, although it was clear that the Lord Marshal would go on discussing plans and strategy all the afternoon if he had his way. "It would be well for me to call upon Lord Hamstell in Elmslaine and sound him out," the Baron said, "if, as you say, Sir Warren has apprised him of the facts. I shall bring you word of him in a few days' time, when I may hope to find Your Lordship more fully recovered. But it would be a braver man than I who would dare the wrath of Viscountess Edenbyrne by disturbing your rest further today!"

Lady Celia had settled her husband on a low couch in the parlor, and left him to his repose, while she went to confer with the seamstress about a new wardrobe for Katin. This took some time, and she was perturbed— but not much surprised—upon her return, to find that Sir Andrew's notion of "rest" consisted of feverishly studying the scraps of paper Rolande had sent him with Hrivas. Their meaning continued to elude him.

Lady Celia fetched a small glass of brandy from the sideboard and handed it to Sir Andrew, then firmly removed the small table where he had spread out the fragments. "You've not been wearing yourself out over those all this time, have you?" she reproached him.

"Nearly," he admitted, "and making no progress, what's more." He leaned back and sipped gratefully at the brandy. "Only Vendeley could saddle me with a maddening riddle like this—and no word from her in all this time. Curse the jade, where has she gotten to?"

Lady Celia turned away, smiling, and poured herself a little brandy before settling on a hassock near her husband. "I expect it's taken her longer than she foresaw to obtain another ship," she suggested.

Sir Andrew glanced over at her. "I suppose so ... although with Vendeley, it's more than likely she's off pursuing some course of her own and leaving me on tenterhooks." He wondered whether he would be more relieved or sorry to lose Vendeley, if some ill had befallen her. True, she was his best hope of ferreting out the Chamber's secrets, his most resourceful and daring agent, but— "Damn it all! I swear to you, that woman's one desire is to devil me!" He rubbed his hand across his forehead, and Lady Celia leaned over to kiss him, then startled him by breaking into laughter.

"My dear, how else is she to captivate you? She daren't seduce you—for one thing, *I* shouldn't stand for it—so she bedevils you. And it serves very well, I'm bound to say. I believe she's more in your thoughts than I am."

Sir Andrew could only stare at his wife in speechless astonishment.

"Well, not *more,* perhaps," Lady Celia conceded, "but honestly, Andrew, have you never so much as suspected that Rolande admires you?"

Sir Andrew found his voice. "Vendeley *told* you that?"

"Oh, no. I don't suppose she knows it herself, and if she did, she'd sooner die than confess to it. But you're in her thoughts as well, or she'd not take such pains to impress you—or devil you, if you prefer. Of course she admires you, and you admire her," Lady Celia added complacently.

"I? Really, Celia!"

"You would be strange indeed if you didn't. Rolande's clever and courageous, an invaluable agent, an amusing companion. She has a most ready wit and a good deal of charm when she chooses to exercise it. And you cannot deny that she's quite pleasing to the eye—as sleek and alluring as a young panther."

Sir Andrew took a swallow of his brandy. "Whether or not I admire her, it's clear that you do," he said, with a bewildered shake of his head. "And I should say, too, that if the creature admires either of us, that one is you, not me."

"There's something in that," Lady Celia agreed, laughing again. "I've exercised some charm of my own on that one—it seemed prudent to do so—and one does grow fond of a wild creature that one has coaxed to take corn from one's hand."

"Wolves," Sir Andrew said emphatically, "do not eat corn. I could as soon admire a ravening she-wolf as Vendeley, and as for her admiring me—I can only say that if her behavior toward me betokens admiration, I should be more than willing to forfeit her regard. If admiration can be expressed by insolence and effrontery—"

"But of course it can, my dear. Our poor Rolande fiercely resents her regard for you, and so cloaks it in disrespect. After all, you have upset her most cherished notions, and that is a wrong not lightly forgiven."

"You are speaking in conundrums," Sir Andrew protested, mystified. "I could hardly follow you at first, and now you have lost me altogether."

Yes, thought Lady Celia, *but you are resting.* "I refer to her notions about the aristocracy," she explained, in a patient tone. "You didn't know, did you, that Rolande comes from the wharf-slums of Avenford, that she spent her childhood as a street-thief, and her youth as a smuggler? She was only Jen Quick then."

Sir Andrew was genuinely surprised at this. No one in Thornfeld had known anything of Vendeley's background, but he had assumed from her manner and appearance that she came from a wealthy merchant family. "How did you find that out? Her habits of speech and dress are hardly those of a pauper."

"Oh, that she *did* tell me, though she didn't mean to. She's told me a great deal about herself." Lady Celia could talk to anyone, and had a positive genius for winning people's confidence and drawing them out—a talent that had proven valuable more than once. "It was the Deprivant Church that educated her above her station, to make a spy of her, before the Uprising. She proved so useful that the Chamber made her one of their chief agents in New Albin, as you know. She's proud of having raised herself by her own wits and daring, you see, and she's never had anything but contempt for those who owe their high position in life to inheritance alone. Dep rhetoric that condemned the nobility as idle, selfish, and cowardly found a ready believer in her, from the start.

"But in Thornfeld she had you to contend with, and she was forced to reconsider her convictions, much against her will. Certainly she detested you, but she was unable to regard you with the scorn she felt you deserved. Arrogant and haughty you might be, but she could see for herself, from your conduct of the colony's defense, that you were anything but idle or cowardly. You were clearly willing to sacrifice your own interests, time and again, to the interests of your fellow citizens, even though you did not consider them your equals. In fine, she found you incomprehensible, and that galled her quite as much as her insolence galls you."

"Vendeley never told you all that," Sir Andrew said with conviction.

"Not in quite those terms, no, but in a roundabout way, she did. She's mentioned upon occasion that you were extraordinarily lucky—that she'd wanted desperately to kill you, and had orders to kill you, but that the right opportunity never arose. Yet it seems to me she had opportunities enough. Once she went so far as to confess that, short of killing you, what she most wanted at that time was to force you to respect her—as she'd been forced to respect you. And in that I should say she succeeded."

"I respected her as an adversary, no more," Sir Andrew insisted.

"And now that she is no longer an adversary, you no longer respect her?"

Sir Andrew frowned uneasily. He had never yet bested Lady Celia in an argument, and had, in fact, no desire to do so. Words were her province, and deeds were his. But a warning instinct told him that it would be as well, in this case, to tread carefully. "I should not call it 'respect,' not exactly," he said cautiously.

"No, no more should I, if I were to speak plainly," Lady Celia agreed, "but to give it its proper name would never do. Still, I trust we are none of us in much danger, for you and Rolande would both think less of yourselves if you admitted to this mutual fascination.

And no doubt it is better so. Yes, decidedly better, don't you agree?"

Sir Andrew did not. Mutual fascination indeed! Vendeley was no better than a common criminal—cunning, yes, in the shrewd way of her kind—and bold enough, if brazen audacity were courage—but the very idea that she . . . that he. . . . But before he could begin to marshal his defense, there was a knock at the door, and Martin, his houseman, came into the parlor.

"Lady Alicen Kendry is here to see you, m'lord, most insistent. She says she's come on a matter of the gravest import."

"Show her to the reception room," Sir Andrew said resignedly, rising.

"How tiresome of her!" exclaimed Lady Celia. They would work Andrew to death among the lot of them. "But I suppose you must see her. She'd not intrude herself at such an hour without good reason."

Sir Andrew nodded. "She may have discovered something about the attempt on her life, and if so, she is right to tell me. Whoever poisoned her very likely attacked me as well."

But Alicen lost no time in making known the true object of her visit. Sir Andrew had no sooner entered than she demanded, without further greeting, "What do you mean, sir, by keeping the Princess Oriana hidden here? The one weapon needed to overthrow the Deps, and you let her pass the time picking weeds and mixing salves! I needn't tell you that such an act could be construed as the basest treachery. She's rightly Queen of Albin—why have you taken no steps to see her crowned?"

At least her loyalty is established, Sir Andrew thought, and asked wearily, "How did you discover this, Lady Alicen? Is Her Highness's identity com-

monly known among the Duke of Wyston's people
now?"

Alicen had been pacing the chamber furiously as she
spoke, but at Sir Andrew's words she sank limply into
the nearest chair and stared at him, her face suddenly
chalk-white. "God's Grace!" she whispered. "It's true,
then."

Sir Andrew closed his eyes for a moment, as if in
pain. "Celia was right—I should have been resting.
Only exhaustion could have made me fall into such a
trap. You only suspected."

Alicen nodded weakly. "It seemed fantastic, but—"
She shook her head abruptly, trying to clear her
thoughts. "You needn't reproach yourself. I'd have
found out the truth one way or another."

"No doubt you would." He was not, in fact, unduly
troubled. He had received a satisfactory report of
Alicen from Sir Warren, and would most likely have
sent for her soon, if not for his wound. Indeed, had her
first loyalty been to the Duke rather than the Princess,
she would have reported her suspicions to him and
awaited his orders before revealing her hand to Sir Andrew. That she had come here openly and alone, thus
putting herself in Sir Andrew's power, in effect, argued
that she meant no ill to the Princess. "Have you told
anyone else what you suspected?" he asked, though he
knew perfectly well what her answer would be.

Alicen gave him an impatient look. "How could I? If
I were wrong, I'd be a laughingstock, and if I were
right I'd be a traitor. Which do you take me for?"

"I take you for the agent of one of the main pretenders to the throne. Now that you know the truth, what
do you plan to do?"

"There would be no pretenders to the throne if the
Princess had asserted her claim! What do *I* plan to do?

It is surely for me to ask that of you. I've been making a bloody fool of myself riding over hill and dale to solicit support for the Duke of Wyston, and all the while you've had the true heir in your garden."

"It was the safest place for her."

"Perhaps. But the only place for her now is the court. She's of age, she's certainly fit of limb and sound of mind—she should be raising an army to reclaim her homeland. As a figurehead alone, she'd be a godsend, though that one is capable of more, unless I miss my guess. A true Obelen," Alicen said in wonder, "but one who was only a child before the Uprising—not accountable, in the eyes of her people, for the faults of the old order. She is the perfect rallying point to unite all of Albin against the Chamber!"

"Agreed," said Sir Andrew, fairly reeling under Alicen's assault. How had she obtained control of the discussion, he asked himself, and put him on the defensive? "But to bring her to the attention of the enemy before we have laid the groundwork of our campaign would put her at too great a risk. And any disclosure of her identity or whereabouts that has not been expressly sanctioned by Her Highness *will* be regarded as high treason, Lady Alicen, I warn you."

Alicen flushed angrily, but said only, "What do you propose, then? You cannot mean to let things go on as they are—you said as much to me at our last meeting."

She had, of course, no right to expect answers to her questions, but Sir Andrew saw no reason to withhold such information from her now. Given what she already knew, he had only two choices where she was concerned—to use her or to kill her. He was convinced that her potential value outweighed her potential threat, but in either case it could do no harm to tell her of their plans. "We are approaching such allies as may

lend strength to our cause, those whose loyalty is un-
questioned. We are well aware that we would be fortunate to count His Grace the Duke of Wyston among
their number. Already, by your own report, he has won
the support of powerful nobles and widespread devotion among the people as well. He could bring a more
powerful force to Oriana's cause than could be
achieved by any other means in so short a time. But
will he set aside his own ambitions to support the Princess? He means to be King."

If he expected Alicen to be nonplussed by his sug-
gestion, he was mistaken, for this was a question she
had already considered thoroughly. Without hesitation,
she said, "The Duke's ambitions are not for himself
alone, but for Albin. I cannot, of course, pretend to answer for him, but I am nevertheless certain that he
would do all in his power to serve the Princess Oriana,
if he knew that she lived."

Sir Andrew nodded thoughtfully. "Sir Warren says
the same."

"Am I to carry word to him, then? Delay can serve
no purpose in this matter. Every day that he remains in
ignorance of her existence will only mean more work
done that must be undone, and the enemy will profit
from our confusion." Alicen understood that, if Sir Andrew regarded the Duke as a dangerous rival claimant
to the throne, she would never reach him alive with
tidings of the Princess. But she also knew that he'd be
a fool to antagonize the Duke of Wyston, and she did
not think Sir Andrew was a fool.

Before Sir Andrew could reply, Katin slipped into
the room through the curtained doorway to the side
chamber. Alicen stood and bowed, flushing a little at
the thought of the way she had stalked and harried her
sovereign in the workshed, like a cat with a cornered

mouse. "Your Highness," she said, "I trust I have not offended you beyond redress by my clumsy attempts to get at the truth."

Katin laughed. "Truth be known, I was more offended by your treatment of my poor little dog. I'm afraid I forget that others may not be accustomed to fending off flying watchdogs. Pray be seated, Lady Alicen."

Sir Andrew had not troubled himself to stand at the Princess' entrance. She did not expect such formal courtesies, and he was too damned tired besides. Katin sank into a chair herself, remarking, "What a wearisome business this is, to be sure! First I needs must spend myself to prove to one that I *am* the Princess, then to prove to another that I'm only an apothecary. It's a wonder that I can remember who I am, myself, from hour to hour."

"Lady Alicen offers her services as courier to the Duke of Wyston," said Sir Andrew. "What is Your Highness' will concerning this?" The question was meant for Alicen's benefit. He and Katin had known the answer for some time.

Katin smiled warmly at Alicen. "My *view,* sir, if not my will, is that we are fortunate indeed to have Alicen Kendry with us now. The House of Kendry has ever been steadfast in its loyalty and honorable in all its dealings. We must know the Duke of Wyston's mind in this matter, and Lady Alicen is his trusted agent—who better to learn his intentions and report them to us faithfully?" Her meaning was not lost on Alicen. She was expected to betray the Duke, if need be, to serve her sovereign. "After all," Katin said, with a sudden grin, "I need fear no treachery from one who owes me her life!"

Katin soon left them, explaining ruefully that she

must dress for dinner. "I trust you will join us, my lady?" she said to Alicen, but since her words were a command, not an invitation, she didn't wait for an answer.

Alicen looked after her for a moment, still hardly able to believe her own discovery. Then turning to Sir Andrew, she said, "I see the mansion is nearly completed. Have you given a name to the estate?"

Sir Andrew would have preferred to discuss his message to the Duke of Wyston, but he answered politely, "Folk hereabout have taken to calling it 'the Governor's.' There seems little point to our naming it now—who knows how much longer we'll be here?"

But Alicen was not really attending to his words. "If I had the naming of the place," she said, "I believe I'd call it 'Wyldendale.' "

* * *

Captain Brodery filled the doorway of Blythe's makeshift surgery and glared at him threateningly. "What makes you so long about it, damn you?" he demanded. "There're three more waiting for your attentions!"

Blythe wiped his forehead with the back of one bloody hand. He'd been at work in the cramped and airless confines of the cabin belowdeck for hours, for the sloop *Windspurge* had put up a brave defense, and casualties had been heavy. The very inadequate assistance of Brodery's surgeon, Grindley, did little to alleviate matters, and Brodery's goading was the last thing Blythe needed. He glanced up at Brodery and snapped, "You're standing in my light. How do you expect me to extract the ball from this man's shoulder if I can't see what I'm doing?"

With a surprisingly swift movement for a large man, Brodery took two steps forward and struck Blythe a blow with the force of a boom. Blythe staggered back, slipped on the slick planking and crashed into the hold wall. Towering over him, Brodery said, "You'll do your job and hold your tongue, or you'll be the one needs a surgeon."

Blythe wiped the blood from his mouth and refrained from pointing out that he could do his job more effectively standing up. Why couldn't it be Brodery who lay helpless under his knife, instead of the sailor whose shoulder he was attempting to stitch with waxed shoemaker's thread? Brodery had been in the thick of the fighting, by all report, and the bastard had come out unscratched. Blythe glanced at his patient— mercifully still unconscious from loss of blood—and asked, "May I attend to him while we continue this discussion?" Grindley, he saw, had prudently vanished.

Brodery stepped back to allow Blythe to get to his feet, but when he did, the captain suddenly grabbed him by the collar and thrust him back against the cabin wall, snarling, "I don't like you."

Steeling himself for another blow, Blythe said, half-choking, "I had gathered that, but if you've nothing against your crewman there, you'll let me finish with him before it's too late."

Brodery let him go, but continued to glower at him as he bent over the hapless sailor on the table. " 'Twas you who gave evidence against Strasser and his crew, when the *Mandrake* was taken. You as good as hanged the lot of them."

"That was none of my doing," Blythe insisted, wiping his hands on a cloth that did not make them appreciably cleaner. "The navy captured the ship on their own when she was limping back after the attack. When they tried us, the magistrates examined the contracts. They showed I'd never signed on as a pirate."

Captain Brodery gave him a look of mingled suspicion and scorn. "Oh, aye, and neither had the cook, Carmine—still he was hanged with the crew, and you were not."

"I've explained that. There was testimony that he'd taken part in the attack, and that I had not done so. I was engaged only in treating the wounded, which is not a crime." Blythe began to search the wound with a long, curved probe.

"Informing on your crewmates is a crime, at sea," said Brodery. " 'Tis Providence has delivered you into my hands. . . . I'll need an able surgeon when the pay fleet is taken—we'll be hit heavy, hunting men-of-war." He spoke matter-of-factly of the danger, but his face broke into a cruel grin as he added, "But when that engagement's behind us, there'll come a reckoning, remember that. And don't think that Vendeley can protect you. She's no say in the matter—it didn't happen on her ship." Abruptly the captain turned on his heel and strode from the cabin, leaving Blythe to brood on his words.

If his life depended on proving to Brodery that he hadn't betrayed the *Mandrake*'s men to save his own neck, then his fate was sealed. There was no proof he could offer, and Brodery would discount any claim he made in his own defense. He had hoped to find some means of escaping the *Black Swan* before the attack on the pay fleet, but Brodery had made sure he was kept under strict watch this time, and now events were moving too rapidly for him. The captain had first seized a brig bound for Baradon and carrying thirty guns, and just now a second vessel had been taken, a sloop of some forty guns, bound from Acquitania. Blythe was still treating the wounded from this melee, but the captured ships were already being outfitted for the coming conflict. Brodery had ordered their course shaped for the Tintich Channel, and the attack on the pay vessel would come soon now.

Blythe picked up a scalpel and regarded it critically. He had managed to salvage most of his equipment from the *Azora,* only to be forced to abandon it on Needle Isle. Not only was this thing a poor surgical instrument, it wouldn't make much of a weapon either.

Corey, Ivy, and Raphe stood together on the foredeck of the *Black Swan,* looking toward the newly-taken *Windspurge.* She was to be Rolande's ship for the attack on the pay fleet, and a score of Brodery's men had been sent aboard her, under Rolande's direction, to fit her out for another battle. But the three of them were still awaiting orders, and Blythe was still occupied below.

"We're true pirates now," Raphe said with ill-disguised anticipation, leaning over the rail to watch the preparations on the *Windspurge.*

"Not a bit of it," said Ivy. "The pay ship belongs to the enemy, and we're within our rights to take her, under the authority of the colonial warrant."

Corey laughed at Raphe's crestfallen expression. "Well, don't be too disappointed, lad. In the Chamber's eyes we're pirates, right enough, and if we're caught, they'll hang us as high as the rest."

"They won't, then," Ivy said confidently. She'd been picklock, footpad, bandit, and pirate in her day, and had an experienced criminal's grasp of the fine points of the law. "We've not signed on under Brodery. We serve under duress. Of course," she added wistfully, "that means we won't get an ember of that great cargo of gold, either."

"As long as we get a ship," Corey said. "That's what the captain's after." Among themselves, "the captain" meant Rolande.

"Do you think Brodery will let Blythe ship with us?" Ivy asked. "A good surgeon's rarer than gold."

Corey looked uneasy. "I don't know. The captain's worried over it. Brodery doesn't like him."

"Neither do I," said Raphe, and spat over the rail. "Smug bastard. Brodery can have him, for all of me."

"I don't say I like him, exactly," Corey said with a shrug, "but I'll be glad enough to have him by if I take a musketball to the chest, and so will you, boy, trust me. That one knows his job."

"Aye, I just say he's a sly'un, that's all."

Ivy laughed. "Don't you know what our Raphe has against the good surgeon?" she teased. "Only that the captain takes him to bed, instead of her cabin-lad, eh?"

Raphe, flushing furiously, attempted to deny it, but made little headway. "Never mind, youngster," Corey chuckled, "maybe in ten years' time you'll be ripe enough for her tastes!"

Then, to Raphe's relief, Ivy spotted Rolande and Captain Brodery coming up on the forecastle from the gun deck of the *Windspurge*. "There they are at last," she said. "It won't be long now!"

"She's yours now, Vendeley," Brodery said in a faintly mocking tone. "I'll leave her to you. Be ready to weigh anchor as soon as the rest of the powder's stowed."

"Send my people aboard, then. I'll be ready."

Brodery shook his head. "And then what's to keep

you from taking your well-fitted new ship and sailing off, leaving me too short to take the pay fleet?"

The idea had certainly occurred to Rolande, but she'd reluctantly dismissed it as impracticable. She'd have only a handful of crew loyal to her, and all the rest Brodery's men. And even if they were willing to desert Brodery, *and* lose their chance at the pay fleet, she'd then have to outrun or outfight Brodery's other two ships. All in all, not bloody likely.

She pointed these facts out to Captain Brodery, adding, "I'd stand to lose more beside. It's not this forty-gun sloop I want, but one of the Chamber's men-of-war."

"You shall have one, if we take them," Brodery promised, "and hands enough to sail her, as we agreed. But till then your lot stays aboard the *Black Swan,* and if you try any treachery, Vendeley, 'tis they who'll suffer for it. I'll gut them myself, one by one."

There were, Rolande reflected, advantages and disadvantages to dealing with idiots. It was easy to bluff them, yes, but it was well nigh impossible to make them listen to reason. This trick of Brodery's would serve no purpose, but he'd never be brought to believe that. The more she argued, the more suspicious and stubborn he'd become.

"I don't say you'd play me false," Captain Brodery said, with his vicious grin, "but if I keep the kittens, I can better trust the cat. You abide by your orders, and you'll get your people back hale and whole when this engagement's done—I can't say fairer than that."

If any of us are hale and whole at the end of this engagement, Rolande thought grimly. But aloud she said only, "As you like, but let's get about it. It's been near a month since I sank one of the Chamber's vessels, man—I'm perishing of boredom!" He'd like that, the dolt.

Brodery did like it. Indeed, he thought well of Rolande, and would have been honestly surprised at her low opinion of him. He clapped her amiably on the shoulder, roared out, "We'll find you some game, then!" and swung down the ladder to the waiting long-boat, leaving her in command of the *Windspurge,* with a strange crew, and the others held hostage on the *Black Swan.*

There was nothing for it now but to go ahead, no other way to get her people out of Brodery's hands. But if she did her part, she reasoned, there was a good chance that Brodery would keep his word. He was known as one who dealt ruthlessly with his prey, but honorably with his fellow pirates, according to their own code of unwritten laws—and he regarded Rolande as one of his own kind, colonial charter or no. He had offered her her rightful share of the pay fleet's cargo, but she had bargained instead for a man-of-war and two score crewmen to sail her to South Oriana. She hoped to salvage some crew from among those pressed into service on the Chamber's vessels as well, for Brodery would probably herd them all onto the worst-damaged ships and sink the lot, if his reputation was to be believed. It was not Rolande's way, or the way of most pirates, but Brodery was in command of this venture, and he'd decide the fate of any crews they took captive. These were warships, after all, Rolande reminded herself. Their crews were the same who'd be sent to sink the ships of New Albin, when the expected invasion came to pass. Sir Andrew would see nothing wrong in her decreasing the numbers of the Chamber's navy—on the contrary, he'd be forced to commend her for such a result.

Not having the benefit of Lady Celia's insight on the subject, Rolande did not know why she so often viewed her actions in terms of their effect on Sir Andrew. Circumstances, she would have said, had compelled her to do so. And who wouldn't enjoy ruffling the feathers of that pompous, stiff-necked guinea-cock? She had told Lady Celia more of the truth about herself than she had ever told any other living being, but she had not revealed that she knew Sir Andrew was harboring the rightful ruler of Albin. That he was, in fact, a good deal more than a colonial governor made it all the more satisfying to be able to nettle him with impunity. Sooner or later, she knew, Sir Andrew would move to overthrow the Chamber and place the girl on the throne—and the intelligence Rolande had been gathering on conditions in Albin suggested that the time was approaching. Destroying the pay ship and its escort of military vessels could thus be regarded as service, not only to the Colonies, but to the Crown.

Rolande laughed aloud, wondering what Brodery would think if he knew that their three pirate vessels were, at least for the present, the Queen's Royal Navy of Albin. Perhaps they were both of them Admirals now. . . .

She thought again of her lordly rank a fortnight later, when the pay fleet was sighted, but this time her laughter held little mirth or amusement. What a joke that she who, since childhood, had hated the monarchy and the order it represented, should now be about to *die* in the service of the Crown! At the shout of the lookout high above the main mast in the crow's nest, "Man-of-war to starboard!" Rolande had raised her spyglass and made out several fast approaching vessels in the distance. Not long afterward, the Chamber's ship hove into view, accompanied by three massive fifty-gun men-of-war.

We're for it now, Rolande thought, eyeing the defenders of the pay vessel. The score of pirate ships still held moored at Needle Isle could have surrounded the pay fleet and made short work of the escort, but carrying out the same strike with three ships would be madness. Yet what choice had she? Captain Brodery was committed to this venture, and Rolande had no doubt that he would let them all die before he backed down. He had ordered her to attack from the point, hoping to spare his own ships the worst blows of retaliation, and she could do nothing else, lest he visit his vengeance on those of her crew who were held at his mercy. Then suppose that, in spite of Brodery's threat, she did order retreat . . . would the crew of the *Windspurge* obey her . . . ?

"All hands to your stations!" she bellowed from the quarterdeck. "Look lively!"

By the time they closed with the approaching Albinate ships, the pirate vessels were flying the flags of Castilian traders. With just three ships, the only logical strategy was to draw as near as possible before receiving a direct challenge, then strike at once without warning. They fell in with the pay fleet at nightfall and kept near till morning, when the trumpets from the men-of-war broke the stillness of dawn. Seeing by daylight that the three ships were closing with them, the captain of the *Burning Brand,* the foremost of the men-of-war, grew suspicious, despite the display of Castilian flags. The foreign vessels might, of course, be hovering near the well-armed pay fleet for protection from pirates, but if so they should have identified themselves by now. He hailed the *Black Swan,* demanding to know her name and her business, and Captain Brodery had a Castilian among his crew answer that they were Castilian merchantmen who had banded together for defense in these dangerous waters. Still dissatisfied with the look of Brodery and his crew, the captain of the *Burning Brand* ordered them to stand off and send a boat with their charter of ownership, proving that they were as they claimed, or else approach at their peril. Brodery's answer was to fire a broadside at the *Burning Brand,* then turn his vessel and sail off, hoping to draw the Chamber's ship after him into the *Dawn*'s range. If they could disable one of the Chamber's vessels, it would make it more difficult for the others to mount an effective defense while having to maneuver around her. The lead man-of-war, the *Burning Brand,* turned to pursue, but as she made after Brodery, the second pirate ship, the *Dawn,* commanded by Brodery's lieutenant, opened fire upon her. The initial shot cut the halyards of the approaching vessel, but the other men-of-war swiftly drew into a line, adding their fire to the *Burning Brand*'s, forcing the pirates to draw back.

Rolande brought the *Windspurge* around, coming up astern of the *Judgment,* the hindmost of the three men-of-war in the line, and fired a barrage of chain and bar shot at the *Judgment*'s rigging. The engagement raged for hours, fiercely fought on both sides, but the Albinate sailors discharged their guns so smartly that the pirates were unable to close sufficiently to board. It was past noonday when a well-aimed volley from the *Burning Brand* hit the powder store of the *Dawn,* and the vessel blew up in a great roar of fire.

Amid the smoke and flames from the burning *Dawn,* the other men-of-war closed toward Brodery, coming about so that they could hammer the pirate sloop with

their guns broadside. Behind them, the pay vessel
tailed around, firing eighteen-pounders toward the
Windspurge to prevent her from coming around to aid
her sister ship.

When at last Captain Brodery realized that he could
not prevail against the better armed vessels, it was already too late to flee. He tried to fill sail and make an
escape, but a volley from the *Judgment* caught the re-
treating *Black Swan* broadside with a decisive blow,
making a great hole in the hull. Seeing that all was
lost, Brodery gave the order to abandon ship, and pirates raced toward the longboats, struggling to cut the
gripes that held them in place, before the ship sank.
Blythe, who had been attending to the wounded below,
scrambled up on deck, hoping to escape. The *Black
Swan* tilted ominously to starboard, and Blythe's coat
was hooked by a mizzen brace. Fearing he would be
pulled down with the ship and drowned, Blythe slashed
frantically at the cloth with a scalpel, until he was able
to cut himself free, then leaped into the ocean and
swam to one of the long boats, which the pirates had
finally succeeded in lowering.

Seeing the *Black Swan* foundering, the other two
Albinate men-of-war turned their guns full upon
Rolande's ship. The first mate of the *Windspurge,* stationed not far from Rolande, was killed at once and fell
to the deck almost at her feet. Rolande ordered her
gunners to return fire, and the rest of her crew to maneuver the vessel into a position from which they
could break away from the other ships and flee. Dis-
tantly she could hear the captain of the *Judgment* calling to his officers to prepare to board the pirate vessels
and take their crews prisoner. One man-of-war bore
down on the *Windspurge,* coming in close as she continued to fire her heavy guns. The *Windspurge,* racked

by round after round of fire, careened. All about was the screaming and moaning of the wounded and dying.

On the foundering *Black Swan* Captain Brodery called for quarters, attempting to surrender, but the first mate of the *Judgment,* ignoring his signal, ordered another round of fire, killing two more of the pirates still lowering longboats on deck. He would have continued the assault, but the Captain of the *Judgment* ordered a halt, and called for a boarding party. Drawing up to the ruined pirate ship, the Albinate sailors boarded the vessel and quickly forced Brodery and his pirates back to their own vessel as prisoners.

Rolande dispassionately surveyed the rigging as the *Windspurge* tried to speed away, dully noting the shattered bowsprit, shredded sails, broken stays, cut ratlines, split staves, and the dead and wounded strewn about the deck.

She should have been able to outrun the heavier men-of-war, but her ship was too crippled for the chase, listing so far astern that her topmast was scarcely out of the water. No, the fight was thoroughly lost, she'd known it since the *Dawn* was blown to bits, and its remains sunk below the waves. She'd seen Brodery's ship foundering, the survivors of his crew herded aboard the *Judgment*. Whether her people had lived or died in the battle and its aftermath, they were beyond Brodery's wrath now. When the man-of-war hot in pursuit of her came up beside her beleaguered vessel and fired a single gun in warning, Rolande turned to her second mate and ordered the *Windspurge*'s colors struck. Rolande stood poised near the forecastle rail, staring at the approaching man-of-war. As a final barrage racked the vessel fore and aft, she was thrown off balance, plunging into the roiling waves below.

It was almost with relief that the pirates viewed the naval seamen come aboard the obviously sinking ship, but such feelings were short-lived as the prisoners were taken aboard the *Judgment* and clapped in irons. When the victors had scoured the *Windspurge* for all living souls, they turned their attention to those who were adrift in the sea, having fallen or jumped from the doomed vessels.

The icy water shocked Rolande from her torpor so that she found herself fighting against the waves, searching desperately for something to grab onto. A plank from the hull bobbed by, and she clutched at it, but her fingers were stiff from the cold water and it slipped from her grasp. As the board was carried beyond her reach, she began to swim desperately after it, held back by her sodden boots and her numb, heavy limbs. There was nothing else nearby to cling to, and she thought, as the cold sapped her strength, *Why not end it now?* So much easier to let herself sink than to keep up this painful, useless struggle. So much better to let the sea take her than her enemies. . . .

A yard snapped off the ship nearby and fell into the sea with a great crash, barely missing her. A wall of salt water poured over her, and she flailed wildly, certain that she was on the point of drowning. Knocked underwater by the broken crosstree dangling from the yard, she made a last effort to break the surface again, disoriented in the icy darkness, and unable, despite herself, to surrender to death without a fight. Then she felt hands gripping her, and she was hauled from the water into a longboat, coughing and desperately sucking down air—and thinking as she did so, *Fool!* A worse death than drowning surely awaited her at the hands of the Chamber.

* * *

The hold of the *Judgment* was illumined only by an oil lamp their captors had left hanging from the rafters, to allow them to see that all the prisoners were secure when they ventured into the hold with food and water. When her eyes were used to the half-darkness, Rolande peered around her, looking for any of her own crew among her fellow captives. She made out Blythe lying not far from her, but was alarmed to see no sign of the others. The prisoners had been divided among the men-of-war, and she had no way of knowing whether those of her crew who were not on this vessel had survived.

Blythe was watching her, and now they crawled toward one another through the press of bodies, dragging the chains that were threaded through rings on the wall. "I thought you drowned," said Blythe.

"I tried. What of the others?"

"Take care!" He grabbed one of the chains dangling between the manacles about her wrists, as it swung toward his face. "Corey and Raphe were taken—they must be aboard the *Burning Brand.* But Ivy . . ." He hesitated, then said flatly, "A cannonball—it took half her head with it."

Rolande understood him. He was not telling her that Ivy had died a particularly gruesome death, but that she had died quickly and painlessly. She nodded. "She was luckier than the rest of us, maybe. Blythe . . ." Rolande gave a weak laugh. "I hope it's some consolation to you to know that you were right, after all—it was a harebrained scheme, and no mistake. I'm sorry you were caught in it."

But Blythe shook his head. "I'm not complaining. If we'd stayed on Needle Isle, Brodery would have made port there and been snared by Tyrrel with the rest of us. I'm better off here than trapped on two square miles of island with that one. His notion of justice is worse than the Chamber's."

Rolande huddled against Blythe for warmth, shivering in her wet clothes. The hold, below the waterline, was dank and chill, and their captors had not seen fit to provide them with blankets. *What's it to them if a few of us die on the way? Just that many less to hang.* "It looks like being a long trip," she muttered. "Why don't you tell me why Brodery was so keen to keelhaul you? It wasn't because you escaped from his ship by swimming to shore!"

"No," Blythe admitted. "It's because the man's a pig-headed, thrice-damned fool. I may as well tell you the tale, I suppose—it can do no harm now. When I was still serving by force on the *Black Swan,* Brodery determined to capture at one stroke a pair of Albinate merchantmen, both of them well-armed and promising vast stores of goods. He first seized a small gun boat of the Castilians, the *Mandrake,* and put his first mate Nief Strasser aboard as captain. With the two vessels he was certain he could take the Albinites—"

"Aye, why not?" Rolande interrupted. "I'd have done the same."

"Oh? You've a warrant to attack Castilian vessels now, have you?"

"I mean, I *could* have taken the merchantmen with those two ships. If I were a pirate, that is, not a privateer. . . . Go on with your story, man, can't you?"

"Aye, Captain. I daresay he could have done it, at that—I saw him win against worse odds. But he didn't know that the merchant ships had recruited a man-of-war to meet them at Bell Point and serve as escort between Albin and the Colonies. The attack was already underway when the third ship arrived and joined the battle, moving to trap Brodery between her guns and a merchantman's. He'd no choice but to retreat under full sail and make away. I was with Strasser, and we tried to do the same, but we didn't get far. The man-of-war made a direct hit on our ballast compartment, and the *Mandrake* only managed to limp a short distance away before she careened, and we were forced to abandon ship. The man-of-war hauled in those not drowned, and took us back to Albin to stand trial. The lot of them were hanged."

"But your name didn't appear on the crew roster."

"Of course not. I could prove I'd been taken off the *Glory* when Brodery sank her—I'd my sailing orders from Captain Stanwyck. The magistrates released me without so much as an argument—but Brodery won't have it. He's convinced I somehow betrayed his crew, as if there was any need for that, when they'd been caught in the act! But once that one gets hold of an idea, however crack-brained, there's no turning him from it, not with a capstan."

"Aye, that's why we're here," Rolande agreed. "But why didn't you tell me that in the first place? I never believed the bilge you did tell me."

Blythe laughed. "Why would I have told you the truth? As far as I was concerned, you were just another murdering, witless pirate like Brodery. My experience of pirates was rather limited in those days," he added, clapping his hand about Rolande's arm. "I've come to think better of the breed, since."

Thinking of her lost crew, Rolande said bitterly, "I told you you're a bloody fool, Blythe. My people might better have gone begging than signed on with me."

"You didn't kill them, you know. Tyrrel did that. As for the rest of us, I tell you the magistrates have no reason to hold us—we're not of Brodery's crew. We'll be dismissed, as I was before."

Maybe you will, Rolande thought, *and the others, if they claim Brodery took them from some merchant ship. But what of me? If the magistrates can't bring this charge home to me, they've a dozen others to chose from.* Yet Rolande knew that there was still one way she might win the Chamber's clemency and pardon. As she lay shivering on the bare boards of the dark hold, fettered and helpless, she no longer had the luxury of disregarding that last chance to escape execution for treason and piracy. In exchange for her life and her liberty, she could tell the Chamber what she knew about the Princess Oriana.

Chapter 8

From a far corner of the large communal cell came a continual whimpering plea, "Kill me, please ... someone ... have mercy ... kill me...." Every so often one of the other prisoners would threaten to comply if the fellow didn't hold his noise, but the begging went on, and no one attempted to silence him.

"Ivy said we'd not be hanged," Raphe whispered, crouching back against the stone wall, with his arms wrapped around himself for warmth. Lichfield Prison in Avenford was, if anything, more dank and cold than the hold of the man-of-war, with only heaps of straw between the prisoners and the bare stone. "But maybe we'll never have a chance to address the Magistrate. They say the warden here shows no mercy to pirates, because his son was killed by them on a voyage in the Perango Isles. I've heard that he'll take them out at random and set them up as a mark to shoot at! There's a man here says he knows of several who were killed thus—shot down in cold blood for target practice."

Rolande had heard the same tale about highwaymen, footpads, and smugglers. "Rubbish," she snapped. "The guards tell such stories to keep their prisoners cowed, and calfbrains like you believe them." She herself had believed rumors even more lurid when she'd first been imprisoned for theft, but she'd been at least five years younger than Raphe, and she'd soon figured out for herself that the truth was bad enough without embellishment.

"Then . . . then they don't torture prisoners just for a wager?" Raphe said hopefully, "to see how long they'll—"

"No! Just keep quiet and do not spread tales," Rolande ordered, and he lapsed into uneasy silence.

Raphe was no coward, as he'd been at pains to demonstrate during every engagement since he'd joined the *Azora*'s crew. As a bondsman on an Albinate merchantman, he'd fought bravely to repel Rolande's boarding party, though the ship had soon been forced to surrender. One of the privateersmen who'd relieved him and his fellows of their weapons had noticed the fascinated way he was gazing at Rolande and dragged him forward, calling out, "Here, Cap'n, you've made a proper conquest of this one!"

Rolande had glanced his way and ordered, "Let him be—if the rest had fought like that one, we'd not be in possession now. I could use a dozen such lads."

Raphe had not been the only sailor to desert the merchantman for the *Azora,* but he was certainly the most eager. He'd proven his courage at every opportunity since—indeed, Rolande had more than once rebuked him for his foolhardiness—and it was not the danger of their situation that unnerved him now, but the gnawing uncertainty. He could have faced a definite threat, even a death sentence, as bravely as any, but he was unused to inaction, to being held in check. He needed to fight this captivity, even if he couldn't win, but Rolande had forbidden any such attempt to escape. Were they just supposed to wait patiently to be tortured or slaughtered by the Dep guards?

Looking around the large, open cell, stone on three

sides, iron bars and guards on the fourth, Raphe could see that there was no possible way for unarmed prisoners to break free, but he had confidently expected Rolande to have some plan of escape, nevertheless. All during the many weeks of the wretched journey to Albin in the hold of the *Burning Brand,* he had told himself that when all the captured pirates were delivered to their destination, and he and Corey were able to rejoin the captain, she would explain how the three of them were to get away. Blythe must surely have been drowned, he reasoned.

But what Rolande had told them, when he and Corey had found her—and unfortunately Blythe—in Lichfield Prison, was that it would be safest for them to acknowledge no connection with her. They must not address her as captain, or by her name. They were to tell the Magistrate that they'd been crewmen of the *Black Swan* when Brodery had first captured her and kept her in place of his much-damaged vessel, the *Wild Stag.* He'd forced their crewmates onto the *Wild Stag* and watched her sink, keeping only the two of them— because they'd fought boldly, he'd said—to replace a man and a youth of his crew who'd been killed in the battle. They had never signed onto his crew, however, or profited by his piracy. They must claim to know nothing of Rolande, if asked, and she in turn would deny that they were her men. Brodery's crew roster would bear them out, and there was no reason for them to be disbelieved. As for her, she would try to give a false name, and if that didn't answer, she'd another card to play—never mind what. They were to remember the tale they had to tell and stick to it, that was all.

It was not the sort of plan Raphe had been anticipating. He wanted to take action—*now*—not wait until the law saw fit to give him a hearing, then try to lie his way to freedom. Worse than the disappointment of finding Blythe with Rolande had been finding that she expected him to be patient and crafty—traits that were not at all in his nature—instead of bold and daring. He huddled against the wall, beset by a host of dire apprehensions, and trying to be as calm and impassive as his captain.

His misgivings would have been twice as strong had he known that Rolande, despite her cool and collected manner, found their confinement every bit as hard to bear as he did. The memories of her ill usage at the hands of her gaolers here, in the past, had never left her, and now they assailed her with insistent, merciless clarity. *I'm not a helpless child any longer,* she told herself, but that was exactly how she felt. Only the knowledge that it could be fatal to show weakness, either to one's enemies or to one's followers, allowed her to maintain a facade of undaunted confidence.

Then the soft, desperate pleading began again, from the dark recesses of the cell, followed by groans and curses from the other prisoners.

"Shove a fistful of straw in 'is face!"

"Do it yourself!"

"I *will,* 'fore long, if he don't leave off."

Raphe brought the dying man a dipper of water, and stayed by him for a time, but after a while the sufferer didn't seem to know that anyone was there, and Raphe came away more worried than before.

"Well, but what about him?" he asked Rolande hesitantly, fearing to anger her again.

"What *about* him?"

"*He's* been tortured—he told me so just now, though anyone could see it."

"If he was, 'twasn't for sport," Rolande said impatiently. She was in no mood to offer reassurance to the boy. Like a caged animal, she wanted to strike out at whoever came closest, but she told herself, *it's your fault he's here,* and said, "Look here, they don't put folk to the question here without a reason, and being a pirate's not reason enough. It was so even before the Uprising, and the Deps are all the stricter about such things. I know them. They'd enjoy torturing the lot of us, no doubt, but luckily they've laws to forbid anything they'd enjoy."

And it was true, Rolande reflected, that Lichfield Prison was a less dangerous and brutal place, now that the Deps were in power. As a rule, she had little use for the Deprivant creed of self-denial and abstinence, but the Governors of the prison were sure to be high-ranking members of the Church, who enforced Dep discipline on the officers and guards under them. Much as she hated to give credit to the Chamber, still a lad like Raphe was far safer from abuse here now than she had been as a youth, within these walls.

But Raphe was not convinced. "Then why did they torture him? He's only a thief, he says. He doesn't know anything about warships, but they thought he did, so they must have taken him for a pirate, too, and—"

"Fetch some more water!" Rolande ordered, and strode off toward the far corner of the cell, kicking Blythe as she passed him, and gesturing him to follow. At first she thought the thief was dead already, but when she leaned closely over him, she could just make out his labored breathing. "Can you do aught for him?" she asked Blythe, making room for him to kneel beside the contorted figure.

After a cursory examination, Blythe gave a low whistle, and shook his head. "Not even if I had my instruments, or medicines . . . no one could. He'll not last the night. I can't tell you why he's still alive now."

Rolande took the water from Raphe and looked down at the dying man uncertainly. It seemed unpardonably cruel to rouse him from that merciful stupor, but such a chance was not likely to come again. She carefully raised his head and tipped a little of the water into his mouth, then let the rest run over his face.

"That's not going to help," Blythe told her. "You'll only—"

"Quiet!" Rolande ordered, as the prisoner opened his eyes. But his gaze was vague and unfocused. If he saw anything at all, it wasn't the people around him.

"Please . . ." he whispered, "kill me."

Rolande touched his hand, and he started as if she'd struck him, peering at her with an unexpected clarity. "You're an officer," he said, and made a feeble attempt to turn away from her.

Am I? "I don't serve the Chamber," she assured him hastily. "I'm captain of a colonial vessel."

The man's voice rose to a trembling wail. "I'm not a spy!"

"No, no, I know you're not. It's all right!" Rolande's heart seemed to be galloping. *The papers she'd sent Sir Andrew had been on a ship bound for Avenford.* "Can you tell me why they thought you were a spy? Why did they ask you about the warship?"

"I don't know about any ship!" he gibbered, half sobbing. "I never saw it!"

"Vendeley, for pity's sake—" Blythe began.

Ignoring him, Rolande said softly, "Listen to me, man. Try! We're not the enemy, I tell you. Do you understand?"

That one fact seemed to reach him, for he looked at

Rolande again, and begged, "If you're a friend—kill me!"

Rolande did not answer at once. When she did, her words were slow and deliberate, and she looked the man in the eye as she spoke. "Very well, if you tell me what I need to know, I'll kill you. I swear it."

"I don't know anything about it," he cried weakly. "I *told* them that!"

Blythe grasped Rolande's arm and tried to pull her away. "This is unconscionable—I can't permit it! Kill him or let him die in peace, but stop this—"

"*I told you to be quiet!*" Rolande broke his grip with a sharp jab of her elbow, and turned on him with a look of such savage fury that he withdrew a few paces. "If you can't help, stay out of the way, imbecile! Do you think I want to do this? Let me get it over with!" Turning back to the wretched prisoner, she said with astonishing gentleness, "I'm sorry to hound you. I know you didn't see the ship—never mind about the ship, it doesn't matter. Just tell me what happened. How did they come to arrest you? That's all I want. Just try to tell me that much—*please!*"

He licked his lips, still dark with dried blood. "Then you'll . . . ?"

"My word on it. Do you want more water?"

"No. I can't. Martingale Pier. The warehouse there, so many guards. I thought, gold shipment. But they're *building something there,* that's all I saw. Then they caught me. . . ."

He broke into a racking cough that brought fresh blood with it, and Blythe knelt beside him again, one arm beneath his shoulders, to ease the strain. "Are you *finished* with him yet?" he spat, glaring at Rolande.

"Yes," she said evenly. "Tell me, what's quickest, strangling or smothering?" The man lay limp now,

eyes closed, his breath a rasping wheeze. Rolande
would have given anything she had for a sharp knife.

"You'd better let me see to it. I know what I'm
doing."

Rolande nodded, showing neither reluctance nor relief. Then she leaned over the hapless thief again and
said, "You've done well this night, friend. What
you've told me may save many lives, and help bring
down the Chamber." But she couldn't tell whether or
not he heard. Blythe flexed his skillful, surgeon's fingers, and Rolande turned away and left him to his
work.

* * *

The stone hall where the Magistrate presided was
drafty, but it was warmed by the great press of people
who'd come to see the trial of the infamous pirate
Brodery and his confederates. They filled the long
rows of wooden benches on both sides of the hall and
stood packed against the walls, filling the space to the
broad oak door.

*And a much greater crowd will gather by the gibbets
on Pittman's Wharf, to watch the mass hanging,*
Rolande thought grimly. As a child, she had profited
by the opportunity to pick a good many pockets on the
occasion of such festivities, and even then she had
taken for granted that she would one day provide the
same opportunity for other pickpockets. As she stood
with the other prisoners in the dock, her hands bound
once more with manacles and chain, she wondered
whether that day was now upon her.

The Advocates for the Chamber and the Accused,
seated at carved mahogany tables toward the front,
looked full of self-importance in their long silk

robes, and even the clerks on their stools held themselves with a deliberate, dignified air as they prepared
their quills to record this momentous proceeding. The
Magistrate had already taken his place upon the dais at
the very front of the chamber. From the massive, high-
backed chair behind his long table, he commanded a
clear view of the Advocates, the witnesses, and the
prisoners in the dock. Rolande, looking at his severe
and disapproving visage, was under no illusion as to
the sentence he planned to impose, once the legal formalities were concluded. The Chamber certainly
wasn't going to recognize the commission empowering
her to sink their ships, nor were they like to show
mercy to one who had been their trusted agent, then
turned traitor to their cause.

But there remained the possibility that the Chamber
didn't know she was on trial here. It would have been
a different matter if she'd been captured at the command of the *Azora*, but as it was, she had been taken
for merely a member of Brodery's crew, and had seen
no reason to correct her captors' error. The Magistrate
and his Advocates would not expect to find the well-
known freebooter Rolande Vendeley in the service of
another captain, unless they learned it from Brodery.
The ordinary crewmen would only be questioned as to
their own identities, and nothing else they might say
would be taken into account.

Rolande had some grounds to hope that Brodery
hadn't given her away. He had not been thrown into
the common cell with the rest of them, but imprisoned
separately, as leader of the malefactors. If he had revealed Rolande's identity to the authorities, she, too,
would surely have been isolated from the others, but
she'd been treated as just another of Brodery's followers.

It would be no safer to be tried as a pirate than as herself, however—either way would end on the gallows. *And if I'm going to hang,* Rolande brooded, *it will damned well be for an offense I intended to commit, not for something I was forced into by a scrofulous sea bandit with the wits of a jellyfish!* Far better to avoid the hangman altogether, and it was to this end that she had lied about her identity when she had been brought forth for trial, and warned her people not to acknowledge her. As the sergeant at arms called for order and silence, Rolande let her spine and shoulders slump, and hung her head so that her hair fell into her eyes. The shallow head wound she'd received in the battle had nearly healed, but she'd had Blythe bandage it nonetheless, in such a way as to partly cover her face. If her anonymity could save her, she would not have to bargain for her life by putting the noose 'round Oriana's neck instead of her own.

When the Hall of Justice had settled, and a prayer had been read, beseeching the intervention of the Good God in all matters magisterial, the Chamber's Advocate proffered a parchment to the Magistrate seated behind the high oak table on the dais. "I have here an exact accounting of the abominations committed by the notorious pirate, Nicholas Brodery, his officers, and their company," the Advocate intoned ponderously. "Herein is a comprehensive list of the vessels brutally attacked and ransacked by these Godless adventurers, with the provisions and lading of the vessels lost."

The Magistrate took the document and studied it, then passed it to the court clerk to be read aloud. The spectators listened enthralled to accounts of fortunes pillaged and ships' companies slaughtered, vessels set alight and left to drift with all hands aboard, prisoners subjected to hideous tortures. Brodery listened also, standing apart, in shackles and under special guard. He appeared impassive—indeed uninterested—but he laughed aloud at the description of himself ripping the heart from a living man and devouring it raw. The crowd was not disappointed in Captain Brodery. They would be able to report to avid listeners that the nefarious buccaneer had laughed, yes *laughed,* at the remembrance of his monstrous deeds.

Rolande didn't doubt that Brodery was responsible for attacking most of the vessels in question, and it was true that he rarely left living witnesses, but then how had these vivid details of his supposed atrocities been obtained? *But he'll not deny any of it,* she thought. Why should he? He knew he was going to hang—he might as well leave behind a reputation so fearsome that his name would live on after him.

At the conclusion of this bloody recitation, the Magistrate raised his eyes in silent communion with a God no less offended than he, and proclaimed, "Such fiends, scarcely meriting the name of men, perpetrators of every outrage against the innocent, have cast themselves out from the grace of our Good God and given themselves wholly in thrall to the Evil One."

The Chamber's Advocate was clearly much gratified at the reception his carefully prepared materials had received. If he had been planning a long summation, he now determined that it was unnecessary, for he concluded simply, "In very truth, My Lord, they are sowers of chaos, the subjects of no nation, obedient neither to God's law nor man's. It is our God-given duty to punish such malefactors for the salvation of their fellows and the peace of all God-fearing people. By making an example of such as these, we may impress upon others of their kind that they assault our ships and citizens at their own peril, and by the same means may honest mariners be saved from the temptation to adopt their evil ways."

When the Chamber's Advocate had resumed his seat, the Magistrate turned to the Advocate for the Accused and asked whether he had anything to say in defense of the prisoners. The question, his tone implied, was purely ceremonial, and he did not look pleased when the prisoners' Advocate rose, bowed, and replied that duty compelled him to bring forward a few matters of apparent significance.

Of the guilt of the company in general, he allowed, there could be no reasonable doubt whatsoever, as they had been taken in the very act of unprovoked attack against vessels engaged in lawful commerce. However, a careful examination of the contracts and crew roll of Captain Brodery's ship the *Black Swan* had revealed that there were some few among the prisoners who were not listed thereon, and who might therefore be presumed to be serving under duress.

The Magistrate sat back with a sigh, for all those who sailed the seas, excepting the officers of the Chamber's navy, were undoubtedly unreliable trash, and drawing such fine distinctions among vermin seemed to him an utter waste of time. Yet he could not deny the weight of his charge, which forbade that he should falsely condemn one who was innocent in the eyes of the law. Reluctantly, he turned again to the documents before him. "To which of the accused do you refer?" he asked in a bored tone.

"In the first place, My Lord, be it observed that the ship's roster shows no women contractually signed aboard as crew. We may thus safely conclude that those females captured with the pirates are merely women of the type commonly found on such vessels, who take part in neither the pirates' depredations nor their profits, and so are generally accounted guiltless for the crimes of the crew."

The Magistrate waved this aside impatiently. It was a matter that usually went without saying, or at least without saying at such length. "Yes, yes, that is generally the case," he agreed. "And the reports of our officers who were present confirm the presumption?"

"They do, My Lord, with the one exception of claims made to them by some of Captain Brodery's men that the known pirate and spy Rolande Vendeley was aboard one of the attacking vessels."

Rolande did not flinch at the mention of her name, though the sound seemed to strike her with the force of musket fire, and she could only hope that her people had remembered her warning not to look at her if she were spoken of. She felt sweat soak her matted hair and trickle between her breasts, and she wondered, *how can that be, when I'm cold as ice from scalp to sole?*

The Magistrate addressed the Chamber's Advocate once more. "Has this matter been made known to Their Excellencies of the Chamber of Statesmen?"

"It has, My Lord, and it needs nothing further to be done, as the traitor Vendeley perished in the battle at sea, by the just judgment of our Gracious God." He referred to his notes and read, "Captain Wolverton of the *Burning Brand* recorded in his log after the battle that: 'The body of a woman armed for battle was recovered from the deck of the *Black Swan* and identified by the leader of these freebooters as Rolande Vendeley of New Albin, who, being without a ship, had joined his crew in hopes of winning a man-of-war to her own use in this enterprise. As the features had been much ravaged by artillery fire, it was deemed useless to attempt to preserve the corse for judicial examination, and it was consigned to the sea along with those of our dead and the enemy's.' "

Called upon to confirm the truth of this account before the God of the Righteous, Captain Brodery spat on the floor and said in tones of deep disgust, "Aye, 'twas Vendeley—or another wearing her clothes and weapons! Rot the luck! Half my crew were her men, and it took the heart to fight right out of them, when that one fell. I might ha' known the witch would bring me bad luck."

A hushed murmur of excitement ran through the crowd. Brodery in the dock, and Vendeley at the bottom of the sea! The effort to secure a place in the Hall of Justice for this event had paid handsomely, all agreed.

So I'm dead, then, Rolande thought feverishly. *No wonder I'm so cold.* She clenched her teeth to keep from breaking into giddy laughter.

The Magistrate picked up his quill and made notations upon the bill of charge before him, then said to the Advocate for the Accused, "The women, then, may be released. Are there others who must be brought to the attention of this proceeding?"

"Three only, My Lord, one Edward Blythe, surgeon—"

But the Magistrate interrupted him. "That has been arranged for. Captain Wolverton sent information regarding this Blythe." He took up a letter from among his documents and read, "Among the prisoners was an able surgeon, who gave the name Edward Blythe and offered his services to treat our wounded as well as those of the enemy. So favorably impressed were our ships' surgeons with his skill and the extent of his medical knowledge, that there can be but little doubt that he is as he represents himself. As only one sur-

geon, Arnold Grindley, appears on the roster of
Brodery's crew, and he has already been identified as
another man, it is the respectful recommendation of
myself and Captains Maxwell and Babson that the said
Edward Blythe be released from custody, as one serving aboard a pirate vessel only under duress." Again
the Magistrate made a notation, then asked with an air
of great patience, "And the remaining two?"

Corey and Raphe were quickly dealt with. Speaking
for both, Corey told the tale of their capture by
Brodery, then produced the rating papers he carried
from his days in the Albinate Navy. He could not read
them himself, but they were precious to him as proof
that he had been taught such skills as made him a worthy boswain's mate, and brought him higher pay. Now
they proved even more valuable because they bore his
name—a name that did not appear upon Brodery's
crew roll or contracts.

Raphe, having broken his contract with the merchantman, had no such papers. They had gone down in
the wreck, he explained, hoping that he would not be
asked to clarify which wreck he meant. But the Magistrate, at this point, did not much care to engage in a
long search for the boy's true history. It was Brodery,
the scourge of the seas, not some half-grown lad, who
represented the matter of import to the Chamber.
Corey's sworn oath that Raphe had served with him,
and was not Brodery's man, was deemed acceptable by
the Magistrate and the Chamber's Advocate, when
Corey humbly added, "Master Blythe, I am sure, will
confirm what I say, for he was aboard the *Swan* when
the boy and I were taken."

The Magistrate handed Corey's papers back to the
clerk, then nodded at the Prisoners' Advocate. "Thus,
Edward Blythe, Corey Rijnland, Raphe Comstock, and

the sundry female prisoners are free to go. Sergeant at Arms, release them."

As the manacles were removed from their wrists, the Magistrate's gaze turned to the other prisoners in the dock. "As for the rest, there is no doubt from the evidence so scrupulously presented," the Magistrate nodded at the Chamber's Advocate, "that the godless wretches appearing before this tribunal have themselves and in consort with diverse others as wicked, committed many great piracies upon honest vessels, to the discouragement of trade and the danger of all innocent travelers upon the seas. Such crimes not only stand in violation of the laws of nations, but are an affront to the Good God, in whose name I shall now pronounce sentence." The Magistrate smoothed his gray robes and turned to face the prisoners for the first time, his face stern and unyielding. "The accused are condemned to be hanged by the neck, and their bodies to hang on the gibbet at Pittman's Wharf for a fortnight, that others may take warning thereby, to what end such villainies will lead them."

* * *

Once Ruthven had received the brass cylinder from the gypsy child Arya, and was able to examine it, he'd realized its significance at once. It confirmed his suspicion that the attack on Sir Andrew, if carried out by a gypsy, as rumor had it, had nonetheless been instigated by someone else. Fenton would not have shown it to the gypsies if it were not somehow connected to the assailant, and Ruthven knew of only one assassin in the Chamber's employ who was likely to possess such an object.

Unlike Katin, Ruthven remembered well where he

had first seen a like cylinder. But he had better reason to remember, since he had been attacked with something taken from it, and barely escaped with his life, on that occasion. *No more could you ever catch me in Albin after that—no more shall you do so now. Kendry and I shall trap you between us like a hare between two hounds.*

He thought of clever, deceitful Alicen—a hindrance to his efforts on behalf of the Duke of Halkin, but a useful ally in this endeavor, for if he was correct as to the assassin's identity, it would need both of them to counter the threat. Nonetheless he was determined that, this time, he would be the one holding the weapon.

Dropping the cylinder into the top drawer of his room's single chest of drawers, he tapped his knuckles restlessly on the walnut top, frowning in frustration. Why had he been able to find no trace of the one he suspected anywhere in the colony? He could not be mistaken—it was absurd to suppose that the Chamber had engaged another spy of precisely the same background, and set both of them after him. The odds against such a thing were overwhelming, and he had discovered no other in Oriana who bore the right signs.

Then what was his next move to be? He'd sought to share his suspicions with Alicen, as they'd agreed, only to find that she, too, had vanished from Oriana. What was he to make of that? With no great pains, he'd been able to find out that her belongings were still at Hannah Franesh's house—a place Alicen believed he did not know about, he thought with satisfaction. If she was off on a mission somewhere, then, she did plan to return, but not knowing what she was about rankled, all the same. She had tricked him once, and he did not mean to let it happen a second time.

But why were Kendry and the Chamber's agent *both*

gone, devil take it? Reluctantly, he considered the other possibility . . . that the enemy had already succeeded in disposing of Alicen, without his knowledge—and just when she could be of use to him! If her body had been left in the great marshes beyond Oriana, it could go undiscovered for years, as he himself had pointed out to her. *If I've been cheated of my vengeance on Kendry, I'll make that one pay for it,* Ruthven vowed.

Chapter 9

Caught in the press of spectators leaving the Hall of Justice, the released prisoners soon lost sight of each other, and Rolande found Raphe and Corey waiting for her on the street outside the courtyard gates, surrounded by questioners eager for further details of Captain Brodery's atrocities. Blythe was nowhere to be seen.

Rolande pushed her way through the crowd to them, put her arm possessively through Corey's—much to his surprise—and rebuked the onlookers, "Get along with ye—'tisn't decent to relish such things! My man's no pirate, nor never was. We're God-fearing folk as mind our own affairs, and let you do the same, as you hope for God's grace!"

Any of the women of the ship—most of whom were in fact washerwomen or cooks—might have taken up with Corey or Raphe, and now that Rolande had been declared by the highest authorities to be one of them, there was no need for her to avoid the others. "Do you come along to my kin in Harborside," she urged Corey. "Aye, and bring th' lad along with ye, or he'll fall in with trouble, sure."

The guards at the gate of the Hall of Justice, devout Deps all, had approved of the tenor of Rolande's remarks, and now they helpfully cleared away the curiosity seekers for her, allowing her to herd her people off toward the wharves without interference. The crowd, who did not want to listen to a sermon in any case, abandoned them to cluster 'round the rest of the ship's women instead. The cleverest of them, Rolande knew, would invent tales even more horrific than the testimony heard at the tribunal—in exchange for food and coin. Captain Brodery's vile reputation was assured for posterity.

Around the corner of a nearby alley, Rolande dropped Corey's arm and called a halt. "What the devil's keeping Blythe so long?" she complained.

"The Magistrate stopped him, when all was over, to thank him for his efforts on behalf of the Chamber's seamen," said Corey. "More than that I didn't stay to hear. He might linger if he liked, but I was for taking myself out of there, before they changed their minds about hanging me."

"Well, I can't wait about while he passes the time with the Chamber's lackeys. I have to get to the wharf. You'd best watch for him here, and I'll meet you after dark in the rear yard of the sailors' hostel on Limekin Wharf."

"Maybe I should go after them," Raphe suggested hopefully, pointing to the group of people moving away from the Hall of Justice, most of them still clamoring and gesticulating excitedly. "They might give me some money if I spin them a few wild tales, and we could buy some food. I'm near-starved."

Rolande grinned. "Why, I thought you might be, and you a growing lad. I'd not say no to a meal myself. Here." She took a half-filled purse from her shirt and handed it to the astonished Raphe. "That lot of fools was so taken up with the news, they were a pickpocket's dream come true. I plucked one gull before we were out the door, and another in the courtyard. We were packed so close, shoving this way and that, 'twas no trouble in the world." She took a few of the coins from the second moneybag, then gave it to Corey, and warned them, "Put the money in your pockets and throw away the purses. I daresay it's not much, all told, but it will buy us a feed. Till nightfall, then."

She started off down the alleyway, but turned back long enough to say, "You did bravely, you two, and cannily. I'll see you paid as you've earned, you know, when we—"

"Wait, there's Blythe now," Corey interrupted, and signaled to the surgeon to join them.

"Time enough you turned up," Rolande greeted him. "Come on, then. We'll buy some food on the way to the wharves."

Blythe hesitated. "You mean to look for passage back to Oriana?"

"In good time. First, I mean to pay a visit to Martingale Pier, then we'll sail for New Albin on the first ship out, whatever she is. We should find a berth quick enough, with the skills among us."

"Then I'd best replenish my medical kit, for the Good God knows we're bound to have need of it. I've friends here who'll obtain supplies for me on credit. Shall I set about that now, and meet you later? It will save time."

"You're right," Rolande agreed. "Let us meet behind the sailors' hostel on Limekin Wharf at nightfall." Blythe, she assumed, knew where to steal what he needed, and evidently he thought he could best accomplish this alone, which suited her plans admirably. She did not for a moment believe that a man who found it necessary to take work as a ship's surgeon had friends among the respectable physicians of the capital, but she didn't care where and how he got his supplies, as long as he was ready to sail when she found a ship willing to take them on. For now, her one concern was to find out what was going on at Martingale Pier that required such rigorous secrecy.

The dock she sought was at some distance from the others, at the far end of the Avenford shipyards, and entirely surrounded by a high stockade fence. But a quick walk past the pier had shown her that a well-staffed guardhouse stood beside the gate through which supplies and newly recruited labor entered. As few laborers came out from the compound, she assumed they were lodged within the fortresslike enclave. She could not pass for one of them, then. She would need some contrivance to gain admittance, a token of authority. . . .

The solution, she decided, lay within the Customs House, which rose in stately authority at one end of the harbor. But before she dared attempt to pass among the merchants and officials there, she would have to acquire decent clothing, and pay a visit to the public baths. The money they had left, after buying food, wouldn't pay for the sort of clothes she'd need, even if she were willing to wait to have them made. Reining in her impatience, she returned to the hot pie stall where she'd left Raphe and Corey eating spiced meat pasties, and settled back to eat her share and watch the traffic on the wharf, like any laborer idling over a meal. For over an hour she observed the sailors, tradesmen, clerks and captains coming and going among the moored ships, before she spotted the one that would suit her purpose.

A narrow-faced, long-nosed man, dressed all in plain Deprivant gray, strode up to the purser of a mer-

chant ship being unloaded on the wharf, and began at
once to upbraid the seaman. "I've reviewed the account books, Swain, and I find you've been cheating
me. I've seen the crew roster, and the quantity of slops
you ordered would never have clothed so many—yet
you've taken credit from me against your warrant.
When I advance you money, I expect to have the benefit of your trade in return. That, I believe, was our understanding."

Rolande noted with satisfaction that his clothes,
though sober in color, were of the highest quality wool
and linen. She quickly explained to Raphe and Corey
the part they were to play in the undertaking.

"I've done no wrong," the purser insisted, cringing
away from his accuser. "Most of the crew were experienced seamen who had served for some time and
needed no new clothing."

"You think I don't know how you pursers work?
You're thieves, the lot of you! You buy the smallest
quantity of clothing needed to make the purchase seem
sufficient, then on the sly you procure cheaper cloth
and sell it to the crew at a higher price—and gain more
profit as the journey goes on."

"That's not so, sir! I've ever been honest in my dealings. I tell you, we had an easy voyage, and there was
little need to replace crew with new sailors requiring
outfitting."

The merchant snorted in disdain. "You shall see
what comes of trying to cheat me. I can and will cancel
the surety I put up for your warrant. You may seek another gull to secure your merchandising ventures."

"Please, Master Gosdown, I've never cheated you of
a single coin, I swear it," the purser protested, grasping
at the merchant's sleeve. Gosdown merely raised his
ebony cane and fetched the man a sharp blow, then

turned away without another word or glance and continued down the dock toward the Customs House.

Raphe was at his heels on the instant. "Master Gosdown, might I make bold to have a word with you, sir?" he asked, when the man stopped, looking at him with annoyance.

"Well, and what do you want of me, boy?" he demanded.

"I know of something it'd interest you to see, I think," Raphe said earnestly. "'Tis proof of the bad-dealing of Purser Swain, sir. You could charge him before the Magistrate with such evidence, my mates say. He made me help to bring the chests ashore and hide them, 'fore dawn, lest you should examine the hold—but 'twas his doing, sir, and none of mine!"

Gosdown's greedy eyes fairly glowed. "Ha! Hide them, eh? Just as I suspected. Where are they?"

"I'll show you," Raphe said eagerly, and started away toward the end of the pier, without giving his quarry time to consider. Blinded by his own suspicions, the merchant followed him into an empty fish shed, where Corey seized him from behind, and Rolande smote him a great blow on the head with a marlin spike.

"Good work. Don't drop him, now, we don't want to muss his clothes." She swiftly stripped the garments from the merchant and made a neat bundle of them, wrapped in his cloak. There was plenty of rope in the shed to bind him with, and Corey's neckerchief served for a gag. There was no need to kill him, Rolande decided. He was unlikely to be found till the fishing fleet returned that night, for these sheds were used only at daybreak and dusk when returning fishermen sorted their catches for sale and used the tools there to patch their nets. This one had been locked, but Rolande had dispensed with that obstacle with no more than a bent nail, and now she locked the door behind her in the same manner.

"Now for a wash," she said with keen anticipation. On the way to the public baths, she told her crew how she meant to get access to the guarded shipyard. By now, nothing that Rolande proposed to do could surprise them.

At the Customs House, the hurrying stream of people ebbed and flowed among the large, wooden clerks' tables arranged throughout the vast marble chamber between the great stone pillars. Here bills of lading from incoming ships were examined and fees assessed, claims filed, cargo lists reviewed, and documents notarized. The tables themselves were covered with the appurtenances of the work in progress—parchment documents, ink wells and quills, heavy leatherbound ledger books and the brass seals which each customs official carried as the symbol of the authority of his office. Rolande, now bathed, kempt, and dressed in the costly gray garments, waited until she saw one of the clerks stamp a document and lay his seal upon the table. As soon as the captain left with his bond, Rolande strode forward and accosted the clerk before anyone else could reach the man's table.

"I am Elliseth Moore, of Dyserth, owner of the merchantman *Deception*," she said imperiously. "My ship arrived in port today, and I understand that she is embroiled in some dispute about the duty owed on her cargo."

The clerk looked sternly back at Rolande. "The rates are set by the Chamber on imports. We've nought to say about them. We just assess the values according to the categories."

"That is apparently the difficulty," Rolande insisted. "The vessel's recently returned from Xanistee with many rare and exotic items, and it seems that some of them have not been categorized correctly. If I were to pay the assessment to have the goods released as things stand, it would cost me a great deal more than it ought, you see." Rolande placed her hands on the desk and leaned close to the clerk. "Some of my cargo is livestock and must be removed in a timely fashion. If I suffer losses as a result of this confusion, I shall have to report the matter to the Chamber council."

The clerk, looking most put upon, protested, "There is no need to distress yourself. I am certain that if we go over the list of items in question we can resolve this matter to the satisfaction of the law." Taking up his quill and a piece of parchment, the clerk gazed importantly at Rolande. "Very well, what is the first item which you feel is in question?"

"First there are the spotted cheetahs."

"These are animals?"

"Jungle cats."

"Can you eat or ride them?"

"Certainly not ... although, of course, they might eat you."

"Then you must pay duty on them, as for luxuries. Is there anything further?"

"Indeed there is. The chief contention is over some two hundred casks of Groolean allpa."

The clerk laid aside his pen and looked up at Rolande with a pained expression. "I beg your pardon?"

Rolande impatiently tapped the merchant's ebony cane on the stone floor. "Groolean allpa. It is a spirituous drink commonly used by tribesmen of Groolea, in Xanistee, as a tonic."

"Indeed."

"The agent who assessed the cargo at the dock claimed it as an intoxicating beverage and as such subject to the highest tax rate under the Chamber's ruling."

"But it is such, is it not?"

"It is a medicine—and as such should not be charged duty."

The clerk was beginning to sense the direction of Rolande's remarks. "The matter is more involved than at first appears, I see. I shall have to inspect the fluid in question myself."

"Ah, now that is exactly what's wanted," Rolande said enthusiastically. "My captain and your agent have apparently been thrashing over the matter all morning without settling it, so I came here in hopes of persuading someone with experience and authority to come make an informed decision!" Her tone grew conciliatory as she added, "You understand, with cargo of this nature, delay could be ruinous. My man will conduct you to the anchorage. I shall just pay the duty on the cheetahs and join you there."

She escorted the customs clerk to the street, where she looked around in evident annoyance and exclaimed loudly, "Where the devil has the fellow got to now?"

At that, Raphe came barreling around the corner of the building, with Corey in hot pursuit, and collided with the clerk, throwing him against Rolande and nearly knocking the two of them to the ground. Raphe kept running, and Corey chased after him, shouting curses and threats, but soon gave it up and returned to Rolande, who furiously demanded an explanation.

"Little bastard gave me the slip," he grumbled. "Got away with my winnings, the poxy brat. I'm not so fast as I was, since I took a wound to the knee, and they can tell, the—"

Rolande delivered an impromptu tongue-lashing on the evils of dicing, apologized profusely to the customs clerk, and sent the chastened Corey to lead the man to the dock where the fictitious *Deception* lay at anchor. Halfway to the wharves, however, they would catch sight of Raphe slipping into a side street ahead, and Corey would dash off after him again, with a hasty "Just wait here half a minute, sir—!" But the clerk would wait in vain if he thought to see Elliseth Moore or her manservant ever again.

Rolande waited a quarter-hour, watching the visitors to the Customs House come and go, then strolled off toward the harbor district, with the clerk's official seal safe in her pocket.

From her observation of Martingale Pier, Rolande had decided that the gate through which supplies passed offered her best hope of gaining entry. She had sent Raphe and Corey to Limekin Pier to seek word of ships setting out for New Albin, that might be approached for work. "I'll meet you there when I've done," she said, then added as an afterthought, "If I've not come by nightfall, meet Blythe by the hostel and all of you take passage to Oriana. Go to Lorin's pawnbrokery, and he'll see you paid for me."

As she approached, the guardsmen standing beside the gate brandished their muskets, and the captain of the guards came forward when she was still some steps away. "What is your business here?"

Rolande stared back at him disdainfully and waved the clerk's seal of office under his eyes. "My business is no concern of yours," she said firmly. "I am an official of the Chamber's government, here on state business. You will let me pass."

Though he could not read, the guard recognized the seal of the Chamber of Statesmen. He hesitated, not certain whether to lower his gun and comply with her orders. He had no wish to run afoul of the Chamber, and he was well aware of the guardsmen behind him, watching the exchange. They would be ready witnesses, if he refused entry to the Chamber's lawful agent—or allowed an unauthorized person to pass the barricade. Which would be the worse offense?

Rolande could see him making up his mind to refer the question to a superior, and this was the last thing she wanted. As if relenting, she said in explanation, "I am already well aware of the nature of the work being undertaken here, Captain. I am arranging for shipments of materials necessary to the construction of the . . . weapon, and I must confer with the Commander here to be certain of what is needed—lest the arrival of critical supplies be delayed. Now stand aside and delay me no further. Time is short, and I've no more to waste."

Her evident knowledge of the work, coupled with her implacable air of authority, decided the guard, who stepped back and nodded for the gate to be opened. Rolande strode inside, like one who has nothing to hide and is not accustomed to being challenged. She was half expecting to be shot in the back or taken into custody at any second, but no one paid any further heed to her. All around her, master shipwrights, carpenters, coopers and sailmakers were busy at their trades, assisted by dozens of apprentices. At one end of the shipyard, wooden planks were being bent and planed. At another point, canvas stretched taut on wooden frames was being cut and sewn. There was an air of urgency about the extraordinary efforts underway, as if all there worked under immense pressure to complete their tasks by some particular date that was approaching. They had no time for curiosity about a visiting official, and Rolande thought that her words to the guard, *Time is short,* had been better-chosen than she knew. Time was running short for the people of New Albin to prepare their defense against the coming invasion. . . .

The largest, most astonishing warship she'd ever seen stood almost complete in the drydock, with four masts, nearly two dozen sails, four gun decks filled with bronze cannon, and an enormous hull of black oak already bearing a brass plate engraved with the name *Invincible.* With such vessels at their command, the Deps would be a devastating enemy, and Rolande did not doubt that now, as ever, the Colonies of New Albin would be the target of their aggression and their avarice. This was the secret weapon by which the Chamber hoped to replenish its coffers and prosper on the resources of the New World.

Can a ship that large stay afloat? Glancing from the mostly fitted ship to the vast warehouses lining the yard with their store of materials, Rolande realized that this vessel was intended to be but one of a fleet, the flagship of an armada. She was reminded of the tales of hardship and want she'd heard from those who'd come in recent years to the New World from Albin. The Chamber would surely not have expended the immense sums needed to build such a warship unless they were sure of her seaworthiness. But how could they be sure?

This, then, would be the first, the one they would test before constructing the rest. The intent hinted at in the scraps she'd taken from the Deprivant messenger suddenly took on a clear meaning. It was the confirmation of an intended destination for the test of the ves-

sel, and the coast of New Lindness would be perfect
for such a trial. It would prove the ship's ability to
cross the sea to the New World, yet take her to a point
sufficiently desolate that she would not be seen by the
colonists and alert them to this new design. And if the
test should be successful, a fleet of such vessels would
easily make the Deps undisputed masters of the sea.
Not only would it become more difficult to defend
New Albin against another invasion, but it would become impossible to invade Albin itself from the sea.
Sir Andrew had of course told Rolande nothing of his
plans of conquest, but she could not imagine that he
meant to leave the Chamber in power when he had the
rightful heir to the throne under his roof. The girl must
be nearly of age by now, and there were other claimants to the crown as well. But there would never be a
coronation, if the Deps succeeded in launching a fleet
of these monstrous battleships.

Gazing at the sleek lines and powerful hull of the *Invincible,* Rolande was overcome with desire for her.
Here, by God, was a ship worthy of her! But somehow she would have to stave off disaster to New Albin, if she were ever to gain command of such a vessel.
Well, she knew the proposed location of the trial—but
not the date, and this information she now determined
to have. Reluctantly, she turned from her inspection of
the ship and looked around for someone with authority
in the yard, only to see that such a one had already noticed her. A man dressed in the martially-cut gray
jacket and breeches affected by the Chamber's officers
was striding across the yard toward her, and his manner did not appear welcoming.

"You are the Master here?" Rolande demanded of
the Deprivant, before he could question her.

"I am," the man replied, examining her costly garb suspiciously. "And who might you be, then?"

Again Rolande produced her seal. "I am an agent of the government, charged with seeing that there are no irregularities in the accounting of the work carried on here. More than that it is not necessary for you to know, at present."

The man examined the official seal, and finding no fault with it, returned it to her with an air of resignation that suggested to Rolande that such inspections by the Chamber were not unusual. "I received no word of your visit here," he said apologetically.

Rolande smiled, rather unpleasantly. "I'd hardly be in a position to find irregularities if my arrival were announced in advance," she pointed out. "And if there are none to find, it matters little whether one is *forewarned*."

"I've committed no irregularities," the Deprivant officer declared, bristling. "Such intrusions, announced or unannounced, merely take time from my duties here and hinder the completion of our efforts, to no purpose."

Rolande's smile vanished, and her eyes narrowed. "Very well," she said coldly. "As we both have our duties to perform here, let us both be about them, with no further waste of time. I am charged with examining your accounts books for the Chamber, and the sooner I finish my task, the sooner my *intrusion* shall cease to hinder you. Pray lead the way."

"Is it not enough that they burden me with more than can be accomplished in the time allowed, but they needs must send plagues of officials upon me?" the Master complained, but he showed Rolande to his office in a rickety wooden building at one end of the pier. Here he removed from a shelf a thick leatherbound account book, which he placed before her defiantly.

"Very good," Rolande said. "I'll not keep you from your duties longer, sir. I shall send for you if I find anything that requires explanation." Scrutinizing the neat columns of entries, she wondered where the Master kept the book with the real figures, but fortunately for him, that was not her concern. Moments later, she heard his raised voice in the shipyard, as he vented his pent-up anger at her on some poor carpenter's lad. She let just enough time pass for him to find himself well-occupied, then turned her attention from the ledger and began instead to search the plain oak desk.

The box containing the correspondence from the Chamber, with the Master's instructions, was of course locked, and with a lock much less crude than the one that had secured the fish-shed. Nearly ten minutes had passed before Rolande found what she sought.

". . . construction of said vessel must and shall be completed by the end of the sixth month of the new year that she may be fytted out and sailed to New Lindness at the beginnynge of Summer and her sea worthyness thus put to the proof," Rolande read. *Yes, you bring her to me—I'll be waiting for her!* she exulted, as she replaced the letter just as she'd found it. When she'd relocked the box, which was rather more difficult than unlocking it had been, she bent over the ledger again for a while, turning the pages, and trying to spend as much time at the task as if she were actually studying the figures. At length, when she could no longer resist her impatience, she affixed her seal to the bottom of the last column, to affirm that all was in order to that point, and returned the book to its shelf, as soon as the wax had hardened.

The Master of the Yard was nowhere in sight as she

made her way to the gate, and Rolande decided that there was no need for her to take leave of him. Let him think as he liked—she would be far away before anyone would think to make inquiries. With a stern nod, she passed through the portal and back onto the road that led to the main part of the wharves.

At last, her course was clearly laid out for her. First to find Corey and Raphe, decide on a ship—she'd have to get rid of these fine clothes, worse luck, and rig herself out in sailors' garb again—then meet Blythe at nightfall, which was not far off now. Thus far, circumstances had favored her, and she had been quick to take advantage of them, but everything depended on reaching Oriana with her information as soon as possible. If necessary, she would jump ship to do it, or even entrust the message to another traveler—though in that case, it would have to be so cryptic as to be almost useless. Closer to the New World, though, she might be able to find a Yerren messenger to carry word to Sir Andrew. . . .

So engrossed was she with congratulating herself on the success of the day's ploys, and with formulating plans for the future, that she was not as observant as she might otherwise have been. It was not until she heard the furious shouting behind her that she suspected that something was amiss.

"That's the other one! See, the brazen jade parades in my clothes and carries my very stick! Seize her!" shouted Master Gosdown.

Corey and Raphe were already in custody, Rolande saw, and she was surrounded by stout officers of the Watch before she could attempt to break away. *This,* she thought bitterly, as her arms were pinioned by two of the officers, *this is what comes of leaving living witnesses!*

* * *

The Magistrate of the Harborside district saw nothing unusual in their case, and wasted no time in disposing of it. They had been made to state their names and origins for the court record, but he assumed that they had lied—as indeed they had—and it was a matter of indifference to him who they were and where they came from. As far as he was concerned, they were just three more of the nameless, dangerous trash that infested the waterside like rats, and appeared before him at every session. He had the word of a prominent and wealthy Deprivant merchant that they had assaulted and robbed him, and that was evidence enough of their guilt, in God's eyes and his own.

"Before the just and benevolent rule of the Chamber of Statesmen, such an offense as yours would have been expiated upon the gallows," he admonished them. "Give thanks to our All-Merciful God that you are brought to judgment in these enlightened days, and may yet, with God's grace, have occasion to repent of your misdeeds."

As a point of strict fact, he was right, Rolande admitted. In victory, the Chamber and the Church had not shown themselves just or benevolent, but the Magistrate's words reminded her that she had had reasons to throw in her lot with the Deps, in the early days of the Uprising. Had she not been betrayed by one of her confederates, during the invasion of Thornfeld, she might well have been Governor of that colony now, instead of a prisoner waiting to be sentenced by a minor magistrate of the capital.

"You yourselves have admitted to coming to this city from the colonies of the New World," the Magistrate continued, scowling deeply, "and I've little doubt you were transported there for good reason. Therefore,

I am ordering you returned to those lawless shores, as you have again shown yourselves unfit for the society of the God-fearing and righteous. A convict ship bound for New Albin will sail on the high tide tomorrow. You shall be upon it." The Magistrate signed the order with a flourish of his quill and handed the document to his clerk. "Sergeant at Arms, see that the prisoners are secured till morning."

Rolande had not been looking forward to sailing under another captain's orders, and the prospect of traveling as a transported felon was even less appealing. But they would be returned to New Albin—and at the Chamber's expense. It was even possible that they would reach their destination sooner as prisoners, for the convict ship would sail directly to the New World, without conducting business at any other ports along the way. Rolande could almost have laughed at this peculiar turn of events, had it not been for the thought of Blythe, waiting for her at Limekin Wharf.

* * *

Katin fidgeted uneasily in the hard, high-backed reception room chair, then caught herself, and smoothed down the folds of the cream-colored satin dress she'd donned for the formal meeting with Lady Alicen. Alicen was watching her, waiting for her answer. They were all watching her. People would be watching her for the rest of her life, she thought. Best to get used to it.

Alicen, abandoning pretense, had returned to the colony in her own identity. Now, as the Duke of Wyston's courier, she had brought his response to the news that the Princess lived, and that response was very much what Katin had anticipated. It was the obvious solution to their situation. Yet now that it had been put before her, she found herself unprepared to answer, despite her expectations.

"And if I refuse?" she heard herself saying, much to her own surprise. A slight intake of breath from Lady Celia told her exactly what was expected of her. Her future had been determined already, by others, and it remained only for her to accept the inevitable. But she had always known that it would be so. What was the use of pretending otherwise?

An experienced diplomat, Alicen replied dispassionately, "His Grace has sworn fealty to Your Highness regardless, as is declared herein." She laid her hand on the document she'd brought with her from the Duke. "He most willingly acknowledges Your Highness' claim to the throne—but . . ." She paused, casting a sidelong glance at Sir Andrew, who had thus far imparted to her nothing of his military plans, "the question then becomes, can Your Highness win it?"

"If the Duke of Wyston regards himself as my vassal, he can hardly refuse me the support of his soldiery," Katin observed.

"Such soldiers as he commands are indeed at Your Highness' disposal," Alicen agreed. "But much of the Duke's support comes not from the army, but from the populace. I am afraid that if you would succeed, you must win the hearts of the people—"

Katin shook her head, not in contradiction, but in simple wonderment. "That an Obelen should have to woo her own subjects . . . !" she murmured.

"Granted, many of the people would follow an Obelen unquestioningly, but if Your Highness will bear my speaking frankly, others will view you as part of the old order, and there are powerful factions among the commoners who have come to the Duke's cause because he has promised them a new order. This is not a promise that can be easily taken away once given." Alicen pushed the parchment between them aside. "If what you plan is a return to the past, then His Grace cannot promise you the support of his followers without betraying his word—and neither can he himself oppose you without betraying his Queen. You see the difficulty of his position."

"I see nothing but difficulty on all sides," Katin said wryly. "Indeed, I see the *impossibility* of governing even a township, much less a country, when every decision must be referred to an ill-informed and undisciplined citizenry. I cannot but wonder whether the Duke of Wyston has fully considered the consequences of his promises."

For a moment, she thought she saw a flash of admiration break through Alicen's impassivity, but Alicen said only, "Such a concern is understandable, Your Highness, and I believe that your fears will be much allayed when you have become more familiar with the Duke's proposal. He has promised the commonalty a voice in their own affairs, no more."

Why, that's more than I have! Katin thought, but she did not so much as smile at her own wit. To say such a thing aloud would be in the worst possible taste.

"The people desire to be *heard*," Alicen was saying, "to be assured that their concerns are made known to those in power. For too long, their overlords prevented this, and now the Church does the same. They will look to you to protect them from the abuses of both." Alicen seemed to recite these arguments almost by rote. Her passion was for the downfall of the Chamber, not for the rise of the commonfolk. But she spoke with conviction when she added, "The Deps profited from our errors, and now we may profit from theirs. If you are ever to wear the crown, it is the people who will give it to you, and His Grace believes that a certain *recourse* is not too much to give them in return."

Katin did not answer at once, though there was nothing awkward or uncertain in her stillness now. It was her prerogative to let others wait while she weighed their words.

At length, Sir Andrew broke the silence. "I mislike the notion as much as any, but we cannot afford to dismiss it out of hand. In the days to come, Your Highness may need the common people as allies rather than as mere subjects."

Alicen pressed her advantage. "Alone, the Duke might have succeeded in driving the Deps from power. Alone, you may succeed in doing so. But if those who support his cause are united with those who will support yours, then together you *cannot fail.* The Chamber's forces will be overwhelmed, the Chamber crushed, the Church brought to heel. It will be so if Your Highness wills it so!"

Katin looked around at each of them in turn. "Marriage it is to be, then?" she said softly. Why was it so difficult to get the words out?

"I would urge Your Highness to consider it," said Sir Andrew. Lady Celia merely smiled at her, a smile that said implacably, "I know that you will do your duty, my dear."

Alicen's face revealed nothing of her exultation. *She doesn't want to do it, poor girl, but she will. She's an Obelen.* She thought of Katin saying cheerfully, at their first meeting, "It's a wonder I can remember who I am, myself!" There was little of that offhand gaiety about her now. She had remembered who she was.

Katin abruptly stood, signifying that the audience was at an end. Turning to Alicen, she said calmly,

"You recognize, Lady Alicen, that I can give no more than a conditional assent at present. There is a great deal yet to be arranged before such a decision as this may be taken."

Alicen rose and made her a solemn bow. "I am instructed to open negotiations, Your Highness. None but yourself and His Grace can conclude them." Then in a not unsympathetic tone, she added, "But if I may be of service to you in any way, you know you have only to send for me."

Katin gave her a small smile. *Already I am gathering about me courtiers.* And the trouble with courtiers is knowing how much they do for your interest, and how much for their own.

After changing back to simple clothes, Katin threw open her window to observe the weather, and found Lucifer sheltering under the eaves, out of the wind and rain. At once he scampered down and over the sill, whining resentfully at such ill treatment. He was accustomed to being able to climb in and out of Katin's window at will, but since the storms had started, he often found himself closed out, his shrill barks unheard in the lashing wind and the thunder. He shook himself thoroughly, hitting Katin with spray from his wet coat, then leaped down from the windowsill and made for the hearth, where he curled up before the blazing fire with an indignant grunt.

"It is perfectly warm in the kennels, you pampered creature," Katin scolded him, as she pulled her hooded cloak around her. "You've plenty of straw there."

Lucifer sneezed scornfully at her and settled himself more comfortably for a nap.

Mindful of Lady Celia's orders, Katin looked into the parlor and reported to Her Ladyship that she would

be working in her shed for a time, if she was not
wanted at the moment. How much easier it was to play
the part of a dutiful household retainer than that of a
Princess of the Realm!

"It's poor weather for you to be out," Captain
Fenton protested, preparing to accompany her. He appealed to Lady Celia, having learned that only she
seemed able to exert any control over Katin's behavior.
"My Lady, pray tell her she's not to. Who would venture out to seek a cure on such a day, I ask you?"

But Lady Celia said complacently, "If we were to
wait for fine weather before venturing out, we'd be
within doors until the spring. This is the storm season
with us, Captain. We may not see the sun for weeks."

"It's in just such weather that my simples are most
needed," Katin put in. " 'Tis the season when agues
and fevers abound more than in any other, and my supplies of all medicaments are fearfully low. I've much
work to do." And she had been hoping to slip away
without the captain's company, for once. She could not
expect him to wait for her outside the shed in weather
such as this, so she'd have him underfoot all the while,
when she longed above all to be alone. She could order
him to remain behind, of course, and ignore the others'
disapproval, but that would be mere childishness. They
were right, and she knew it—the Governor's apothecary might go about without an escort, but it was out
of the question for the heir to the throne of Albin. The
time for such freedom and privacy was over. Soon
there would be nothing left of the Governor's apothecary except a collection of medicinal herbal recipes
and a pack of soarhounds. After all, there was no such
person as Katin Ander. There never had been.

At least the wild weather kept the captain from trying to make polite conversation, as they made their

way through the dripping orchard to the workshed. Katin huddled in her cloak, thinking of the many times she'd walked with Jerl here, talking and eating the fallen fruit. *I told Jerl the truth, after all.* She was indeed betrothed to a lord of one of the great noble houses, and Jerl would have to be told that she could not break the engagement. She realized now how unfair she'd been to let him believe there might be hope for the two of them, hope he'd tended as carefully as his farm, all these years. . . . She had told herself that she wished to spare his feelings, but she saw now that she simply hadn't wanted to let him go.

She had always known that she must one day make a dynastic marriage, very likely to a stranger, certainly to a man for whom she felt no particular affection. If, for a few years, here in the New World, she had allowed herself to believe that it might be otherwise, she had only been playing a child's game of pretense, and now it was finished. The Duke was not completely a stranger, to be sure, though she knew him little enough. They had met, of course, for they were cousins, but he was older than she by a dozen years at least, and she had never passed much time in his company. Her one clear impression of him, indeed, was that he was a skilled hunter—at one time, she had classed everyone by their aptitude for the chase. But he was popular with the people, by all accounts, and that, it seemed, was to be the deciding factor in her choice of a husband.

There was nothing to be gained by dwelling upon the fact. The thing to do now was work, to keep herself occupied and not to think overmuch about matters that could not be mended. She waited patiently in the rain while Captain Fenton lit a lantern and satisfied himself that no threat lay within the workshed, then she hung her wet cloak on a peg and set about checking her supplies of various medicaments. *Who will see to this after me?* she wondered. *I ought to have trained an apprentice.*

"And you expect this weather to last for a *season?*" said the captain, settling himself at the table.

Perhaps it was just as well he was there, Katin thought. Having to talk with him would keep her from brooding. "Oh, we in New Albin don't fret ourselves over a storm or two," she laughed. "Why, in Thornfeld we had Yerren attacking, then a plague of dragons to contend with, and we'd no sooner rid ourselves of them than the Chamber's army landed on our doorsteps. So, you see, it takes more than a few months of rain to trouble us."

Much as he would have preferred to ask about the dragons, the captain instead dutifully returned to the subject of the Princess's safety. "Still, in these dark days, it is more than ever necessary to be cautious. The more you stay within the mansion, the less the cause for concern."

Katin looked up from lighting the brazier and tugged at the chain around her neck. "Are you forgetting that I have this to protect me?" she asked mischievously, pulling from her blouse the eye-charm the gypsy girl had sent her. "No evil can befall me while I wear it, and I promise you I don't mean to take it off. So you see, you—"

She broke off as the dry bits of wood in the brazier, charred into coals, burst into flame at the spark from her flint and steel, and a great mass of bluish smoke suddenly began to billow around her like a cloud. Katin had no more than a moment to be astonished at the mysterious vapor filling the shed before she fell senseless to the floor.

Captain Fenton jumped to his feet the instant he saw the dark smoke and leaped to the door, which Katin had pulled fast against the gusts of wind that would blow her powders and dried herbs about. But when he tried to throw it open and draw the noxious fumes from the hut, the door would not give, and he realized that someone had slipped the bolt into place outside. The poisoned smoke rising from the brazier was not an accident, then, but a deliberate attempt to murder the Princess—and he could do nothing! Again and again he threw himself against the door in an agony of frustration, struggling to stay conscious even as he dropped to his knees, helpless, in front of the door.

Chapter 10

The same ship that had brought Alicen back to New Albin had brought news for Ruthven as well— news that was at once enlightening and infuriating. Rumors had begun to be whispered among the higher military and political ranks that the Princess Oriana was not dead, but in exile in the New World and planning to attempt a return to the throne. The Duke of Halkin's spies had as yet been unable to confirm or disprove the reports—and that was one of the tasks the Duke had set for Ruthven. According to Ruthven's report, Viscount Edenbyrne was to be found in the colony called Oriana, and to whom should the Princess go for protection if not to the Lord Marshal? The very name of the settlement might be a sign to her followers to seek her there. Ruthven was to determine whether Sir Andrew was hiding the Princess, and, if he found her, his other task was to remove her as a barrier to the Duke's own aspirations.

This message was the one clue that Ruthven had needed to resolve the riddle of the Governor's household. Captain Fenton's arrival was explained, and his attendance upon a girl with an imperial manner that ill became her menial position. Ruthven had never seen the Princess, but only coins struck with her likeness; so that, unlike Alicen, he was not led astray by the changes in her height and coloring. Without other reasons to suspect, he would certainly never have marked the resemblance, but now it struck him with the force of a revelation. Her age was right for her to have been a girl of eleven or twelve at the time of the Uprising. . . .

Ruthven had continued to keep the Governor's Mansion under observation, and he knew that Baron Graydon and other dignitaries had been calling there of late. Indeed, Alicen had taken up residence there since her return, and now he recalled that she had visited the Mansion just before she'd left the colony, as well. Was Kendry a step ahead of him again, already acting as liaison between the Princess and the Duke of Wyston? If so, he would have to act quickly, or the Duke of Halkin would soon face an unconquerable alliance among the heir of the House of Obelen, the Lord Marshal, and the Duke of Wyston.

Ruthven had decided to strike at once, before Sir Andrew and the rest could learn that their secret was out, and take precautions. If the haughty, fair-haired minx were indeed Oriana Obelen, the resulting furor at her murder would tell him that he had hit the target. And if his suspicions were ill-founded after all, at worst his actions would result in the death of an insignificant apothecary, and he would have to find the right victim and strike again. There was one way to be certain.

His spying had made him familiar with the daily routine that Katin followed, and he knew that she visited her workshed without fail, however foul the weather. But nowadays—since the spread of these rumors, in fact—she never went there unescorted by Captain Fenton. A direct attack was thus out of the question, and would call too much attention to itself besides. If the girl proved to be no more than she seemed, he might need to make another strike on the estate, and the less suspicion aroused by the herbalist's death, the better. What was wanted was something subtle, something that could be taken for an accident. . . . It was a challenge, but not, for Ruthven, an insurmountable one.

He had waited until the deepest part of night, then, dressed in his darkest clothes, he had stolen silently as a shadow across the garden to Katin's shed. The door did not lock, for Katin expected no one to steal herbs only an apothecary would know how to use, but a stout iron bolt high on the side kept curious children from the more dangerous specimens. Ruthven slipped inside and shut the door behind him before lighting his lantern.

One of the first and most critical skills a clandestine agent acquired was a knowledge of drugs and poisons. As Ruthven swiftly searched the shelves until he found a jar of dried twigs of oleander, he thought again of the trick Alicen Kendry had played him. But now the last act of that drama was about to be performed. *When the Duke of Halkin has ascended the throne, I'll be in a position to make her regret it.* Or to secure a pardon for her, perhaps even have the Kendry estate returned to her. . . . It would be almost irresistibly amusing to have the highborn little vixen in his debt, though of course the Duke—no, the *King*—would never be able to trust her completely. Perhaps he himself would be a Baron before long. . . .

Clutching the jar of oleander, Ruthven had made his way to the brazier, where a thin layer of ashes and partially charred bits of wood had been left to serve as kindling for the next day's fire. He had broken the oleander twigs into small pieces, crumpled the dry leaves,

and intermixed them with the cold ashes. Then he blew
the residue of dust from the bottom of the mortar and
returned it to its place on the shelf. In a moment, he
was bolting the door of the workshed after him.

The wind whipped his cloak about him, and he had
smiled, thinking that he had contrived to turn even the
wretched weather of the New World to his advantage.
Winter was the season of storms, and it had been blus-
tery and rainy for many days now. Tomorrow, he had
reasoned, was unlikely to be different. When the
apothecary and her noble guardian entered the shed,
they were sure to close the door behind them, to shut
out the wind—then Ruthven, hidden nearby, would
bolt it against their escape. With any luck, the weather
would be forbidding enough to discourage visitors to
the garden who might observe him.

Back at his own lodgings, with a fire in the grate
and a mug of mulled ale before him, he had settled
down to compose a letter to the Duke of Halkin, to report that his orders had been carried out. Then at last
he was free to attend to the matter of his own security.
To this end he had quickly drafted a note to Alicen and
paid a boy from the kitchen a few pennies to deliver it
to her, early next morning, at the Governor's Mansion.

* * *

Waves smashed against the hull of the convict ship,
washing over the rails and carrying every loose object
across the sea-slicked decks into the ocean. The sky
was rent by flashes of lightning, while booming thunder like the echo of cannonfire had to fight with the
roaring wind to make itself heard. *They were mad to
try this crossing now,* Rolande thought, *but then what
do they care if a boatload of criminals is lost at sea?*

The colonies of New Albin were often referred to as the Summerlands, because Albin's undesirables had always been deported to the New World in the summer months, when the sea was calmest. It was only now—with the founding of new colonies like Oriana in the warm southern part of the continent—that the Chamber had decided to try sending a ship in the winter as well. It was surely more merciful in God's eyes to transport the condemned than to hang them, and the sooner they were transported the less God-given foodstuffs must be expended to feed them.

The folly of this experiment was now becoming clear. The crossing from the Old World to the New had never been easy, for the sea could be violent at the best of times, but in the winter all her fury was unleashed against the frail wooden vessels that dared attempt to cross her.

Rolande, along with the rest of the transportees, had been called to the deck to help batten down the ship against the gale, and she was clinging desperately to the foremast, attempting to tighten a clewline. They were not far off the coast of New Albin, Rolande knew, but if the ship went down now, they all risked drowning as surely as if they'd been hundreds of miles out at sea. Her curses were lost in the raging wind as she pulled the line still tighter through the block, and she could barely hear the shouting of the ship's officers ordering that the rigging be doubled on the mainsail and the smaller sails trimmed, that the masts and spars might not be broken totally away. On the morrow, if they survived the night, those men would not be able to talk above a whisper.

A blast of wind and rain shook the ship so violently that she came close to oversetting, and Rolande grabbed wildly at the drenched rigging, fearing that

she would be swept overboard. This time there would
not be even the Chamber's navymen to pull her from
the sea. Anyone who went over now was doomed, for
it would be impossible to accomplish a rescue in this
gale, even if hands could be spared to attempt it.

The captain ordered the ship put before the wind. It
took two men at the wheel and two at the tiller to keep
her head to sea, but having left only the smallest side
sails, this was the only way she might be worked at all.
But despite the best efforts of all aboard, the main mast
snapped like a twig under the force of the wind, and
the ocean poured over the deck in a torrent, from bow
to stern. The jib boom was torn away, then the jigger
mast, then the maintopgallantmast. Finally, the entire
ship shuddered as it was thrown against the boulders in
the shallows near the shore. The keel struck the jagged
edge of a partially submerged rock, and the hull was
rent with a deafening crack.

"Abandon ship!" the captain cried to those who remained. "She's going down for sure!"

While seamen and transportees struggled to free the
few longboats that hadn't already been washed away,
Rolande, still clinging to the foremast, looked around
wildly for something she might use to keep her afloat
long enough to reach the shore. But even as she
grabbed for the lower yard, the brace holding it in
place broke. She was hit first by the swinging knevel
block, then as she gasped in pain and pressed her hand
to the gash over her ribs, the fore yard snapped, and
the free-swinging crossbeam smacked her hard in the
chest and carried her over the side.

Then she was vaguely aware of lying on something
soft and wet. Water dripped onto her face and ran
down into her eyes and mouth. With an effort she

forced her eyes to open, but she saw only vague, dark shadows moving around her. Perhaps she was dead, she thought, and these were demons come for her—but the thought brought no alarm with it. Her mind was curiously numb. Even the pain in her side did not seem important. Then a larger shadow loomed over her, wings outspread. She gazed up at it in rapt contemplation, but as it drew nearer, blackness covered everything again and she slipped back into the fathomless darkness.

Corey had been squatting beside Rolande ever since he and Raphe had pulled her from the sea, but now he rose and ran, sloshing through the mud toward the boulder where, moments later, Hrivas landed with a thrashing of wings. Corey could not have explained how he knew this was Hrivas, for most *Ysnathi* found it impossible to tell one Yerren from another, but he had not the faintest doubt of this one's identity. Hrivas, for his part, had known since the storm struck that Corey was nearby, and in danger, but he could no more fly in those storm winds than a leaf can float upstream, and not till the calm of morning had he been able to set out to find his friend.

Raphe was horrified to see Corey run to greet the unknown Yerren like a long-lost friend, for he himself had no way of knowing whether the newcomer was indeed his shipmate or a stranger. Didn't the fool know that most featherfolk hated humans and would attack any they found alone and defenseless? None of the other survivors who lay on the shore, too injured or exhausted to go farther, made any move to approach the armed Yerren. Raphe snatched up a rock to use as a weapon and ran after Corey, yelling for him to wait,

but when he reached the two, he found them already
trading news.

" . . . been flying by the coast each day since I
reached Oriana," Hrivas was saying, "but none from
the ship have come back."

"No, nor no more they will, *tsivihr,*" said Corey, using a word he had learned from Hrivas. He was not
completely certain of its meaning, but he thought it
was "comrade-in-arms," or something of that sort.
"You were right about Tyrrel's isle. Only four of us got
away from there with the captain, and now it's only
Raphe and me left—"

"And the captain's hurt bad!" Raphe put in, tossing
down the stone and pointing to where Rolande lay. "If
we can't get her to help soon, she's sure to die."

"Aye, we were in hopes a salvage ship might come
by, or that some of the others who went to seek a settlement would send back help, but there's been no sign
of either. We didn't like to leave the captain, but we
don't dare carry her, without so much as a sling or a
cart. How far be we from a town?" Corey had no idea
whereabouts they had washed up, having lost all sense
of the ship's bearings in the storm-blasted sea.

"For me, 'tis an easy flight, but for you wingless
beasts it would take days—and a boat. This is the east
side of the river. Oriana lies to the west."

"Curse the luck! You can fly there and fetch help,
but by the time folk get back here, it may be too late."

Hrivas was silent for a minute, and when he spoke
again he pointed, not west toward Oriana, but northward, where the swamp stretched on till it lost itself in
scrubby forestland. "Gypsies—there's a gypsy camp
nearby here. And I saw some hunting when I was flying across the forest from the town. They have a cart

to haul the carcasses back to camp in. I'll fetch them to you, then fly to Oriana."

He began to spread out his wings, but Corey said, "No, wait! You know the gypsies and the Yerren hereabouts are sworn enemies. If you fly yon, they're as like to shoot you as not."

"But the captain . . ."

"Tell me exactly where they're huntin' and I'll go to them. The captain's partners with that fellow Lorin runs a pawnbrokery in town. Gypsies trade with him all the time. I can convince them that he's like to reward them if they save her. You wing back to Oriana and tell the Governor she's shipwrecked here, and that we'll try to take her to the gypsy camp. Tell him . . ." Corey hesitated. Rolande had not openly told him what she'd been about, but he knew what Raphe had heard in Lichfield Prison, and he himself had witnessed Rolande's ruses after their release. And she'd been eager to return to Oriana as soon as she discovered whatever was a-building at Martingale Pier. If she wasn't spying for the Lord Marshal, then he, Corey Rijnland, wasn't a boswain's mate. "Tell him she was bringing him some secret information about the enemy's warships. Maybe that will fetch him. Where'll we meet?"

"I'll fly over the gypsy camp and look for you when I return. Watch for me, and I'll lead you to a safe place."

Corey knew what he meant—a place far enough from the gypsies for his own safety, and far enough from the marsh-Yerren for Corey's. "I'll look for you, then," he agreed. "Just stay out of range of arrows and musket-shot."

"Do not," Hrivas said gravely, "try to teach the fish to swim." He gave his friend as precise directions to the gypsy hunters as he could, then climbed the boulders to the highest point and launched himself into the air. Raphe watched as Corey trudged into the marsh, and Hrivas flew off to the west. Then he turned back to stand watch over Rolande.

* * *

Captain Fenton had not been overcome by the fumes of the burning oleander as quickly as Katin. He was larger and heavier than she, and had not been standing directly over the brazier when it gave forth the noxious cloud of poison. But he could not summon the strength to break down the barred door, and he had finally collapsed to the floor, too weak and dizzy to rise. Then he felt his head begin to clear somewhat, for the air near the floor was not choked with the deadly smoke, and he thought: *I can't let the Princess die in here!* Crawling across the floor to her, he dragged her away from the brazier, all the while trying frantically to remember what was in the shack that he might use to save her. He'd seen her douse the brazier with sand, at times, and that was surely the first thing to do, to keep more of the poisonous fumes from filling the small room. Then maybe he could hack a hole in the wall, or the edge of the door, to let in untainted air. He must *keep awake.* . . .

Where was the sack of sand? Hanging from a peg in the wall . . . ? Leaving Katin by the door, where he hoped some fresh air might be seeping through, he held to the doorframe to pull himself laboriously to his feet, and tried to look around the smoky shed. His eyes were watering badly, and a crippling wave of dizziness smote him again, leaving him reeling and light-headed. He fell back against the door, thinking *too late—*

But the door fell open behind him, sending him tumbling headlong onto the grass. Rolling to the side to escape the clouds of smoke now billowing from the hazy interior of the shed, he took one great lungful of fresh air, then dove back into the hut, seized Katin and pulled her through the doorway to the safety of the damp garden. Exhausted, he collapsed to his knees beside her and finally took time to ask himself, *how is it possible?*

"She's not dead, is she, Captain?" a girl's voice asked from beside him. "I ran as fast as I could!"

Fenton glanced sideways and saw to his surprise the gypsy girl who'd stopped him on the way back from the Common. But he had no time to spare for her now. He passed his hand before Katin's mouth, and felt her breath, faint but present. Pressing his head against her chest, he heard that her heart still beat strongly. "She lives yet," he gasped, still fighting off the stupefying dizziness. "Run to the barn there and have one of the grooms ride for Doctor Justin at once."

"I've done that, sir. I had to fetch a gardener I saw, to pull back the bolt—for I couldn't reach it—and he's gone for help."

Katin sighed without waking, coughed, then began to breathe more deeply and evenly. To the captain, who was well acquainted with death, she looked much less like a corpse and more like a girl asleep. Now for the first time, he turned his attention to Arya. "How did you come to be here, child?"

"We brought the horses that are broken now. The Governor's steward—"

Fenton shook his head impatiently. "How did you know to open the shed? How did you know about the poison?"

For a moment Arya was silent, then she said slowly, "I didn't know about any poison, sir. Only, that the . . .

the leaf-lady was in danger." Evidently, Katin's profession was a difficult one to translate. "So I ran here to find her."

"Why here?"

The girl looked at him innocently. "But she's always here, no?"

Only his own weakness kept Fenton from seizing the child and shaking a sensible answer out of her. *"How did you know she was in danger?"*

"Oh, I'd always know that, wouldn't I?" She seemed rather surprised that he found it necessary to ask, and she held up the leather thong she wore about her neck. " 'Twas this, you know, sir, that told me. It wept," she said matter-of-factly.

As Fenton stared at the metal eye, twin to the one the Princess wore, a drop of water did indeed gather and fall, like a tear, from the edge of the charm. But then, it was still raining steadily. "But—" he began.

"Here are people from the house, coming to help you," Arya said suddenly, jumping to her feet. "Goodbye!"

There were still other questions Captain Fenton wanted to put to her, though he suspected that it would be a waste of time. Possibly judicial torture could extract a straightforward answer from this evasive waif, but he doubted it. Still he did not intend to let her get away this time.

But how to catch her, in his weakened state? "Wait," he said hastily. "The Governor will wish to reward you for rescuing his ward. He'll be most grateful."

Arya hesitated. This was business. She didn't know what a "ward" was, but she assumed that it must be an aristocratic way of saying "bastard." There might be a gold piece to be had for her part in the affair. That would go far toward appeasing the others, who would be angry at her for running off when there was work to be done. His Excellency was said to be a generous man. . . .

While Sir Andrew carried Katin to the house, and Captain Fenton was assisted by two of the household guard, Arya trailed uncertainly after him, ready to bolt on the instant. She was reassured to find that no one paid her the slightest heed, however, and when another of the guards tried to turn her from the door, she stood her ground and insisted, "The captain said I was to come!"

"Oh, aye, and did he say you could steal Her Ladyship's silver spoons, too, gypsy brat? Be off with you!"

Dancing with rage, Arya shouted, "You ask him! I'm the one saved them both, I am! He'll tell you so!"

She was made to wait outside while Fenton was consulted about her, and by the time she was admitted, she was determined to get in and see the Governor, if she had to break a window to do it.

"Very well. Captain says to let you in," the guard admitted reluctantly, on his return. His tone said *might as well throw everything of value in the house right down the well now and be done with it.* Arya glared at him as she stalked past, but her triumph was short-lived. As soon as the door had shut behind her, the man added, "He says to make sure you *stay* in, too," and seized her by the wrist. She was dragged to a small, furnished anteroom, told, "You'll wait here till you're wanted," and locked in.

Arya waited. Now that she was inside, she wanted to break a window and get out, but the only window was in the door the guard had pushed her through, and when she stood on a stool to look out of it, she saw that he was standing sentry on the other side. She crept to the far door and peered through the keyhole at the parlor, where Katin lay, still insensible, on the cane-backed daybed, surrounded by the others. Arya knew them all by sight. On either side of the daybed were the physician Doctor Justin and the old man called Carlo, who was sometimes to be met with in the marshes. The gypsies considered him crazy because he paid good silver for specimens of the snakes and large insects that infested the swampland, but he was harmless enough, Arya knew. He and the physician seemed to be arguing about the best way to waken the medicine-maker, while the Governor and his lady looked on anxiously. The captain sat in an arm chair by the fire, sipping from a glass of brandy and looking somewhat stronger. Arya considered whether to cast a curse on him, but decided to wait and see how the Governor dealt with her. At least it was warm in here. Finally, she curled up on a bench and fell asleep.

She dreamed of the hostel in town, where her older sister Darkliss sometimes told fortunes to travelers. Arya had never been abovestairs there, but now she found herself climbing the stairs as bold as you please, and no one challenged her right to be there. She stopped before a certain door, which she knew would be locked, but among her charms was a key that would open it, and she slipped quickly inside without being seen.

She had felt sure that no one was within, and she was alarmed at first to see a man lying in the bed, with his back to her, completely still. She froze, staring at him, then gradually realized that there was no danger of his waking, and she remembered the old riddle, "What city is most crowded, though nobody lives there?" Her instinct had been right—there was no one in this room.

She wanted to run away before she could be found

there, but instead she drew nearer, against her will, and looked down at the dead man's face. She recognized him. "I warned you," she whispered, "that it was an evil charm."

Suddenly she heard voices and footsteps approaching the room, and she looked about frantically for someplace to hide. But already someone was opening the door behind her. . . .

She woke, panic-stricken, as Lady Celia opened the parlor door and escorted Doctor Justin and Carl out through the antechamber and into the hall, giving Arya only a distracted glance in passing. Before Arya could decide whether to dash into the parlor and confront the Governor, or race through the other door and try to outrun the guard, Lady Celia returned, locking the outer door behind her. Arya rose and curtsied to her, with a cringing air, begging, "Please m'lady, I've done no wrong. Why have they locked me in here?"

"I haven't the faintest idea," Lady Celia said wearily, "but I daresay we'll find out soon now." She was carrying a large peach, which she gave to the startled girl, then stood regarding her critically for a moment. She took Arya by the chin and gently raised her head, remarking, "Stand up straight when you address someone, child, and for heaven's sake *never* whine like that. If you behave like a cur, you'll be kicked like one."

Arya clutched the peach and stammered, "Yes, m'lady. Thank you, m'lady." She was not easily surprised, but the Viscountess was something altogether beyond her experience.

Lady Celia locked the parlor door behind her again, leaving Arya with a great deal to think about. As she devoured the peach, she tried to listen through the keyhole to what was being said, but they spoke in low tones, like conspirators. The medicine-maker was

awake now, she saw, and looked little the worse for the
danger she had passed. That was good. She'd be a sad
loss to the community, for the gypsies found her more
willing to treat their ailments than Doctor Justin, and
less particular about payment. Folk said she'd marry
that proud captain, but Arya hoped it wasn't so.

She sucked the peach-stone clean and put it in her
pocket, for it could be carved into a new charm. Perhaps she'd make one for the Governor's lady, she
thought, though she had never encountered anyone
who needed one less. Ruthven had done Arya an injus-
tice at their first meeting. A thief and a liar she might
be, betimes, but her charms were not altogether rubbish.

When she was at last admitted to the parlor by Captain Fenton, she took care to stand up straight and look
as defiant as she dared, but she no longer felt at all
sure of herself. She had been taught that it was safest
to avoid the notice of persons of authority, yet here she
was, the object of attention of the Governor and an
officer—to say nothing of the terrifying Lady Celia.
Katin smiled at her, the Governor looked frankly puzzled, and Lady Celia asked, "But what has this child to
do with the business, Captain?"

"That is what I myself would most like to know,
Your Ladyship. She seems to have been party to it
from the first, in one capacity or another. It must have
been she who stole that brass cylinder from me—the
one clue we had to—"

"I didn't! I'm no thief!" Arya protested. This was
worse than she'd feared. She moved closer to Katin,
for protection. She had already noted that there was
another door at the back of the room, but was it
locked? Where did it lead? Could she reach it before
she was caught?

"Arya," said Katin, placing her arm around the girl's shoulders, "listen to me, little one. I know you're a pickpocket, remember, but I also know you saved my life—and the captain's—so I won't let any harm come to you. No one here is angry with you, but we must know why you took the brass piece."

"I didn't want to—he made me!" Arya cried, trying not to whine. "I told him it would bring bad luck!"

"Who made you?" Sir Andrew demanded.

"One of the gypsies?" Captain Fenton said eagerly, at the same time.

"No! No gypsy—a stranger, in a velvet coat, *you* know," she appealed to Katin, "the man who caught me, and you told him to let me go—"

"Why, it's Oliver Ruthven she means," said Katin, for she had seen Ruthven—though he had not seen her—when he met with Sir Andrew. "But why would he want the thing?"

"Did he shoot the arrow at me?" Sir Andrew asked Arya.

"I don't know anything of that! He didn't tell me why he wanted it." Suppose they didn't believe her? She turned back to Katin. "But he locked you in the hut, mistress. I saw him." She hadn't meant to volunteer information—another thing she'd been taught not to do—but she had to tell them something, and she felt sure that she wouldn't be able to get a lie past Lady Celia.

For a moment, none of them said anything. Captain Fenton had expected to spend hours, if not days, merely trying to find out whether the girl had seen anyone near the shed, and now he suddenly had the answer to a question he hadn't even thought worth the asking. The others were silent also, for though there was a great deal that needed saying, none of it could be said in front of Arya. Ruthven could have no possible reason to kill Katin unless he knew who she was—and if he knew, did that mean that the Duke of Halkin knew? If not, he soon would. Ruthven must be questioned, and then he must be silenced. . . .

"They'll not tell him I said he was the one?" Arya asked Katin timidly. She had no charm that could protect her from the likes of Ruthven.

"No, they won't tell him anything," Katin assured her. "Don't you fret about that one—he'll not be after you or anyone else, ever again. Just you stay here with me until His Lordship has him under arrest."

"That," Sir Andrew said grimly, "will be within the hour." He turned to Captain Fenton. "Are you yet strong enough to accompany me? I don't wish to resort to the militia in this matter."

The captain was already on his feet. "Nothing could dissuade me," he said.

Lady Celia selected a key from the ring at her waist and opened the back door of the parlor for them, as that way was more convenient to the stable. But before they had reached the door, Alicen burst through it, wild-eyed with alarm, and threw herself on her knees beside Katin. "You're all right, then?" she cried. "They said you'd been poisoned, or suffocated, or burnt—I couldn't make sense of it!" She had spied Arya barely in time to stop herself from addressing Katin as "Highness," but she could not conceal her relief at finding her sovereign only a little wan, after the confused reports she'd received in the stable-yard.

Touched, Katin kissed her and said, "I'm quite safe now, thanks to my little friend here. I'll tell you all about it later."

"The child bears witness that Oliver Ruthven was behind the attack," Sir Andrew told her, "and we are on the point of running him to ground. I take it you will join us?"

"Ruthven?" Alicen got slowly to her feet. "But that's impossible—unless—when did this happen?"

"It must have been at much the same time you left for the docks," Lady Celia said, with a slight frown. She would have sworn to it that the child was telling the truth. "For just after you rode off, a gardener came running to fetch help."

"Why do you say the thing's impossible?" Sir Andrew demanded. "Explain yourself! There's no time to be lost."

"It was him," Arya whispered to Katin, nervously. But who was going to take her word against the Lady Alicen's?

"Perhaps it was just possible," Alicen said thoughtfully. "I was some time at the docks, and he might have struck then, and still reached the hostel before I did. But someone else was there before me. By the time I arrived for our meeting, he was dead."

There was another marked silence. Then Katin, insisting that she was quite well, took Arya off to the kitchen for a meal, allowing Sir Andrew to exclaim, "You say you went to *meet* with the Duke of Halkin's agent?"

"We'd an agreement," Alicen said defensively. "Someone was trying to kill us both—and you as well. We'd agreed to work in concert to find the Chamber's assassin, nothing more." But instead the assassin had found Ruthven. She had no doubt that she would be next, unless she could somehow outwit the killer. Alicen cursed the swiftness of the enemy who had struck just in time to prevent her from receiving Ruthven's warning. "He sent a message early this morning, bidding me meet with him. And I'd give something to know who his informants at the harbor were," she added, in evident vexation. "He must have known I was back the moment I set foot on the dock!"

"How did he know about the Princess?" Sir Andrew demanded.

Alicen spread her hands helplessly. "I don't believe he did, when I last spoke with him. He must have received new instructions regarding her." As if to herself, she said, "I didn't think it of him. I never doubted he'd kill me, if so ordered, but the Princess . . ."

"Then we've no choice but to assume that the Duke of Halkin knows of Oriana, and regards her as a threat. At least we know where we stand with him. But who killed Ruthven? Who told you he was dead?"

Alicen shook her head. "No one, for I saw him myself. After the meeting here this morning, I composed my report to His Grace, as you know, and went straight to the harbor to see that it sailed on the first ship out of port. Then I conferred with my spies on the docks, about the latest arrivals—and learned nothing of interest. If I'd only gone on to the hostel at once, I might have arrived in time, for I think he couldn't have been long dead when I found him. He didn't answer my knock, so I let myself into his room with the key to the room I rent there. He appeared to be asleep on the bed, but when I tried to wake him—" Alicen grimaced. "He didn't die peacefully in his sleep, that's certain. The bedclothes had been pulled up to cover most of his body, perhaps to dclay discovery as long as possible, but he was struck from the front—stabbed in the chest. Whoever did that must have been hiding there when he came in, and surprised him."

"Did you see anyone there—or any sign that might tell us who killed him?"

"No, nothing." Although she'd wanted only to be

away, she'd made herself search Ruthven's chamber for any clue to his murderer. "There was no one about but some serving maids—no one was near the room but me—and I didn't kill him."

"Of course not," Lady Celia said soothingly, handing her a tot of brandy. Alicen hid it well, but Lady Celia could see that she was shaken by the day's events.

"Among all Ruthven's possessions there was not a single document to be found. Someone took every scrap. But I found nothing else untoward about the room, beyond his dead body."

Sir Andrew frowned in frustration. "We're too late, but we'll do what we must." Sharply he called a servant and sent him after the Watch. "We'll see to it that the landlord and all the inhabitants of that rat trap are questioned—and have all his possessions held there until we can go over them."

When Katin returned, she heard Alicen's story, and told her about the attempt on her own life. "What's become of the child, Your Highness?" Alicen asked.

"I gave her a gold ember and had a groom take her to the Common. Some of her people are camped there for the night."

Without going so far as to criticize the Princess' actions, Captain Fenton objected, "She might have been able to tell us more about Ruthven. She never did explain her connection to him."

But Katin shook her head. "I asked her how she came to be thieving for him, but it was only that he'd been spying on you when you questioned the gypsy men on the Market Green. He paid her to go after you and steal the thing you'd showed them, but she'd never seen him before that, except for the time she'd tried to pick his pocket. I told her to say only that she'd seen smoke coming from under the door of my workshed and pulled it open herself."

"That was wise," Alicen approved. "We don't need rumors going about, that you're the target of assassins. But what of the gardener who unbolted the door?"

"He's to tell others that he saw what was happening, and ran to the house for help, no more," said Lady Celia, who had seen to that particular untruth herself.

"Will the girl keep the secret, do you think?" asked Captain Fenton doubtfully.

Katin shrugged. "Will the gardener? Would you have us keep them under lock and key until the coronation?"

Having no answer to that question, the captain raised another. "But why did Ruthven want the brass piece, unless it was he who tried to shoot Sir Andrew?"

"That's no mystery," said Alicen. "We both thought that whoever tried to kill us probably attacked Sir Andrew as well. He must have thought the thing would lead him to the Chamber's agent. And maybe it did— but now we'll never know."

One thing was certain, however. Ruthven's clothes with their silver buttons and buckles had not been touched, and his money pouch had still been hanging from his belt. Whoever had killed him, it had not been for purposes of thievery, and this told Alicen all she needed to know.

Chapter 11

The gypsies who tended Rolande had patched her wounds as best they might and hung eggshells wrapped in red ribbons and bags of aromatic herbs around the interior of the tent where she lay. Whatever combination of medicaments and charms they had applied had kept her alive thus far, but she remained weak and feverish, dazed with pain. As the hours passed, she grew increasingly uncertain that she could weather this latest storm.

When she opened her eyes and groaned in pain, the girl who watched over her offered her a bowl of broth, but Rolande didn't seem to see it. "Fetch Hrivas to me," she whispered weakly.

The girl scowled in return. "Fetch what? I don't think we have any o' that, mistress."

Rolande tried to pull herself to a sitting position, but soon gave up the effort and sank back upon the straw pallet. "Fetch him!" she ordered in a tone so desperate that the girl, certain that something terrible was about to occur, leaped to her feet and ran to look for Rolande's people. One of them must be the man she wanted.

Rolande lay upon the pallet exhausted. When Corey came, she recognized him and said urgently, "Send

Hrivas to Sir Andrew—bid him come. I have to tell him what I've learned."

"I've done that already, Captain," Corey assured her. "Hrivas flew for Oriana yesterday. I daresay he's on his way back here now, with word of the Governor. I told him to say you'd important news for His Lordship."

Rolande closed her eyes, soothed by the motion of the ship. "Well done. The ... information must not be lost with me. Let him come to me for once, then. I'll not see Oriana again."

"To be sure you will! We'll bring you there in a cart, to the—"

But Rolande heard no more. *What nonsense,* she was thinking, and smiled at the notion of a cart crossing the miles of ocean that surrounded them. Sir Andrew was coming, and so ... something was settled. Something important, though just at the moment she didn't remember what it was. "Tell Will to batten down the hatches," she ordered Corey. "There's another storm brewing."

* * *

Sir Andrew paced the moonlit garden of the Governor's Mansion, thinking over the day's events for the hundredth time. He knew it would be useless to attempt to sleep as yet. The Watch had questioned all the servants and guests of the hostel in Livery Row, but had nothing to show for their efforts. If Alicen were right that one person was behind the attacks on her and Ruthven—and perhaps himself—then that person was undoubtedly working for the Chamber, and the Princess would be the next target if the killer knew of her existence. Alicen had guessed her identity, and

Ruthven had learned of it somehow. Rumors were abroad. The assassin had succeeded once, and might do so again. He had to ferret out the enemy in their midst before the Princess could fall prey to another of these cowardly traps.

Without thinking, he turned his footsteps toward Carl's cottage. He was sure to be awake yet, for he often worked half the night away at his studies, without seeming to notice the passage of time. *And if there's anyone who may shed light on some point I've overlooked, it will be Carl,* he told himself. As he walked, he examined, yet again the details of the different attacks, searching the evidence for a pattern, as Carl had long ago taught him to do. The only *direct* strike, he mused, was the one upon Ruthven. That had required daring as well as skill, for the risk of detection would be great if the first blow did not kill at once. . . .

There were indeed lights showing within Carl's cottage, but when Sir Andrew pushed open the door, what he saw in the dim lamplight completely drove from his thoughts the orderly accounting of events he had meant to lay before Carl. There, hanging by one long limb from a ceiling beam, was a monstrous, shaggy creature the size of a bear.

Sir Andrew had never given a moment's credence to the tales of a huge, tree-dwelling man-beast that was said to haunt the swamps, but he could not deny the evidence of his own eyes. It turned its head to regard him balefully, and he saw that it was chewing something. For an awful moment, he wondered if it could have eaten Carl. He drew the pistol from his belt slowly so as not to alarm the beast further, but before he could advance, Carl pushed aside the deerskin that hung from the doorway separating the inner and outer rooms, and hurried to place himself between Sir Andrew and the creature.

"*What* is the meaning of this, m'lord?" the old man demanded, fixing his patron with a look of severe disapproval. "Surely you know better than to fire upon any animal, save in mercy or necessity? Why, I might never find another, if I lost this specimen."

"I wasn't going to shoot it unless it attacked," Sir Andrew protested, feeling much as he had over twenty years ago, when Carl had caught him betting on cockfights. "But what sort of creature *is* that?"

"I take it to be a giant spotted swamp sloth, m'lord," said Carl, mollified. "But classification is difficult, the beasts are so exceedingly rare."

"Thank the Good God for that."

"Oh, no. He's the most peaceable animal imaginable, and completely herbivorous. A baby would be quite safe with him." Carl reached up and stroked the great beast's flank. It slowly shifted its eyes to Carl, then took hold of his neckerchief by one end, pulled it loose, and nibbled at it daintily. Finding it unpalatable, it tossed it back onto Carl's shoulder and looked about for something more appetizing. Carl uncovered a large earthenware jar and removed a handful of water-ash leaves, which he offered to the creature.

Sir Andrew returned his pistol to its place as Carl fed the greenery to the swamp sloth. "How did you come by the thing, if they are so hard to find?"

"Ah, he was completely hidden by foliage. Note the unusual greenish cast to the fur—rather difficult to see in this light, but sunlight brings it out—and the black markings, the very hue and pattern of swamp verdure and shadow. I should never have seen him if I hadn't been hiding within a hollow tree at the time."

Sir Andrew set to clearing a lethal-looking assortment of lancets, bone scoops, pincers, and forceps from the oak bench by Carl's worktable, before he dared sit on it. "Hiding from what?" he asked idly, thinking that the marshes could scarcely be home to anything more fear-inspiring than the giant sloth.

Carl considered the question while he watched the great creature move ponderously overhead, till it had positioned itself over the closed jar of water-ash leaves, with one long arm dangling toward the lid. "As I recall, I was trying to avoid being seen by a pair of gypsies," he said slowly.

For the moment, Sir Andrew forgot the swamp sloth. "What were they about that you felt you must hide from them?" he asked sharply.

It was Carl's turn to look abashed. "I overheard them plotting to kill someone, I believe," he admitted. "I meant to report their conversation to you, but in my excitement over the discovery of the sloth, I'm afraid I forgot their very existence. In the light of an event of such magnitude, the incident was comparatively insignificant, you see."

"Possibly," said Sir Andrew. "As it may very well have been my death they were conspiring at, however, the affair admits of a certain consequence, in my view. I may, of course, be mistaken."

His heavy-handed sarcasm made no impression whatsoever upon Carl. "*Yours*, m'lord?" he gasped. "I would have thought, one of their own— How could you have fallen afoul of such folk?"

"That is what I, too, would like to determine. Tell me exactly what you heard."

When he had brought the scene clearly to his mind, Carl recounted quite accurately for Sir Andrew the conversation between the two men in the swamp, but it contributed little to the inquiry. "Would you know them again if you saw them?" Sir Andrew asked.

Carl looked doubtful. He could distinguish any of thirty species of hawthorn at a glance, but people were all one to him, for the most part. "Well, one was little more than a lad, the other a grown man ..." he offered.

Sir Andrew never did ask for Carl's view of the situation, nor did it occur to Carl to ask the reason for his visit, but he had received his answer nevertheless. He returned to the manor house convinced that he would have to find out the truth of the gypsies' involvement, even if he must travel to their encampment himself. Their leader, Kedzier, was no fool. It should be possible to reason with him.

With at least one unknown killer at large, the Princess in danger, the alliance with the Duke of Wyston to be effected, and the Chamber planning another invasion with a weapon of unknown power, he had quite enough to occupy his mind, yet he had not even entered the mansion before Lady Celia met him with the news that Rolande's Yerren crewman had brought word of her at last.

Hrivas was waiting on the rear portico, where Lady Celia had left him, knowing that Yerren were ill at ease within walls. "I fear for the captain's life," he told Sir Andrew. His face and voice remained expressionless, as if he remarked merely, "I fear it may rain," but Sir Andrew had had dealings enough with the Yerren to disregard their seeming impassivity. "You must go to her, for she is too hurt to travel here from the gypsy camp. She has information of much importance for you. She has learned of the enemy warships."

Sir Andrew put a few questions to him, but learned little beyond what Hrivas had already told him.

Rolande had been shipwrecked in the last storm, washed up on shore to the east, on the far side of the river. She was most grievously wounded, Hrivas repeated. She had been bringing him secret information.

By now, Katin and Captain Fenton had joined them, and Sir Andrew told them Hrivas' message, adding, "According to the reports I've received, the ship that broke up offshore to the east was the *Seafarer*—an Albinate convict ship. If Vendeley was aboard, she was certainly not its captain." To Hrivas he said, "Tell her I myself am coming. I shall start out on the morrow for the gypsy camp."

"Tell the Captain that I, Ander, shall come to her too," Katin put in. Before the others could object, she said firmly, "Vendeley has saved my life more than once. If she's as seriously injured as Hrivas believes, she needs better treatment than the gypsies can provide her. I don't mean to let her die in the swamp if I can do aught to prevent it. I shall expect Captain Fenton to accompany me, of course."

Captain Fenton bowed, trusting to Lady Celia to dissuade Her Highness from such a dangerous and unnecessary journey.

"She will know of your coming on the morrow, by midday," Hrivas promised. He clambered up one of the pillars onto the roof and took flight from the peak of the cupola, much relieved to have his mission over with and return to the heights.

The others hurried in out of the chill, damp night, and Lady Celia sent for some hot mulled wine, as they settled themselves in the parlor. "I do wish," she sighed, "that there were some way to offer hospitality to the Yerren. But they hate to be indoors, spirits are simply poison to them, and I'm told that they find our diet repulsive. I did try to give that one fruit, when he was here before, but he didn't eat it."

"Jerl says they don't feel safe on the ground," Katin explained. "I'm afraid if you can't entertain them on the roof or in a tree, the kindest thing is not to detain them any longer than necessary. They do like fruit, though—and cake. Perhaps I could bring Hrivas some. I daresay he doesn't get much of it." She paused, puzzled. "But how is it that he can come and go in the gypsy camp, I wonder? And how is it that Vendeley was on that convict ship? I know the Yerren don't lie—she must have been aboard, but if the Deps caught her, I don't understand why they transported her instead of hanging her. The Chamber has offered five hundred embers for her capture."

Lady Celia smiled. "They may not have known they had her. Rolande is not one woman, but many."

Dashing Captain Fenton's hopes, she added, "I quite see that *you* must go to her, my dear, but Andrew, what can you do for her? Need you go yourself?"

Sir Andrew set down his mulled wine. "If Vendeley claims to have learned something of importance to our defense, it is most likely so. And if she is not a fool—which is one accusation I would never level against her—she will not trust such information to a messenger. She doesn't know Fenton, and Jamison's still at Haremare Point reviewing the progress at the shipyards. This won't wait for his return. We can't chance wasting time." To Katin, he said, "You, I think, will be as safe there as anywhere else—we'll take an escort of militiamen. There can hardly be more predators on the prowl in the swamp than we seem to have in our midst here nowadays. But I've another reason to go, aside from obliging Vendeley and keeping a watch on Your Highness." He told them of his conversation with Carl, and concluded, "It's not just our little pickpocket who's been brought into this business."

Captain Fenton said excitedly, "The gypsies Schellring saw could have been among the men I questioned that day at the Common—yet I've not seen the two I suspect about the town recently. I've wondered if they were deliberately staying away, lest they be recognized."

"Decidedly, it is time I had a talk with Kedzier myself."

Clearing his throat nervously, Captain Fenton began, "But if, as seems likely, the enemy has accomplices among the gypsies, is it wise, Your Highness, for you—"

In as regal a tone as Fenton had ever heard her use, Katin interrupted, "That has been settled, Captain. We shall leave as soon as possible. I had better see to my medicine kit at once. I may need remedies for fever, festering wounds, and weak blood, as well as splints and bandages." She rose, kissed Lady Celia, bowed to the others, and swept from the room with a majestic dignity that her rough attire and disheveled hair did nothing to dispel.

Corey, meanwhile, had been employed about some diplomacy of his own, persuading Kedzier to allow Hrivas safe passage to and from the gypsy encampment.

"This one's tame, is it?" Kedzier scowled. "I've lost people to those cursed featherlings. Folk won't like having one of them among us."

"Tame" was not the word Corey would have chosen for Hrivas, but he didn't mean to start an argument with Kedzier. He assumed, with good reason, that the gypsy leader was a sort of captain to his tribe, and thus someone to be approached with respect. "Well, they're not all the same, you see, sir," he explained. "He's a sailor, Hrivas, the same as me. He doesn't make war on the *Ysnathi*—I mean, on humans—because he's used to living among 'em—us—on board ship. He's not killed any of your people, sir, on my honor."

The gypsies knew, of course, that there were Yerren who worked the ships. There were even a few who came into Oriana now and then to trade furs for weaponry and the few sorts of *Ysnath* food they liked. But their visits were rare, and they didn't linger any longer than they must. Kedzier had never had a good look at one, and he was curious to do so. As Sir Andrew had noted, he was not a fool, and Corey's claim that the Yerren were not all the same had struck a chord with him. Other people were all too quick to assume that all gypsies were alike, after all—that all were thieves and charlatans because some were. . . .

"If they'd let us be, we'd let them be," he told Corey. "What those feather'uns don't know is that they're gypsies like us, now most of their people are gone. They should have peace with us." He shrugged. "But how are we to tell them anything? I'll give the word that if one of them comes among us alone, while your lot are here, and conducts itself peaceable, it's not to be fired on. But you'll be answerable for the creature, mind."

When Hrivas swooped over the gypsy camp the next morning, he expected Corey to follow him, but instead, to his surprise, Corey and Raphe signaled him to land. Hrivas flew lower, warily, watching the groups of gypsies clustered beneath him. They pointed to him, talking excitedly, but none aimed a weapon at him, that he could see.

Raphe ran off to tell Rolande of Hrivas' arrival, and

Corey again signaled to the circling Yerren to descend. Hrivas at last alit atop a tree at the edge of the clearing, from which he could take flight on the instant if need be. Corey, he knew, would not have beckoned to him unless he believed it to be safe, and he could sense no warning of danger from his friend, but only reassurance. The others, he noted, still made no move against him. He began slowly to descend the tree. To come to land on such uncertain ground went against all his instincts, but Corey was *tsivihr,* and Hrivas was incapable of doubting him.

Then suddenly he realized that he was also receiving impressions from some of the Ysnathi that Corey called gypsies. They felt curiosity about him, and some apprehension, but there was no threat directed at him. For whatever reason, they did not intend to attack. When he came within shouting distance, Corey called, "Come on, featherpate! These folk have sworn a truce with you!"

Hrivas landed beside him, clutching Corey's arm to steady himself. Like most of his people, he was awkward at alighting on flat ground. "Get your damned talons out of me," Corey complained. "Are you trying to shred me, man?"

"You are trying to get me killed," Hrivas pointed out, looking around at the gathering gypsies. Nothing in his manner expressed tension, but Corey was well aware of it.

"Nay, I tell you I've the word of their captain they'll let you be."

Hrivas tried to ignore their stares. They were only more Ysnathi like his crewmates, he told himself. "How fares Captain Vendeley, then?" he asked.

"Eh—I don't know, lad. She's alive yet, but I don't like the look of her. Sometimes she knows where she

is, sometimes she doesn't. What news do you bring?"
He led Hrivas toward the tent where Rolande waited,
devoured by fever, drifting in and out of delirium, but
clinging to life with the same fierce determination with
which she had always lived it.

"The Governor's on his way—said he'd set out this
morning. I'll go back and look for them, to make sure,
when I've rested some. And the female called Ander
will come, too—the one who used to come aboard the
Azora whenever we made port in Oriana."

"That's good news—". Corey pushed aside the hide-
flap of Rolande's tent and announced, "Governor's
bringing his 'pothecary, Captain. She'll fix you up
smart."

Rolande, who had been lying on the pallet with her
eyes closed, opened them and looked at him uncertainly. "He's bringing her?" she mumbled. "Here?"

"Aye, they'll be here by tomorrow or the day after,
I shouldn't wonder. Here's Hrivas says they're to start
out today."

"She ought not—'tisn't safe . . . she's not really an
apothecary . . . "

"But if the Governor employs her, she's bound to
have some skill, Captain," Raphe said reassuringly.

" 'Twould be better to have Blythe at hand, to be
sure, but the lass must know more than the gypsies,"
Corey agreed.

Rolande only shook her head wearily and lapsed into
silence, which worried her crewmen all the more. If
Rolande had called them a pack of worthless fools and
ordered them to get about their business, they'd have
felt a good deal easier about her.

* * *

The Yerren do not laugh, but when Corey told Hrivas of his conversation with Kedzier, he could sense his friend's amusement, and thought of it as laughter. "What that one does not know," said Hrivas, "is that all *Ysnathi* are the same to us. How could we make peace with these gypsies when we can't tell them from the rest of you?"

"*You* can," Corey said, surprised.

"Because they're here. You know I could never recognize more than a few of our crew—Will was the biggest, Grio the darkest, and the captain, well, she's the captain. If I see hunters in some parts of the marshes, I know they must come from here, and I know that you've a name for the ones who live here, but I doubt that the others of my clan know so much as that."

"Couldn't you tell them? These folk don't think they're *Ysnathi,* y'know—if they think your kind are gypsies of the air, then maybe they're a sort of featherless Yerren. Why not tell your people that? I should think they'd find it an advantage not to have this lot shooting at them."

Hrivas shook his head—a habit he'd learned from his human crewmates, for Yerren used no such gestures. "They don't listen to me," he said.

Yet Hrivas felt that there might be something to the notion. As they walked through the encampment, he saw that the gypsies, like the Yerren, lived far more in the open air than the *Ysnathi* of Oriana. Arrayed in an uneven circle were their canvas-covered carts, interspersed with tents and wooden huts not unlike the treetop dwellings of the marsh-Yerren. Outside of several tents, men sat working on pieces of tin with shears and hammers, while nearby, women in colorful skirts finished the trinkets or stirred pots of food hanging over open fires.

Here and there, Hrivas caught again some traces of the unspoken communion he shared with the others of his clan—and with Corey. He was startled by the sight of a gypsy woman carrying what appeared at first glance to be a Yerren infant, for he had never seen human children except at a distance, and had not realized how much they resembled unfledged Yerren young.

The children, for their part, were eager for a better look at the feathered stranger. They had often been told that a Yerren would carry them off and eat them if they misbehaved, but Hrivas was something of a disappointment to them. He was not even as big as an ordinary person, and did not seem very fearsome when seen at close quarters. When one of their number made bold to ask him whether he himself had ever carried off any bad children, he patiently explained that he could not possibly fly while bearing anything so large and heavy as a child—unless perhaps a very small one were to cling to his back. All clamored to try, at once, but the adults shooed them away.

On the whole, the gypsies approved of Hrivas. Darkliss, Arya's older sister, who was known to have the second sight, announced that there was no harm in him, which satisfied Kedzier. Before he left to search for Sir Andrew's party, she offered him a bright red neckerchief, "so we'll know you from afar," she told him, "and not take you for one of the others."

Corey felt Hrivas's reluctance to accept her gift, and the woman, too, was apparently aware of it, for she stepped back with a puzzled look and said, "Oh ... you don't like it."

"Red is not the color of my clan," Hrivas explained, sensing her disappointment. To wear the color of another clan was a thing unheard of, an act of unimaginable treason. And yet ... he had never so much as seen a member of the Red Rock Clan, and his people would certainly never go to war with them again. To maintain clan enmities was surely madness, now that there were so few surviving Yerren of any color. *And they think me a traitor already, because I left the marshland to travel with the* Ysnathi. *What does it matter, then? Maybe I'll have to be a gypsy instead of a sailor, if the captain dies.*

He could find work on another ship, in time, but he knew from other Yerren sailors that most were tolerated at best, and more often shunned, by their human crewmates. He'd been lucky to take ship with Rolande, who had made him an accepted member of her crew—indeed, something of a mascot. In a way, he realized, the crew of the *Azora* had become his clan.

He reached for the red neckerchief, saying, "I thank you, it is well thought of. The color is nothing. 'Twill serve for a sign between us, that we are not at war."

* * *

The news of the impending visitors swept through the camp in short order, and the two gypsies who had been overheard by Carl took the first chance to confer about their prospects. Sitting on a fallen log in the marsh near the river, the elder of the two cast an appraising glance at his young cohort. "Not any too pleased, that one was, to find 'is Lordship was still with us."

Michat took a swig from a pewter flask and scowled. "How was we to know there'd be a bloody healing-woman right on the spot? He should've died, by rights, the blow he took."

"That's God's truth, but we'll not see a penny of our

money all the same, unless, a-course, we finish the job."

Michat took another drink, looking sideways at his companion. "Think we can, then?"

"You've heard the news, haven't you? The roebuck's coming to the hunters. This time my arrow will find the heart." He took the flask from Michat and corked it. "But more than that, boy. He brings the 'pothecary with him. There's money to be had for her head, too, if you want to try your hand at it."

"Why?" Michat couldn't imagine what good it would do to have the apothecary killed. The Lord Marshal was sure to have enemies, but why the girl? Still, after the trouble she'd caused them by saving the Governor's life, he was willing enough to do the job.

Kamar took a blade from his pocket, pulled open the tortoiseshell guards, and began to pick his nails with the point. "How would I know why the gentry kill each other? 'Tisn't our affair. It's worth twenty embers in gold, that's all I need to know."

Michat gave a whistle of amazement. "More than for t'other one! But how do you plan to kill them at all—they'll not be traveling alone, and we've but the two of us."

Kamar pointed westward with the point of the blade. "I say we wait in the brush near the riverbank, and strike when they're in the middle of the river. No one can row and hold a musket at the same time. We'll pick off our targets—one for you and one for me—and make for the deep woods. By the time they get free of the oars and brace their flintlocks, we'll be out of range, and by the time they reach shore, we'll be long gone!"

"Eh, that *is* pretty, now," said Michat, looking at Kamar with admiration. "But what of Kedzier, though—

he's suspicious already. When he gets word of this, he's sure to blame us, and who'll swear the two of us were somewhere else?"

Kamar spat. "To the devil with Kedzier! What do I care what he thinks, if I've that much money to my name? I don't mean to grow old breaking horses for others to ride. Think on it, lad. We could fit ourselves up with proper gear and strike out for the mountains to the west, where there's gold and silver strewing the creekbeds, waiting for someone to bend down and take it! We would be rich men—"

"Leave the tribe?" Michat said doubtfully. "No one's ever done that. . . ."

Kamar shrugged. "I told Kedzier we should press on further west and gather ourselves a fortune in ore, but he'd not have it. We all have to settle near the hills where the horses run, because *he* thinks that's proper work for a gypsy. Now me, I've a fancy to have horses of my own, and a carriage for 'em to pull, with a coachman to drive it, and a carriage house besides— an' a manor house to go with the carriage house, and me master of th' manor, with a dainty bit in silks to be its mistress, and folks bowing down when I pass. There's nothing you can't have, boy, if you've th' means. But you can stay with the tribe if that suits you. Nay, if you want to spend your life wading through muck in this gnat-ridden swamp, you're welcome to. You can even tell Kedzier I did it, then you'll be—"

"No, I'll go, too!" said Michat, his eyes shining. "Why should we go on living like beggars, if we can live like lords? I'm with you!"

"Good lad. I knew you'd the heart for it." Kamar passed the flask back to him and watched him take a long, greedy pull from it. It did not require the second sight to read his thoughts, the alluring visions of diamond buckles and golden earrings, of red silk shirts and blushing, soft-skinned beauties. *The Good God sent you to me, you brawny simpleton.* Let the lad come along, by all means. Let him carry packs and toil in the mountains for months. Time enough to get him drunk and cut his throat when they'd gathered gold and silver enough to make a man's fortune. . . .

* * *

Sir Andrew and his party trudged through the matted undergrowth, keeping to a course which the gypsies, in their regular passing, had left to mark their path. He had brought two militiamen to act as escort, but he did not anticipate trouble—other than possible encounters with wild beasts—for he planned to stay to the gypsies' trail, well away from the Yerren village deeper to the north. The boat they would need to cross the Wherrisovir River was on a sledge hauled by the militiamen.

Carl, who had been to the gypsy camp, had assured him that the way was well traveled, making it unnecessary to take a guide. But at several points only Katin was able to see the signs that people had passed, and Sir Andrew followed her lead with misgiving until the reappearance of the path showed that she'd been right. After some hours of this uncertain journey, he was much relieved when they were joined by Vendeley's Yerren lookout.

At first, he'd feared that they had after all strayed into Yerren territory, and that the lone Yerren circling overhead was the scout for an attack party. Sir Andrew had his people ready their muskets, but the Yerren was unarmed, and seemed to be trying to catch their attention rather than evade it. "It must be Hrivas," Katin said, waving to him, and when the others had laid aside their weapons, he swooped low enough to call a greeting.

But even with Hrivas for a guide, the way was far from easy. They slogged uncomfortably through the heat that soon caused their clothes to become sweat-soaked. The swamp was choked with thick tangled vines and close-grown brambles, and pitted with bog holes that could swallow them down if they chanced a misstep. Savage beasts reportedly lurked in the thick dark growth, and Sir Andrew sent Hrivas to spy out the terrain, from time to time, and warn them of dangers ahead. The trip would take two days, Sir Andrew estimated. If they could travel by night, they might arrive sooner—or they might not arrive at all. The swamp, murky at the best of times, was too treacherous to negotiate in the dark.

Just before dusk they stopped near a stream to make camp and gather wood for the fire. They had brought food enough for the journey, but Katin would have liked to find some fresh game for their supper. She had her bow and quiver, but she knew better than to suggest to Sir Andrew that she might go off into the marshes to hunt, even with an escort. Once she would have tried, but now she had responsibilities to more than herself. Sitting down on a rock, she rummaged through her pack for something to eat and found the carefully-wrapped half cake she'd brought in case she should find Hrivas at the gypsy camp. "Lady Celia sent this for you," she told him. "I hope it's to your liking." Katin couldn't tell whether or not he was pleased, but before he left them for the night, he offered to catch some marsh-hens for them in the morning, when the birds left their hidden nests among the reeds.

Katin checked on the packet of medicaments that she'd left in the boat, wrapped in waterproof oiled cloth, for safekeeping. Then she finally settled down and stretched out her feet to the fire to dry, remembering the first trip she'd made into the wilderness, with Rolande complaining about her wet boots the whole way. And all the while she'd been planning to betray them to the Chamber . . . *but at the last she snatched me out of the enemy's hands instead and took me along on that ill-fitted merchantman to capture the Dep munitions brig. 'Twas better sport even than hunting wild boar!* By the time Rolande and her ragtag crew of bandits had made off with the vessel, Katin had been all but ready to sail away with her, too. Her distrust and scorn of Rolande had turned to reluctant admiration. She desperately hoped that she would reach the gypsy camp in time to aid her.

She'd questioned Hrivas at length about Rolande's injuries, and he'd described her condition as best he could—a description that was far from reassuring. Katin had little doubt that the wound was festering, for the gypsies' knowledge of medicine was primitive at best. Poison from an untreated wound could kill a person in a matter of days. . . .

Abruptly an unearthly animal shriek brought Katin to her feet, bow in hand, but Sir Andrew stopped her before she could leave the circle of light cast by the fire. They all stood rigid, weapons at the ready, listening to the loud thrashing and howling coming from the brush by the bank of the stream, all too close to their camp.

Without a word, Sir Andrew and Captain Fenton had moved to flank Katin. Now the two militiamen started toward the source of the bloodcurdling sounds, but in a moment, further investigation became unnecessary.

The screen of reeds between the campsite and the water was suddenly crushed down by the massive, lashing tail of a seven-foot-long lizard that was fighting with a great gold-furred cat the size of a calf. As Captain Fenton raised his musket and fired, Sir Andrew seized Katin and half lifted, half threw her into the fork of the nearest tree, shouting, "Climb!" The cat appeared to be getting the worst of the fight, and the wide, squat lizard didn't look as if it could pull itself up a tree.

The wildcat abruptly ceased its screaming, as one of the musketballs fired by the militiamen found its mark, but the gigantic lizard, though wounded, was far from dead. Blood poured from wounds in its ridged, leathery, green hide, but it crawled forward with surprising speed and snapped viciously at Captain Fenton's boot with long, jagged-toothed jaws. The captain jumped back, using his empty musket as a bludgeon to beat the beast back as the militiamen frantically reloaded and Sir Andrew braced his musket against the split branch of an ash tree and fired a ball that penetrated the great reptile's skull. It thrashed wildly once more, then lay still.

Katin clambered down from her perch and joined the others to stare at the nightmarish creature and the great mauled cat. "The pelt's ruined," she said regretfully, "but could we take the giant lizard back for Carl?"

It was already late afternoon when they arrived at the Wherrisovir River, an unappealing muddy green barrier that sliced through the swamp from north to south. The Yerren name simply meant "reedy," but the colonists had already begun to refer to the river as the Wheresoever. Sir Andrew, the memory of the giant lizard still fresh in his mind, was cautious in his approach to the crossing. While the militiamen set the boat upon the bank and slid it into the water, he sent Hrivas to survey the span of the river they would pass, for their small vessel could be easily upset if such a beast attacked it. But the Yerren reported that the river appeared safe, then flew to the top of a basswood tree on the far bank, to watch and wait.

With Katin and Sir Andrew in the bow and Captain Fenton in the stern, the two militiamen took up the oars and began rowing across the sluggish water. Only the thick weeds impeded their passage, and when they had passed the midpoint of the river without encountering any further monstrosities, Sir Andrew observed, "It seems there are no sea serpents or kraken about, at least. I suppose we should be thankful for that much."

Katin chuckled. "I pity one of those green creatures if Vendeley ever sees it. She'd have its hide for boots in no time at all—" She broke off and asked anxiously, "Is it much farther to the gypsy camp, do you think?"

"Once we land, we should have but a short distance to go," Sir Andrew assured her. "I expect we'll be there well before dark, if nothing occurs to delay us."

Just then there was a warning cry from Hrivas, and Sir Andrew pushed Katin to the bottom of the boat and threw himself over her, as Hrivas nocked an arrow in his bow and let it fly. A moment later Michat tumbled from one of the tall clumps of rushes along the river bank, clutching at his wounded arm, where the arrow had slashed it. Kamar charged from another clump of reeds with his crossbow aimed at Hrivas, but at once a shot rang out from the trees behind him, and he fell lifeless to the muddy ground.

As Corey burst from the tangled stand of green hawthorn, Michat forced himself to his knees and pulled his musket to him, pointing the weapon first at the boat, still defenseless and exposed upon the water, then at Hrivas, the more immediate threat. Hrivas dove into the air, making himself a most difficult target, but he could not fire a weapon upon the wing. Captain Fenton tried to brace his flintlock across the side of the rocking boat, but before he could steady his aim the wounded gypsy had gained his feet and disappeared into the swaying reeds. Seeing that his way was blocked in all directions save one, Michat dropped his heavy musket, drew his pistol, and ran into the woods to the north, desperately pushing his way through the densely interwoven branches.

Having reloaded his own pistol, Corey raced after him, but the thick underbrush made it impossible to see which way the man had gone, and Corey soon lost his trail. Hrivas was not encumbered by the need to search from the ground, however, and he soared in pursuit, clutching his bow mid-wing in one taloned hand. As he swooped from tree to tree, he could not see all the way to the ground, but he soon marked where the underbrush was being disturbed by the passage of his quarry. With a long, piercing war cry, he veered about in the air and landed in a tree just in front of the disturbance that marked the gypsy's passing.

As Michat broke his way through a clump of red maple to emerge in a tiny clearing, a sixth sense for danger made him look up to where Hrivas perched on a branch, bow in hand. The gypsy raised his pistol, and suddenly the air was full of great wings as a score of Yerren landed in the trees all around him. Arrows flew from everywhere at once, and when they stopped, the gypsy assassin lay dead, his body riddled with a dozen shafts.

Hrivas knew why the others had come to his defense. They were of one clan, and could sense one another's feelings all too well. If he'd been hurt, so close to the Yerren village, all the clan would have suffered with him, and that they could not allow. But now that the threat was past, Hrivas felt their hostility and scorn directed at him as strongly as ever. They gathered around him, and their leader tore the red neckcloth from Hrivas's throat. His wordless fury fell like a blow. Hrivas had disgraced himself and his clan.

In the excitement of the attack and the chase, Hrivas had forgotten that he was wearing the neckerchief. "It means nothing," he protested. "The clan-across-the-river bade me wear it as a sign that I am a messenger, no more."

The others knew that he spoke the truth, for falsehood was impossible among members of the same clan. But such an explanation, though true, was not acceptable to them. Hrivas could sense the sneer behind the war leader's words as he said, "So now you serve even our deadliest enemies. I thought you were a Yerren of the floating cities."

"I am! But some of my *tsivihri*"—there was no Yerren word for *shipmate*—"have taken refuge from the storms in the village across the river. I must carry word for them, to and from the city Oriana."

"Let the *Ysnathi* carry their own messages! We are at war with the clan-across-the-river!"

"They want peace with us," Hrivas insisted. "Their High Priest has said that they draw bow against us only because they are attacked."

For answer, the leader pointed to the body of the gypsy Michat. "Had you attacked that one?"

"No . . . but—"

"You believe whatever the *Ysnathi* tell you. As much a traitor as you are, you are even more a fool. Come with us and ask the Elders to forgive your folly."

Once, such acts of treason would have earned him exile, but now that the Yerren were so few, even a renegade like Hrivas could hope to be welcomed back to his clan. And he was tempted to go with them, to be one with his people again ... *If the captain dies* ... but how could he take up arms against the gypsies, who had welcomed him? How could he spend his life hunting the marshes, when he had sailed the ocean?

There was no need for him to answer. The Yerren leader sent a silent signal to his band, and they took flight together, leaving Hrivas to watch them wing away to the north. He knew they felt his sorrow, but they could not share it. He swooped low over the ground and snatched up the red neckerchief, then flew back to the river, to tell Sir Andrew that their second assailant was also dead.

" 'Twas just that I knew the wing'un was in trouble," Corey explained, as he led the way along the bank past the moored rafts the gypsies used to cross the river, and through the forest to the encampment. "It just come to me sudden, y'see, like rememberin' something, but it was happening now, not before." He shrugged. "Thought I'd best come and meet 'im." To Hrivas, perched in a tree ahead of them, waiting for them to catch up, he called, " 'Twas a good thing for you, featherpate, that you brought me that pistol from town!"

Hrivas, who had gathered some nuts, shied one at him and answered impassively, "If you plucked'uns weren't such a bloodthirsty lot of savages, you wouldn't need one."

Sir Andrew marveled that Corey was able to take his uncanny ability so much for granted. In Thornfeld, where the zealous Scrutinor sect had held sway for a time, such an admission had nearly resulted in Jerl Smit's being hanged for a witch. Even Carl could shed no light on the actual nature of the phenomenon, though he insisted that there was nothing unnatural in its operation. "I've long suspected the existence of some such communal sympathy in colonies of ants and bees," he'd told Sir Andrew. "Perhaps it exists, unbeknownst to us, among more highly developed animals as well. Perhaps, indeed, the wonder is not that some other orders of beings possess this ability, but that the order of humankind does not."

It would certainly make negotiation easier, Sir Andrew thought, not long afterward, when faced with the inscrutable Kedzier. Hrivas had flown ahead to tell Rolande of their coming, and by the time the party reached the encampment, it was clear that the gypsy leader, too, had been warned of their arrival. He came forward to greet them himself, looked through Captain Fenton as if unable to see him, and addressed himself to Sir Andrew with obsequious politeness. "Lord Governor, you honor our camp by your visit."

Sir Andrew would have given much for the ability to tell what Kedzier was feeling just then. Was the gypsy leader surprised to see them alive? Before he could reply, Katin demanded, "Where is Rolande Vendeley, please? I must attend to her at once."

"Aye, I'll show you, lass. Come with me," Corey said eagerly.

"Captain, take Dugan and Hardison and accompany Mistress Ander," Sir Andrew ordered, then turned to Kedzier and said coldly, "I am aggrieved that I must fear for the safety of my people here, but two of your men attacked us as we crossed the river. You will find the body of one by the riverbank. I shall expect to be told who he is. The other fled northward and was killed by a party of Yerren."

He had hoped to learn something from Kedzier's reaction, expecting protestations of ignorance or denial, but instead Kedzier broke into a stream of invective in his native tongue, his face a mask of frustrated wrath. "You have saved me the trouble of killing them myself!" he told Sir Andrew. "I warned that pair of devils' sons—!" He shouted orders to some of the men working nearby, and explained, "I have sent them to fetch the body, but I can tell you who he is without seeing it. If 'tis a youth, then it must be Michat, if a man, it will be Kamar."

"If you knew who tried to kill me before, it was your duty to inform me," Sir Andrew rebuked him. "Had our Yerren guide not flushed them, they might well have succeeded this time, and fled into the brush before they could be stopped. I expected better of you."

Kedzier mantled at Sir Andrew's tone, but could not deny that the Governor had grounds for displeasure. "If I was sure of their guilt, my duty was to punish them myself, for bringing dishonor on us, and putting us all in danger of retribution. But I was not sure, and there was nothing to be gained by telling my suspicions to outsiders. We are held in enough mistrust as it is. I warned them, I asked questions, I had them watched."

Again, Sir Andrew wished for the Yerren sense that would have told him whether the other was lying. *But it would not avail us, in any case. We belong to different clans.* "Why was I attacked, then?" he demanded. "I have not allowed your people to be ill treated at the hands of the colonists. What was their quarrel with me?"

Kedzier shook his head sadly. "You were not the enemy. Kamar was ever too hungry for gold, and the boy too easily led."

"They were paid by someone, then? Who?"

"I tried to find that out. I set one of my sons to keep a watch upon them, but one day I found him asleep near the wagons, at noonday, like a drunkard. I know they must have drugged his food. But then the child Arya—the same," he added pointedly, "who saved the lives of those two with you today—she told me that a man had paid her to steal that brass charm that belonged to the killer, and that the man was dead. So. He must have been the one, I thought, and there is no further danger now." He spread his hands resignedly. "I was wrong, it would seem. But if he did not tempt Kamar to the deed, I know no more than you who it was. If I find out, this I will tell you, upon my honor, for none of my people could have been behind it."

Sir Andrew had no reason to disbelieve him. Kedzier would have little to gain and much to lose from a foolish attack on those whose good will he depended on. "I shall rely on you to do so, then," he said. "Now I must speak with Vendeley." He offered payment for Rolande's care and keep, but this the gypsy leader thought it wisest to refuse.

Arya watched wide-eyed as Katin applied a poultice of moldy bread to Rolande's wounded chest. She had seen some strange magic used by wisewomen of her tribe, but nothing as peculiar as this. " 'Tis to purify flesh that's mortified," Katin told her. "Such a wound leaches poison into the blood, and the poison of the mold somehow undoes the other. Carl calls it a counter-poison. I can't say that I understand it, but I know that it works. Now I must brew a decoction of willow bark to break her fever—run and fetch me hot water as quick as you can."

Katin had been horrified to find Rolande lying in the dark, close tent, and had fastened up the canvas over the doorway at once, to let in light and fresh air. Rolande had opened her eyes for a moment and regarded Katin incuriously, but gave no other sign of life as Katin examined her wounds. *At least she's reasonably clean,* Katin thought. She had made the others stay outside, but admitted Arya, who had come running as soon as she heard that the herbalist was in camp.

By the time Arya returned with the hot water, she had heard all about the attack on the party, and hastened to take credit for Katin's safe arrival. "You see, my charm saved you again!" she crowed.

"I shall never take it off," Katin assured her. She looked up at the eggshells hanging over Rolande's pallet. "Are those your charms, too?"

"No, those are Janna's. Mine only protect, they do not heal," Arya explained. She looked critically at the eggshells and frowned. "I don't know if Janna's do either," she added, "but don't tell her I said so."

Katin smiled. "I daresay you're right, but I won't tell her. I think you'd better start coming to me for reading lessons, little one, and I'll teach you some healing charms, too."

Sir Andrew knelt beside Rolande and looked down at her uneasily. She was much thinner than he last remembered seeing her, and her face had an unhealthy, unnatural flush. If she was aware of his presence, she gave no sign of it. "Can you save her?" he asked Katin softly.

Katin pushed the hair out of her face with a weary gesture that was somehow unlike her. "Her heartbeat's strong," she said, "and her breathing seems unhindered. They've not been making her drink enough, but I've given her willow-bark tea and broth and boiled-apricot cordial, and a good bit of water. She's kept it down so far—that's a good sign—but she should have a drink of water every hour tonight, all the same. I'll see to it."

"Indeed you won't," Sir Andrew interrupted. "You'll get some sleep."

Katin waved this aside indifferently. "Arya can help me with her. She's better than I at getting her to take it when she doesn't want it."

Sir Andrew sighed. "I should have brought Doctor Justin. I didn't imagine that she was as ill as this."

"One doesn't," Katin agreed. "It's as though this is someone else, and Vendeley's off at sea, harrying the Chamber's merchantmen. Weak and helpless as she is, how could she be Rolande Vendeley?"

She was right, Sir Andrew realized. He had always thought of Vendeley as an indomitable force.

"But I doubt the doctor would have agreed to tramp through the marshes to treat a pirate," Katin continued. "He won't come to attend to the gypsies. And the merchants wouldn't like it, besides. He'd not care to lose their custom—they pay in currency, you see."

"If I'd known she needed him," Sir Andrew said heatedly, "I'd have brought him at gunpoint, if necessary."

Katin smiled a little at his vehemence, but said only, "Well, I don't know what more he could have done, but I'm no physician. She may do very well without him—I expect we'll know by morning. When the bread mold works, it works quickly."

"Has she said anything?"

"Oh, yes. Curses for the most part. Last time she woke, she seemed to know me, and she asked for you."

Sir Andrew felt like doing some cursing of his own. Suppose he'd come too late? Suddenly he thought he understood what Lady Celia had been trying to tell him about Rolande. "Damn the witch! After all the times I wished her dead, in Thornfeld, I believe she'll die now, just to spite me!"

"I *am* dead," Rolande said, without opening her eyes. "Killed in an engagement with three men-of-war, and buried at sea. So declared the court, so it must be true." She laughed weakly.

"She's raving again," sighed Katin. "She told us before that she was Admiral Quick of the Royal Navy. I thought the fever had abated, but I must have been wrong." She began to bathe Rolande's face with cool water.

"The Quick and the dead—that's what I am—" Rolande insisted. "How very witty. I must tell Celia that." She opened her eyes, looked at Sir Andrew, and frowned. "Your Lordship . . . ?"

"I'm here, Vendeley."

Rolande tried to raise herself on her arms, then quickly changed her mind and lay back, grimacing with pain. The effort had exhausted her, and she lapsed into silence again, lying as still as before. Katin checked to see that the poultice was undisturbed, and answered Sir Andrew's questioning look with a shake of her head. "Let her rest, My Lord."

He nodded and started to rise, but Rolande grasped his sleeve with one hot, dry hand, and said faintly, "I have to tell you—before it's too late . . ."

Sir Andrew hesitated. He didn't want to tax her strength further, but if there was any risk that this might be his last chance to find out what she'd learned, he dared not let it pass. There was too much at stake. He knelt beside her again and said to Katin, "Leave us for now—but don't go far."

Katin frowned, but she understood as well as he that there was no other choice. *The future of Albin may depend on Vendeley's information . . . and she may not speak in front of me. She doesn't know that I'm party to Sir Andrew's plans.* She nodded reluctantly, then took up a tin mug and slipped her arm behind Rolande's head to raise it, so that she might drink. Rolande sipped weakly at the water. She tried to take the cup from Katin and hold it herself, but her hands trembled too much, and she lay back again, muttering to herself, as Katin slipped from the tent.

Sir Andrew bent over her. "Can you tell me what you've found out?" he asked softly.

Rolande drew a deep breath, coughed, tried again and gasped, "The Chamber's new weapon . . . a great warship . . . *Invincible* . . ." She rested for a moment, but then spoke again, determined to impart what she knew. "Bigger than any navy's ever had . . . four decks of bronze cannon . . . vengeful beasts upon the channels . . . flaming torches upon the bow . . ."

Was she delirious again, or was this the truth? Four decks of cannon . . . ?

"The test—'tis the first month of summer!" Rolande whispered, and fell silent again.

At last, a fact—a fact he could build a plan on. The scraps of paper he'd studied so hard suddenly made sense. There was a vessel of some new design, and it would be tried for seaworthiness in the first month of summer off the coast of New Lindness. Now that he knew what the Chamber was about, he could find a way to thwart them.

"Well done!" He looked down at Rolande and saw that she no longer heard him. She lay still in a death-like slumber, her eyes sunken, her cheeks hollow. It seemed as if she had held to life only long enough to impart her secret, and having done so at last, could now give up the painful, exhausting struggle. Pausing only to assure himself that she was still breathing, Sir Andrew hastily went in search of Katin.

Chapter 12

It was dusk before Katin joined Sir Andrew on the rough-hewn bench, made from a split log, that sat outside the tent Kedzier had offered him. "There is no more I can do now," she said. " 'Tis in the hands of the Good God. But Vendeley is strong—and stubborn, which is even more in her favor. I expect she's a hard woman to kill."

"Many have found her so," Sir Andrew agreed.

Someone had brought Sir Andrew bread and a bowl of stew, and now Arya came scampering up to Katin and tugged at her jacket. "Mistress Ander, my sister says you're to come and eat with us!" Suddenly remembering her manners, she dropped a hasty curtsy to Sir Andrew, then seized Katin's hand to pull her toward the center of the camp, where the cook pots bubbled over open fires.

Sir Andrew watched Katin walk away, hand in hand with the frisking gypsy girl, and marveled at the change the last few months had wrought in her. Where once she had seemed a child of the wilderness, even when dressed in silk, now there was something regal about her, even in homespun. It was not an air of authority or condescension—though she knew how to assume those, at need—but the true nobility of spirit that was born of discipline and self-sacrifice. His own family had always been loyal supporters of the House of Obelen, and Sir Andrew had followed the same course unquestioningly, yet he found himself thinking now, *she will be a better monarch than her forebears were.*

But if she were ever to ascend the throne, he had to do more than protect her from assassins. Seeing that Captain Fenton was watching her from nearby, he turned his mind to what he'd learned from Rolande. There were still many details he wished to ask her about—if she lived—for two things must be accomplished if they were to triumph. If the trial of the *Invincible* was a success, they must convince the Chamber that it had failed, that their deadly vessel was not seaworthy. Then they must somehow gain the knowledge necessary to design such warships themselves, to give their small navy an advantage when they launched their own attack. Neither of these tasks would be simple, and without Vendeley, they might be well nigh impossible.

Darkliss was stirring thick chicken stew in an iron pot hanging from crossed poles, and Katin gratefully accepted a bowl of it, realizing that she'd eaten nothing all the afternoon. She saw that Darkliss was studying her closely, and in a moment the gypsy woman sent Arya on an errand and said to Katin, "The little one has told me you wish to teach her to read and to heal with herbs. Is this so, mistress? Sometimes she makes up stories, that one."

"It's quite true," Katin assured her. "I need a 'prentice, and she seems to me quick and clever. If she learns to read, she can teach herself much from my books and the notes I've made."

Darkliss nodded thoughtfully, then remarked, "I

have warned her that if she learns to do these things, her charms will no longer work."

Katin set down her bowl and stared at the woman, an angry flush rising to her face. "How could you tell her such a thing?" she demanded. "Why do you wish to prevent her from bettering herself?"

Sounding genuinely surprised, Darkliss replied, "I have no such wish. I think it would be a good thing for her. If she had such skills, she would win respect for herself and for our tribe. But she ought to know what will come of her choice, no?"

She believes it, Katin realized, at a loss for a reply. To say "I'm sure her charms will still work" would be tantamount to admitting that they did work—which seemed dishonest—but to say, "Come now, they can't stop working, because they've never worked in the first place," would be heartless—and probably futile. At last she asked, "Are you sure it would happen that way?"

Clearly, the woman was too polite to exclaim over Katin's ignorance but she said, "Why, how else could it happen? It has always been the way, that the new wisdom drives out the old. My grandam used to say that in olden days the people"—an expression that referred only to gypsies—"could fly like birds or breathe water like fish. When they learned to make fire and work metal, those old powers left them, but the people lived many years longer than they had before." She shrugged, not committing herself to the strict historical accuracy of the tale, but acknowledging its essential truth. "It is for Arya to choose. But she is very young—I think she should learn the new ways if she can. Maybe in her grandchildren's day all the people will know how to read and write, and no one will need charms or soothsayers any more."

Katin started to eat her stew again. "Ah, I was forgetting that you can see the future. In some colonies already there are schools for all the children."

Darkliss shook her head, setting the bangles on her earrings jangling. "No one can see the future. I can tell fortunes—that is not the same thing at all." Her dark eyes seemed to look into Katin's very thoughts.

"How is it different?" Katin asked, dropping her gaze uneasily and applying herself to her stew.

"Oh, I could tell you a few things about yourself, mistress—that great changes are coming to you, that you think to make a long journey, perhaps soon, perhaps never to return. But I need not see the future to know that."

Katin put down her empty bowl and stared at Darkliss, frankly startled. "Then how *do* you know it?"

"Why else would you decide to take a 'prentice now, if not to take your place when you go? And she must learn to read, you say, so that she can teach herself from your books. So, you may not be here much longer, to teach her yourself. 'Tis the present, you see, that reveals the future." She took up Katin's bowl and filled it again. "I don't say as I don't sometimes *see* things," she added, as she gave the stew to Katin, "but it's only things that *are*. What's not there yet can't be seen."

To offer money for the food would be an insult to the hospitality of the tribe, Katin knew, but it was acceptable to pay for a service. She took some silver from the pouch at her belt and held out her palm to the gypsy woman, saying, "Tell me more."

Running one long fingernail along the lines of Katin's hand, Darkliss studied the pattern as intently as she'd watched Katin herself earlier. After a minute or so, she looked up and said, "You've survived many dangers these few years past."

"So I have."

"And there are more dangers to come, but you will weather those as well. You will know sorrow, and it will make you strong." The gypsy peered down at Katin's hand as if into the depths of a well, then she looked up and met Katin's eyes. "You are not what you appear to be," she said finally.

Katin snatched her hand back as if she'd been scalded. "What do you mean by that?"

"I couldn't say what it means, mistress, unless I were to keep looking for the answer. But what would be the use in that, when you already know it? Shall I try?"

"No. I've heard enough. Thank you for the stew, it's very good."

Katin was relieved when Arya returned, walking slowly and carefully, so as not to spill the heavy pitcher of cider she carried. When she had settled down with a bowl of stew, Katin asked her, "And have you decided to come to me for lessons, then, little one?"

"Yes, mistress, whenever you say. It won't so much matter about my charms—no one wants them anyway. But, you know, the one I gave you might not protect you anymore."

"Never mind," said Katin. "I plan to be very careful in future."

* * *

Rolande began to recover sooner than Sir Andrew would have thought possible. Before long, he was able to question her about her discovery and satisfy himself that he was in possession of the facts. When he was not questioning Rolande, she was questioning Katin about all that had passed in the colony during her long absence.

Katin told her of the attacks on Alicen and Sir Andrew, of Captain Fenton's visit to the gypsies, Arya's theft of the etched brass cylinder for Ruthven, and Ruthven's mysterious death. But of the attempt on her own life, she said nothing.

"Curious . . . !" said Rolande. "And Ruthven's killer took the brass cylinder, I suppose?"

"No, Lady Alicen saw it among his possessions when she found his body at the hostel. Either the Chamber's agent wasn't looking for it, or hadn't time to find it."

"I wonder what it could be," Rolande murmured thoughtfully, and fell silent for so long that Katin thought she was asleep, and slipped from the tent quietly, so as not to wake her. But when the girl who brought her meals next entered, Rolande sent her to fetch Arya. "I've a job for that one to do," she said, with more animation than she'd shown since the shipwreck, and when Arya appeared, she asked eagerly, "You remember the little brass case you stole from the captain for this man Ruthven?"

Alarmed, Arya protested, "He made me steal it! I wanted no part of the thing—"

"Listen to me, sprat," Rolande interrupted. "I don't care what you steal or why—I'm a pirate, I steal for my living." If the girl ran off, Rolande was in no condition to catch her. "I want you to carry a message to town for me, that's all. You know the trader Lorin, whose shop's on Livery Row?"

Arya nodded. Darkliss thought well of Lorin, for all

that he was an outsider. "My sister knows him well," she told Rolande.

"I'll just bet she does." Rolande took a few coins of the money Sir Andrew had given her and offered them to Arya. "As soon as you can get yourself to Oriana, seek out Lorin and say I've sent you. Tell him just what that brass piece looks like, for I want him to get it for me, and hold it against my return. Ruthven's goods are still at the hostel, locked up somewhere, I daresay, and he's to buy it from the landlord no matter what the cost. When you've delivered the message, he'll pay you as much again, for we've an understanding about such things."

Arya frowned. That thing again! Why did they all want it? The money Rolande offered was a good price for a small service, but Arya's own idea of honor balked at taking advantage of the woman if she didn't know what she was asking for. At last she said, "I'll tell him if you want me to, mistress. I can go to market with the others tomorrow. But that brass thing is unlucky, I swear to you. I warned that man of it, but he didn't believe me, and now he's dead."

"I believe you," Rolande said, with a grim smile. "Don't fret yourself over that, sprat. I intend it to be very unlucky indeed, for someone."

With the passage of a week, Rolande, tightly bandaged, was able to wander around the gypsy camp and sit in the sun—whenever the stormy weather permitted. She was unquestionably on the mend, but even such mild exercise as this still exhausted her, and there could be no question, as yet, of her trekking through the swamp on foot. Sir Andrew and Rolande were equally impatient at their forced inactivity when there was so much to be done, and after a few more days,

Katin agreed that Rolande might cross the river on one of the gypsies' rafts and make the journey in one of their carts.

Rolande had planned to stay with Lorin until she had the prospect of a ship and the strength to sail her, but Katin would not hear of her being taken anywhere but the Governor's Mansion while she was yet so weak. Sir Andrew agreed, since there was still much to be discussed regarding the exact details of the design of the vessel and the ways in which it might be possible to capture it, and he felt that he might as well have her where he could keep an eye on her. Celia, he knew, would raise no objection to having a lowly privateer under her roof.

Indeed, far from objecting, Lady Celia welcomed Rolande with relief, for she'd been worried about her, despite the encouraging reports Sir Andrew had sent by way of Hrivas. She installed Rolande in elegant quarters more befitting a distinguished visitor than a bastard daughter of the Avenford slums. Doctor Justin was summoned at once, declared that her wounds were healing cleanly, ordered a week of bed rest, and left a tonic that Carl examined suspiciously then dismissed as rubbish and discarded. "Feed her," he advised Lady Celia.

After the grueling journey through the marshes, Rolande did not feel equal to anything more than bed rest, and even eating the rich meals that were brought her seemed too much of an effort at first. But once she'd recovered from the journey, she began to enjoy the unaccustomed experience of being waited on and pampered. She no sooner had her strength back, than she began to hound Sir Andrew for a new ship.

* * *

"The Devil—! Look at you, woman," Lorin complained, regarding Rolande in the morning light that filtered through the one grimy window of his room. "Hardly an ounce of flesh left on you, and what there is covered with scars."

Rolande stretched lazily. "You didn't mind my looks last night."

"Couldn't see you in the dark, could I?" He carefully touched one scarred breast. "That's not sore, then?"

"I'd let you know quick enough if it was." She leaned back against his comfortable bulk, still in a cozy half-doze. "Cold . . ." she mumbled.

Lorin put his arm around her companionably and asked in an offhand tone, "Did that sly-eyed surgeon of yours find you?"

Suddenly alert, Rolande said, "Blythe? What do you mean?"

"He was in Oriana some days ago, came by the shop looking for you."

"Why didn't you tell me that before, man?"

"I didn't think it was so bloody important, that's why! I told him you were at the Governor's. Thought he'd look for you there!"

"Did he leave any message?" Rolande said impatiently.

"Said he was staying at the Brazen Horn, but he might be gone for a few weeks. He wanted you to know he'd be back. What's so special about that one, I'd like to know?"

Rolande was already pulling on her clothes. "I told you, I want to be at sea again soon," she said evasively. "I need to have my crew in place."

Lorin gave her an appraising look, but said only, "See if you can find me some more fancy cloth, then. There'll be a call for it soon, for the grand ball in honor of the Governor's Mansion being finished at last. Everyone of any consequence is to be invited, they say."

"Aye, even the more influential merchants," Rolande agreed. "We've come a long way from Albin, when the likes of Sir Andrew and Her Ladyship mix with common tradesfolk, no?"

"Well, I've not been invited, that's all I know. And see you don't plunder any Acquitanian ships for cloth this time, or those influential merchants will use their influence to see you hanged. They're up to mischief of some kind."

"I'll be careful." Rolande took up the brass cylinder from the windowsill where she'd left it, tossed it in her palm thoughtfully, and put it in her pocket.

"What is that thing? For what I paid, it should be gold, not brass."

"It doesn't matter what it is—but I've an idea whose it is, and if I'm right, there's going to be a reckoning." Rolande leaned over the bed and kissed Lorin's stubbly jaw. "I'm off to look for Blythe and see about the provisioning of my ship. I'll see you tonight."

"Oh, will you now?" Lorin said darkly. "What if you find curly-locks, eh?"

Rolande grinned and kissed him again. "I shouldn't say so, vain as you are, but the truth is you're worth two of him."

Rolande asked at the hostel, but found that Blythe had not been seen recently, though he'd paid the landlord to keep his room against his return. She would worry about him when he reappeared, then. She had other matters to attend to, in the meantime. She meant to exact revenge from Tyrrel for the crew of the *Azora*, but before that could be accomplished she had to train her new crew to her liking.

The *Shraik,* the ship she'd obtained from Sir Andrew, was a fifty-gun sloop, but many of the hands she'd had Corey and Raphe recruit were untried as yet, and might prove unreliable. Rolande knew that the loyalty of a privateer's crew depended greatly on the amount of booty they thought the captain could gain for them. To this end, she drilled her gunners hard and kept all hands busy learning the ropes until she was satisfied that they would weather an engagement. Then she set about finding a suitable target—one that would serve both as a test of their ability to work together and a taste of the rewards to be gained thereby.

They cruised for six days east toward the islands that were scattered along the near part of the trade route between New Albin and the Old World, and then Hrivas, on the masthead, spotted a ship in the distance. He flew to investigate, and reported that she was the *Carnelian,* a moderately-sized but well-fitted merchant vessel, flying the Albinate flag. Rolande ordered her crew to man the guns and take a bearing on the same compass point, sailing on a course to intercept her, since Rolande's ship was the swifter of the two. By tacking whenever the *Carnelian* turned in her attempt to sail away from them, the *Shraik* was eventually able to catch her. When they came up to their quarry and fired across her bow, the captain immediately struck his colors. The *Carnelian* was outgunned by Rolande's vessel, and her captain, reasonably enough, did not intend to sacrifice his men—and possibly his ship—in a futile effort at resistance. Drawing alongside the Albinate vessel, Rolande ordered the lashings made fast and the boarding planks put in place.

The main hold contained such luxury goods as had

begun to be in demand in the more prosperous colonies, but still had to be imported from the Old World. There were elegant furnishings, silver hand mirrors, fine glass perfume bottles, ivory fans of exquisite workmanship, musical instruments of wood and silver, and bales of rich cloth that Lorin would appreciate. The rest of the cargo consisted of hogsheads of Acquitanian brandy, barrels of rare spices, and kegs of Castilian wine. In a small chest in the captain's quarters, Rolande found a cache of gold, no doubt intended to promote the activities of the Chamber's adherents in the New World. There was no way to prove such a suspicion, however, for she saw nothing else to suggest that the ship was engaged in anything but a commercial venture, so she had to content herself with loading the cargo and sharing out the gold among her people. After taking the ship's papers and flag to present to Sir Andrew, as proof that the *Carnelian* was her lawful prey, she set sail back to Oriana with her booty and a highly contented crew.

* * *

In preparation for the ball that night, servants and townsfolk hired for the occasion polished silver platters, hung ribbons and greenery from the balustrades of the staircase, and placed bowls of flowers on the mantelpieces of the mansion's first floor rooms. The musicians were received, the hothouses and orchards pillaged for their fruits, the floors and windows polished till they shone, and the soarhounds banished to the kennels.

While Lady Celia was busy supervising the final preparations, Alicen returned from a trip to the docks and immediately drew Katin and Sir Andrew into the reception room for a conclave. "I have this day received a message from Albin," she informed them, "and I thought it right to deliver it at once." She glanced meaningfully at Katin.

"It concerns the marriage proposal?" Katin asked, but it was not really a question. She'd put off making a definite response to the Duke of Wyston, but she'd known it was only a matter of time until he—quite rightly—demanded an answer.

Alicen nodded soberly. "Rumors are spreading in Albin that Your Highness is alive. His Grace was forced to let his senior advisers know the truth, for he couldn't very well abandon his campaign without some explanation—not while Halkin lurks like some hungry lion in Acquitania. The Duke of Wyston cannot define his strategy without some formal declaration from Your Highness in this matter."

Sir Andrew said nothing, merely glancing at Katin, waiting for her to speak. She toyed with the oil lamp on the table, turning it round and round so that the flame danced on the polished mahogany surface. In the distance she could hear the first faint notes from the musicians tuning and practicing their instruments. She had discussed the matter of the Duke's proposal with Sir Andrew at length since Alicen's return, and she knew in the end that she really had no choice but to give the Duke the formal commitment he deserved. She raised her eyes to meet Alicen's. "Tell him that he is to continue to lay the groundwork for a conjoined effort, but not to reveal to the leaders of the popular factions that I am indeed alive—not just yet."

"That's wise," Sir Andrew agreed. "We will want to choose our time to reveal your whereabouts very carefully, when they are less prepared—preferably after we've dealt with the threat of this new warship."

Alicen nodded. She knew that Sir Andrew had set every able-bodied craftsman in the colony to constructing and outfitting ships, as soon as word of the Chamber's planned invasion had been received. He planned to adopt the innovations in the design of the Albinate vessel, to give their navy the advantage when they attacked the Chamber's seaforces. "I will tell him so," she replied, but she made no move to rise, and continued to regard Katin with an air of polite expectation. Then, when Katin said nothing more, Alicen ventured, "Does this mean that Your Highness will accept all the terms of the Duke's proposal?"

Katin raised her head again and fixed Alicen with a hard stare. "It means that I shall marry him," she said flatly. "Lady Alicen ... "

"Your Highness?"

"I've not seen my cousin Wyston for many years. What is he like?"

Alicen was taken aback, despite her diplomatic experience. It was not the question of a monarch to an emissary, but of one woman to another. Sir Andrew, recognizing the fact, discreetly withdrew as Alicen said smoothly, "I can assure Your Highness that there is nothing in the Duke's person or character to make you regret your decision."

But Katin did not want a polished answer. "Would *you* marry him?" she demanded.

Again, Alicen had no ready reply. "Why, I daresay any woman would, Your Highness—"

Katin sighed and abruptly stood up. "Let be. It was a foolish question. I must go dress, or Lady Celia will scold me—and I suggest that you do the same."

Alicen bowed. "Were we at peace," she said hesitantly, "no doubt His Grace would have commissioned a portrait and sent it with me. But suppose it done, and the picture altogether true to life, I believe that Your Highness would not be disappointed."

"Thank you," said Katin, dismissing her.

The mansion shone with light. All the windows on the ground floor were ablaze with candles in tall brass holders, and lanterns hung from the trees lighting the way up the drive for the carriages that brought Oriana's most important citizens to the ball. Inside, the household servants replenished the polished silver platters of oysters and scallops, roast pheasants and joints of venison on the stretchered tables of native oak and walnut.

Unlike some of the merchants who graced his home that night, Sir Andrew had not the means to furnish his house exclusively with pieces imported from the Old World. Still, all the furniture was gracefully carved and inlaid by local craftsmen. The house was large and handsome, and the ballroom was a scene of gaiety and splendor. On the recently laid parquet floor, dancers executed the graceful steps of a cotillion to the music of violinists and flautists in a small gallery above. The town's most prominent merchants proudly mingled with the nobility of Oriana and the nearby colonies. Herrel Richter, Mistress Cardif and Goodman Trudet were there in clothes of damask silk adorned with lace and embroidered ribbons, their differences with the Governor momentarily put aside. When Lady Celia swept down the wide staircase from the second floor, in an elaborate gown with a draped overskirt trimmed with satin bows, all heads turned to admire her. Those who knew their hostess only as the practical, capable mistress of the manor hardly recognized her, transformed into a ravishing, gay enchantress.

Katin, drinking a glass of punch after a dance with

Captain Fenton, watched Lady Celia talking graciously with her guests and marveled at her air of unfeigned enjoyment. Katin herself was intolerably bored, and it did not help matters to reflect that innumerable formal court functions such as this lay ahead for her. As soon as she could do so, without giving offense, she turned her back on the music and the bustling servants scurrying by with fresh platters of glazed cakes and went into the terraced garden outside the ballroom.

She was of course followed by Captain Fenton. "You cannot mean to walk in the gardens alone and unprotected," he protested.

"I shall not be alone—Jerl Smit is waiting for me," she said firmly. "I require no further protection." She knew he did not consider Jerl sufficient escort, but her tone left no room for argument, and he had no choice but to bow and withdraw.

Jerl looked up at the sound of Katin's approach, then rose hastily from the bench when he saw a stranger coming toward him—an elegant lady with jewels in her hair and a graceful tiered ball gown that swept the ground as she walked. He had never before seen Katin in the dress of a fashionable young noblewoman, and when he realized that it was indeed she, he knew exactly why she had sent for him. It had been absurd to hope that there could be any other reason. It was just as well, he thought, that she looked so unfamiliar. That would make it easier. "I got your note," he said awkwardly, gazing at her with painful resignation. "You look awfully pretty like that."

He was right about Katin's reason for summoning him. She had meant to tell him at once that she could not break her engagement. She would not weep, she told herself sternly. That would not be seemly. She would tell him as true a tale as was safe, and wish him well, with dignity. But coming from her grim talk with Alicen, and the cold, bright gallantries of the ball, she was suddenly so glad to see Jerl that she threw herself into his arms and said breathlessly, "I've missed you so much, Jerl. I'm *surrounded* by people who are absolutely devoted to me, and don't care a straw for me! You're the only one who—oh, God—stop me talking like this! Every word only puts us both deeper in danger!"

Jerl did not understand her distress, but he willingly stopped her from talking, in the simplest and most expedient manner. Then, finding that this time his kisses were not refused but returned, he drew Katin into a nearby arbor, out of sight of the house. But it was Katin who pulled him down beside her on the bench. *Why not?* she thought feverishly. *It's what I want and what he wants. If we're never to have a wedding night, we may at least have this night to remember. No one has the right to judge me!*

Jerl, kissing her eyes, her lips, her throat, murmured confidently, "We'll be married at once ..." and felt Katin stiffen in his arms. It was an agony to let her go, but he forced himself to pull away from her, and stared down at her, gasping, "Katin! You're going to marry me!"

"I *can't*," Katin wailed. "I can't even stay in New Albin. Jerl, wait—there are others depending on me, I've a duty to them that I can't deny. I have to go back! You—you could come with me ... " she faltered.

"But not as your husband."

"No," she whispered.

"Do you take me for one of your *pets?*" Jerl demanded, gripping her shoulders so hard that she knew she would find bruises there by morning. "Is that what you think of me?"

Katin didn't try to break free. She wanted Jerl to hurt her, to strike her, threaten her—anything to justify the pain she knew she was causing him. "I do love you," she said helplessly. "I love only you, Jerl. But that's all I have to offer you. Not my troth, not my faith, not honor, not even *time*—"

Jerl stood, then bent to grasp her hands and pull her to her feet. He led her by the hand through the garden, back to the terrace outside the ballroom, where the swirling figures danced, bejeweled shadows on the panes of the mullioned windows. "Go back where you belong, Your Ladyship—Your Grace—whoever you are," he said gently, dropping her hand.

Katin had never longed so keenly to tell him the truth, but the memory of the poison smoke suffocating her in the apothecary's hut stayed her lips, for his sake and her own. "Don't hate me, Jerl, please," she begged.

"Don't be silly," Jerl said with simple dignity. "You know if you ever need me, you have only to send word." Then he turned and strode off into the night, leaving her alone in the dark garden.

The ballroom shimmered with the fine silk gowns of the women and the silver-gilt trimmed jackets of the men, but the latecomer who made her entrance just after midnight outshone them all as she descended the stairway from the second floor. She was resplendent in a flowing gown of gold satin decorated with ruffles of cream-colored lace, and her headdress sported a huge plume of ivory-white. Her proud carriage and studied grace proclaimed her a lady of some distinction, yet she arrived unannounced, and no one came forward to claim acquaintance with her or perform introductions.

"Exquisite!"

"But who is she?"

The puzzled whispers passed through the crowded room, as the stranger made her way to the sideboard where Sir Andrew was deep in talk with Goodman Trudet. When he turned to find her standing at his side, he stopped in mid-sentence and stared at her in disbelief. With a smile as sweet as the candied apricots in the dish beside her, she swept him an accomplished curtsey, and said, "I trust I am not come too late to be welcome, Your Lordship. You must blame the storms that have made the roads so treacherous. Will you not show that you forgive me by asking me for this dance?"

Sir Andrew had no choice. Merchant Trudet was gazing admiringly at her, plainly hoping for an introduction. Hastily, Sir Andrew took her hand and led her into the crowd of dancers, where he whispered furiously, "Vendeley, are you determined to ruin me?"

The merchants had made no secret of their disapproval when it became known that the Governor was harboring the infamous Vendeley, who was recovering from wounds no doubt incurred in some illicit venture. Still, that might have been allowed to be an act of mercy, however ill-advised. But introducing her into the society of respectable people, as a fellow guest, could only be construed as a deliberate insult.

Rolande was well aware of Sir Andrew's predicament, and enjoying it thoroughly. She laughed, in tones as silvery and light as any lady's, and said, "Come, none of your guests will recognize me, you know."

Once recovered from the shock of seeing her there, Sir Andrew realized that she was probably right. It was unlikely that these folk knew her by sight, and even if they did, she would certainly not be familiar to them in this guise. Her dancing would not give her away, he had to admit. She swept through the elaborate cotillion as if she were born to it. "It is a foolhardy and unnecessary risk, nonetheless," he rebuked her. "How are you to be introduced to the company, I'd like to know?"

"Why, as Elliseth Moore, of course, a wealthy shipowner of Dyserth. I think of settling in these climes, and I particularly wish to make the acquaintance of the local merchants." As the music ended, Rolande curtsied again, with a flourish of her ivory-and-lace fan. "I have passed unremarked in more exalted company than *this,* I assure you!" she murmured, and turned away to address herself to Mistress Cardif, who was appraising an ornate silver serving bowl with a professional eye.

"A fine example of Tuscan chased silverwork, is it not?" Rolande remarked politely.

"So it is. But for my part, I prefer Acquitanian wares, especially their goldsmithry," Mistress Cardif said loftily.

"Ah, there we agree. One can't go far wrong with gold."

Mistress Cardif gave her a nod of approval, then looked her over more thoroughly. "You must be newly arrived in Oriana," she said. "For I've not seen you before, I believe."

Rolande introduced herself, then added, deliberately probing, "I've had dealings mainly with Hammersfeld and Dunraven, but now that civilized communities have been established here in the south, I've come to see what profitable commerce may be arranged with merchants in these colonies. Still, exporting anything has become a risky undertaking, I'm afraid. What one doesn't lose to storms is stolen by pirates, and no one seems able to contain them."

"Aye, that's the truth, and no mistake." Mistress

Cardif set her plate down atop the sideboard, the better
to express her indignation with a shake of her fist.
"I've lost two shipments to freebooters this past year,
one to pirates and one to the cursed privateer that our
Governor allows—nay, *encourages*—to disrupt trade
'twixt here and Albin. You'd best take warning, Mistress Moore, that His Lordship's pet privateer despoils
ships of Albinate ownership with impunity."

" 'Tis Rolande Vendeley you speak of? A disgrace!
That is but one matter I mean to discuss with Lord
Edenbyrne ere I undertake to deliver goods to traders
in Oriana."

"Don't think we've not tried! There's no satisfaction
to be had from that one. 'Tis not the community's welfare he has at heart, but only his own spite against the
Chamber for ousting him from his high position!"

"I see," said Rolande, deeply interested. "I wonder
that the merchant interests here in Oriana allow this
unsatisfactory state of affairs to continue. In other colonies I've visited, such matters are referred to a council of responsible householders, who determine how
the interests of the citizenry may best be served. They
would not permit one man's whim to deprive the rest
of all goods from their homeland."

Mistress Cardif nodded vigorously. "That is how
things would be done here, if we had our way! But,
you see, Oriana was settled by folk from Thornfeld, the
one colony attacked by the Chamber's army four years
ago, and 'twas Sir Andrew who led the defense. His
word's still law to most here—and the militia would
obey him unquestioningly. I ask you, are we at war
with Albin now, that he should forbid trade, as with the
enemy? But if the authorities won't protect the rights
of honest merchants, we need not give way, for all that.
We are taking matters into our own hands now, and we

plan a few surprises for these cursed freebooters. As a shipowner, you'd do well to join with us."

Rolande took an almond pastry from a nearby tray. "I've heard rumors that some of the merchants here in the south had made common cause against the threat to free shipping, but the idea seemed . . . well, rather vague," she said doubtfully, with the air of one who is willing to listen, but unlikely to be convinced. "To be quite frank, I didn't see how the plan could be put to practical effect." Since she knew nothing whatsoever about the plan, this was true enough.

As she intended, Mistress Cardif took her remarks as a challenge. She moved closer and said in a low tone, "We'll soon see how practical it is. Oh, I don't say it will rid us of this scourge of pirates, but it ought to force those in power to take action against them, instead of turning a blind eye to crimes against ships of other nations. The fact is, as you no doubt know, that the authorities here and in Acquitania will do nothing to curb depredations against Albinate vessels such as your own, and no more will the Chamber's navy defend ships from New Albin and Acquitania."

"Aye, and the same is true for the Castilians and the Empire of Saxony," Rolande said impatiently. "Indeed it has seemed, of late, that no one can be sure to profit by trade except the privateers! But still I cannot see how this alliance of yours will mend matters."

"No? But if we register our vessels under multiple names in multiple countries—"

"Then you can fly the flag of the country in whose water you're sailing," Rolande interrupted, unimpressed. "An old tale."

But Mistress Cardif shook her head. "No, our plan is much more far-reaching than that. We merely invoke the letter of the law to spring the trap. If a privateer takes anything outside his or her charter, we can see them clapped in gaol. And we use our multiple registrations to assure it."

Rolande frowned, remembering the merchant ship she'd recently taken. She'd seen nothing amiss, but still ... "I may have been misinformed as to your intent," she said earnestly. "Pray tell me more."

"But who was it informed you?" Mistress Cardif asked. "I should have thought—"

But this was a question Rolande did not care to answer. "Ah, wait," she broke in, seeing Lady Celia approaching. "I have not paid my respects to our hostess. That won't do." She met Lady Celia with a graceful curtsy and declared, "Viscountess, what an honor to be received in your home! But I do not flatter myself that Your Ladyship will remember me—Elliseth Moore, of Dyserth."

"To be sure I remember you," Lady Celia said graciously. "But it has been rather a long while since we met. You must come and tell me everything about yourself." Taking Rolande firmly by the arm, she drew her out onto the rear portico, where they would be alone, and said in exasperation, "Upon my word, you try my patience too far, Rolande! You are a wicked wretch to come here just to amuse yourself by provoking Andrew into apoplexy—"

She broke off as someone opened the door to the portico, but it was only Alicen, and Lady Celia warned her to be discreet by saying, "Lady Alicen, do you know Mistress Moore, of Dyserth?"

"We've met," Alicen said dryly, and closed the door behind her. Crossing the portico to Rolande, she remarked, "Moore, is it? Strange. You greatly resemble a certain pirate I had the misfortune to encounter some months ago."

Rolande dropped her most accomplished curtsy. "And you, My Lady, an insignificant little banker's clerk I met in the course of a voyage."

Alicen looked her up and down, taking in the elegance of her apparel and demeanor, then said, "An impressive masquerade, I do grant. One might almost take you for something other than Avenford wharf trash, if one knew no better. But then I've seen you in court costume before—"

"So you have. Do you refer, perhaps, to the occasion when you locked me in the catacombs under the palace and left me to die?"

Alicen sighed. "A rash and injudicious act—I've long regretted it. After all, you somehow escaped. I ought to have poisoned you and had done with it."

"That's been tried, too," Rolande said contemptuously. Dismissing Alicen, she turned back to Lady Celia. "But you wrong me sadly, Your Ladyship, to say that I came here tonight only to confound Sir Andrew. His discomfiture was at most only a secondary consideration. My first purpose in coming was to bring you a house-raising gift. That's what delayed me tonight. It had to be transported by cart and taken upstairs before I came down myself."

"A gift? But how intriguing. What can it be?"

"Come and see!" Rolande clasped Lady Celia by the hand and led her back through the ballroom and up the stairs to the sitting room off the main hall, with Alicen trailing behind, still suspicious. With a flourish, Rolande threw open the door and stood aside for Lady Celia, who took a step into the sitting room then stopped, speechless, at the sight of the beautifully carved rosewood Acquitanian harp standing before her chair. In a moment, she was running her fingers lovingly over the strings, and harmonious chords and trills filled the air.

"I paid one of your musicians to put it in tune," Rolande said proudly. "Is it right?"

"It could hardly be better." Sitting down, Lady Celia drew the harp to her and began to play, tentatively at first, chords and scales and runs, then fragments of remembered melodies and airs of favorite ballads. The others stood transfixed by the ethereal strains of the music that flowed from the beautiful instrument.

Sir Andrew had seen the three leave the hall, and followed, worried that something might be wrong. It was not like Celia to leave her guests, and Vendeley was probably up to no good. Alicen, he knew, trusted Rolande even less than he did himself, and would not be accompanying her for the sake of her witty conversation. He half expected to find the two bent on fighting a duel, and Lady Celia intent on dissuading them.

But when he heard the strains of harp music, he knew exactly what had happened. When he entered the sitting room, Lady Celia looked up with tears in her eyes and said, "Andrew . . . isn't it splendid?"

His wife's obvious pleasure in the instrument somewhat tempered his frustration that Rolande, and not he, had procured it for her. He managed to smile and say, "Very beautiful indeed," before pointedly asking Rolande, "And come by legitimately, no doubt?"

"I took it from the *Carnelian*, under the order of my warrant. She carried a shipment of fine Acquitanian musical instruments, and this one I knew Celia must have, as soon as I saw it." Watching Sir Andrew pretend not to be shocked at her familiar way of referring to Lady Celia, Rolande wisely decided that he'd been goaded enough for the present. "But you mustn't feel

slighted, My Lord," she said with a grin, "for I've
brought you a better gift than this one."

Lady Celia rose. "Ah, the real reason for your visit,
my wicked one—I thought we should come to it in
time. But I must not neglect my guests this way. Nor
must you, Andrew. Pray don't be long gone, or they'll
take offense and talk scandal. Such a bore." She
laughed. "I've looked forward to this ball for months,
and now I only wish to stay here and play my new
harp! I thank you for it a thousand times, my dear," she
said, and wafted from the room with a radiant smile.

"What is this gift?" Sir Andrew asked with a frown,
suspecting another of Rolande's tricks.

"A plan." Rolande closed the door to the room, then
sat on the chair in front of Lady Celia's slant-front sec-
retary and regarded Sir Andrew seriously. "A means of
capturing the Chamber's new warship without destroying her, for that's our only hope."

Sir Andrew nodded, all else forgotten. "What do you
propose?"

"What we need is a fleet crewed by sailors who
know—as pirates do—how to take a ship without
blowing her to splinters. Your colonials couldn't do it.
Half are green landsmen and the rest trained for war. A
pirate crew's aim is to seize a ship as a prize, not sink
her as an enemy."

"That's all very well, but we need a fleet, as you
say, not a dozen rival ships under as many commands.
We've no pirate navy to call upon."

"Not yet," said Rolande, "but one thing I learned
from my experience with the pirates on Captain
Tyrrel's isle is that they can be convinced to work together if it suits their needs. I am of a mind to return
to the channel isles, now that spring is upon us and the
storms of winter are ending. Great numbers of pirates

will be sailing now, and I mean to persuade them to form a fleet for the purpose of capturing the *Invincible*."

"But how will that be to their benefit?"

"If the Chamber builds a fleet of those vessels, the Albinate Navy will hunt the pirate ships down and devour them like sharks chasing minnows. Come, 'twas you who gave me the idea—you made use of the forest bandits to save Thornfeld. They'd no love of the Deps, and no more have the sea bandits . . . and I have another incentive to offer them as well."

"What is that?" Sir Andrew asked warily.

"When we have done your bidding, while we're all together as a great force, it will provide the chance to drive Captain Tyrrel from his lair on Needle Isle. They'll not have forgotten how he kept them from going after the Chamber's gold—and they covet the fortune in treasure he's said to have hoarded on the island. Without Tyrrel, they could use the isle as they see fit in future, and answer to no one."

"And what do you stand to gain, Vendeley?" Alicen demanded. "Are we to believe that you've nothing at heart but the welfare of your fellow scavengers?"

Rolande rose, moving about the room restlessly, her fists clenched. "I want a chance to gut the bastard who murdered my crew," she said stonily. "I led them into his trap, but I couldn't lead them out again. I had to leave them there at Tyrrel's mercy, and that's not a thing I can ever forget—but I can make Tyrrel pay for it at least, and I will, I swear to it."

It should have been strange to hear such an oath from the tall, elegant lady in satin and lace who stood before them, but Rolande's finery served only to accentuate her ferocity, while her fierce resolve made her seem all the more splendid. But then she stopped, resting her hand on the carved scrollwork of Lady Celia's harp, and turned to Alicen with a smile. "It is a matter of loyalty and honor," she said evenly. "You wouldn't understand."

Lorin roared with laughter when Rolande returned at dawn to his room and swirled about to show him her splendid gown—then he wasted no time in helping her to get out of it. She slept most of that day away, then stayed in bed, since she was already there, and let Lorin ply her with food and ale.

He was much amused by her account of the Governor's Ball. "Here's to our dauntless privateer," he toasted, "braving not only the terrors of the high sea, but the terrors of high society!" He swigged from his mug and chuckled. " 'Twas the fox in the henhouse, right enough, decked in feathers and saying 'cluck-cluck' to the biddies! I'd give an eye to have seen it."

"Aye, but there's fox hunting afoot, you know. It's as you told me, the merchants have banded together. They've some plan to trap pirates and privateers alike."

Lorin set his mug down on the square table that stood beside the bed. "What did you find out?"

"Not enough. It has to do with the way they're registering their ships, but I couldn't press for details then and there. You must see what more you can ferret out."

"So! What the gallant fox can't catch, maybe the sly ferret can. We'll see. I know a few 'prentices who don't scoff at earning an ember or two for passing along a bit of gossip. If the merchants paid a decent wage, their secrets would be a deal safer."

Rolande stretched luxuriously. "Ah, greed's been the undoing of many a trader."

"And many a pirate, too. I warned you to stop hunting those Acquitanian merchantmen."

"I *did* stop, as soon as I got a decent ship for my use. Since I took the *Azora*, I've only hunted enemy ships or ships on enemy business. So you needn't preach at me, just find out what this alliance of merchants is about, if you can. I don't like the sound of it."

"I'll find them out, never fear. But they can't catch you so long as you let neutral ships alone." Lorin dropped back onto the bed beside her and gathered her into his arms again. "What a world it is, where the chickens chase the fox! But my wager's on the fox. On a cunning, sleek-shank vixen . . ."

Rolande grinned and snapped her teeth at him.

By the time she left Lorin's, next morning, she had transformed herself once again from a highly respectable personage into an infamous adventurer who would not have been allowed to set foot within Mistress Cardif's gates. Lorin was right, she thought, they would never outfox her. Soon she'd know what trick they had planned, and she would use the information to her own advantage, trap them in their own snare. Meanwhile, she'd have her crew make ready to set sail on the next high tide.

The street was full of fishermen, victuallers, and gypsies selling tin goods from carts, as she made her way to the docks absorbed in half a dozen plans at once. She could go directly to the channel islands, and pick up what sport she could on the way, or try her luck in nearby waters and return to Oriana once more before setting out for the channel. That would allow her to confirm once more the terms on which Sir Andrew would deal with the pirates, and to find out what Lorin had learned about the merchants' scheme . . . and to have another look for Blythe. . . .

She'd just stopped to buy a pastry from a stall on

the wharf, when a man in the uniform of an officer of the Watch stepped out from the doorway of one of the nearby shops. He was accompanied by two militiamen, and he approached her with such clear intent that Rolande knew he meant trouble even before he spoke. "Captain Vendeley, I've been waiting for you to return to your ship. I'm charged to apprehend you for piracy, in the matter of an attack on the Acquitanian vessel *Carnelian* by the ship *Shraik,* under your command."

"Rot!" Rolande said sharply. "Food for gulls! The *Carnelian*'s an Albinate trader, and I took her under the Governor's warrant, as everyone knows. Apply to Sir Andrew for the proofs."

"No doubt he can sort the matter out for you, Captain. I am only sent to collect you so that you may answer the charge. Here is my warrant. You will find that it is in order."

Rolande was surrounded. They had waited for her to reach the middle of the wharf, where the water would cut off her escape on three sides. The officer, musket at the ready, blocked the way to shore, and the militiamen had positioned themselves to prevent her from reaching the *Shraik.* If she tried to swim to safety, in broad daylight, she'd be an easy target even under the water.

The merchant alliance was behind this deliberate mistake, of course, but there was no point in arguing with the officer about it. He had his duty to carry out, and no authority to disregard his orders. She thought for a moment of offering a bribe, but that could be presented as evidence of guilt, and for once, by the Good God, she *wasn't guilty.* A fight with the three of them was out of the question as well—she'd taken more than enough of bruises lately.

"Very well, lead the way," she said reluctantly, dreading another stay in prison.

* * *

"Ought you to accept gifts from a privateer employed on behalf of the colony?" Alicen asked Lady Celia abruptly. It was not her place to question or criticize the Viscountess, and both knew it, but Alicen had convinced herself that she had a duty to speak.

Lady Celia went on softly stroking the strings, allowing the soothing sound of the harp to float about them. "Of course I ought not, my dear," she said placidly. "But Rolande has such good taste, how is one to refuse? I daresay she'll bring you some trifle next time, and you'll find it's the very thing you've been wanting."

Alicen felt that the subject was not a fit one for levity. "I don't want anything from that arrogant, treacherous upstart! I can't understand why Sir Andrew trusts her."

Lady Celia had thought that playing for Alicen might be a pleasant diversion while Andrew was away at the navy yard at Haremare Point, but now she was beginning to regret her own impulse of hospitality. "Andrew does not altogether trust her," she explained, "but he finds her exceedingly useful. Without her help, Thornfeld might well have fallen to the invading army—and when she was the Chamber's agent, she was a formidable enemy."

"There it is," Alicen said grimly. "If she betrayed the Chamber, what's to keep her from changing allegiances again, when the whim takes her? The woman's not to be relied upon!"

"You may of course be right, but I think it very unlikely that the Chamber would ever trust her again, after the way she turned on them. She's under sentence of death now, for treachery and heresy. She'd be mad to take the chance."

"She *is* mad! I tell you, she's capable of anything, if it amuses her. It was madness for her to appear at your ball as she did, just for the sake of an extravagant, ostentatious gesture. I've crossed paths with her before, and every time she does something unaccountable, as if just to plague me."

Lady Celia ran her fingers down the harp strings and sighed. "I see. So you, too, are under her spell. Really, I begin to think there's some truth to the rumors of her demonic powers. Do you realize that ever since the ball you've talked of her to the exclusion of all else?"

"Why, I—but that's—" Alicen stammered.

"My dear, if Rolande takes the trouble to plague you, it's because she finds you worth the trouble." Lady Celia paused, trying to think how best to suggest to Alicen the reason for her preoccupation with Rolande's behavior. But just then, to her relief, there came a knock on the door, and she rose to open it.

An agitated manservant stood there. "Your Ladyship, the Captain of the Watch is downstairs in the hall," he announced in tones of dire apprehension. "He wants Lady Alicen, he says."

Alicen frowned. "What does he want with me?"

"He wouldn't say, m'lady, but he showed me a writ." Such documents held an almost sacred authority for those who couldn't read them.

"Well, let him come up and state his business," Lady Celia ordered, glad of any distraction from Alicen's tirade. How refreshing it would be to meet someone who was simply indifferent to Rolande, she thought, half amused and half nettled.

When the captain was admitted, he bowed awkwardly, looking as if he'd rather be battling drunken, knife-wielding ruffians in an alley than accosting two ladies at the Governor's Mansion. Nevertheless, he resolutely stepped forward to address Alicen. Clearing his throat, he said, "Lady Alicen Kendry, I have orders to take you into custody, on the charge of the murder of Oliver Ruthven."

Chapter 13

Rolande lay stretched out on a wooden bench against one of the stone walls of her cell, attempting to relieve her sense of confinement by cursing the perfidy of the merchants and imagining the terrible retribution she would deliver on Mistress Cardif and the rest, once she was free again—as she soon would be, she assured herself. Sir Andrew would see to it. He was the highest authority here, after all, merchant alliance or no. He would not allow his most valuable agent to be tried and hanged for piracy— would he? She remembered uncomfortably his words of some months past, warning her that if she overstepped her limits and gave the merchants due cause for her arrest, he would not be able to intervene on her behalf. But that had been merely an attempt to intimidate her into obedience—he would not really abandon her to the hangman. Celia wouldn't let him. Besides, the *Carnelian* was *not* an Acquitanian ship, and she could prove it! He'd have no choice but to demand her release. She found herself wishing, however, that she hadn't gone out of her way to vex him quite so much, on the night of the ball.

Then she all but forgot her own troubles, a moment later, in her astonishment at seeing Alicen led into the cell as a fellow prisoner. "I refuse to be immured with this beastly pirate!" Alicen protested. "I demand a separate cell!"

"We've only the two cells, m'lady," the gaoler explained uneasily, "and the other's for men, so you'll have to share this one." He locked the door securely and hurried back down the narrow hallway.

"Lady Alicen, welcome!" Rolande said, sitting up to make room for Alicen on the bench. "So they've decided that you're a pirate, too, eh?"

"Certainly not," Alicen snapped. Being arrested was demeaning enough, but having Rolande be party to her humiliation was mortifying. Her reservations about the Duke of Wyston's proposition for reform had never been so pronounced as at this moment. She would not have been subjected to such an outrage under the old order. Sitting down on the bench as far away from Rolande as she could get, Alicen told her stiffly, "I've been accused of murdering Oliver Ruthven."

"The Duke of Halkin's agent? You surprise me— I've never known you so careless before."

"I didn't kill him!"

Rolande smiled. "And I'm not a pirate."

"No? Then why are you here?"

" 'Twas a scurvy trick on the part of the merchants. I raided an Albinate merchant vessel. I had her papers and her flag. Now they're claiming she's an Acquitanian ship, that it was an act of piracy to attack her. But the *Carnelian* was Albinate when I took her, whatever she is now!"

Alicen shrugged. "Well, if it hadn't been this one, no doubt they would have caught you for something else eventually."

"Why, thank you for your sympathy, Your Ladyship. They do say that the true test of a lady is how she conducts herself in adversity."

Alicen flushed. There were some grounds for the rebuke, she could not deny it. Rolande might have gloated a good deal more over Alicen's predicament, after all, as Alicen had fully expected her to do. But instead she seemed almost subdued as she sat staring at the one tiny window in the stone wall. It struck Alicen that Rolande was behaving better than she was herself, and the idea was galling. *I'm damned if I'll apologize to the likes of Vendeley!*

"I believe you didn't kill Ruthven," Rolande said suddenly.

"Why?" Alicen spat, before she could stop herself. "Did you kill him yourself?"

Rolande continued to watch the window, where the small square of sky was now darkening to deep evening blue. "No. You know I was away from Oriana then."

"Oh, yes, I forgot. But then, folk do credit you with demonic powers—"

"If I had them, I'd not stay locked in this cage!" Rolande said, with a passionate vehemence that took Alicen by surprise. Alicen turned to her, startled, and, for a moment, caught a desperate, haunted look in Rolande's eyes that she'd never seen there before. Rolande looked away, then abruptly rose and began to pace about the small cell, her fists clenched tightly.

Watching her, Alicen said, "You're right, Vendeley, prison doesn't bring out the best in my temperament. But then, I'm not as used to it as you. No doubt you've been in many."

She had expected to provoke Rolande to a sharp retort, but Rolande hadn't the heart to bandy words with her further. "Aye, too many," she said, without a break in her restless pacing.

Alicen sighed. "Well, if the *Carnelian* is really an

Albinate ship, Sir Andrew will be able to set things straight for you when he comes for me," she offered.

"You've sent for him then?"

"Lady Celia has."

"Good." Rolande paused and drew a ragged breath. "How ... how long do you think he'll be?"

"A day or two at most, I expect. He's gone to the shipyard at Haremare Point."

Rolande started pacing again. "Then we'll just have to fend for ourselves till then. A pity you're so small, but listen, Kendry, don't worry, I can protect you. We may be unarmed, but we're not defenseless. I don't think they'll dare use weapons against us—they'll threaten to, but with only two of us here, they can't claim not to know how we were wounded. Just remember, that sort are always cowards. They expect you to be cowed, and if you defy them, they don't know what to do. I can—" Rolande broke off as she saw that Alicen was staring at her as if she had no idea what Rolande was talking about.

"Have you taken leave of your senses?" Alicen asked her. "The guards won't interfere with us! Why, Sir Andrew would—"

"Sir Andrew is not here," Rolande pointed out stonily. "In God's name, I used to believe you were brave, but now I can see you're just so smug and sheltered, you think nothing can happen to you! Well, *I've* been in prison before, My Lady, as you so kindly reminded me, and trust me, I know what to expect!"

She's terrified, Alicen thought in amazement. She had never seen Rolande show any sign of weakness or fear before, but now she was visibly shaking. *Yet she was worried about me.* What was it Lady Celia had said ...?

"Well, you've never been in *this* prison before, have

you?" Alicen asked reasonably. "Perhaps things are different here. Come, don't cry till you're hurt. I daresay they'll let us be, and if they don't, they'll wish they had. Sit down here and stop wearing yourself out."

Rolande paused in her pacing and regarded Alicen with uncertainty. Was the haughty little bitch trying to *reassure* her? Remembering the deference with which the guard had spoken to Alicen, Rolande said curtly, "True, they may be afraid to tamper with you. They know you're a lady, and the Governor's guest. But I'm just pirate scum as far as they're concerned."

"Why then, I'll protect you." Alicen rose and laid her hand on Rolande's arm. "*Will* you stop stalking about? What ails you? Yes, they know I'm a lady—and they know you're Rolande Vendeley! They'd probably sooner cross an enraged bull than you. Come, sit down."

Rolande pulled away, shamed at having let Alicen see her fear, and distrustful of her unwonted forbearance. "I'm fine. I've no patience for being walled in, that's all."

"Vendeley," Alicen said patiently, "I'm not the enemy."

Rolande turned around to look at her. "No?"

"No. Not unless you give me cause."

"I see. And I suppose you swear that upon your *honor*?"

Alicen laughed. "That's better. Come along, let's have peace."

She sounds like Celia. Rolande gave in and let Alicen take her hand and lead her back to the bench. "That ship was no more Acquitanian than I am," she muttered.

Alicen squeezed her hand. "Rest," she suggested, leaning against her comfortably. After a time, feeling calmer, Rolande put her arm around Alicen's shoulders. "All right, now tell me," said Alicen, "how did you escape from the catacombs?"

Despite herself, Rolande grinned. "I knew better than to trust you," she began, then stopped, listening. "Someone's coming." There was nowhere to hide in the small cell, and she could only wait, holding herself tensely ready for anything.

From the corridor came an appreciative whistle, and a man's voice growled, "You do get the luck, Vendeley! I've never been locked up with a tasty bit like that—only poxy pickpockets and cutthroats, reeking drunkards—"

Rolande leaped to her feet. "Lorin! Ha! Watch what you say, man. This one's a lady."

Lorin snorted. "As if a lady'd be in the town gaol, along with the likes of you. And you'd not be here either if you'd listened to me."

Rolande walked pointedly away from the barred door. "If you've come just to tell me I've been a fool, you can take yourself off again."

Lorin looked put out. "Not bloody likely I'd pay two whole embers in bribes to get in here, just to tell you that. I can tell you what a fool you are anytime, for free."

"It's about the merchants' plot then? Their claim is false?"

"Aye, right enough, but I don't know that you can prove it. It's an arrangement 'tween the merchants here and abroad. They have contrived to register vessels under multiple names in multiple countries. Each vessel carries both a true set of papers and a false set for different countries at odds with each other. When a ship is taken by a vessel of another nation, the captain turns over the false papers corresponding to the flag he's sailing under. Later, a true set of papers for a friendly country is produced, and a charge sworn out against the privateer, who thus appears guilty of piracy."

"Then there is no doubt that the papers they have are legitimate," Rolande said grimly, "the conniving swine."

"And I daresay even if the Magistrate takes the time to seek verification in Albin, there is no ship with the name that matches the papers you produced. The merchants can prove the ship you took was Acquitanian. You can't prove it otherwise."

Rolande cursed herself for having fallen prey to such a ploy. "You should have wagered on the hens, it seems."

"They've not won yet. What do you mean to do now?" Lorin asked, confident that Rolande would have some plan to meet the situation.

"There's only one way out now—Sir Andrew will have to intercede for me. They can prove the cursed ship came from the moon if they like, but if he declares a pardon, there's nothing they can do about it."

Lorin frowned. "Will he, though? He'll set 'em all against him if he does."

"He won't like it, but he'll do it. He expects to have another war to fight soon, and he knows how much use I can be to him." *And if that doesn't persuade him, I know what will. . . .*

It didn't sound a very secure plan to Lorin, but it was worth a try. "Shall I go see him, then?"

"No, he's away from Oriana. He'll come straight here when he returns, never fear."

"What am I to do, then?" He lowered his voice. "Some of these merchants could meet with accidents, you know."

"Such things have happened," Rolande agreed, feeling almost cheerful at the thought. "But for now, just deliver a message to my ship for me. The crew's no doubt heard of my arrest. Tell them that I will soon be free, and that they're to stand ready to make sail at once."

* * *

Sir Andrew commandeered the Watch Captain's small, dark office, the only room where he might interview the gaol's prisoners in privacy. He naturally sent for Alicen first, and was much surprised to find that she seemed more concerned with Rolande's plight than with her own.

"Why was Vendeley not summoned, too?" she greeted him. "Your Lordship cannot mean to leave her here, surely?"

"I shall deal with Vendeley in due course," he assured her, "though she has little enough claim on my sympathy. I warned her what would happen if she became more a hazard than an advantage to our cause. She brought this on herself."

Alicen shifted uncomfortably on the edge of a hard, straight-backed chair. "But she claims the merchants tricked her somehow. . . ." Even as she said the words, she realized how unconvincing they sounded. Why had she believed them?

Sir Andrew clearly did not. "No doubt she would make such a claim. It is the one tale she hasn't tried before," he said impatiently, dismissing the matter of Rolande. "I am more concerned at the moment, Lady Alicen, to hear your response to the testimony against you."

"But what testimony can they have? They've told me nothing since I was brought here."

Lady Celia had made inquiries at once on this point, knowing that the Magistrate would not have ordered Alicen's arrest, without first consulting the Governor, unless there were strong reason to believe in her guilt. She had been able to inform Sir Andrew of the details of the case as soon as he arrived.

"It seems that a serving girl at the hostel has given evidence against you," he began.

"But they were questioned by the Watch before, and none reported a thing!" Alicen protested.

"That was before the Magistrate offered a reward to anyone who came forward with information about the killing." He was well aware of the suspicion in which the Watch was held by servants and laborers, many of whom supplemented their meager pay by petty thievery. "Then this woman claimed that she saw you enter Ruthven's room, and leave in a rush, not long before he was discovered to be dead."

Alicen recalled the servants working about the hostel when she'd gone in. "So she may have done, for I wasn't in hiding, but he was already dead when I entered his room, as I told you."

Sir Andrew met her eyes, his face serious. "Unfortunately, she's also told the Magistrate that there was bad blood between you and Ruthven. She claims to have overheard a raging argument between the two of you, including an exchange of threats, when she was cleaning the upstairs hallway, some time back. Is there any truth to this?"

Alicen cast her mind back to her confrontation with Ruthven, on the day she'd sneaked into his room at the hostel. Hadn't she passed a girl on the stairs? If that one had still been there when Ruthven returned, she could not have avoided hearing him shouting Alicen's name and slamming the door. And if the chit had then listened at the keyhole as long as she dared, she might have heard. . . . "I daresay there is," she admitted. "I still suspected Ruthven of poisoning me, then, and he blamed me for the attempt on his life. But even if this servant's tale is true, it doesn't prove I killed him! And if I'd done so, I'd have told you. I'd no reason to keep such a thing from you, not once I'd learned—" she lowered her voice—"that he'd tried to kill the Princess!"

Sir Andrew nodded. "If you'd killed him, you'd have done us a considerable service," he agreed, "but I can't very well explain that to the Magistrate, not yet. And at present, you're the most likely culprit they have. Well, I shall have you out of here one way or another." He believed Alicen's story that someone had been after both her and Ruthven. After all, she'd nearly died of poison in his own yard. And if the killer learned of Oriana's presence in the colony, she would undoubtedly be the next target. No, the time had not come to reveal the Princess' secret to the authorities. He considered the situation briefly, then summoned the Captain of the Watch. "Lady Alicen Kendry is to be released to my custody. I shall stand surety for her, and see that she is held secure in my household until this matter is resolved."

The captain had been expecting something of the sort, and was prepared for it. He'd had no choice but to carry out the Magistrate's orders, but it stood to reason that His Lordship wouldn't leave a noblewoman to the keeping of the gaol, like a common criminal. All the same, he needed proper documentation before he let her loose. "I'll require a written authorization from you to release her, sir," he said firmly. "To satisfy regulations, you understand." Of course, if the Governor refused, that would be that, but it was as well to ask.

But Sir Andrew only snapped, "Yes, yes, go to the Magistrate's clerk and have the proper document drawn up, then bring it to me for signature. *Now.*"

"At once, sir." Quailing as many a militiaman had under Sir Andrew's glare, the captain fairly ran from the room in his haste to send a messenger to the Magistrate's house.

While Sir Andrew waited for the matter of Alicen's disposition to be settled, he decided that he might as well see about his other problem. Having ordered one of the guards to take him to Rolande's cell, he followed the man down the fieldstone corridor, leaving Alicen under the eye of another watchman stationed outside the office door.

If there was indeed such solid evidence pointing to her as Ruthven's murderer, Alicen wondered, would it require more than Sir Andrew's intervention to set it right . . . ?

Rolande strode to the door at the sight of him, and gripped the bars so hard that her fingers visibly whitened. "You took your sweet time!" she shouted, without waiting for him to speak. "I thought I'd rot in here!"

"As you well may," Sir Andrew said sharply, too furious at her insolence to see the ill-disguised desperation that prompted it. "I understand there's reliable evidence of your piracy. I warned you before, I can't go about pardoning criminals on a whim."

"It's your damned merchants who are criminals! That ship was as Albinate as you or I when I boarded her—for the rest, 'tis all their subterfuge." Quickly,

Rolande recounted the details of the merchants' plot while Sir Andrew reluctantly heard her out.

"You've no proof of any of this," he said at last, rubbing his temples to alleviate the pain he felt starting.

"I *gave* you the ship's papers, and her flag!"

Sir Andrew was silent, weighing the possibilities. Rolande was an invaluable asset, and he needed her expertise if they were to succeed in taking the Albinate warship. Yet if she had turned rogue, she was no longer trustworthy, and he might free her only to set loose a renegade worthless to his cause and dangerous to the colony. She'd been the Chamber's spy long enough to know how to acquire false paper, to justify her in seizing the ship. And anyone could lay hold of an old Dep flag. "You've no proof that they're genuine," he pointed out. "I take it the Captain will deny it."

"Lies!" Rolande insisted. "You're the Governor— you have the power to override their testimony."

"It's not so simple as that, Vendeley, and you know it! If I free you without cause, if I further antagonize those with power in this community, they may stir up the colonists against me. I can't afford to resign the Governorship now, when I need the resources to build a navy that can challenge the Albinate armada. By God, you ask a great deal, if you expect me to put the future of the colony at jeopardy, for the sake of one treacherous turncoat whose only loyalty is to her own interest!"

Rolande had reached the end of her tether. "You *dare* say that to me, you bloody, prating fool—? If I'd looked to my own interest, I could have sold your precious Princess to the Chamber at any time, these four years past, and made my fortune by it! I had her in my hand, I had her *nailed in a crate* after I rescued her from Pryce. She'd be long dead if not for me, or have you forgotten that? I had her aboard my ship, too, after your last battle with Hough, and a dozen times since. I could have sailed off with her straight to Albin if I chose—I'd have been the Chamber's darling if I'd given them Oriana Obelen! But I've never betrayed her, not so much as told a living soul of her secret, and you question my loyalty? Thank the Good God there's iron and oak between us, man, or I'd rip out your heart for that! If you don't get me out of this hole, 'tis you who are a disloyal hound, and you'll pay for it!" Some instinct of self-preservation made her stop just short of threatening to expose the Princess' secret if he failed her. Let that remain unsaid.

Sir Andrew stared at her, stunned. "You've known ... *all this time?*" he choked out at last. "How?"

Rolande sighed, exhausted by her own outburst. "After Pryce convinced Hough I'd betrayed the Chamber, I did some spying on my own account. I found a letter Pryce had written Hough, saying only that he had the Princess—and then I discovered that he was holding young Ander prisoner. But I never did find out how he knew about her." She shrugged. "So I stole her away from him. I could have delivered her to Hough then and there, and instead I brought her to you."

"Why?" Sir Andrew asked helplessly, still trying to get his bearings.

"It didn't suit me to pander to the Chamber, after I'd had a taste of freedom. I meant to be my own master."

"But then, why pretend not to know about Oriana?"

"Because," Rolande spat, "I knew that one day I'd need this card to play, to prove my *loyalty,* My Lord!"

She had certainly done that, Sir Andrew thought. This revelation of hers had put everything in a new light. Pirate or no, Vendeley had served and protected the Princess—knowingly, it seemed—and kept her se-

cret faithfully for years. There were few enough Her
Highness could count upon, in these uncertain days.
"Very well," he said resignedly, "for the Princess's
sake, I shall see you pardoned, much as I might prefer,
myself, to see you hang. Should the merchants
object—and they will—I shall tell them that you are
engaged upon a mission of the utmost importance to
the colony, and that they shall see the benefits were
worth the cost in the end. It may succeed in purchasing
us time enough to do what must be done."

"It's no more than the truth, that," said Rolande.
"And tell them that you know of their scurvy little
tricks—that will give them something to think about."

Sir Andrew gave her a searching look. "That was the
truth, then?" he asked, surprised.

"*Yes,* I tell you! Those papers were aboard the *Carnelian!* Tell the Cardif woman and her cronies that you
won't countenance their duplicity. I daresay they'll
deny it, but if you hold fast, they'll not be able to come
it wronged and righteous over you."

"Excellent. The very weapon I needed."

"Well, here's another for you. The merchants are
afraid to oppose you openly, so you needn't worry
about a demand for your resignation. Whatever you
may think, *they* think the people of Oriana will follow
your lead, even if it means doing without goods from
Albin. That's another thing Mistress Cardif told
Elliseth Moore, at the ball where I was so unwelcome."

"Most interesting." The one thing Rolande had
never done was bring him unreliable information. "But
if one act can strain the people's faith in me, it will
likely be this pardon. Now if you've nothing more to
tell me, I shall go and arrange for your release." When
Rolande made no answer, he added, "And as soon as
you're free, you're to set about your important mis-

sion, and avoid neutral trading vessels, is that understood?"

"Yes, m'lord," Rolande said meekly, then as he turned away, she asked, "You do mean to invade Albin and put the lass on the throne, I trust?"

It would be pointless to deny it. "Of course—if you've no objection, Mistress Vendeley?"

"None in the world. Then I'll be able to capture Acquitanian vessels with my sovereign's sanction." Rolande smiled. "I quite fancy myself as Queen's Privateer."

* * *

There was an urgent knocking on the door of the captain's quarters, and the first mate's voice could be heard calling for Rolande. She climbed out of bed, grabbed her greatcoat, buttoning it around her, and yanked open the door.

The man took a step back, startled, but hesitated only a moment. "Captain—I know you weren't to be disturbed. But Hrivas' spotted a huge warship—coming from the east."

Rolande's scowl changed to a look of eager anticipation. "How close is she?"

"At the speed she's making, she'll be upon us before the next watch."

"Summon all hands to their stations," Rolande ordered. "I'll be there directly."

The man turned on his heel, heading for the ladder to the deck above. Rolande reached for her breeches, then looked back at Raphe, still tangled in the bedsheets. "Don't loll about—get dressed. There's work to be done!"

A cannonade burst forth with a great crack of thunder and the jib boom on the *Shraik* shattered, spraying Rolande with slivers of wood. Amid the noise of shouting sailors and roaring guns, Rolande signaled her helmsman to pull back, then maneuver around so that the *Shraik* was again approaching the *Invincible,* this time sailing toward the enemy's stern as another vessel moved to fill her place on the port side.

It had been near sunset when the great black shape, still invisible to human eye, had been spotted by Hrivas, soaring far in advance of the pirate fleet. A heavy fog blanketed much of the sea—one of the reasons for the Chamber's choice of the coast off New Lindness, Rolande speculated. Not many vessels would be found sailing the inhospitable waters of this far northern sea, so the *Invincible* might go unobserved, and the Chamber already assumed that their new warship could weather the natural elements that brought other ships to grief.

Well, it's up to me to show them the error of their ways. At Rolande's signal, the ships to the rear of the *Shraik* drew up close. Before long, Captain Bannion put before the wind, accompanied by Captain Payne's two sloops, sailing out of the fog, following in the wake of the *Invincible* after she had passed. When their quarry sailed into the trap, no escape route back would remain.

Now the other pirate ships closed in from every side, swarming around the massive black hulk, like a flock of buzzards around the beached carcass of a whale. Turning to meet the onslaught that came first from her port side, the *Invincible* sent out volley after volley of heavy fire that shattered the masts and rigging of the nearest ships. The longer they were engaged, the greater grew Rolande's admiration for the designers of the magnificent warship. She counted forty broadsides fired in an hour by the *Invincible,* more than twice the rate of any ship she'd ever known. No matter what the cost, she vowed, she must have that vessel.

All around the dark warship the pirate vessels closed in, fired, and withdrew, leaving the *Invincible* unable to sail in any direction without running the gamut of yet another volley of cannonfire. The continuous blasts of artillery fire splintered the wood of the poop, quarter and forecastle decks, and carpenters and crewmen scurried to and fro through the narrow passages on either side of the lower decks, trying to patch damage to the vessel's hull before the ship could take on water. But the net of pirate ships drew in closer.

The officers and sailors of the *Invincible* had hoped to become familiar with the workings of the new vessel on her maiden voyage, as well as test her seaworthiness. Their number included gunners, for the trial of the cannon, but the Chamber's Admiralty had anticipated no trouble beyond perhaps an encounter with a stray pirate ship. Operating her guns in a full-scale engagement with a veritable fleet of ships was altogether beyond the crew's experience, and before long they were firing so wildly that only a tenth of their hundreds of rounds of shot found their mark.

Rolande smiled in satisfaction as she received the reports of the embattled ships, brought promptly by Hrivas. All the work of the past weeks was now bearing fruit. The *Shraik* had cruised pirate-infested waters from White Hern Island to Dunraven, hailing ships in sail and making port wherever pirate vessels were known to take on supplies. In all, Rolande had convinced fully a dozen other pirate captains to fall in with her plan. Some had joined her because they feared the rise of a navy that could drive them from the sea, some for a share of Captain Tyrrel's treasure, and some from sheer pride and bravado. Indeed, the greatest difficulty had not been in finding enough allies for the venture, but in finding those willing to accept Hrivas as part of the plan. On that point, however, Rolande had held firm. Pirate crews were largely unaccustomed to cooperating with other vessels, and immediate communication carried from ship to ship by a Yerren, when signals might be obscured by fog or smoke, could make the difference between success and defeat for a concerted effort such as this one.

And Rolande was well pleased with the fleet of twelve ships she had finally assembled—two of which even had Yerren lookouts of their own. Whatever their reasons for joining with her, she was determined that her force of cutthroats and seaborne brigands would bring the proud *Invincible* to the point of surrender. Her pride was surely a match for the Chamber's.

The most vulnerable parts of the *Invincible*'s hull were now armored with metal plates, which made it difficult to find a critical spot to strike. Shouting over the pounding gunfire, she ordered a targeted hit upon the *Invincible*'s gun battery amidships. Her gunners' aim was true, and smoke billowed forth as a shattering explosion shook the *Invincible*'s upper gundeck. "We must have hit powder there," Rolande thought with satisfaction, but she thanked the Good God that the commander of the enemy vessel had observed good naval procedure and only allowed enough powder for one shot to be stored by any gun during the engagement. Had there been any quantity on the deck when it was hit, the ship might have undergone too large an explosion, and suffered worse damage than she wished. It had been a calculated risk, but well worth it, and now all throughout the *Invincible* there was terror and confusion as sailors raced about wildly, seeking to extinguish any sparks which would set other powder stores alight, while other crewmen tried to prepare for further attempts to blow up their guns.

"Now!" Rolande commanded, and Hrivas set off amidst the smoke from the thundering guns, flying low over the other ships, his presence the signal that they should attempt to board. The pirate captains in the vessels nearest the *Invincible* drew closer in, attempting to lash their bows to the larger vessel and extend boarding planks to the lower decks. In the *Invincible,* sailors climbed up the rigging to the tops and rained musketfire down upon the attacking ships to repel the boarders.

Rolande ordered the gunners on the *Shraik* to fire high, driving the defenders from the masts and rigging. The *Invincible* responded with a low volley, attempting to cripple Rolande's ship, but her vessel was the more maneuverable of the two, and she had already drawn back out of the way. The *Shraik* closed in again, with Captain Bannion's vessel close beside, and they succeeded in anchoring their grappling hooks in the *Invincible*'s shrouds. Then lashing their vessels to the enemy fore and aft, they gained the deck of the monstrous warship and battered back the defenders with small arms fire. Rolande caught hold of a backstay and swung herself over the rail onto the forecastle deck, where the *Invincible*'s captain waited, erect and calm in his soot-stained gray uniform. Unfaltering, he raised his pistol, the muzzle toward Rolande's breast, but even as he cocked the weapon, her sword swept in an arc, slashing through his coat sleeve at the wrist. His gun hit the deck and she swung again, this time slicing through his throat. One by one, other ships drew near and joined the boarding party until the attackers over-ran the decks of the *Invincible*.

The enemy sailors were now in total disarray, outnum-bered and surrounded, their officers dead or captured. Most fled to the galley, holds and shot lockers, or surren-dered where they stood. Finally Raphe climbed up the foremast rigging to the flagpole and pulled down the Chamber's torch-and-sword flag, to replace it with Ro-lande's black banner, emblazoned with a golden shraik.

As the Chamber's surviving sailors were rounded up and locked in one of the ship's great holds, Rolande surveyed the carnage. The effort had cost dearly in lives, and the sea all around was strewn with wreck-age. When a muster had been made, it was found that more than a hundred of the pirates' hands had been killed or wounded and several of the ships damaged, four of them wrecked beyond repair. But Rolande was resolved to carry out the strike against Tyrrel's isle as planned, without delay. Sir Andrew would be awaiting the arrival of the Chamber's warship at the hidden cove that had been made ready for her near Haremare Point, and Rolande meant to deliver her as promised— after she'd achieved her vengeance on Captain Tyrrel.

They sailed as soon as they had repaired and re-stocked their ships with timbers and stores salvaged from vessels too damaged to be seaworthy again. Lost crew members were replaced in the same way, until new vessels could be captured, at sea or at Needle Isle. Using the cover of the fog to disguise their passing, they made their way south until they cleared the last of the fog banks, then crossed an expanse of open ocean, silent except for the occasional forlorn cry of a lone seabird. The pirate ships escorting the *Invincible* easily surrounded and commandeered any vessel luckless enough to cross their path, gradually bringing the pirate fleet back to full strength, though many of the ships were sailing short-handed.

The voyage to the islands was a windward passage and took but a fortnight. They soon reached the cluster of islands where Needle lay, and maintained thenceforth a heading that would take them by those shores that were least inhabited. Rolande had convinced the other pirate captains that the *Invincible* must be kept out of sight as much as possible, if they were to have the advantage of surprising Tyrrel with her unexpected power. But staying far from the main shipping routes meant that there was little quarry to prey upon.

Then on an evening when they were but a few days from their destination, the dark hulk of a galleon hove into view, and Captain Payne at once signaled Rolande of his intent to attack. Examining the vessel through her spyglass, Rolande noted with suspicion the ship's pitted brown hull and the row of nine pound cannon in its gunports. And why had the captain chosen a course off the main trade route, where it would be difficult to find supplies? The vessel was sitting low at the water line. *Fully laden then,* she thought, *with an unusually heavy cargo.* Livestock, perhaps, or people . . . ? She could be a convict ship, but, if so, she was far off course. More likely a rogue slaver, commanded by a captain who obtained his wares wherever he could find unprotected victims, and sold them to those who weren't particular about their history. Rolande sent Hrivas flying across the short distance to Captain Payne's ship, to say that she would join him in attacking the unknown vessel.

At the approach of the pirate ships, the slaver clapped hard upon the wind, making a run for the island to the east. A brig or schooner might have outrun the massive *Invincible,* but the old, heavily-laden galleon could not put enough distance between them to make an escape. With her multitude of masts and sails, Rolande's ship gained steadily upon the smaller vessel until she came within firing range, and Rolande sent a single shot over her bow, warning the captain to surrender.

The captain of the slaver, however, reasoning that he had nothing to lose, responded instead by firing a barrage of cannon at the *Invincible.* Incensed at the lesser vessel's refusal to yield, Rolande ordered a volley to be fired high at the slaver, so as not to endanger those below. The artillery fire raked the slaveship, and one panicked hand leaped overboard as the deck was torn open behind him. When Captain Payne opened fire off the slaver's stern, her captain realized that the attackers were determined to take her, and would not be discouraged by resistance. Further combat would only shatter his ship plank by plank, and the captain ceased fire and struck his flag.

The *Invincible* was lashed to the bowsprit of the slaver, and Rolande and her boarding party clambered down onto her decks, soon joined by Captain Payne and some of his pirates. They took possession of the ship in short order, for slavers were notoriously parsimonious when it came to paying more crew than was required by necessity. Rolande, followed by Raphe, made straight for the main hatch.

When they descended the ladder to the hold, lamps in hand, they were greeted with a great clamor from those chained together in the dark chamber, waiting to learn the outcome of the battle that had raged overhead. Rolande was about to order Raphe to fetch the keys to the chains, when he exclaimed excitedly, "Captain! Look, it's Will—and there's Peg!"

Peering into the gloom to where he pointed, Rolande saw that he was right, and she gave a triumphant shout of giddy elation. Most of the crew of the *Azora* were among the captives, and hailing her on all sides. A crushing weight lifted from her heart as she greeted her lost crew, battered and bruised, but yet alive. "The keys, lad, and more light!" she ordered Raphe, who hastened up the ladder and returned almost at once with Corey, both of them laden with lanterns. "Why so surprised to see us?" Rolande laughed, as they set about freeing the prisoners. "Don't tell me you doubted I'd come to the rescue!"

One man managed to get to his knees with a rattling of chains, and Rolande recognized Captain Varrett. "So, you live yet, too!"

"Aye, Vendeley—we thought you'd been washed out to sea. There wasn't so much as a longboat missing, and Tyrrel had every ship in the harbor searched stem to stern. How the devil did you get off Needle?"

"Didn't you know I've demonic powers? I just changed myself to a black swan and flew away."

"Black swan? Brodery? But where—"

"Off the headland," Rolande explained, inserting the iron key into his manacles. "That one did me a good turn, for all he was a monstrous fool. Hanged in Avenford, he was, and could have taken me down with him, if he'd a mind to." She tossed the key to one of the captives and climbed up out of the teeming hold into the clean air above.

Captain Varrett followed, shaking his head in bewilderment. "And did you use your witchcraft to find us?"

"In truth, I wasn't looking for you," Rolande admitted. "I thought that cur Tyrrel would have killed the lot of you."

Stretching his cramped limbs, Captain Varrett grimaced and said, "Not he, not when there was a profit to be made. He used us as slave labor to build up the harbor fortifications on his island. We felt the weight of his whip on that job, and once the work was done, he sold us to this plaguey flesh-peddler." He noted with approval that the captain of the slaver had been lashed to the mast, while his people stood by, under guard, until they could be herded into the hold to take the place of their cargo. "I've a score to settle with Captain Tyrrel, if I can get at the bastard."

"Why, I was on my way to Needle now, with a fleet of our fellows, to avenge the *Azora.* Mayhap you'd care to join us, eh? It's a pity his fortifications have been strengthened, but I think my new ship will be a match for them."

For the first time, Captain Varrett turned and regarded the *Invincible,* her vast bulk looming over them and dwarfing the slaveship like a whale beside a dolphin. For a moment he only stared, then he turned back to Rolande with a broad grin. " 'Tis witchcraft, right enough, for there's no such ship afloat, nor ever has been. Only you, Vendeley, could disappear in the middle of the ocean and come back at the helm of a dream . . . ! But about those fortifications, now, I had my people make a few improvements in them here and there. In some places, the wood's held together with shortened nails, and parts of the stockade are supported with posts braced with wood that's soft with rot. I knew someday I'd go back and attack them, but I did not expect the day to come so soon."

"I see we have much to discuss," Rolande said, "when you've refreshed yourself. I expect the captain's cabin of this scow will have what you need for now. When we've sorted matters out here, we'll plan how best to pay Tyrrel for the way he's used you all."

The rescued sailors were shared out among the ships of the pirate fleet to fill those crews short of hands. Rolande took her own crew aboard the *Invincible* with much celebration, and left the fate of the slavers in the hands of those left aboard the galleon, under Varrett's command. She did not inquire about his plans for them. All that remained was to put an end to Tyrrel's tyranny.

The fortifications overlooking the harbor at Needle Isle did, indeed, look as if they had recently been reinforced. The stockade rose higher and was armed with heavier cannon—eighteen pounders that were fired as soon as the pirate fleet came 'round the point that sheltered the inlet from the open sea. Rolande was not surprised at this greeting. No doubt Captain Tyrrel had received warning from one of the pirates she had attempted unsuccessfully to enlist in her plan. Then again, he would probably assume that any armada approaching Needle had come with unfriendly intent.

Captain Tyrrel was taking no chances—and neither was Rolande. She remembered, all too well, the weapons shanty where Tyrrel kept the guns visiting pirates brought ashore. Wouldn't he store his own spare powder there as well, secure under lock and key, and constantly guarded? Her ill-advised attempt to capture it before had nearly killed them all, and she remembered every aspect of the ordeal, including her own regrets that she had no Yerren at her command, as she scaled the deadly precipice. But this time she had three, and she had as well the example set by Sir Andrew during the Dep invasion of Thornfeld, when he had made use of Yerren warriors to destroy the enemy's powder magazine. By doing the same, she would not only destroy

Tyrrel's supplies, but make it impossible for him to re-arm the visiting pirate crews, to aid in his defense.

At her signal, Hrivas and the other two Yerren swept into the sky, clutching their bows and pitch-dipped arrows. Landing in the high branches of the trees on the cliff, they ignited the arrows with bits of flint and steel, and shot the flaming shafts into the roof of the weapons shanty. They took flight before Tyrrel's people even realized that an attack had been made, and in a space of minutes the fire ate its way through the dry wood, spreading to the contents of the shed. The guards had no means to extinguish the blaze, and no time to save the powder. From her vantage point on the forecastle deck, Rolande saw them dashing down the hill to escape, a moment before the powder caught and the shed burst in a great explosion that sent firebrands flying in all directions.

When the plume of smoke from the weapons shanty rose over the trees, the pirate fleet entered the harbor with cannons blazing, sailing past the vessels at anchor. Amid the shouted orders and outcries of the pirates manning the fortifications, the invading vessels positioned themselves to strike most strongly at those weak points in the stockade that Captain Varrett had revealed to them. Rolande ordered a steady barrage of cannonfire aimed at the joints where the timber walls met as the palisade followed the jagged line of the coast.

The *Invincible*'s cannon were not only more numerous than those carried by any ship previously, but also more advanced. They had been provided with gunlocks, a device that enabled the gun captains to judge when to fire with far more precision than was possible with traditional linstocks. Rolande, observing the accuracy of the cannonades issuing forth from the *Invinci-*

ble, was more than satisfied with the effect of this new invention, and looked forward with keen anticipation to demonstrating its use to Sir Andrew.

Section after section of the fortification shattered and fell away, sending Tyrrel's cutthroats screaming onto the rocks below. Soon there were panicked men running wildly in every direction, seeking to escape from the collapsing bulwarks. Seeing the rout that was taking place, Captain Tyrrel exhorted his minions to hold their ground, for he stood no chance if his defenses failed. Surrender would avail him nothing against a foe bent on vengeance, and though he did not know that the pirates he'd sold had returned, he knew that Vendeley had sworn to avenge her crew. But he was a commander who inspired fear rather than loyalty, and his people, finding themselves outnumbered and outgunned, had no intention of dying with him. Those who were only sojourning on the island, still unarmed, wisely preserved their neutrality and kept to their own encampments.

Rolande bade the Yerren climb to the maintopgallant yards of Captains Payne's and Bannion's ships, which had drawn near to the shore, now that there was little danger from artillery fire. From this height, Hrivas and the others sent flaming arrows into the damaged fortifications, setting the remaining timbers alight and exploding any reserves of powder that remained there. Against the noise of the crackling fires springing up around him, Captain Tyrrel shouted curses at the pirate fleet, then, mad with rage, seized an abandoned musket and fired at his own people who were in retreat.

Rolande was in the first longboat to reach the shore, and Tyrrel raced toward her, through charred logs and splintered timbers, his pistol raised to fire as soon as he came within range. She threw herself from the boat onto the shore, just as he fired, and his shot went over her and lodged in the wood of the longboat, directly behind her. Drawing her own pistol, Rolande gained her feet and ran toward him, but by now other boats had also arrived. Before Tyrrel could reload, he was surrounded by scores of angry pirates. In no time, he was disarmed and bound, then dragged into the woods and hanged from the branch of a large oak on the cliff, near the burnt remains of the weapons shed, and in plain sight from the open sea.

When the remainder of Captain Tyrrel's men had been rounded up and disarmed, a conclave of the pirate captains took place, to decide how the island would henceforth be governed, and how Tyrrel's wealth would be allotted among them. Some of the ships moored in the harbor belonged to Varrett and the other captains who'd taken part in the failed revolt against Tyrrel, and these they reclaimed without dispute. Others were Tyrrel's property, and it was agreed that they would be turned over to those captains who had lost their vessels when the *Invincible* was seized. Each decision was toasted liberally, for many kegs of rum and brandy had been taken from Captain Tyrrel's stores. But Rolande didn't stay to find out how amicably Tyrrel's treasure would be divided. She provisioned her two ships, returned her new crew to the *Shraik,* sent her old crew aboard the *Invincible,* and ordered both to make ready to sail without further delay. The delivery of the *Invincible* was now long overdue.

She had one last matter to lay before her fellow captains, however, before she set out for Oriana. "Do not forget," she urged, when she took her leave of them, "to spread the rumor that a monstrous big Albinate warship was seen to sink like a stone, in the northerly sea, at the first sign of rough weather."

"Why, the only wonder was that the thing stayed afloat as long as it did," Captain Varrett put in, "for any sailor worth his salt could see that she was too big and ungainly to ride out a storm."

The others laughed. " 'Tisn't possible to provide proper ballast and balance for a ship that size, as everybody knows!" one of them agreed. "Only a lot of lubberly loons like the Deps would try it."

"Aye, that's the stuff to give 'em," Rolande said, pleased. "Tell that tale and stick to it, or the Deps'll seize our domain as they did Albin, the thieving gray beggars."

Clearly, it was in the pirates' interest to convince the Chamber that their fearsome new weapon was unseaworthy, and the captains carried out Rolande's plan with enthusiasm, when they went their separate ways. Before long, the news was known widely throughout the ports along the sealanes, all the way to Albin.

Chapter 14

Messages had been arriving from Sir Warren with increasing frequency, now that preparations were under way for the Princess's return to Albin. His informants all reported that in the wake of the loss of the *Invincible*, the Chamber had altered their plans. They would continue to build their fleet up to invasion strength, but relying on conventional vessels instead. It was unlikely that construction could be completed before the storms of winter came again, but the Deps were determined to strike by the time summer returned.

This gave Sir Andrew but little time to complete his own preparations. He discussed strategies for defense with Captain Fenton and Commander Jamison, and spent a good deal of time in the navy yard, observing every stage of the shipbuilding operation, and growing more worried and impatient with each day that brought no sign of the *Invincible*. Thus, when the message arrived that the *Invincible* had at last been sighted, Sir Andrew left immediately for the hidden harbor, to meet with Rolande and inspect the Albinate warship.

Captain Fenton accompanied him, for it had been seven years since Sir Andrew had left Albin, and Fenton, in his work for Sir Warren, had been in a position to observe the activities of the Albinate Navy far more recently. His ideas about meeting the threat of the enemy armada would be worth hearing, but before they left, Sir Andrew exacted a solemn promise from Katin that she would remain within the mansion until he or the captain returned.

Sir Andrew's reaction to the *Invincible* was all that Rolande could have wished. All that he saw amazed him, and he grew more impressed with every innovation she showed him, particularly the gunlocks. For once he did not stint in his congratulations that she should have captured such a prize and somehow brought it back nearly unscathed. He wisely forbore to mention how long it had taken her to sail from New Lindness. Rolande in turn refrained from reminding him that the *Invincible* would still be in enemy hands if he'd left her in prison, as he'd threatened to do. When he'd examined the fabulous vessel inch by inch, Sir Andrew divided his shipbuilders into teams and set them to copy the *Invincible* in every detail.

Rolande had sent her old crew, and the pick of the new, directly back to Oriana on the *Shraik,* with messages for Lorin—and for Blythe, should he be found in the colony. The *Shraik* would have arrived by now, and she herself planned to return to Oriana with Sir Andrew and join her people there. She hoped he appreciated the considerable sacrifice she was making for the royalist cause, for the *Shraik,* though a fine ship, could never satisfy one who'd captained such a vessel as the *Invincible.*

Sir Andrew did perhaps take into account this further evidence of Rolande's loyalty and reliability. Gazing up at the *Invincible,* he said, "She'll be the flagship of the fleet when we meet the Chamber's armada. And you'll take command of her, Vendeley, if you can sink ships as well as you steal them."

* * *

Jerl had conscientiously avoided Katin since the night of the ball. He had work enough to occupy him, overseeing the digging of wells, splitting wood for new corrals, plowing fields, and attending to the manifold daily duties of the farm. As he guided a plow through the rocky soil of the westernmost field, he told himself that Katin had made her choice, that she had her reasons, and that he had no time to waste in pursuit of a hopeless dream. He was realistic enough to keep his behavior in check—he would not go to Katin's workshed to seek her out—but it was another matter, he found, to govern his thoughts and wishes. Again and again he heard in his mind the words of his last conversation with her, and found himself trying each time to think of a way to change her mind.

He knew better, of course, for he knew Katin. Had it been merely a matter of something she wanted to do, he might have persuaded her to give it up, but this was something she did *not* want to do, and so she was determined to see it through. Nothing he might say could sway her. She was lost to him, and he knew it. Why couldn't he stop thinking about her? He'd had a goal and purpose in life before he'd known Katin, and he had them still—more, he had accomplished a great deal, he had made something of himself. Why, then, should he feel that his hard-won home in the New World meant nothing if Katin would not be there to share it with him?

Suddenly Jerl was thrown forward as the iron tip of the hickory plow jammed under a large rock. When the heavy draft horse pulling the plow felt the resistance, it gave a lunge forward, and the metal blade twisted and snapped, pulling Jerl off-balance. He tumbled into the half-turned furrow, slashing his hand on the broken blade as the horse galloped off, the loose reins dangling behind. Jerl rolled over, swearing, clutching at his gashed hand. Blood flowed freely from the wound, which was ripped deeply down his entire palm. Tearing off his shirt, he bound the wound as best he could and made his way toward the house, as blood continued to seep through the makeshift bandage.

But before Jerl had reached the doorstep, one of the field hands, who'd seen the accident, had run to the stable and sent the lad to fetch Doctor Justin. "Tell him 'tis bleeding hard, he must make all haste!" she ordered.

The stableboy mounted one of the sturdy farmhorses and galloped for town at once, only to find that the doctor was away at a distant household, treating a serious gunshot wound, and would not be free for hours. There was only one thing to do, in Oriana, when Doctor Justin could not attend to a sufferer. The lad remounted without delay and rode off to the Governor's Mansion to seek Katin.

Sir Andrew and Captain Fenton had not yet returned from Haremare Point, and Katin, true to her word, had stayed safely within doors, bored to distraction. She had been passing the time playing with Clara and Imp, the soarhound pup Katin had given her for a pet, with Sir Andrew's reluctant consent. But the child had been taken off for a nap, Lady Celia was out, and Alicen, confined to the premises until the question of Ruthven's murder should be resolved, was poor company. Katin repaired to the kitchen to cadge a piece of cake from the cook, who liked to spoil her. She had hardly entered, however, before she was told that a youth had come from Jerl's homestead to fetch her. The boy, failing to find Katin at her workshed, had come to the kitchen door to ask for her.

"The master's hurt," he cried as soon as he saw her, "and Doctor Justin's away. You'll come and help him, Mistress Ander, won't you?"

Katin's breath caught in her throat. If Jerl could not come himself, he must be badly injured. "Hurt? How?" she demanded.

"He took a great wound from a plowshare—Maggie said it was bleeding terrible."

Her promise to Sir Andrew forgotten, Katin raced to her workshed, dragging the boy after her. As she gathered up salves and bandages, she thought of sending the boy for Carl. He was no surgeon, but he could stitch up a wound if necessary. But then a better idea occurred to her. "Ride to the harbor and seek Edward Blythe of the sloop *Shraik*," she said decisively. "Captain Vendeley says he's a surgeon of some skill. Here's some silver, so that he can hire a horse from the livery stable near the docks. Fetch him to your master, and I'll meet you there." She had visited the *Shraik* with balms and tonics soon after it made port, but had found that her services were little needed, because Blythe had returned and taken up his duties again. As a privateersman, he must be well used to treating dangerous wounds, she assured herself.

Riding as recklessly as when she was a youngster, Katin reached Jerl's farmstead quickly and found him standing at the well in the yard, sluicing water over his wounded hand from the raised bucket, and trying to remove the splinters of hickory from his palm. He looked up at the sound of her approach and, in his surprise, drew back his hand, so that Katin saw blood welling in his palm and dripping over his fingers. She threw herself from her horse and ran to him, demanding, "What have you done to yourself, Jerl? Let me see that! Why, 'tis no more than a nasty cut!" She was so relieved to find Jerl alive and standing that she added without thinking, "And here I was half mad with grieving! Your lad had me frightened into fits—I thought you were dying!"

So she'd been that much afraid for him? She must indeed have ridden like a madwoman to arrive so soon. "No, I've only torn my hand on the coulter, but I can't stop the cursed thing from bleeding."

Katin examined his hand, which was washed clean now, but had an ugly ragged wound running down the center of the palm. "That wants stitching, but at least I can stop the flow of blood, I think, for now." Scolding cheerfully, she took a jar of witch hazel from her pack and poured it over the wound. He winced. "There, that'll teach you not to be dreaming behind the plow," she said.

"I can't help dreaming." It had been hard, but not impossible, to renounce the stranger in the Governor's garden, the elegant young lady in jewels and silk ... but this wild-riding, windblown firebrand was the girl he'd known for years, his closest companion. . . . How was he to give her up? Jerl winced again as the burning witch hazel cleansed the wound, but said boldly, "If I'd known that such an accident would bring you to my side, I'd have cut my hand all the sooner."

"More fool you!" Katin snapped, pulling a roll of bandages from her pack. She folded some to make a pad, which she pressed into the center of Jerl's palm, then began to wind the rest tightly around his hand. "You know that you needn't spill your life's blood to fetch me to you!"

Jerl brought his other hand up and squeezed her hand between his two, ignoring the pain in his palm. For a moment, Katin returned his gaze, and all the tenderness she felt toward him could be seen in her face. But only for a moment. Forcing her eyes from his, she lifted the edge of the partially strapped compress and looked down at the wound, from which blood still seeped, though more slowly. Then, to her relief, she heard the sound of hooves beating across soft turf, galloping toward them. "Doctor Justin's away," she said brusquely, "so I sent your lad for a ship's surgeon who's supposed to know his business. That must be they." She peered down the dirt track that ran between the homestead and the surrounding forest.

Soon Blythe and the stableboy rode up to them, and Blythe leapt down, tossing his reins to the boy. Katin released Jerl's hand and stepped aside, saying "Master Blythe, thank you for coming so promptly. 'Tis not as serious as I feared, but a surgeon's skill would not be amiss, I think. I've treated it with witch hazel and a compress."

"Very well, as I'm here, let me have a look," Blythe said curtly. He unwrapped the bandage, nodded in approval at Katin's work, then examined the wound, probing Jerl's hand to be certain that nothing had been broken. Katin flinched at his roughness, but Jerl remained perfectly still, his face as impassive as a Yerren's. "A clean gash, but a deep one," Blythe concluded. "You're right—it could bear stitching." He took a length of waxed cobbler's thread and a curved needle from his leather instrument case, then gripped Jerl's wrist with his left hand, so tightly that blood ceased to gather in the wound, and Katin was able to wipe Jerl's palm dry with a fresh piece of bandaging, as Blythe instructed her.

Now that he could see exactly where the edges of the wound were, Blythe began to suture them together with deft, quick motions, never slackening his grip on Jerl's wrist. The pressure not only kept the wound dry while he worked, but also numbed Jerl's hand to some extent. Katin, who was generally most interested to view such procedures, found that she could not watch at all. She clutched Jerl's other hand in both her own, though whether to steady Jerl or herself she could not have said.

Jerl clenched his teeth, determined to show no weakness in front of Katin. When Blythe finished, Jerl thanked him and said with a rueful smile, "I shan't offer to shake hands, but pray come to the house and have a drink, and payment for your services."

But Blythe waved this aside. "I'm in something of a hurry. I came away unexpectedly and have work waiting. Mind you keep that wound clean." He reached out to take the reins from the lad who was still holding them, and said to Katin, "Allow me to escort you home, Mistress Ander."

Offended at his dismissive treatment of Jerl, Katin replied, "I thank you, no. As you're in a hurry, I shouldn't dream of taking you out of your way."

Blythe gave her an arch look, and shrugged. "As you wish. But Goodman Smit should get some rest." Without further delay, he mounted his horse and rode down the track into the woods.

Katin realized that she was still holding Jerl's hand, and hastily dropped it. "Oh, of course—it's most improper for me to be alone with you, and you only half-dressed. I daresay he'll spread scandal about me, and *what* will Lady Celia say then?"

She had spoken lightly, but Jerl said, frowning, "If

he does, someone will have to sew *him* together when I've done with him."

Barechested in the sun, Jerl glowed like a burning brand in Katin's sight. *It isn't fair!* she thought in childish despair, but outwardly composed, she said brightly, "Nonsense—I was only chaffing. But he's right that you should be resting. From the look of that shirt, you lost a quantity of blood. Come along. I've brought willow bark to brew you a draught against the pain. Jerl . . . you really are a stalwart one. I've seen others—soldiers—howl like babes when they weren't in nearly so much pain as you—"

"But they didn't have you to hold their hand," said Jerl.

* * *

Rolande was weary when she finally returned to Oriana from Haremare Point, and she went directly to the *Shraik* without even stopping to see Lorin. She received the report of her first mate, and learned of Blythe's return, but he had been fetched by a farm-lad to attend to an injury, so she ordered, "Send him to me directly he's back," and went below. Making her way down the dark-paneled passageway to her cabin under the poop deck, she could hear the sound of a fiddle being played in the forecastle and the noise of boisterous singing. The crew of the *Azora*—now the crew of the *Shraik*—were still celebrating their escape and the victory over Tyrrel, and for a moment she was tempted to join them. She too still felt thankful for the turn of events that had reunited them.

Corey and Raphe had done their best to muster replacements, but most able hands had been recruited by Sir Andrew for his shipyards and navy, and she'd been forced to take on many who were far from the equal of her lost crew. Hrivas had quickly learned to stay out of their way, and he was as pleased as any to have his old shipmates back. Rolande could hear his clear, reedy voice above the others, joined with them in song.

But what she needed most was rest, not company, and she went on to her cabin alone. Her quarters were comfortable, furnished with a bedstead, a stretchered mahogany table flanked by two carved straight-backed chairs, a low chest of drawers of inlaid olive wood, a dropleaf writing desk, cedar storage chests for linen and plate, and a tall cherrywood wardrobe—all bolted securely to the floor. She reached for the door of the wardrobe, but something stopped her, and she realized that she had seen a smudge of black powder below the latch, as if someone had closed it with a powder-stained hand. Rolande had not been aboard the ship since the capture of the *Invincible,* and she never kept weapons or powder within the wardrobe. *It's latched—no one could be hiding there,* she told herself, but there was no harm in being cautious.

Drawing her sword, she stepped back and pressed herself flat against the wall to one side of the wardrobe. Then she extended the blade so it rested just beneath the latch, and carefully lifted it. As the wardrobe door swung open, there was a sharp crack, and a puff of black powder from the interior of the cabinet, as a lead ball shot over the blade and embedded itself in the wainscotting opposite, at chest height. Rolande slowly lowered her sword and waited, but nothing more occurred. Neither did any of the crew appear, for all were on deck or in their own quarters, far to fore of the vessel. When she peered cautiously around the wardrobe door, she saw there a flintlock pistol held in a brace, its brass barrel pointing straight at her. The lock on the gun, which must have been cocked, was now closed, but it had been attached to the inside of the wardrobe door with a wire that would pull the gunlock forward when the door was opened, causing the flint in the lock to hit the iron filings in the pan in the usual manner and fire the gun.

Rolande carefully removed the wire, then tossed the pistol in her sea chest and went toward the forecastle to question the crew, her tiredness forgotten. Her immediate concern now was to find out whether anyone had been seen about her cabin since the ship's return.

* * *

"I think the pain's better than this brew of yours," Jerl told Katin, making a wry face.

She laughed. "That's what Sir Andrew says, but he asks for it all the same, when he has the headache." She began to gather together her supplies and return them to her pack.

"Stay a bit," Jerl urged, as he and Katin walked through the house to the front door. "You needn't run away."

"No—I oughtn't to be here at all. I promised Sir Andrew that I'd not leave the house till he and Captain Fenton returned from Haremare Point. If he comes back before I do, I'll get a tongue-lashing. And besides, Blythe's right—you simply must rest now."

Gratified to hear that Katin had defied Sir Andrew to come to his aid, Jerl asked no questions, but only leaned close to kiss her cheek, and promised that he'd rest. He meant to keep his word, but after he'd made sure that the plow horse had been recovered. He watched Katin walk down the path toward the forest's edge, then when she was out of sight, he started out for the westernmost field. Despite her words on the night of the ball, he couldn't help feeling hopeful and happy about her now, as if they had come to an understanding that would somehow resolve all their differences.

Katin had told a farmhand to tether her horse to the fence that bordered the forest and marked the boundary of Jerl's land. It was contentedly cropping the sweet clover that grew there, as Katin approached, and she stood beside it for a time, stroking its glossy neck and gazing off into the forest, lost in thought. Though she had told Jerl that she must lose no time in returning to the Governor's Mansion, she seemed in no hurry to mount and be off. *There must be a way,* she was thinking.

Not until she'd thought that Jerl was dead or dying had she understood what it would mean to lose him. Her duty to her people must come first, yes—for an Obelen, there was no escaping that duty—but must it cost her all freedom forever? She was needed now, as a symbol, but once the monarchy had been firmly reestablished, and peace secured, would it matter whether she or another occupied the throne? Wyston wanted to be King, and she was not at all certain that she wanted to be Queen. . . .

Wild, impractical schemes crowded her thoughts, of abdication, of disappearance, even of a feigned death that would leave her at liberty to return to the life of Katin Ander. But the difficulties presented themselves to her as readily as the possibilities. Surely she must leave Albin an heir—and if she bore a child, Wyston would never be more than Prince Regent. Could she trust him to safeguard the welfare of one who stood between him and the throne? For that matter, would she herself be safe with him? If she were to die without issue, he would be in a position to declare himself King.

Not for the first time, Katin wished that she knew more about her affianced. Had he, too, someone he was reluctant to leave behind? Lady Alicen would know, and just as certainly, she would not tell what she knew. *Perhaps I'll ask Arya's sister about him,* she thought, half in earnest. *There's no telling what that one knows. . . .*

And perhaps Darkliss had been right about Arya's luck-charms, the Princess thought later, for certainly on this occasion the silver eye did nothing to caution its wearer of impending danger. As Katin stood musing at the forest's edge, only the snap of branches at her back warned her that she was not alone, and before she could turn, she was suddenly seized from behind. Her assailant clamped one arm across her throat, choking her and pulling her head back, and in a moment she saw the flash of a knife as he raised it toward her neck.

In a display that Baron Graydon would have been proud of, she swiftly drew her dagger from her belt and brought her hand straight up. With the pommel of the hilt, she struck her attacker a sharp blow on the wrist just below the ball of his thumb, as the Baron had taught her, so many years before.

As the shock ran through the assassin's wrist and arm, Katin heard a yell of pain, and she broke free, giving a wild scream herself, in hopes that the noise would bring help. But she wasted no time in waiting to see if anyone appeared. Racing into the woods, she glanced back only once and saw Edward Blythe holding his injured hand in his good one.

He must have doubled back through the woods after he left us—to lie in wait for me. And if he now took her horse and pursued her mounted, it would only be a matter of time until he ran her down. Still, she would not make his task easy for him. Intent on putting distance between them, she ran on, ignoring the whipping of the branches across her face and the thorns tearing at her clothes.

Blythe, however, was still struggling to untie the reins, for his right hand was yet numb and all but useless. Losing patience, he snatched up the knife from the ground where he'd dropped it, and started to hack at the leather with it, cursing furiously. Who would have expected the chit to know such a defense? Still, she was alone and on foot—he'd soon catch up to her.

But before he could mount and ride in pursuit, he was knocked to the ground with one stunning blow to the point of the jaw, losing hold of the knife yet again. For a moment his vision blurred, then he found himself looking up into the face of Jerl Smit, who demanded, "What have you done to Katin Ander? I heard her shout—where is she?"

"There is no Katin Ander!" Blythe spat, scrambling to his knees. "She's Oriana Obelen, boy. Help me catch her and your fortune's made!"

To his astonishment, Jerl laughed. "That's who she is, then. I might have known. But you'll not catch her, while I live." He kicked out and caught Blythe in the chest with one hobnailed boot before he could get to his feet. Then, catching sight of the knife Blythe had dropped, Jerl lunged for it and turned on Blythe with the weapon clutched awkwardly in his good left hand.

Blythe had hoped to work silently and disappear into the forest unseen and unheard, but he had reckoned without Katin's training or Jerl's interference. He struggled to his knees again, as Jerl came at him, and this time he abandoned subtlety in favor of safety. In the space of a few heartbeats, he had dragged the pistol from his vest, steadied it against his stiff right hand, and pulled the trigger. His aim was thrown off by his injury, but the ball pierced Jerl's chest and sent him sprawling to the turf, with his lifeblood seeping into the soil and staining the sweet clover.

Wasting no further time on Jerl, Blythe climbed astride Katin's horse and galloped into the woods, but he searched in vain for Katin. Jerl's intervention had given her a chance to hide, and Blythe had no time to comb the thick foliage for a sign of her. The shouting and the gunshot had brought others to the scene, leaving him no choice but flight, for if Katin succeeded in reaching the Governor's Mansion, the authorities would be at his heels in no time. Leaving Katin's horse in the thicket where he'd hidden his own, he spurred his hired gelding to a gallop and made for the harbor at a desperate pace.

Katin, from her perch high in an oak tree, watched Blythe race off, and shifted position for the first time since she'd heard the horse moving through the underbrush. Thank the Good God, he didn't know much of her habits. As Lady Celia had so truly observed, should the Princess' enemies seek her out, they would hardly expect to find her in a tree.... For all that Her Ladyship despaired of Katin's rough country ways, the skills she'd learned in the wilderness had served her well.

As soon as she was sure that Blythe had gone, Katin climbed down and hastened back to Jerl's farm. She'd heard the pistol shot and feared that one of his people might have been injured.

Jerl smiled when he saw Katin bending over him, despite her look of anguished despair, and the tears coursing down her face. As a surgeon, Blythe had known where to strike, and Katin, as a healer, knew that there was nothing she could do for Jerl.

"You're safe, then," he said weakly. "I tried to stop him—" Jerl broke off, coughing painfully.

"Hush, don't talk—listen," Katin whispered urgently. "I'm safe thanks to you, Jerl. You did stop him. You gave me time to get away." Nothing in all the world mattered, except that Jerl should understand what he'd done.

Jerl's eyes gleamed, but then a worried look came over his face and he struggled to warn her, "He knows who you are."

"Yes. But now I know who he is," Katin said earnestly, stroking Jerl's face, "and he'll not have another chance. You saved me, my darling. You, and no one else." She kissed him, sobbing, "Jerl, I'm so sorry . . ."

Jerl reached to touch her face. "Don't be," he murmured, and smiled again. "I'm not."

When she rose at last, leaving Jerl's people to see to him, the Princess's eyes were dry and her manner calm and composed. Jerl Smit was dead. And so was Katin Ander.

* * *

Blythe rode directly to the *Shraik,* and, after confirming that Rolande had returned, went at once to her cabin and found it empty. It was not too late, then. He walked slowly to the wardrobe, not touching it, but bending to peer closely at the junction where the two doors came together. That was how Rolande found him as she came quietly up behind him and asked, "Looking for something, are you, Ned?"

His guilty start was not lost on Rolande, but he answered brazenly enough, "Yes—I'm looking for a place to hide! Thank the Good God you're back." He was still slightly out of breath from the mad rush back to the ship, and his face was flushed. "There's been an accident—worse ... I was in a fight with a farmer— Jerl Smit—he attacked me—and now, I fear, he's dead. You must hide me, and get me away from here!"

"Must I?"

He crossed the cabin to her and clasped her hand in his. "You'll not fail me now," he said confidently. "After I've stuck to you through every kind of disaster, and crossed the ocean to find you. You're not that sort."

Rolande gazed at Blythe appraisingly. "If that's all that happened, you were only defending yourself, and Smit's in no position to bear witness against you, so what's the hurry to be away?"

Blythe looked uncomfortable under Rolande's scrutiny. He glanced uneasily toward the cabin door, expecting a party of the Watch to come barreling through it at any moment. "There's more to it than that," he admitted reluctantly. "That lass was there—the—the Governor's brat—"

"You didn't harm her?" Rolande broke in anxiously.

"No—why should I? I merely offered to escort her home, but the silly chit mistook my intent and took offense—then her great oaf of a swain came along to defend her honor. He knocked me down, and I lost my temper and shot at him. The girl ran off, no doubt to His Lordship, who'll put the Watch onto me swiftly enough. And I don't mean to hang for what was an act of self-defense, as you say."

Rolande waved this aside. "If your account's true, Sir Andrew will see you used fairly. The girl may be a favorite of his, but he won't let that interfere with his duty."

"She's more than that!" Blythe said desperately. "She's the Princess Oriana. Would I tell you that if I didn't trust you, woman? Sir Andrew will do her bidding, whatever it is. You must—"

"The Princess . . . ?" Rolande interrupted, sounding doubtful. "Now how do you know that?"

"I intercepted a report that Oliver Ruthven was planning to send to Halkin."

"I see! That would be when you killed him, would it? I suppose you bribed the hosteler to let you into his room?"

"Nothing so crude. Such a transaction is too likely to be remembered. I'd taken a room of my own there, and kept the key by me."

"Of course. And you tried to kill the Princess just now, I take it." Rolande ticked off Blythe's crimes on her fingers, like a child making a calculation. "Then there was Sir Andrew, at the Harvest Fair—you hired the gypsies to shoot him. Don't waste your breath denying it, for I have this, you see. One of them must have stolen it from you." From the pouch at her belt she took the brass cylinder and held it up. "And you've another in your case there, don't you?"

Without taking her eyes away from him, she picked up his leather instrument case and dumped the contents over her bed. Cuvettes, probes, and extractors rolled across the blanket, and among them was a silver cylinder, embossed with the physician's emblem of twin serpents coiled around a staff. "That's a lancet case, isn't it?" said Rolande, pointing to it. "They fold up and fit inside. I've seen you take them from this old brass one, when you were operating on my ship. It's empty now—I've no doubt the gypsies found a use for the knives, but the case itself is quite distinctive."

Blythe was silent, and Rolande went on with her catalog. "You tried to poison Alicen Kendry, and now you'll let her hang for Ruthven's murder."

"What's that to you? The royalists are no friends of yours. In time they'll rid themselves of you—"

"Like the Chamber? Do you think *they'll* keep faith with you, now you've failed to assassinate the Princess? You've tried to kill all of us, and only succeeded in—"

"Not you, Vendeley. I've never played you false."

"No? You'd not have met me at Limekin Wharf with a squad of the Chamber's soldiers, after you'd reported to your masters?"

"Don't be a fool! I could have betrayed you a dozen times over, by then, if I'd meant to do so. On board the *Judgment,* in prison, in court—"

"Not without giving yourself away. The Chamber doesn't care to have every sailor or prison warder or minor advocate know who their privy agents are. If we'd not been released, would you have left me to hang, when your friends arranged for your pardon?"

"I would have helped you to escape, as I expect you to do for me now!"

Suddenly Rolande signed him to be silent and stood rigid for a moment, listening intently. "You're right," she said quietly, "they're coming for you. Those were hoofbeats on the wharf, and someone's boarding. Quick—hide in the wardrobe, as you planned—I'll send them away." She strode to the door, then glanced back to see Blythe still standing before the wardrobe, one hand outstretched uncertainly. "Hurry, man, what ails you?" she snapped.

"Vendeley, I—"

Rolande turned back, pushed him aside, and yanked open the door of the wardrobe, then watched without surprise as Blythe dove to the floor by the bed, his hands covering his face. Deliberately, she removed the pistol from her belt and pointed it at him. "There's no need to worry about the gun in the cabinet blowing you to bits. I found your little love token and disarmed it."

Blythe struggled backward across the floor until his back was resting against the cabin wall. "Listen to me, Vendeley. There's no need for us to be enemies any longer. We can help each other. I have access to the Chamber—you have access to the Princess. We can take her together, share the honors and rewards. There'll be glory enough for us both and to spare, if we can deliver Oriana Obelen to the Chamber! Think of it!"

Rolande remained motionless, holding the gun on him steadily as he struggled to his feet, gripping the edge of the bed. Her stance dared him to try to reach for a weapon. "I've thought of it from time to time, over the years. I've known who she was since the Deps invaded Thornfeld," she boasted. "I've had a score of chances to abduct her if I wished."

"Then now is the time to act! You can choose to have riches and honors, or to take your chances in the bloodbath to come. I know your history, Vendeley, you're no royalist. Why should you shield Her Bloody Highness at the expense of your own welfare?"

"You're right," said Rolande, "except in one detail. The royalists are going to win this time—and I mean to turn their victory to my advantage."

"And you think that lot of nobles will give you the chance? You forget what you are, woman—but they won't. They'll use you and throw you back in the gut-ter where the Chamber found you. But they won't win without the Princess. We can stop them, I tell you!"

"I don't doubt it," said Rolande.

Encouraged, Blythe took on a more coaxing tone. "You know it was the Deps who made you, and so 'twas with me. We're the same kind, we have to look to our own interests, and the Deps offer us the best prospects. Why should you scruple to change sides once again?"

As he took a step toward her, Rolande motioned with her pistol for him to keep his place. "I had reason to cross the Deps, and I'll turn against the Princess' lot when they give me reason, and not before. If you knew me at all, Blythe, you'd know that much."

Blythe leaned back against the cabin wall again, and studied her, almost smiling. "And what do you plan to do with me, then, Captain? The last time I asked you that, you had a proposition for me, and left me little choice but to take you up on it."

"I propose to hold you here till Sir Andrew's people come looking for you, and I suggest that you offer them every cooperation, when they do. For my part, I need you to prove Alicen Kendry innocent of Ruthven's murder, but I don't need you alive for that."

Blythe shook his head, looking faintly amused. "I'm afraid that's not a proposition I can accept."

"I'm not leaving you a choice this time either."

"No?" Blythe started toward her again, ignoring her warning gesture. "But we're not miles from shore now—how will you stop me from jumping ship? I don't think you'll shoot me to save some noblewoman who thinks less of you than of her prize lapdog. We're too much alike for that. You know as I do that we should have made a match, and maybe will yet, when the dust clears." He stopped a few feet from her and faced her, smiling. "But for now I have to get away, and you won't stop me, love, though you're welcome to come with me." He stepped confidently forward and made as if to pass her.

"I told you you were a bloody fool, Blythe," Rolande said, as she aimed the pistol square at his heart and pulled the trigger.

* * *

Messages had been flowing back and forth between Sir Andrew and Sir Warren, carried in relays by the winged messengers employed by Sir Andrew. But word of the approach of the Albinate fleet came sooner than Sir Andrew had anticipated. The growing strength of the royalist alliance must have forced the Chamber's hand, he reasoned. But whatever the cause, before many months had passed, a great armada had left Avenford and was sailing toward Oriana, obviously intending a swift and decisive strike.

It seemed certain that the enemy knew about the Princess. Ruthven had evidently been acting on the Duke of Halkin's orders when he'd tried to assassinate her, and there was no telling what Blythe had reported to his superiors. If the rulers of the Chamber of Statesmen knew about Her Highness, then secrecy had lost its advantage, and it was time to reap the benefits that disclosure could afford. An open declaration of Oriana's identity, and of her betrothal to the Duke of Wyston, could cause havoc among the Chamber's forces, and bring many new adherents to the royalist cause. With the Princess' consent, Sir Andrew gave orders for the news to be heralded abroad at once.

He had called for a redoubling of the efforts at the navy yards, to complete the vessels on which their defense depended, though he knew that the sailors would have little opportunity to train on them. Would their ships be ready in time? Sir Andrew asked himself. Would they be sufficient to stave off the attack? If only the colonial forces could defeat the Chamber's armada now, it would be the first blow in the war that would one day place the rightful ruler on the throne of Albin.

The first encounter took place when the Albinate fleet was just approaching Oriana, having cleared the islands where Sir Andrew's Yerren messengers flew in relays. When the first of these winged informants brought word that the invaders had been sighted, Sir Andrew sent couriers far and wide, mobilizing the colonial fleet.

Before engaging in a major strike, Admiral Congdon of the Chamber's navy sent a vanguard of ships toward South Oriana to harry to colonial fleet and test its strength. Rolande, aboard the *Invincible,* ordered only a convoy of conventional vessels to sail out to meet the attackers. She didn't wish to tip her hand until the main Albinate force was committed to the battle, for only then would she have her chance at destroying them all.

A dozen ships of the colonial fleet went forward, but did not draw up in a line to fire, in the traditional formation. Instead, the lead colonial ship raised its helm and cut in and out among the ships in the fore of the enemy's vanguard. The other colonial vessels, following her example, did the same. They maneuvered swiftly in their light craft among the heavier Albinate ships, bombarding the Chamber's vessels with cannonshot. Then they slipped around the rear of the vanguard and sailed back toward the bay on which Oriana was situated.

Rolande's vessels had received far less damage than they'd inflicted, for the enemy had been unprepared for such tactics, and the Chamber's larger ships had been unable to mount a concentrated retaliation upon them as they wove in and out, lest they damage their own vessels more than the colonials'. Admiral Congdon, who stood upon the deck of the Chamber's flagship, was enraged by the gall of the colonials, while at the same time convinced from what he'd seen of their fleet that they were inferior in both numbers and construction. He lost no time, therefore, in sailing straight toward the bay where the colonial navy had retreated. Thus, the Chamber's Admiral, now confident of victory, was lured inexorably into Rolande's trap.

When the Dep ships hove into view, Rolande sailed forth to meet them, this time leading the fleet herself with the *Invincible*. At the sight of the approaching colonials, the Chamber's ships—true to their standard tactics—drew up into a line, close-hauled, but carefully arrayed so that none obstructed the adjacent vessel's line of fire. There were full seventy-five warships, and they were an awe-inspiring sight. Despite Sir Andrew's having solicited funds from loyalists throughout the Colonies to purchase additional ships, Rolande had little more than half that number at her disposal.

The vessels that were aligned with the center and starboard portions of the enemy's line, Rolande ordered to remain far back, so that they were out of artillery range, then she brought the balance of the fleet abreast of the port side of the Chamber's line of ships. She ordered her officers to attack at once, keeping to the windward, so that if the tide of battle should turn against them, they might escape with the bulk of their force intact. Being far inferior in numbers, they could ill afford to lose any ships that might be saved. The Chamber's armada, lacking Yerren lookouts, had no way of knowing that those ships out of range of their spyglasses included five more of the *Invincible*'s make.

The ships on the port side of the Chamber's line turned, moving forward to intercept the oncoming colonial vessels, while those on the other end of the line turned as well, planning to sweep around to the rear of the attackers. Given the superiority of their numbers, such a tactic might have worked, but at that moment, Hrivas took flight from the topmast of the *Invincible*, sweeping back toward the colonial vessels still out of range.

Recognizing his signal, the remainder of Rolande's vessels sailed toward the enemy, led by the five great warships constructed in the image of the *Invincible*. They sliced through the center and starboard sections of the enemy's line as the Dep ships tried to bring themselves about yet again to fire broadside at the attacking vessels. Rolande's strategy depended on the swift and decisive destruction of a large portion of the Chamber's navy—evening their numbers as far as possible. Then with her own superior ships, she hoped to be able to destroy those that remained. The colonials' conventional ships, being smaller and swifter than most of the Chamber's vessels, dove among them, struck in the most obstructing locations and, leaving disabled ships behind them, sailed out of range yet again. Those of the invaders still able to fight were trapped in their single line among too many crippled vessels to be able to mount a coordinated attack against the colonial fleet. The *Invincible* and her sister ships, meanwhile, made a massive attack at the midpoint of the enemy line, an action that cost many crew on both sides, but accomplished its purpose of leaving the center of the battle zone so jammed with immobile vessels that the ships on either end of the Chamber's line could not possibly join forces. Rolande counted every one of her own vessels that was crippled, praying that they had enough firepower to maintain the battle until she won it.

The engagement continued until late into the night. By now there were large numbers of disabled ships on both sides, their broken masts and shredded sails making maneuvering impossible. Most of the smaller colonial vessels were damaged, and many were useless, with shattered rigging and yards. All six of the great warships, however, were still maneuverable, their armored hulls and massive guns protecting them from all challengers. But despite her immediate advantage, Rolande could not allow the enemy time to repair their damaged vessels, for in a war of attrition, she was sadly outnumbered. She needed to strike now and put a decisive end to the threat.

Rolande turned the *Invincible* in the direction of the Chamber's flagship, the *Holy Sword*, a man-of-war bearing a full hundred guns. Still the *Invincible* dwarfed the other warship, and through her spyglass, Rolande could see the officers on the forecastle conferring in consternation as the mighty *Invincible* bore down upon them. From the starboard side, the *Indomitable*, one of the *Invincible*'s sister ships, moved into firing position, while the other warships engaged those of the Chamber's double- and triple-deckers that were attempting to defend the flagship. On the *Holy Sword* the gunners fired wildly, volley upon volley, at the approaching warships, who answered with cannonades of their own, but still came on. *Fools*, Rolande thought, *this will teach you never to plan your strategy by rumor.*

The *Invincible* closed with the flagship from the port side, while the *Indomitable* sailed past her stern to the starboard, effectively cutting off the Chamber's flagship from the rest of the line. For every volley fired from the *Holy Sword,* the *Invincible* continued to inflict twice the damage, for her armored hull was far stronger than that of her enemy, and the number of her guns far superior. All around, men prayed aloud or shouted for the Admiral to surrender before the ship was blown to pieces, but Admiral Congdon believed implicitly that the Good God favored the righteous, and ordered his men to give no quarter. Rolande closed the distance between the two ships, firing the guns of her upper deck, and there was much bloodshed as vast numbers of the Admiral's crew fell amidst the crashing of yards and spars and the shattering of wooden deck planks and rails.

On the *Invincible* the topmainmast and mainyard crashed to the deck, but the ship was already close enough to the *Holy Sword* to attempt a boarding. Small arms fire cut down sailors on both ships' decks, but finally Rolande's crew succeeded in securing grappling hooks in the *Holy Sword*'s port shrouds, and a short time later the boarding party overran the flagship's decks. The Admiral commanded his routed sailors to stand their ground, but a ball from Rolande's pistol caught him in the throat and put an end to his exhortations.

The boarding party had now begun to set fire to the flagship's sails and yards, and as soon as the blaze caught in the rigging, Rolande ordered her people and their prisoners back aboard her own ship and severed the lashings, sailing off as the fire crept down to the powder-strewn decks. Rolande, her coat and breeches smeared with powder and blood, stood upon the fore-

deck of the *Invincible*, watching as the *Holy Sword*
burst in a massive explosion like a fireball upon the
sea.

The fleet was seized with confusion at the sinking of
the flagship and the death of Admiral Congdon. There
were more experienced seamen among the Chamber's
crews than among Sir Andrew's, but the invading sailors could not match the steadfastness and dedication of
the colonials, who were protecting their own shores. In
one Dep vessel the crew, panic-stricken, seized control
of the ship from her officers and sailed her out of action, heading for the safety of the channel islands. This
movement was mistaken for a general retreat, and they
were followed by more than a dozen other ships, leaving a gap in the Chamber's line. Shortly thereafter,
three of the Albinate ships ran afoul of each other, attempting to flee, and were bombarded and sunk by artillery from two of Rolande's great warships.

The *Invincible* and her sister ships made short work
of the scattered remaining attackers, then Rolande ordered the remnants of her weary fleet to chase down
the ships that were fleeing, for they had to ensure that
the destruction of the Chamber's navy was absolute.
By now the Dep captains had grasped the colonials' intent, and one by one those vessels that were still whole
turned and formed themselves into a solid line, firing
back at the colonial fleet, in an attempt to allow the
more critically damaged vessels to sail toward the open
sea. Rolande understood their determination to stand
and fight. *I shouldn't like to be the one to report to the
Chamber that I returned with my ship whole and able
while the rest of the navy was destroyed.*

She stood upon the foredeck, sailing into the final
engagement as dawn came, and the wind rose. With the
favorable wind, the colonial fleet was able to bring

their heavy warships up to pound the Chamber's vessels with broadsides from the windward, leaving their lighter ships free to attack from the leeward side. Relying on their superior speed and maneuverability, the small sloops sank or captured the Chamber's vessels all up and down the line. It was late afternoon by the time the last of the Dep ships struck their colors, and the colonial fleet accepted their surrender in triumph. But the victory had not been without its costs, and amid the smoke and roaring of the cannon, more than one of the defenders' ships had foundered in the unheeding sea.

Sir Andrew wiped the sweat from his brow as he stood on the main dock in Oriana in the heat of the summer sun, anxiously scanning the horizon for the returning fleet. Yerren messengers had brought word of the victory, but no exact accounting of their losses. The shore was lined with townsfolk awaiting the defenders, and when the first of the returning warships hove into view, a wild cheer rose from the milling crowd. Before long, more vessels sailed into the harbor and dropped anchor.

As Commander Jamison marched his militiamen to the shore to assist with the prisoners, Sir Andrew greeted the returning captains, all the while assessing the damage to their vessels. He was already counting them as the core of the Queen's navy.

Lady Celia laid her hand upon his shoulder. "Are there enough?"

"I think so. The Chamber should have few left at home to fend us off—if we strike soon, before they have the chance to rebuild their armada. If we can win a foothold in Albin now, with Graydon's troops and Wyston's followers, we stand a fair chance, and we seem to have most of our large warships still." Indeed, Sir Andrew could see that five of them were now within sight, but he frowned as he realized that the *Invincible* was the one not yet accounted for.

Lady Celia took his hand. "Vendeley?"

"I don't know."

Princess Oriana waited on the wharf to receive her victorious officers and tender them her congratulations—and she, too, gazed out to sea in search of the *Invincible*. From the reports of the returning captains, there was no doubt that Rolande had performed brilliantly in battle—but had she survived?

Now that her true rank was known, the Princess was guarded by a detail of militiamen, but Arya was at her side as well—much astonished to find herself a royal favorite—and Lady Alicen was also in attendance upon her. "Don't worry yourself over that one, Your Highness," said Alicen. "She's more lives than a cat, and sharper claws."

The Princess smiled. "When she was in the gypsy camp, Arya made her a luck-charm with a cat's tooth and a scarlet thread."

"But I don't know that it will answer, mis—Princess," Arya put in solemnly.

Princess Oriana turned to her. "Tell me, little one, all the while you served me for a 'prentice, did your sister never tell you who I was?"

"Did Darkliss know that?" asked Arya, startled.

"To be sure she did, for she read my palm and told me, 'You are not the one you seem to be.'"

Arya suddenly blushed and said uneasily, "I don't think that she knew any more than that, Your Highness."

"Why do you not look me in the eyes, Arya? You are hiding something. Do you not trust me?"

"You will be angry with Darkliss," Arya whispered.

"No indeed. It is not a crime to have the second sight, whatever the Deps may say. Tell me the truth now."

Arya did not seem reassured, but she dared not disobey a royal command. "Darkliss has the second sight—sometimes—but many tell fortunes who do not," she explained falteringly. "We always tell folk they are not as they seem, for here in the New World most don't tell their neighbors what lives they led in the Old. 'Tis not really a *lie.* . . ."

To her relief, the Princess did not seem angry to find that she had been gulled by a glib-tongued fortune-teller. Indeed, Her Highness and Lady Alicen were laughing so hard that at first they didn't hear the cheers that were raised by the crews of the vessels moored in the harbor. Then a longboat pulled into view, sailing in and out amid the ships at anchor, and a tall figure in torn and dirty coat and breeches stood up in the prow, waving a gay plumed hat.

Oriana wanted to race to the end of the pier, as the longboat bumped against it, but instead she waited with regal dignity for Rolande to come to her. Leaping onto the dock, with the feathered hat still in her hand, Rolande saw her at once, and she strode up to her sovereign and made her a sweeping bow. "Your Highness, the fleet is at your disposal!" she declared.

The Princess gave her a gracious smile. "Well done indeed, Captain Vendeley."

"The troops as well are in readiness," said Sir Andrew, approaching the group. "They but await Your Highness's command. With your leave, I shall sail for Castilia, directly a ship can be fitted out for the journey."

Oriana knew that the Lord Marshal planned a conclave with Baron Graydon and the Duke of Wyston, in the secret mountain fastnesses of Castilia, where they would establish their battle plan for the deliverance of Albin. "Very good, My Lord," she assented. "Much as I've profited from my sojourn in the hinterlands, in due season comes the time to journey home."